SHADE FOR LOVE

The Shades of Beckwell: Book 1

SHELLY CHALMERS

For Grandpa, Uncle Bob, and everyone else who refuses to let age define them.

WE ARE the Shades of Beckwell. Though shadows of ourselves, we remain a force to be reckoned with. We take no crap, sugar in our tea, and cookies if you have them.

Mission Notes: It has become apparent that our services are needed. Our old enemy is back. But we aren't the men we once were. We're going to need some help. Notice has been sent, plans have been set in motion. We will find a way to protect our town...and paranormals worldwide from a repeat of the devastating genocide we prevented years ago. We need our leader.

Additional Note: It's Pancake Tuesday. Get there early before Mrs. BossyBody and her crew take all the best tables.

Chapter One

SURPRISE WEDDING

MARRYING a man she'd never technically met was bad enough. The fact that her best friend wasn't there to either congratulate her or talk her out of this insanity made things worse. She, Cara Jenklow, was not made for love.

Cara stood in the quiet second-kitchen of the Beckwell Senior Center in a wedding dress, staring into the mirror propped between an open drawer and the upper cabinets. The wide-eyed, gray-hued woman reflected said this whole thing was insane.

The lingering scent of roast chicken wafted beneath the door from the main kitchens across the hall, the murmur of voices and clank of bins signaling the kitchen had long since shifted to post-dinner clean-up. To everyone else, this was an ordinary Monday evening. Heck, for most of the day, going through the motions of leading art classes here at the Center, she'd pretended it was an ordinary autumn day, too. You know, except for the part where she was getting married.

She sucked in one unsteady breath after another, none

of which did anything to reduce the urge to puke, run, or maybe both.

Her reluctant chauffeur, Maddy Hatt, stood near the door, appearing equally uneasy.

"Um, Cara? Are you, uh, sure this is a good idea? The whole arranged-marriage thing," Maddy said, her ever-present, elbow-length black gloves in place as she wrung her hands together, her dark eyes wide in a pale elfin face. Possibly, she'd taken up the position nearest the door because she wanted to make a run for it, too. Possibly because she'd noticed the grayish hue to Cara's skin and wanted to avoid the splash zone.

"I shouldn't have dragged you into this, Maddy. I guess this would be easier if I'd met him first." Technically, she'd seen her soon-to-be husband many times, she'd just never met him. Unless dreams counted. They probably didn't. He'd appeared for years in her dreams…increasingly X-rated as she'd gotten older. Gorgeous square-cut jaw, chiseled features, soulful blue-gray eyes, the full package. He'd appeared in her visions, too, which she got when she painted.

Her paranormal abilities, despite being the granddaughter of a full-blood dryad nymph and a Baba Yaga descendant, could be counted on one hand. Occasional visions of the future when she painted, not that they were anything special in a town where everyone learned about interpreting visions in elementary school. Literally, there was a class. Ditto for the prophetic dreams—although that was a middle grade class. Hers always featured William Best.

She also had skill with potions, which anyone could do with a little practice and help. She'd learned from Dom, the most almost-magical thing about her. Dom, her best friend that'd been like a consolation prize after Mom died and who insisted Cara trust the visions about William. Or had, before they'd vanished and stopped answering Cara's calls two days ago.

Cara smoothed damp hands down the cool satin ivory dress that had been Gran's so many decades ago. It'd been important to include Gran. Besides, this dress had been part of Gramps and Gran's happy marriage…other than the part where Gran was disowned by her family for marrying Gramps. Sure, Gran and Gramps had known each other and stuff first. Minor details. Maybe if Gran'd had the same kind of visions while painting, had been dreaming and fantasizing about the same man for years and then her grandfather set her up in some arranged marriage scheme, which might or might not finally secure Cara's place among an elite group of protectors, maybe Gran would have jumped for the chance, too.

Or, you know, not. Because who did that kind of thing? Other than her and…her.

Cara let her head drop into her hands. Geezus, Josie, and George, this was bonkers. *Dom, if only you were here.* Dom always knew what to say.

Maddy crept closer, a frown and unusual fierceness in her expression. "You're not being forced into this, are you? Because if you are—"

"Oh, Goddess, no!" Cara faced her mostly friend, took Maddy's hands, and tried for an everything-is-fine smile. "I, um, am totally up for this," she croaked.

A knock scratched at the door. "Hey, sweetie. You ready in there?" Gramps called from the other side. "The boys are getting restless. Henry's holding them off, but we're going to have a fight on our hands over who performs the ceremony."

The "boys" being Gramps and his group of retired paranormal soldiers, the Shades. Something between a group of grandfathers…or maybe fairy godfathers. After Mom'd died and Dad ditched Cara here in Beckwell when she was six, each of them had gifted her with their time, their talents, and their love. These days, the boys were more schemers than soldiers, a male version of the *Golden Girls*, and there had to be some reason they wanted her to marry William. *Nothing came for nothing*, Gramps was fond of saying. She'd been trying for years to prove she was ready to become a Shade. Maybe this was their way of finally initiating her into their ranks. After all, William had led their squad once. Their very own immortal soldier.

"I'll be right out," Cara called back, smoothing the cool satin again. *Deep breath in, slow breath out…* Dom said she should trust William.

"Cara? Are you sure about this?" Maddy repeated.

Maddy wouldn't find herself in this situation. First, because Maddy avoided human contact other than twice-weekly visits to the Senior Center to run her two classes and visit her mom. Second, despite what most people—including Maddy—believed, Maddy was a level-headed woman who didn't make rash decisions based on paranormal-induced visions. At least, not so far as Cara knew. Third, Maddy had a car, something Cara didn't possess. Since she lived centrally in Beckwell, when the old one died, she hadn't bothered replacing it. Perhaps most importantly, though, she'd known Maddy for as long as she'd lived in Beckwell, someone else who'd never left. Maddy was the only one of their rapidly shrinking circle left in town, and she'd answered the phone when Cara had called half an hour ago. If entering an arranged marriage with a stranger wasn't bad enough, walking across the highway in the blowing October wind and light rain in a wedding dress made the whole thing crazier.

"I wish Ainsley and Jessie were here. They could talk you out of this."

Cara scowled at herself in the mirror, her tight, dark curls partially pulled up, mostly wild as they preferred. Back in school, she, Maddy, Ainsley Chaimek, and Jessie Eldrit had made up the Four Misfit-teers, like Cara's own version of the Shades, protecting each other and other outsiders on the schoolyard. In a small town where some families measured how long they'd lived here in centuries, not being born in Beckwell meant you were forever "new."

Of course, that'd all fallen apart when Jessie ditched Beckwell after high school and dragged Ainsley off with her. These days, Maddy was better at keeping in contact with the others. Cara had Dom…emphasis on the "had."

"That's sweet, but Jessie is probably building a house or something, and Ainsley probably found someone to mother." She squared her shoulders. "We shouldn't bother them." Yesterday when Gramps had brought up the idea of marriage, for a moment, a calm certainty had descended. A kind of "knowing" that settled over her with the same sense of rightness and truth of a vision when she painted. Not magical influence from outside—the Shades had trained her to recognize that—but more an internal knowing that didn't require precise understanding. Even without Dom there, with their steady confidence promising that William was the one for her, Cara had just known she should marry him. With a calm she usually only felt during painting and visions, she'd agreed to marry William. Calm which, admittedly, vanished as quickly as it'd come, leaving plenty of time for second-guessing. The knowing said this was right. Dom said there was something between Cara and William. But Dom was missing, unable to give that assurance now.

"Oh. Um, so I didn't think we'd be bothering them.

They'd want to be here. Are here. Now," Maddy mumbled, holding out her phone. "Ta-da. Video call."

Cara turned, blinked at Maddy, then at the small screen.

Ainsley's cute, freckled face and wild hair took up most of the screen, whereas Jessie's blonde head was down, probably on her phone or computer as usual.

"Cara, I can't believe you didn't tell us you were getting married!" Ainsley cried. "Maddy, hold the phone farther back so we can get the whole dress and everything. Jessie, look how gorgeous Cara looks."

Maddy gave a slightly apologetic shrug but backed away, while Ainsley oohed and ahhed before Maddy came closer to Cara again.

"You look so beautiful, doesn't she, Jessie?" Ainsley said.

There was a grunt—sounding a lot like Ainsley had elbowed Jessie in the ribs—and Jessie's blue gaze and almost too-perfect face, brow raised, stared out through the screen. "You look great, Cara. Congrats, hope things turn out, all the happiness and stuff to you." She turned back to her phone.

"Thanks, Jess. I can tell you really put your heart into that," Cara said dryly. Big surprise. She and Jessie had never been close, mostly because Jessie hated Beckwell and thought the Shades were interfering, manipulative old frauds, and refused to hear reason when Cara explained otherwise.

Not looking up, Jessie just snorted. "Come on, Cara. Happy endings are for suckers. But, hey, hope the sex is good. And I'm sorry, but I've got to run. I've got a meeting with a new potential supplier, then I've got three billion other things on the list for today." She glanced up. "Seriously, though, good for you and all the best." Jessie disappeared from the screen.

Ainsley centered herself in the screen and tried to compensate with an especially bright smile, as usual trying to keep the peace and take care of everyone. "We're so thrilled for you, really. Don't mind Jessie. She's super stressed with the new company and stuff. Hopefully work will bring us back to Beckwell soon." Something dulled her expression, an unusual brittleness edging her smile. "I need to talk to my folks and Grandfather. The kind of talk that needs to be in-person." She blinked, then, like flicking a switch, snapped the wattage up on her smile. "Lots of love, kiss the groom for us, and hopefully, we'll see you soon-ish!" She blew a kiss before the video call ended.

Silence filled the room a second as Maddy tucked her phone away. "I... I hope that was okay," she whispered.

"Oh, Maddy, that was perfect, thank you," Cara said, eyes burning at the thoughtfulness, especially with Dom missing, and longing to give her friend a hug but instead squeezing her hands together. Touch was hard for Maddy. "You're always so thoughtful. You didn't have to pick up the phone this morning after I've been such a neglectful friend. Give me a call, and I swear I'll make it up to you. Help get some of the antiques online to sell, manage the repairs to the roof, whatever you need."

It wasn't just Maddy she'd been neglecting. It'd been a couple of months since she'd last emailed Ainsley to check in. There was no sense emailing Jessie, who never answered emails and was prickly as a porcupine, but kind of cute and vulnerable in a way you couldn't just abandon. Besides, they'd been friends forever...even if Cara had never worked up the guts to introduce them to Dom.

Color stained Maddy's pale face, and she dropped her gaze, twisting her gloved hands in front of her. "That's kind of you, Cara. Thank you. But unnecessary. I... I manage."

Maintaining a rambling old Victorian stuffed to the eaves with antiques for the business her mother had started, never mind her mother and Maddy's own condition, Maddy's life wasn't easy. A pang settled through Cara. She'd do better. She'd be better, for her friend, for Beckwell, to earn her place as a Shade.

She turned toward the door, hands fisted. All right then. She could do this. Three steps would take her out the door, where Gramps waited to take her to meet her groom. Three steps that just needed three reasons why she wanted to marry him.

First, there'd been that weird "knowing." Maybe it was vague as hell. But in that moment of calm knowing, there'd been a sense that marrying William was necessary and would set everything right. He was the first step on a path that would put everything back to where it'd been, where she and her best friend worked together to make a place for Cara in this town, helped her to matter.

One step toward the door.

Second, there were the visions. She'd studied those chiseled features and blue-gray gaze in countless canvases. He'd always been there for her in her dreams, ensured no other man could compare.

Another step forward. Palms damp.

Which led to the third reason. Thanks to Gramps and the boys, she could write a dossier on William MacIntyre Best. Former soldier, current P.I. He helped the paranormal underdog, fought the bad guys. Nothing like the heartless bogeyman some people claimed. William had led Gramps and the boys' squadron, the Shades, back in the Second World War...because he was an un-aging immortal soldier and all. He wasn't even 150 yet, and years didn't count the same way for immortals. Cursed or blessed by a god, all because one of them had answered his mother's desperate pleas for a child that survived infancy. A child that wouldn't die. He'd been alone so long, and she could change that.

Cara closed the distance to the door, her hand firm on the knob.

Her best friend Dom's only physical form was a necklace. Weirdos couldn't cast stones. Especially in a town where normal need not apply. And Cara was more normal than not. Other than being more spirit than person, at least Dom understood why Cara wanted to be a Shade and protect Beckwell like Gramps and the boys. Well, in a Dom kind of way. Until two days ago. When Dom stopped answering. Not because they were in a foul mood or didn't feel like answering. Dom had said something ominous about trouble, town, and to find the nymphs, in that order, message broken and staticky, then silence like a wall settled between them. It wasn't like Cara could ask for help finding Dom or the nymphs, but the knowing said William was the answer to her problems. Even in Beckwell, where weird came with the territory, telling people your best friend was a necklace was, well, *too* weird.

One problem at a time.

She marched out of the kitchen. "Time to get married."

Chapter Two

FIVE OLD MEN AND A WEDDING

YOU LEARNED IN WAR—AND in PI work—that if you didn't pivot when you'd been outflanked, outmaneuvered, and your best plans shot to hell, you ended up dead. Neither an arranged marriage nor seeing the Shades, his former army squadron, had sounded dangerous. However, the second Albert Jenklow's granddaughter, Cara, walked into the windowed Beckwell Senior Center dining hall after the dinner rush, William MacIntyre Best knew he'd been had. His palms dampened, his heart sped, and the world flipped. The paranormal world might fear him, but he'd just blundered into the biggest damned trap of his life. He needed a plan B, and fast. He reached for his tin of mints, fingers unsteady as he found one, but the sweet chill on his tongue did nothing to calm him or steady his thoughts like it usually did.

Cara Jenklow glowed with the promise of everything he could never have. Beautiful. Loved. Mortal. Undoubtedly female, the way the ivory gown hugged her curves, contrasting stunningly with her dark skin. She walked, tall and statuesque, down the makeshift aisle on Albert

Jenklow's arm, his figure hunched and shrunken, light glinting off his bald head.

William couldn't look away from Cara. She had trouble written all over her. Hell, it was in the way she held her head high and glided toward him, no hesitation in her step, determination shining in those dark eyes. The fading sunlight played with her dark curls, creating a warm halo around her face and causing a lurch of his innards that made him want to pull at his collar and smooth his hair.

Made him wish he was as young as he looked and believed in the possibility of happy endings.

He straightened and narrowly avoided that collar-tug.

Behind his bride-to-be a slim, dark haired pale woman slipped into a seat as witness. The only other guests were the snoring old man who'd been there since before the dinner rush and the big, dark-haired guy with the stethoscope and lab coat, Doctor Quilan.

His four old friends stood behind William, backs to the windows like choirboys, dubiously innocent considering this setup. Four men who'd once been eager to prove themselves, protect their country and their kind. Four men who'd gotten old, frail in the years since they'd last met. They'd said she was lonely. That she was in danger. That she needed him.

The woman striding toward him didn't look like she needed anyone. Her grandfather, Jenklow, leaned on her slim, bare arm, yet her stride remained strong, back straight, shoulders back. Worse were those delectable lips of hers that twitched as though enjoying a private joke, her dark gaze steady on him.

A small curl of something dangerous flickered to life inside, an old fire flaring. Heat burned through him, low and hot, hungry. He wanted that smile on him, for him. It'd been a long time since he'd felt pure, old-fashioned desire. His hands grew damp at his sides. Something more insidious lurked in that desire. Something that lit up the dark corners and cobwebbed dreams of getting married and settling down. Of a bride and a woman who'd love the real him.

He shifted. Blast. He had a mission to focus on. For too long, he'd had more enemies than friends, and any time he'd gotten attached, someone else paid the price. There was a damned good reason he'd dedicated his life to bringing down the Guardians, and it wasn't time to let personal attachments get in the way now. He had to cap those feelings and that lust. Dangerous or not, whether she needed him or not, he needed her.

For bait.

Rumor was his old enemy was back and headed this way. The human-hating Guardians had destroyed dozens of sanctuaries like this one during the war, and sources said they were after a rising power, a unique hybrid right here in Beckwell. Hybrids historically had manifested unusually strong abilities…and they typically lacked protection from powers stronger than the gods and purebloods who usually made up the Guardians. They were the perfect target for the Guardians, who'd used many like them during the war. Like strapping bombs to rats, hybrids were a disposable weapon the Guardians could always find a use for. Rumors being unspecific things, his source hadn't known what species or what person.

Lo and behold, Albert and his old team, the Shades, contacted him about concerns they had about their beloved granddaughter. An unusual nymph-Yaga hybrid. Her growing abilities. New threats to their town. It'd all clicked. *She* was the hybrid the Guardians were after. The Guardians liked nothing better than turning a uniquely powerful paranormal into a weapon no one would see coming. They'd destroyed countless sanctuaries and lives throughout their history in the same way.

Agreeing to this faux marriage had seemed logical. The Shades knew he'd do anything for the cause, anything to bring a stop to the Guardian's atrocities. Including follow through with their demand that he marry a woman who had no clue about any of it. His name and reputation would provide her some protection, but more than that, he needed to stick close, let the Guardians come to him when they came after her.

His skin itched and his chest tightened. The Shades would want to hide her away. He was knowingly putting her in danger. He'd lost to the Guardians before. Hell, if they got to her using fey magic or other mind control, there might be no saving her. But this was his chance to have the Guardians come to him instead of the fruitless chasing he'd done for years. Even if he couldn't save their target, her handler would have to be physically close, and he'd follow that handler up the food chain.

Cara stopped beside him, giving Jenklow a sweet kiss on his wrinkled cheek and a squeeze of his liver-spotted hands. Her expression was guileless and sweet as she faced William, not a flicker of an eyelash to indicate she'd heard a word of the stories they told about him.

While Jenklow took his place with the rest of the Shades, she offered him a shy smile, a hint of a dimple in one cheek. She was tall, but he was taller. Tall enough to admire the robin's egg sized amber pendant that lay on her chest, trailing into the shadows between her breasts. He swallowed, throat thick, and it wasn't the only thing. Hell and blast.

"Hi," she said. "I'm Cara, and I'll be your bride this evening."

If he'd believed in hell, he was headed there…if

anyone figured out how to kill him. His lips twitched in an almost smile, the muscles stiff from disuse. He'd appreciated strong women long before it was fashionable. "A pleasure. I'm William, your groom."

Her lips curved more, that dimple deepening. She leaned closer, a tendril of dark hair caressing her neck, her sweet floral scent twining around him, luring him closer. "I know who you are. Don't worry."

Ice water rushed through his veins, and his smile cracked. Ah hell. If she'd heard the stories about the real-life Van Helsing, a paranormal being who sometimes tracked and hunted his own, stories that kept most people distant, was she flirting with him because she was one of those women? Some saw him as the ultimate conquest, a notch for their belt.

Before he responded, Henry Einar cleared his throat, tall and straight-backed, once-blond hair now white. Attention caught, he nodded at William and Cara. "Please join hands."

William reached for Cara's hands. Her fingers were long and strong, skin as silken as he'd imagined.

"Dearly beloved, we are gathered here today to witness the union of our dear friend, William MacIntyre Best, and Cara Rose Jenklow, a granddaughter to Albert and all of us. We will collectively perform portions of the ceremony."

Oh, hell.

Bal Liko, weapons officer, stepped up first, skin light brown, a thin dark moustache all that remained of his hair. He was more belly than muscle these days, but he crossed his arms and gave William a hard look. "You promise to take good care of our princess? Never go to bed angry, and don't hurt a hair on her head or else?"

"That's not a vow, Liko, that's a threat," Einar said mildly.

"Which is why it matters," Liko shot back, gaze narrowed on William.

Years of training, situations facing down demi-gods, deranged pixies, glamour-sick yuppies, and the worst the Guardians sent after him kept William's expression neutral despite the hard thud of his heart. The Shades would never forgive him if they found out why he'd really agreed to marry Cara. If he didn't keep his distance, they'd realize he was the monster everyone believed he was. "I do."

Liko's gaze narrowed like he wanted to continue his interrogation.

Dapper George Chaimek, though, with all his silvery hair and a fuller moustache, strode up and prodded Liko, his former brother-in-law and permanent nemesis, in the side.

"You've had your turn. Move it," Chaimek said.

Liko glowered but returned to his spot in the line.

Chaimek, the old sorcerer, stuck his tongue out at Liko. They'd bickered long before there'd been wives in the picture, both of them long since widowed.

A small pang settled in William's gut. All he knew of any of his friends' wives were the black-and-white photos, the letters Jenklow sent, and the hollow sentiment of sympathy cards.

Chaimek's dark gaze settled on William. "I don't have to threaten you. You know what I'm capable of if you hurt Cara. Even without visits, you still remember who we are, don't you?" He bestowed a glowing smile on Cara. "Darling Cara, do you promise to give William the benefit of the doubt when he makes a mistake, which he will, and give him the chance to explain?"

Cara nodded. "I do."

"Doyoupromisetorespect,honorandbelieveineachother?" Ted Zaki squeaked, stringing all the words together and barely stepping forward before jumping back, his narrow, ageless face red. The djinn was the oldest of the team, but he could have been someone's beanpole college kid, with a mop of dark curls, thick glasses, and prominent Adam's apple. Ironic he'd always been cool as a cucumber as their transport and coms man.

"I do," Cara and William said at the same time.

Damn it. Every time his gaze bumped into Cara's, that flare of desire ignited, burned a little hotter. She looked tastier than apple pie a la mode, or chocolate cake steaming from the oven.

Albert Jenklow was the last to take center stage, heart and soul of the Shades. Like Liko, time had stolen most of his hair, leaving bushy eyebrows and a white fringe around his ears. The weight of the years had stooped his once tall frame. Still, mischief and intellect shone in that blue gaze, and ten to one, odds said it was he who'd come up with this scheme. "Cara, William, I know this marriage is unusual, but don't let that dim it's potential. May the gods bless this union with love and joy, and may you both remember that sometimes there's magic where you least expect it."

"I now pronounce you husband and wife," Einar said. "You may now kiss."

"So say we all," echoed the rest of the Shades.

Something old and expectant crackled in the air as the words hung there a moment. William turned to his bride.

The sun set the ends of her dark-brown curls on fire, her dark gaze luminous.

The way she regarded him was more guileless than conquest-seeking, yet how could she calmly hold his hands if she knew the stories? This close, he spotted the gold flecks in her brown gaze, felt the tremble in the fingers he clasped. This wasn't a real marriage. He couldn't... He shouldn't...

"With your permission, I'd like to kiss," she whispered.

"Really?" He stepped closer, the heat of her soaking through that satin.

She made a surprised kind of laugh, dark eyes dancing. "I'm sure."

Her laughter stopped. That weightiness of the moment held them as she leaned forward, and he lowered his lips to brush hers.

She was the perfect height for kissing, her lips soft and moist, not sticky with lipstick. He brushed his mouth against hers once, her lips moving beneath his. Sparks and potent need chased through him, drew his hand to her satin-wrapped body, the warm curve of her back to gently tug her closer. Kissing her was like it was his first time. She tasted of mint and sweetness, better than any treat he'd enjoyed. The heady rush and burgeoning desire, the spark of energy that promised this was only beginning, a sweetness that was more intoxicating, more addictive than any of the treats Dad had always banned.

Kissing Cara was like a promise that somehow, after all these years, all those lonely nights on the road, all the rumors and legends... In this moment, with this woman, he was safe. He'd finally come home.

He yanked away, lips burning. Fire raced through his body, his pulse pounded in his ears, and desire for her body and for that insidious hope she inspired battered at his defenses and control. Hell no. He'd ridden that pain train too many times. Mother and Dad had proved love soured around him. He was too old for relationships. Too old for her. There was no home other than the road and the next case, and she deserved a hell of a lot better than him.

She was a means to an end. A tool to use against an old enemy. Nothing more.

The Shades cheered loudly, other silver and white heads poking their faces around the dining hall doors curiously.

Cara remained frozen where he'd left her, eyes closed for a moment before they fluttered open, her gaze finding his. A bemused sort of calm curved her lips.

New arrivals swarmed toward them, most of them silver-haired like the Shades, making this less like a formality and more like a party. Or a wedding. A real one.

All of the residents knew Cara, giving her hugs, offering kind words. He was pressed back by the swarm of silver- and white-haired residents, all so mortal, so fragile with age.

Then there were the whispers, the stares, the questions of "why him?" Why would their sweet Cara Jenklow marry the bogeyman of children's stories, a threat that if you didn't stay in line, if you broke the rules of their paranormal world, the Abomination would get you. Not quite human, not quite paranormal, something in between he'd never understood himself.

The room faded to grayish blurs, and he couldn't have picked out the faces of people who greeted him from a suspect line. They'd hate him, too, when they uncovered the truth. But he'd protect them from the Guardians anyway because that was the mission.

His gaze lingered on his new wife. A mission he'd sacrifice anything—and anyone—to complete.

Chapter Three

DANCING AND PLOTS

KISSING WILLIAM BEST in real life eclipsed every dream she'd ever had. The rest of the wedding thing was exhausting. In a normal marriage, weren't you supposed to save your energy for the wedding night? Cara gave a small wave to Mr. Einar, who worked the other side of the room. Unfortunately, even if she did want to know if other activities with William were better in real life, too, she'd lost him a half hour ago or so after Center residents swamped her, all of them always happy for any excuse to party or talk about their newest grandbaby. If she and William were meant to be together like Gramps, her visions, and Dom believed, they'd eventually connect, right?

Cara's face ached from the effort of holding a polite smile while standing near white-haired Mr. Filipov and Mr. Kozel, who had less hair and a wispy beard, both of whom sat while insisting she mediate their discussion of inter-dimensional reality bubbles. The only way she had any idea what they meant was because of Mr. Zaki's kind tutoring and all the articles he forwarded for her to read.

She shifted awkwardly, seeing as her left foot ached where Mrs. Silver's cane had connected when Cara saved her from a fall after overly enthusiastic dancing. The poor dear couldn't afford to break a hip. Or maybe it'd been when Mrs. Helsin's wheelchair had rolled over Cara's toes when she'd headed to a very nervous Maddy's rescue, cornered by a few of the newer residents who didn't understand Maddy needed her space and that she'd analyze their antiques for them during her allotted time slot.

Whatever the case, Mr. Filipov and Mr. Kozel both had the benefit of chairs, whereas Cara did not. Damn toes and reality bubbles. Still, this was what the Shades had trained her for. Know everyone so you were always the first to know, Mr. Einar always said. Mr. Liko probably would have told both Mr. Filipov and Mr. Kozel to stuff it by now, but his lessons on self-defence every birthday were enlightening. She'd learned everything they had to teach her, everything to prove she was a worthy Shade and deserved all that time they'd spent on her over the years. Sure, they only taught her things even someone with limited magic could handle, like defensive spells and tricks to allow her to escape and find someone with real power to help. But she knew she could prove that her love and dedication to Beckwell made her a valuable Shade, impressive ability or not.

Which meant buzzing among all those residents, she was the first to hear the stories they whispered about her new husband. The names they gave him. Abomination. Van Helsing. Death dealer. Most of them she'd heard, but with everyone except Gramps and the boys questioning why she'd married William Best, well, kind of hard not to question that herself.

She reached for the chilled amber Yaga pendant where it rested against her chest. Cold meant no Dom. If only the spirit were around to offer sage advice, with a side of grouchy or not. That was the problem when your best friend went missing and they were the spirit of the ancient Yaga house, Domoroy Yaga—or Dom for short—that lived inside a pendant. People gave you weird looks if you told them you talked to jewellery. In every other way, Dom was real, even defining themselves as outside of the binary, identifying as they/them, and with strong opinions on *everything* that could be tiresome…but which Cara missed.

But for two days, right after Dom told Cara that William was part of her destiny and to find the nymphs, it'd been radio silence. Not in the sullen, didn't-feel-like-answering silences Dom would pull, either. Not a word, no explanation, gone. After two decades of always being there when Cara needed them, Dom was missing. If they didn't return, Cara would lose her consulting position with Doc Quilan, working with the doctor on potions and alternative healthcare based on species-specific history for paranormal patients. All her hard work would be for nothing. The consulting paid better than teaching art classes alone. Dom was the one who knew that Yaga history, was basically a bodyguard/encyclopedia and helped with the diagnosis. It was because of Dom that Cara had finally made a place for herself in Beckwell, started to feel like she could fit in… even if she wasn't born here and didn't have the ability everyone seemed to expect.

"Has anyone seen my bride?" The deep baritone rolled over Cara like chocolate on ice cream, sending a small shiver of heat straight to her core.

William stood just behind her, broad shoulders filling out that gray suit jacket, close enough the heat of him warmed her bare skin, made the hairs on her bare arms prickle. He raised a brown-blond brow over that storm-blue gaze.

She shivered. "I, uh… I was seeing to our guests."

Doing the usual things, including what she'd picked up from the boys, seemed suddenly silly for her wedding day.

His fingers brushed hers, sending more sparks shooting through her like deranged fireflies before he linked hands and tugged her closer. "Gentlemen," he said, politely cutting into Mr. Filipov and Mr. Kozel's heated discussion. "I have to steal my bride away for a dance."

The two residents scowled a minute before returning to their convoluted discussion.

William tugged her after him.

"Are we really going to dance?" she asked, trailing after him.

"We are."

Her heart pounded, and too many other visions and dreams that'd involved dancing followed by the horizontal mambo rushed through her head. *New husband, stranger, take things slow*, she reminded herself.

The hum sliding through her body, the tingles and the heat settling low in her belly said her hormones and libido hadn't gotten the memo…or had and burned that bugger to ash.

They reached the makeshift dance floor, and William pulled her into his muscular embrace, one hand clasping hers, one on her lower back while she got to check, nope, no shoulder pads filling out his suit jacket. Just lean, hard muscle.

Her brain stuttered, focused on the scalding heat of his fingers in the small of her back through the satin gown. Goddess, she'd had this dream so often. The slight pressure of his hand was all they needed to move in sync, as though they'd done this a hundred times. In her dreams, sure. Chalk one more up for better in real-life. The heat of him wrapped around her, the shift of his muscles beneath her fingertips, his faintly clean, spicy scent. Heat curled low in her belly, growing ever more fervent as his gaze snared her.

"You're an excellent dancer," she said, voice breathless…and better than the "do me now" her libido suggested. Frick's sake, you'd think she was a virginal teen with her first crush. Although, technically, William *was* her first crush.

"You must know everyone around here, and they you."

Heaviness settled over her, and she grimaced. She'd spent too long playing nice, and she'd neglected William, who couldn't know many people in Beckwell. "I do, thanks to Gramps and the boys." She forced herself to meet that blue-gray gaze. "I'm so sorry. I guess since I work here it's habit to mingle and check-in with everyone, but that's no excuse for my bad behavior."

"I thought you were avoiding me." He said it without heat or censure, as though he'd expected she'd avoid him.

Heat climbed her neck. Crud. Focusing somewhere near his ear, she pasted on the usual rueful smile that worked to placate the boys or others in town when she'd broken one of their unwritten rules. "Not at all. This whole arranged-marriage thing threw me little, but I shouldn't have abandoned you to the mercy of Beckwell seniors."

There was a long pause, leaving them moving to the music.

"Cara, can you look at me?" that deep voice of his rumbled, the sound of her name on his tongue making it somehow sexier.

She found his ear again.

"My eyes."

She swallowed, forced her gaze to meet those stunning eyes, gold flecks and a darker ring around the iris. The spiciness of him curled around her, and the faint crinkles around his eyes made her want to kiss the skin there, ensure those were laugh lines. How did you stare someone in the eye when you'd had sex dreams about them and now they were here, married to you?

"Why did you marry me?" The words popped out unexpectedly.

A brown-blond brow rose, and while he didn't miss a step, sidestepping them away from collision with another couple, the muscles in his shoulder tensed beneath her fingertips. "Your grandfather is one of my oldest friends, and when he asked for my help keeping you safe, I said yes. Why did you marry me?"

"Because Gramps asked." Mostly true. Plus, there'd been the "knowing" and Dom's advice. Too bad that certainty had abandoned her now. Probably thoughts of the wedding night...and that big difference between dreams and real life. "My best friend also advised I should, and they know me better than anyone. Safe from what?" Beckwell was safe...so long as someone wasn't trying to end the world, which happened more often than you'd think.

He hesitated, the pause making the back of her neck itchy.

Other than the strange sense of "knowing," she wasn't psychic, but Mr. Chaimek had trained her to spot a lie using tells. William's hesitation, the tension in his shoulders when she'd asked why he married her, the convenient timing of his return to Beckwell... He was hiding something.

"You've heard of the Guardians?"

A chill slid through her. "Baddies who pick on the little guy, talk about purifying the paranormal blood lines, getting rid of humanity so paranormals inherit the earth. Nut jobs." A shiver of unease slid down her spine, and the image of one of her paintings from last week came to mind. Dark, faceless shadows, stepping into the light. "Why would they come here? I love Beckwell, but we're the buttcrack of nowhere. There are larger paranormal sanctuaries."

"Since the Veils fell, Beckwell has become a paranormal hub. Beckwell existed in all of the realms—the mortal, Braelyn with the gods, angels, and fey, and Daimoleigh with the demons. The Shades are some of the last people alive who remember how dangerous the Guardians were." Another pause. "We believe the Guardians are after you."

She rolled her eyes. "Me? No way. Sorry to disappoint, but I'm basically powerless. I have the odd vision, but only when I'm painting. Even Normals get visions, and they're not considered a real ability around here. I have no nymph ability at all—no transforming into a tree, communal connection, foretelling the future, nothing. And my Baba Yaga side…" That was all Dom. Dom held the knowledge and power of the Yagas and let Cara borrow it occasionally. Without them, Cara barely belonged in Beckwell at all. "I have some skill with potions, that's it."

William frowned, and something flickered in his expression.

Maybe he was disappointed that her unusual mixed heritage didn't live up to the hype. She'd been too "spooky with that messed-up magic stuff" for Dad and his perfect new family, especially after Mom died. The frozen image of Mom in the hospital after the accident, all those horrible tubes and machines, everything happening so suddenly…the confusion, the pain flashed through Cara. By the end of the week, Dad had shipped her off to Beckwell, and when she'd gotten here, Gramps had given her Mom's pendant, the Yaga pendant, like that was all Mom's life added up to. He'd believed it was just a family heir-loom, a piece of old jewelry with the story from the Yagas but no real power. But then Dom spoke to Cara for the first time…the only one who could explain what'd happened.

"I take it you were expecting someone more para-normal than normal, huh?" she asked, trying not to sound disappointed.

Arriving here, she hadn't been weird enough. No obvious abilities, no paranormal features, and clueless when it came to the unspoken rules that came with living in a paranormal sanctuary. Especially the small class distinctions that made some of the old families in Beckwell powerful, ranked demi-gods and full-blooded paras higher…left families like the Yagas always on the outside as mostly mortals who'd taught themselves magic and refused to follow the rules, respect the ranks. Little wonder she spent more time talking to a pendant than real people. She needed Dom; they were essential to the life Cara had built in Beckwell.

"Cara, I've been in the paranormal world most of my adult life. You don't have to hold back."

She frowned. "I'm not. I make potions for some of the residents, but that's more training than innate ability." And Dom. "Look, I'm getting the vibe you're here more for the Guardians than me. Honestly, maybe it's a relief since getting set up with your grandfather's old army buddy is, well, a little awkward."

This earned her a small smile, like the hint of sunshine from behind a cloud. "Let's make things less awkward, then, and keep this relationship completely platonic. My name and reputation provide some protection, and I'll see to the rest. Consider me…your bodyguard."

Platonic, huh? It would be easier on her heart, less

chance of getting attached… Although a part of her wanted a bodyguard with benefits. That was a thing.

"Sounds great," she lied brightly. The full-color reality of William Best was strictly off-limits. Guess for now, she'd stick to finding the nymphs and Dom. Dreams and one kiss would be her only taste of William.

Chapter Four

FUR BABY

STANDING arms crossed and alone in the deserted circle the residents had formed around him, William watched Cara romp across the dance floor with a still-spry Einar.

Her laughter carried, the carefree sound curling around and resuscitating that younger part of himself buried deep that needed to damn well stay hidden. She hadn't laughed like that with him. Had mumbled something about checking on her grandfather as the song ended before she made her getaway. She didn't treat him like a deadly pariah, but she'd wanted her distance. That'd been twenty minutes ago, but these were her people, her party. She should enjoy it. He'd been on long-haul stakeouts. He'd survive.

He popped a mint into his mouth, never taking his gaze from her, that lithe body, the kindness she exuded. His favorite mints couldn't compare to the taste of her. Maybe she didn't want a platonic marriage. Hell, maybe he'd told her too much about why he was in Beckwell. He'd opted for the partial truth, since it was less likely to get you caught than a full lie.

She'd finished dancing with Einar, taking skinny Zaki by the hand.

He might not know her, but the influence of his friends was obvious. She knew everyone, was liked by everyone, and chatted with ease like Henry Einar. She had George Chaimek's wicked sense of charm and wit. Ted Zaki's intellect to converse knowledgably no matter the topic. She moved with athletic grace and assurance, something that suggested Bal Liko's influence. From her grandfather, though, there was no mistaking the connection. She'd spent most of the evening keeping a ready eye for anyone in need. Had she inherited more from Jenklow?

Jenklow had been a healer, handy with defensive and artillery potions, and his visions had saved the team's bacon several times. The legend of Baba Yaga was full of contradictory information and actions, but she and her heirs had the potential to be extremely dangerous, even cannibalistic. While it didn't look like Cara was eating anyone soon, had she lied to him when she'd said her abilities were nominal?

"You trying to confirm the things they say about you? Or have you forgotten how to talk to people you aren't slicing and dicing?" Liko said, edging up beside him, similar crossed-arm stance.

Either Liko'd drawn short straw, or it was his turn. All of the Shades had approached, offering conversation and friendliness in an otherwise unfriendly room. Many of the residents had trouble with their hearing, so the stories they told about him were less whispered and more shouted. Where he went, death followed. Sometimes his enemies… sometimes anyone close enough to become collateral damage. Still, his presence was no reason his friends shouldn't enjoy the party, so he'd sent them all off with one excuse or another. Eventually, they'd demand a confrontation, but the farther he kept from them, the less likely his purpose with Cara was exposed and the Shades finally discovered what kind of monster they'd called friend. The kind who would use an innocent woman as the means to an end.

William slid his former weapons expert a look. "Don't see you out there cutting a rug."

Liko pulled a face. "Never liked dancing. No point since Dot died."

Another knot twisted in William's belly. He'd sent sympathy cards—only damned kind of card he needed, but he hadn't come for any of the funerals of the Shades' wives. Hadn't called or visited, either, only answered Jenklow's phone calls but never initiated them. He'd seen too many funerals.

The next one could be his new wife's. To the Guardians, her mortal side made her disposable, undeserving of the ability she might have inherited, especially from the nymphs who'd been long-time members. It also made her more vulnerable to magical influence. They'd control her mind, let her destroy this town and others. They'd done it repeatedly during the war, enslaving an unlucky few from the paranormal sanctuaries they destroyed...only making those who'd survived and been used wish they'd died sooner.

Liko nodded toward Cara, the action pulling back William's focus. "What's your excuse? She's young, pretty, and always jumps to your defense. Our princess not good enough for you?"

His friend must have been exaggerating. No one had defended William since Mother. "We've barely met. This is her party, not mine. We're taking things slow, and I want to be respectful."

The other man's dark gaze was long and measuring.

He snorted, unconvinced. "You disrespect her, I'll have your balls. What's your take on the mission, then? You must have heard some of those whispers about the Guardians movements through your contacts."

Shit. Exactly what he didn't want to do. Admit he was there to track down the Guardians…but on his own mission, without looping in his old friends. William adjusted his crossed arms, pretended to be watching Cara, not monitoring Liko's response. "You invited me to stop the Guardians from troubling Beckwell, and I will. I've heard things."

Maybe that would be enough. Better yet, maybe Liko would reveal what the Shades had heard, if they'd kept up with some of their network.

A long silence stretched. Stretched a little longer after that.

Then Liko sniffed, dropped his arms, paced away, then stalked back. "You asshole," he cursed, voice pitched low and vicious, stabbing his finger into William's upper arm to punctuate. "I *told* them you'd do this. Try to cut us out of it, steal our mission, take on the Guardians alone. Same shit you tried to pull first few missions we ran. You took center and the most dangerous positions, left us back where it's 'safe.' That's it, isn't it? You think we're too old for this. That we've lost our edge." He swore again, this time a colorful string that was pure Liko.

Exactly what he'd been hoping to avoid. Liko's temper would only rile up the others more.

"Maybe I'm looking at efficiency and risk," William replied softly, trying to keep his voice and body neutral. If Liko punched him, that'd only ruin everyone's evening, especially for Cara. "You have families, lives here. I don't." It sounded convincing enough. And didn't bring in their mortal fragility at all. Or that he sure the hell couldn't stand to lose them.

Liko leaned closer to hiss, "You are full of shit. Our princess doesn't count, then?"

William was saved from answering as Cara skipped up to them, a warm glow and fine sheen of moisture on her skin.

She looked back and forth between them, obviously sensing some level of tension…probably thanks to the scowl on Liko's face.

The urge to lick the sweat from her skin shot through William—and straight down to other anatomy it had no business visiting. Hells bells, his thoughts were anything but platonic. Forget Yaga. Was Cara part succubus?

"There you are." She extended her smile to William, which made it unclear whether she'd meant the comment for Liko or him. She focused on Liko. "I wanted to say goodnight. I hope everything's all right." A glance toward William, and color darkened her cheekbones. "I thought we could sneak out. You know, before anyone tries making a big deal out of it." She leaned in to give Liko a quick, one-armed hug, and the big man patted her shoulder indulgently.

William shifted. He'd been Shades commander; they'd shed blood together. He sure the hell wasn't hugging them.

Liko, freed from Cara, gave William a dark glower that erased any possibility of hugging…but didn't seem to suggest a coming punch, either. "Through the kitchens and out the front door. Clearest path without interference." He leaned close to Cara. "Did you need anything else, Princess?" The tone and the glare he shot at William asked whether she might want help to, say, dump her new husband and bury the body.

Cara's hesitation lasted a few years until she slapped on

that familiar, careful smile he'd started to recognize and turned it on both Liko and him. "No, we're good." Then she did that thing where she glanced at William but didn't meet his eyes. "Let's go."

She led him surreptitiously through the crowd, acting as though she searched for a friend rather than escape, then they ducked through the industrial kitchens, out into the central atrium, and finally, out into the crisp autumn night and the sudden silence of the gravel parking lot, the hum of the building's floodlights deafening. The privacy of the moment, the significance of the night—their wedding night—closed around them.

Their footsteps crunched in the gravel.

"We should take my Jeep. Don't want to damage your dress." He gestured toward the older model gray Jeep Cherokee, similar enough to the Jeeps he'd driven during the forties to be a small point of familiarity in a changing world.

"Sure. Great. I'm not far," she said, voice high and over-bright, that knife-blade smile in place.

He knew she wasn't far, just across the secondary highway. His research ensured he knew Beckwell's layout and danger spots. He held open the passenger door, and she gathered her skirt to slide past him, close enough he caught the heat of her body, her faint spicy floral scent. Talk about danger spots. Heat stung his body, made him remember how large that front seat was, especially if the seat was laid back.

Cursing himself, he slammed the door and sucked in a breath of autumn air. The wind ruffling his hair wasn't, unfortunately, cold enough to get him thinking straight. Hell, he was tempted to stuff his mouth with chocolate and peanut butter, some other sweet treat...but that wasn't the fill he craved. So much for his vaunted self-control.

Wedding night. Back to the intimacy of her home. Damn and blast. The plan had seemed simple, but he hadn't considered the allure of a beautiful woman, or the pull of tradition and circumstance. Maybe Liko was right, and he'd spent too long hunting and not enough time talking. Talking just reminded you more than a knife to the throat where you didn't belong, who didn't want you. Neither the human nor paranormal world wanted him.

He climbed inside the Jeep and turned the engine over, tapping the wheel a few times. No damned way was he prepared for the intimacy of her house. Telling his new wife he'd drop her off and see her later would likely go over like a lead balloon, though.

Cara cleared her throat, leaving him no choice but to drink in how soft and feminine she looked in his Jeep that was more likely to play host to corpses than beautiful women.

"I was thinking," she said, mustering up false joviality. "You're new in town. Maybe I could give you a tour?"

He probably could have mapped Beckwell himself. But thank the gods for any valid reason to avoid her house a little longer. "Sounds great. Where to first?"

THANK the Goddess William had agreed to her idiotic tour idea. Seriously, who went for a tour at night in the country? There was nothing to see, but it did mean they weren't back at her place. Together. Alone. On their wedding night. Maybe that was why they'd both played along for forty-five minutes while they'd circled the small collection of houses that made up Beckwell woods, down through three-acreage areas, through the center of town four times, and were headed for their fifth circle.

The trees hemming in both sides of the road flashed in the headlights, wind stirring leaves free and flinging them at the Jeep. This was getting ridiculous. His scent, his presence, his body was too close for comfort in the driver's seat. They'd have to go back to her place soon, even if it would be weird and awkward and…

Cara studied William's silhouetted profile.

Far too tempting.

Okay. Plan B—or was that C? Disperse any wedding night-type tension by establishing a firm friendzone. He wanted platonic. She'd been thinking taking it slow, but guess they'd aim for glacial instead.

She cleared her throat, pitching her voice toward chipperness to make this less weird. "Have you spotted signs those Guardians are here? What are we talking, pitchforks and bonfires? I know this town. I'd make a great partner." Partnership established, she'd either get to know him, or he'd complete his mission and skip town. She reached for the Yaga pendant, frowning.

They went through the four-way stop and made two lefts and a right before he answered. "The Guardians are more subtle, at least in the beginning. I have a meeting with the police chief tomorrow. We're looking for petty vandalism, graffiti, small crimes to start. They recruit disenfranchised young paras who feel they don't belong in this world and are feared by the human one."

His use of "we" was favourable. Now a joke to build comradery, like Mr. Einar recommended. "That could be most teens at any school. Heck, that could have been me."

No laugh, not even a chuckle, and it was too dark to see if there'd been a hint of a smile. Crap.

"Seems like you know everyone and they you." Tone completely serious, yet at least he'd taken the bait for conversation.

Conversation was good. Left less room to think about sex. And beds. And all the muscle hiding beneath his suit. And stripping off said suit to reveal—

"I love Beckwell. I always have. But it's not easy to belong here. I was such a misfit," she blurted out before heat stole up her neck. *Super smooth.* She fake-coughed. "I mean, Beckwell is great, but like all paranormal sanctuaries, the class system and nonsense about 'pureblood' plays a part. I used to visit Beckwell when I was a kid, but after Mom died when I was six and Dad dropped me off with Gramps and Gran, I knew more about the Normal world than the paranormal one. I didn't understand all the rules —you know, don't ask about other people's species, don't stare, celebrate your own ancestral magic but don't expect anyone else to, those with the most power win—and like I said, I'm pretty pathetic in the abilities department. Plus, as much as Gramps and the Shades tried to help, their added attention only seemed to make things worse."

No one else, not even Maddy, Ainsley, or especially Jessie had understood why Cara idolized the Shades. Then again, everyone else had forgotten that without soldiers like the Shades, the Guardians would have won the Second World War and destroyed all the sanctuaries like Beckwell, all the paranormals with mortal blood. But, as kids, the Shades' attention had created more complications since two of them at the time were the town mayor and the police chief. Preferential treatment for four unpopular kids who hadn't been born in Beckwell, and worse, all had minimal and unusual abilities didn't earn them friends. On top of that, Cara was a Yaga. Outsiders who'd always lived outside of society, bohemians routinely breaking social mores like sex and kids outside of marriage and celebrating feminine power long before it was cool.

"You should have seen the trouble I got into when I

stuck up for my friend, Maddy Hatt, by bringing Gramps's old field med kit to school and telling the bully I'd use it on him if he didn't smarten up." She'd known it was more first aid than weapon, but the bully hadn't. Nor had the principal or the bully's parents.

Well, upside, describing what a loner she'd been was probably killing all sexual vibes. Like the ones she'd spotted in his eyes when they'd danced, when he'd held the door for her. He'd called platonic, which made any idea that he was attracted to her unfair. Never mind that he resembled a sex god. Or, what a sex god *should* look like, rather than the fat schlubs who usually stole the role.

"You never wanted to leave Beckwell?" he asked.

She shrugged. "No. This is my town. I've never wanted to live anywhere else…not that Gramps ever believed me." Gramps told her he'd abandoned her at the house so he wouldn't hold her back. Back from what? All she'd ever wanted was to protect Beckwell like the Shades and prove her worth to them. Which was too pathetic sounding to explain.

After an exceptionally long pause, William spoke, remaining a silhouette. "I was born in the human world, too. Didn't find out until I was in my twenties that the paranormal world existed, and I was part of it. Turns out, not dying when everyone else around you does gets you noticed, and when word got around, well, I was about as popular as I am now."

His tone was wry, but Geezus, Josie, and George, that must have been awful. She wanted to give him a big hug, hold him tight, and not listen to all the horrible things people said about him. "I'm so sorry," she said, some of that ache inside in her words. "At least you're here now. With your old friends." *With me.* Fantasies were fun, but being in love with a fantasy was pathetic. Learning to love a flesh-and-blood man was real.

Ugh. So not doing well with the platonic thing.

Fortunately, William didn't notice. "Jax, my first paranormal friend, explained things to me—things like those rules you mentioned. He gave me purpose, led me to what I do today." He shot a glance her way. "What about you? Who pulled you out of your childhood angst?"

Damn. The way he talked to her made it seem like he genuinely wanted to know *her* in a way she'd rarely encountered. A quiet, girly kind of sigh slipped over her. Damn the darkness and the fact that he faced the road again so she couldn't read his expression to know for sure.

I spent most of my time talking to my necklace and with my grandfather and his friends. Yeah, they'd wait at least until the third day of marriage before she sprang that on him. "My friend Dom." The truth sans weirdness.

"You mentioned her before. Was she at the wedding?"

Taking an interest in her friends, good. Details about Dom, not good. Although… Cara rubbed damp hands down her thighs. This was all about the buddy experience and getting to know each other on neutral terms, right? "Dom uses the pronouns they/them. And about Dom… since you're my bodyguard and all, I hoped you could help me." She picked through what she could tell him. "Nymphs," she said. "I'd like your help finding some nymphs. Dom is missing, and I have reason to believe nymphs are behind it."

He straightened in his seat, readjusted his hands on the wheel. "Particular nymphs, or in general? Your grandmother was a nymph, wasn't she? They're pretty insular. I haven't encountered any in years. How do you know they're behind your friend's disappearance?"

Careful… "My friend was worried about nymphs the

last time we talked. Yes, Gran was full-blood dryad, but her family disowned her and left the area years ago. If I knew where Dom was, I—"

She caught the faint shadow in the road ahead. The headlights illuminated the red-gold fur of an animal.

"Dog! William, watch out."

He must have spotted the animal when she did.

The dog froze.

William jerked the wheel. Hit the brakes.

The Jeep jolted to a stop.

Her heart pounded, her hands braced on the dash. "Did we hit it?"

He sat frozen, hands clenched on the wheel. "I don't think so." Wincing, he glanced in the rear view.

Cara twisted around, peered through the side mirror.

A four-legged shadow stood where it'd been.

Waiting.

This was Beckwell. Built on a magical vortex that attracted all kinds of lost things and creatures. Weird happened. Not all of it benign.

Yet, staring back at the waiting animal, that cool calm of the knowing settled over her. Made her reach for the door pull. "Do you have a flashlight? We should see if it's okay." She climbed out of the Jeep.

William called after her, sounds indicating he'd scrambled for his door too. "No, Cara, wait—"

She walked toward the animal.

Good news was it didn't rush forward, try to tear out her throat, or tell her it was secretly a god in disguise. It waited. William's cellphone lit up the animal, a scruffy, red-brown dog, tongue lolling, planting itself on its rump to wait for them. It didn't bark. Didn't growl.

Didn't quite behave like a dog.

She knew this dog. It looked exactly like the animal in

the vision she'd painted. The only dog that had ever shown up on her canvas.

William approached from one side, Cara from the other.

The dog looked from her to him, then back again. Wagged its matted tail and cocked its head.

"Cara, we sure this is a dog?"

Nope. But William had a reputation for sometimes shooting first. She needed to know why this creature had shown up in a vision, what it meant. Maybe it had something to do with Dom, or nymphs, or the Guardians. After all, visions of William had increased three-fold the past month, right before Gramps had proposed the marriage plan and William showed up.

"Even if it's not a dog but a shapeshifter or something, we can't leave him here. He's skin and bones, and possibly suicidal, running out into the road like that. We stopped. The next car could hit him," she said. That sounded like a plausible reason to take it home. Besides which, a stinky dog was not conducive to romance.

"We're not adopting a dog. Especially one that's probably not a dog."

"We're not adopting him. We're making sure he's safe. Just for the night. I have a garage."

The dog ping-ponged its gaze back and forth between them, as though following their conversation.

Very undoglike behavior.

When William blew out a breath in defeat, she knew she'd won. "It might try to kill us."

The dog grinned, tongue hanging out of its mouth. Cheeky bugger.

"I've seen this dog in a vision. If he tries to bite anyone, we'll deal with it. But it'll be fine. You'll see." She gave the dog a quelling glance. The least it could do was look less triumphant.

The dog ducked its head and whined.

"Sure. What's one night," William grumbled. "It stays in the garage."

Chapter Five

#STEAMY

THE DOG DID NOT STAY in the garage. The dog did not step one paw in that garage. Cara jabbed her paintbrush into the burnt sienna before smearing it across the canvas with vicious strokes. If lying to her new husband and then leaving him to deal with the probably-not-a-dog wasn't bad enough, after changing into her paint-stained white tank top and cotton boxers, she'd escaped to her sunroom-studio for a quick session. Hopefully, painting would give her some clarity about the craziness of the day.

The setting sun streamed through the sunroom's windows, cutting a stripe of light across the canvas and the initial dark tones of the painting. Life had gotten more complicated since Dom disappeared two days ago. Now she was lying to her new husband, bringing home strange animals, still didn't know what'd happened Dom, and would lose everything if she didn't figure out this nymph mystery and get Dom back. She needed Dom's help to consult with Doc Quilan and make her potions. Teaching art, making potions…that was the place she'd built for herself in Beckwell, so it didn't matter that she didn't have the abilities everyone expected of her. She didn't get visions of the future walking in her garden like Gran. She didn't have glimpses of other people's futures like Mom. Nor brief prophetic visions like Gramps. Without her ability to make potions, without Dom to help prove Cara had worth…

A small shudder chased down her spine. She tightened her lips before rinsing her brush and dipping into the next color, a brilliant cerulean blue. She'd find the nymphs, get Dom back. One thing at a time, she'd get things under control.

Water ran upstairs in the bathtub where William attempted to bathe the dog. There were barks, followed by male rumbles. Then a splash and more rumbles. This time, guessing from the tone, William's swears. His presence shrank the echoing space of the two-story, three-bedroom farmhouse. The distance between her bedroom and the one she'd offered him, two doors down, felt no more substantial than a sheet strung between them.

She let instinct guide her color choice and actions as she once more cleaned the brush and made more bold strokes across the canvas. Visions didn't require refined work, just broad strokes and the gist of a thing. It'd been months since she'd painted what she wanted. These days every painting was controlled by visions. Those paintings were why she'd brought home that probably-not-a-dog, why she'd agreed to the whole marriage.

Not that Mr. Platonic-Marriage cared. William had brought in a single duffle bag from his Jeep and kept it on his shoulder, like he was a tourist and didn't want anyone to steal his few belongings. He'd nodded when she'd pointed out Gramps's empty-shelved den and offered it for his use. Had finally set the bag down in the second bedroom but hesitated to enter any of the rooms she showed him, as though creating a mental map of a museum but never touching the exhibits.

She let the painting and the vision take her, entering that meditative state for a few minutes.

"Cara..." Dom's voice crackled through Cara's mind, staticky and indistinct, as though over a bad connection. *"Nymphs... find... town... threat... marriage..."*

Cara dropped the brush in the water and clutched the pendant. *"Dom? Can you hear me? Are you there?"*

The pendant went cold.

Whatever barrier she'd broken through in meditation was gone. Dom was gone.

Her shoulders slumped. Raising her gaze up to the painting didn't help. She'd painted enough to make out two distinct figures on the canvas. One of them with a bold, blue-gray gaze even more haunting in real life, and firm, hard angles forming his face. William.

The other, smaller and more colourful, burnt sienna touched with umber, oddly amber eyes for a canine. The supposed dog they'd found on the road tonight.

Shaking her head, Cara pulled a sheet over the wet painting and glanced at the stacks of canvases leaning against the outer walls. She'd never painted William and the dog together before, but maybe now because they were together? Three of the canvases leaning against the walls portrayed the red-brown mutt.

In more than half of the remaining canvases, William's fierce features stared out. So much for clear messages from the universe.

She stared out the windows into the black of the back-yard. Too bad none of these visions came with guides. Back in school they used to say visions required patience, that if you were supposed to understand them, you would. Patience had never been her strong suit. William and the dog were together in the painting and literally. Did that mean they were supposed to be? That they were connected? Hell, maybe she painted William because she'd listened to one too many stories and was obsessed.

A sudden shiver raised goosebumps, and her scalp prickled. Her gaze sharpened at the indecipherable dark outside. She swallowed and wrapped her arms around herself. It was her backyard. She'd walked home dozens of times through the dark yard most of her life, always felt safe. This was her land, her home. Even still, she backed quickly from the windows.

As though someone else stared in.

Barking and more splashing echoed upstairs.

She grimaced. Speaking of somethings… There was the possibly-a-dog creature upstairs, one she'd invited inside. The least she could do was help de-stink the animal.

Flicking off the sunroom light, she padded to Gramps's dark study, then the living room with its dark-green chairs and faded floral sofa, Gran's floral scent tickling Cara's nose. She didn't dare glance into the empty former dining room, the room they'd converted to Gran's sick room. The scent of roses and summer, so distinct to Gran, followed her into the foyer with its ticking clock, reminding her she hadn't filled those boxes where the rented hospital bed had stood. Like Mom, Gran had died with the beep and hum of machines. Then a few months after, Gramps announced he was moving into the Senior Center with the rest of the Shades. Freeing her, he said. Abandoning her was more like it.

She pounded up the stairs toward the bathroom faster than she had to, grateful that tonight she wasn't alone in the house. She knocked on the bathroom door.

"Can I lend a hand?"

There was an answering splash and protesting bark.

"That'd be great," William called back, then addressed the dog. "Hold still, will you? We've made enough of a mess as it is. We don't have to make it worse or damage Cara's house. I need to suds you up, then we can rinse, then we're both out of here." He was trying to reason with the animal.

It was so damned cute, she was smiling as she opened the door and stepped inside.

Anything she might have said died a swift death at the sight that greeted her. She sucked in a breath, hand squeezing the doorknob.

Some part of her registered the wet dog covered in bubbles that barked a happy greeting.

All the rest of her couldn't turn from wet, gleaming skin, rippling chest, and back muscles. Like her, William had stripped off his wedding clothes, leaving him in dress pants only, where he knelt beside the clawfoot tub. Scars criss-crossed his back, other puckered flesh made her wish she could kiss away the memory of that pain. Maybe lick it, too, for good measure. Heat spiraled through her, burning away all those good intentions to keep things platonic, focus on the other problems already taking up bandwidth. So much glorious, naked, bronzed skin. Holy centerfold. She had a half-naked fantasy man in her bathroom, right there for the taking.

Cara licked her lips and tried not to drool. "Y-you took off your shirt."

"Figured it'd get wet."

A very inappropriate comment about other things getting wet shot through her. She squeezed her lips and knees together.

The dog barked, water splashing, claws scrambling against the edge of the tub.

"Oh, no, you don't," William muttered, grabbing the

mutt gently by the scruff and keeping him from jumping out. "Sorry. He got out before. I'll clean up." He gave her a nice full frontal, which unfortunately contained dress pants. "I can hold him, but I need some help with the sprayer."

Get closer. To all that naked male flesh. Glorious, lightly bronzed like he tanned or something. Nah, she couldn't see William hanging out in a tanning parlor. Maybe he ran around shirtless most of the time. Now why weren't any of the stories about that? Her head filled with images of a half-naked William running through the streets, doing action-hero stuff with sexy stoicism from injuries that left those scars. Was his skin as hot and smooth as she imagined? His muscles would jump as she pressed her hands over those scars, kissed each one—

"Cara?" William gazed at her in a way that said she'd been standing there drooling a little too long.

"Oh. Yep. Of course." She slipped past the open door and dropped to her knees beside him, face burning.

The dog yipped, wagging its tail and splattering them both with soap bubbles.

Cara laughed. Mystery animal or not, he was cute. "Naughty boy," she said through a smile. "This is a game to you, isn't it?"

The dog yipped again, tongue hanging out in a big doggy smile. It was good at playing the role.

This stinky guest reminded her so much of Lucky, her childhood dog. He'd helped her warm up to life in Beckwell…until he'd developed a tendency to run into roads.

"You okay?" William asked.

She met his gaze that had turned a deep, stormy blue, his focus on her not the animal. Plus, still mostly naked and close enough their thighs brushed.

It was difficult to swallow, harder to speak. "Just thinking about a childhood pet. We should give this guy a name." She reached for the receiver-style sprayer hanging above the taps. She ought to be having a cold shower.

"You spray, I'll hold him and scrub. I thought we agreed he's probably not actually a dog. He doesn't act like a normal dog."

"Then we can call him Not-Dog. I mean, until he finds new owners and all." She turned on both the hot and cold taps, running it over her fingers until it felt comfortably warm. "You don't like dogs?" She lifted the sprayer over the animal's head, who tried to scramble free of William's grip.

"I like dogs just fine. Had one for years," William said, voice gruff.

"Really? I never heard— I mean..." Her face burned. "That must have been good company."

Those beautiful shoulders lifted in a noncommittal shrug. "He was." His gaze grew unfocused in a way that suggested memory held him. "Jack. His name was Jack, named after an old friend." The softness in his expression shuttered, and he focused on the dog, scrubbed the animal again. "Animals, like people, don't last forever. Especially if you're me."

"William, I'm so sorry. I... I guess that's the part they don't tell you about immortality, huh?" She wanted nothing more than to pull him into a hug...and maybe lead him into her bedroom to have her way with him all night until it didn't hurt anymore. Her throat thickened, her eyes prickled, and heat of all kinds suffused her. Oh, Goddess. All the stories, even the ones Gramps told... They'd never given the mighty hero William Best such soft-ness, never talked about the lost friends, the lost pets, the loneliness and isolation he had to feel.

The tips of his ears pinked. "It is what it is." His voice was gruff before he cleared his throat. "This one's not ours. Not-Dog is accurate enough. Hold still, dog. We had a deal." William tried to scrub the animal, which twisted and danced around the tub, tossing its head, yipping, and howling.

"Deal?" She had to raise her voice above the howls.

"The dog acts like a normal dog, it stays the night."

Water splashed over William's arms. Droplets slid in rivulets down the valleys and muscles, over his chest, toward that line of hair leading into his dress pants.

Cara gripped the sprayer, body hot and aching.

"Get this spot behind his ears, would you?" William replied, oblivious to her drooling.

She tried to spray behind the dog's ears.

The dog danced around again, almost jerking William off his knees despite all those muscles and his grip on the animal. Barking again and again, the dog jumped around, splattering William and Cara.

"Stay still," William growled.

Not-Dog jerked again, somehow freed himself.

William reached for him.

The dog scrambled for the edge of the tub, barking. It leapt.

Cara saw where it was headed. Eyes widened, sprayer in hand, she scrambled to move—

The dog hit her square in the chest.

She fell onto her back. The sprayer flew out of her hand, water spraying everywhere.

The wet, soaking dog licked her on the face, then shoved off her chest and dashed into the hall.

"Dang, I swear I had him. Are you okay?" William rushed to her side, grabbing the sprayer and shutting off the water with one hand, scooping her against his chest and cradling her against him with his other arm.

Oh, she was freakin' peachy. Maybe it was the concussion talking, or maybe her libido had drowned out the pain receptors, because every part of her prickled with awareness of William's arm around her, the touch of his fingertips on her face. She stared up into that warm, blue-gray gaze. Damn. There was something about a man who could multitask…and who smelled so good, something a bit spicy, maybe some old-fashioned cologne or something, plus that distinctive minty sweetness of his breath. So much warm flesh, within easy reach of her fingertips, her lips.

"Cara, are you hurt?" He repeated more softly.

So, this was what heaven felt like. Or when something you'd dreamed became flesh. Warm, smooth flesh sheathing hard muscle… "I'm fine," she breathed.

"He got you pretty good." William glanced down toward her chest, his gaze flicking back to hers, color climbing his cheekbones. "You're, uh, soaked through."

She followed the direction of his gaze, down to her white, paint-stained tank top… Oh. Make that virtually transparent tank top that showed off the cute lacy purple bra she'd worn.

Her gaze flicked up. Caught William enjoying the show, his eyes darkening and dilating. From the way his heated gaze stroked over her, he wouldn't mind helping to take that bra off too.

She lifted herself in his arms, slid her hand up that muscular forearm, over his bicep. Muscle tensed beneath her touch. Her hand glided over the hard heat of his chest, her fingertips tracing water droplets across his skin. His heartbeat pounded beneath her fingertips.

William's gaze locked with hers.

For one shuddering, breathless moment, she knew he'd kiss her. Like everything else the stories never talked about, he'd be so damned good at it. He'd know how to touch a woman. Would make her sigh, wring the pleasure from her lips. Maybe he'd carry her across the hall to her bed where he'd make sweet, gentle love to her all night long. Or maybe they'd never get that far. Their touches would turn frantic, tearing at each other's clothes, grasping and caressing, sliding and thrusting, moans and the feel of him, squeezed in her—

"Let's get you on your feet," he said, voice gruff like a dash of cold water all over her fantasies and hauling her to her feet.

Or that.

Her knees were unsteady a moment, but that was probably the lust. Could have been the way her head spun, the way everything had been going so well and now… William helped her to her feet, all business and efficiency. No lingering touch, no hands sliding over her flesh. Hell, it was like touching her burned him.

The second her knees were steady, he stepped back, reached for the bathroom door, and escaped into the hall. "I have to find Not-Dog."

His footsteps carried him rapidly away, the hottest almost-sex moment of her life instantly aborted. A celibate wedding night sucked.

Chapter Six

FIRST STRIKE

KEEPING things strictly platonic between he and his tempting new bride was proving harder than expected—in more ways than one. William stalked through Cara's dark yard after the mystery mutt, a cold North wind flaying his bare skin no less than he deserved. Thank gods the mutt had taken off into the night because he'd been too tempted by Cara's moist lips, the softness in her dark eyes, the promise of both ecstasy and peace in her touch. Forget chocolate and peanut butter. He had a whole new obsession.

He glared into the shadowy darkness, wind rushing through rustling leaves clinging to branches, stirring the fallen into a shushed dance. Where the hell was the mutt? It probably wasn't a dog, but it was as soaked through as he, the wind was cold, and if it'd wanted to be welcomed into Cara's home to set up some plot, it should damn well get on with it.

That made two of them who deserved nothing from her, two wild, homeless creatures she'd allowed into the coziness of her home. His gut twisted. She needed to stop looking at him that way she did. With softness in her eyes, sweet and sympathetic because he'd been dumb enough to say anything about Jack. She wasn't one of those violence groupies who believed the worst of him and lusted after it. Yet, if she'd heard the stories…

How could she look at him like he was worth anything?

As though he was a man.

Not-Dog yipped and rushed out of the darkness, jumping and dancing in the moonlight.

"I should leave you out here to freeze and fend for yourself," he scolded, scooping the shivering wet animal into his arms, damp leaves and mud sticking to his bare chest. "Your dog act stinks. You actually stink, and you're not causing any trouble for Cara, got it?" He strode toward the warm glow of the farmhouse. "I don't care what you are. Stay out of my way. And, to be clear, you're sleeping in the garage."

The dog whined pitifully, shivering harder.

It would be cold in the garage, especially for a wet dog…

"William? Did you find him?" Cara called out into the darkness, a warble sounding her unease.

Blast. Was she out there, soaked and on the porch, too? She wasn't dressed for the elements. He stalked faster around the edge of the house toward her, close enough to see her slim curves silhouetted in the open doorway.

"William? Dog?" Her voice had a fear-sharpened edge. "See?" she muttered. "That's why we should have given him a name. Then at least I'd have something else to call when you both disappear into the dark."

"I thought we'd agreed on Not-Dog," William said, stepping up onto the porch beside her.

She jumped with a small cry, her hand flying to her neck. "Frick's sake!"

"Get inside. It's freezing out here." He edged her back-ward toward the door.

She stilled, staring out toward the darkness and the rustling trees. Her hands fell slack to her sides, and she cocked her head. "Do you hear that?"

The wind rustled again, sending a chill through him. Not-Dog whined and wriggled in his arms.

"It's calling me," she murmured.

Hairs rose on the back of his neck and arms. "Inside. Now," he barked, taking her arm and bundling her inside the doorway, closing and locking the door and positioning himself between her and the outside. "Go upstairs, get dried off, and you may as well head to bed. I'll deal with Not-Dog and get him settled in the garage."

Not-Dog whined again, tried the puppy-dog eyes on Cara.

She raised a brow and set a hand on her hip. "Oh, c'mon. He can stay in the kitchen. I don't think he's dangerous."

"He's a menace who smashed your skull against the bathroom tile. Then, somehow, managed to escape through a locked door. Garage is generous. I'll deal with him. You get to bed."

Alone. On their wedding night. Her body sliding beneath cool sheets, aching and wanting, ready for him... While he gave an animal of questionable heritage another bath.

Yeah, there was no part of his plan to use her as Guardian-bait that led to a happy ending.

Especially not for him. He'd done too many things that walked the line between decent and unforgiveable. Dad might have called him an abomination years ago, but William's actions had proved it true. Using Cara, lying to her was bad enough. He wouldn't make it worse, wouldn't give her anything to regret when he left.

She'd crossed her arms, face mutinous. "I can help you with the bath."

The two of them in that confined space, steam making her skin dewy, her leg brushing his. The scent of her surrounding him, making him think stupid things, like giving up his mission. Making this a real marriage, deserving of a real wedding night. He saw forever in Cara's eyes in a way he never had with Marjorie so many years ago. All because Cara looked at him like he was human.

Obviously, she had poor taste in men, and he was losing his edge.

"I'm good," he said, voice gruff. "It's been a long day. Get some sleep."

She stared a long moment, then finally headed toward the stairs. "Be nice to Not-Dog," she called over her shoulder, one foot on the stairs. "He might not be a dog, but he is…important somehow. We should find out how before we get rid of him, don't you think?"

"Tomorrow he's gone. Good night, Cara."

She half-turned, curls catching on her shoulders, the light from the upstairs hall creating that halo effect again, a picture of sophistication, grace, love, and home that stole his breath. "Good night, William."

Then she was gone. Up the stairs, her door closing with the finality of that click.

AN HOUR LATER, both he and Not-Dog were clean and dry, the animal secured in the garage with a pile of old towels to keep him warm, no sign of intruders outside.

William rolled his shoulders, steeling himself for the task of securing the house for the night.

The creaking wood floors in Cara's house reminded him with every step this was more than a house; it was a home. The kind of home he hadn't had since he was sixteen and moved out to work at a neighboring farm, hoping that removing himself from the picture would allow Mother and Dad to repair their relationship. A relationship damaged by Dad's suspicions that William looked nothing like him, was never sick, stronger than any of the other boys...not quite human. Maybe it'd been too late by then anyway, and it'd cost William the safe comfort home provided, depending instead on roadside hotels, bedrolls beneath the stars, and the front seat of his Jeep.

He padded barefoot through the kitchen, with its worn black and white floor tiles cool beneath his toes, the tiles apparently laid by Jenklow and Einar, a personal touch like the hand-built white cupboards. He shook his mint tin, popping one in his mouth, the sweet chill settling over his tongue.

No attackers awaited him in the kitchen or pantry, softly scented of sweet treats Dad would have disapproved of, the pencil marks on the doorframe noting heights for Cara and, in more faded pencil, Marie, Cara's mother. He popped another mint in his mouth for Dad. Shutting off the light behind him, he moved onto the front closet, shoes and coats tidy, a collapsed dining table peeking from behind them.

The dining room next door was echoing and sad, a few boxes hinting at unfinished business. Cara had been living alone with ghosts for too long. She deserved better. Maybe while he was here, he could help her with the table, help clean out some of these ghosts to make this space her own, to do the things she needed to move on.

Like she'd have to move on when he was gone. Some lucky fella would be blessed to meet her.

Next to that was Jenklow's wood-paneled den, a few dusty forgotten books in a box on the built-in desk, good space for a map behind the door or above the desk beside the window, the room musty but more of an office than he'd had for years, and she'd offered it to him. Last time he'd had an office, a friend had died instead of him. That was what happened when he got too comfortable, let his guard down and thought for one instant the Guardians weren't hunting him…or that he deserved good things.

The next room was a dated but cheery living room, painful in how personal the space was with the dark-green chairs, dated floral sofa and worn floral rug, the mantel and walls crowded with family photos. Jenklow and his late wife. Stages through their lives including a beautiful, dark-haired baby girl who resembled Cara, then photos with Cara in them, that solemn, dark gaze recognizable at any age. He stopped in front of one of the photos, child Cara standing in front of the house with a white dog—probably the one she'd mentioned—between Jenklow and his wife. The little girl was solemn and unsmiling. Maybe not long after her mother died and her father had abandoned her. She understood what it was not to belong.

He left the room without disturbing anything. Those photos, the echo of love in that room made his four tattered photos tucked inside his books more forlorn. A picture of Mom, one of him with the Shades, one of his dog Jack…and the snap someone had gotten of he and Jax, not long before the other man died. That and his battered old rucksack were all his life added up to, the bag so filthy he'd been afraid of it dirtying the handmade quilt in the room Cara had given him.

He stopped in front of the last door, her sunroom

painting studio, Cara had said. The tangy chemical scent of wet acrylic brushed his nose. He reached for the switch, hesitated. With the moonlight streaming through the windows, he'd have spotted any movement or silhouette. Although there was that large shape in the center…

He flicked on the light. An easel with a paint-stained cloth covering the canvas. No vil—

The female scream sawed through the silent house.

He'd flicked off the light and was halfway up the stairs in moments. Threw open the door to Cara's room. Bright light revealed no attacker. Just Cara, body bent and arched in the bed, clutching her skull with low, keening cries.

"Stop! Make it stop," she cried. "Dom, please!'

Pulse pounding, he analyzed the scene. Eyes squeezed shut. Gray-tinted skin, sweat on the brow. Likely psychic attack.

He perched on the bed, tried to keep his voice calm, muscles tensed as though he could fight her attacker. "Cara! Cara, listen to me." Wasn't Dom her friend? Why would they attack her? "Cara, it's a psychic attack. Build your shields." He took her wrists gently in his hands. *Damn it, damn it, damn it.* He wasn't psychic, knew only what basic training taught him. "C'mon, Cara," he coaxed. "Shields. Get them in place."

She moaned again, but the sound softened. Was the attack lessening because she'd gotten up her shields?

Or was she losing?

Hands clenched, he dug out his cell. Did he call in the boys? Jenklow? Someone stronger to help her.

"C'mon, Cara," he muttered.

"Dom…" The name eased past her lips like a breath. Then her body eased with a sigh, and she settled back on the bed. Slipped limp into sleep.

He gently lowered her hands onto her sides, tucked the

blankets around her then stepped back with a frown, his heart still pounding, guilt and something twisting up his gut. Did he wake her up? Call a doctor? Hell, if it had been a psychic attack, there was nothing a doctor could do. Hands trembling, he reached for the tin of mints in his pocket, popping one between his lips and letting the sugar soak like calm against his tongue.

Her breath slowed into the peaceful rhythm of sleep.

He retrieved the straight-backed chair from his bedroom and his notebook. Settling into the chair beside the bed, he opened his notebook, pulled out the pencil and scratched some notes, glancing up to check on Cara. The attack meant someone was already after her. She'd mentioned something about nymphs. Abilities were unknown. Too many suspects filled the Senior Center, let alone the town.

He matched his breath to hers, assuring himself the attack was over. During that attack, she'd mentioned Dom, her supposedly missing friend. Cara was hiding something. If Dom was a threat, whether Cara objected or not, they'd have to be dealt with.

Chapter Seven

A NEW DAY OF MAYHEM

CARA WOKE to find William in a chair beside her bed, dozing with arms crossed, white T-shirt straining across his chest, head drooped. Not-Dog stretched out at his feet, though the animal popped his head up and wagged his tail as she sat. She grimaced. When had they come in here? Standing guard over her.

Even asleep, William could have been a sex god. A tired one. One too many orgies the night before? Her lips twitched. Worse, though, was the innocent sweetness sleeping William had, something that pulled at her, made her want to tug a blanket over him and let him know he was safe.

That gentleness was more dangerous than the sex god. Gentleness snuck into the heart, made her remember behind the stories and the fantasies, there was a flesh and blood man. Accessible, warm… Someone that filled her home and watched over her all night long. Someone who still missed his former dog, who understood what it was like, to never quite fit.

She scowled at herself. This was not the recipe for a

happily ever after. He wanted a platonic, temporary marriage. The way he'd ended last night's almost-kiss emphasized that.

Then there'd been that attack. Nausea twisted her belly. Dom's voice, momentarily loud and clear in her head again, helping defend Cara as they always had.

Not-Dog cocked its head at her as she swung her legs over the edge of the bed.

She put her finger to her lips and slid free of the bedding, every rustle of the fabric thunderous.

Not-Dog glanced at William, then barked, loudly.

William jerked awake, overturning the chair, jumping to his feet, knees braced, hands out, prepared for attack. "What's wrong? Cara?"

Cara glared at Not-Dog, who unrepentantly panted happily, tail wagging.

She turned on William, the height of him, the way he filled out that T-shirt shrinking her room. Her throat thickened. Funny how all that innocence faded once he was awake and conscious. In her bedroom.

"All good," she squeaked, searching the room for something, anything. The glowing numbers on the bedside clock worked. "I have to get ready! I mean, I, uh…" *Play it casual. No need for panic.* "I have work today. Should get dressed."

William's gaze flashed to her white tank top, the boxers skimming the tops of her thighs.

Heat suffused her body. *Eep.* Mentioning clothes—or lack thereof—was a bad idea.

He cleared his throat, avoiding her gaze. The chair banged as he bumped it. "Great idea. See you downstairs." He hurried toward the door. Reached to close it, then frowned back at Not-Dog. "I put you in the garage." He clicked his tongue. "Not-Dog. Out."

Not-Dog gave her one more tongue-lolling doggy grin, then padded out after William.

At the click of the door, Cara sagged. Crap on a stick. One sexy man in her bedroom and she went to pieces. The glowing clock, though, said if she didn't get her butt in gear, she would be late for work. She changed quickly into a clean pair of slacks and a soft coral blouse with a collar that floated around her shoulders. It was feminine and frillier than she'd usually choose, but William's presence made her want to flaunt her girly side. Dumb. Would he notice? Probably not. Unfortunately, didn't stop her. That almost-kiss last night…

She hurried downstairs into the kitchen. Second day of marriage and all, she'd make breakfast. The sound of the running shower upstairs said she had time. She started coffee, the actions soothing, rituals she associated with Gramps and Gran. Then scrambled eggs and bacon. She cracked the eggs on the edge of the pan. The bacon hissed and spat the way she wanted to. Still, the memory of last night, the knives into the skull pain crept up on her, made her stomach twist.

Not-Dog's claws clicked on the tiles, and William cleared his throat to announce their presence.

"Breakfast is almost up."

"I'll pick up kibble for Not-Dog. Help find him some new owners." William snorted. "I locked him in the garage and out of the house last night, yet here he is. Maybe he should buy his own kibble." He paused, and though she focused on the eggs, the weight of last night warmed her neck. "Cara, are you all right? You know that last night—"

"I know what last night was," she said quietly, shoving the eggs hard enough some jumped out of the pan. "A psychic attack. Gramps and the boys trained me to fight them. I never…" Her voice faltered and her hand trembled on the spatula. "It means someone is after me, doesn't it?"

"Yes," he replied quietly. "But you're not alone."

She divided the eggs onto two plates for them and a bowl for Not-Dog, then the bacon. "If he can pick locks, eggs shouldn't hurt him. I want to help with the case. I know this town, I know the people. I won't let the Guardians destroy this town."

"Coffee?" William asked, pouring himself a cup—and ignoring what she'd said.

"No. I don't drink coffee." She brought the plates to the table and set Not-Dog's bowl on the tile with a clink. Her chair scraped the floor as she sat. "Well? What do you say? We can get started on a plan."

William's chair creaked as he sat. "You know the town, but can you believe people you know could be Guardians? That's why it's easier for me. I'm an outsider, which gives me more objectivity." He picked up his fork and started to eat.

She glared, brow lowering. He was doing the same thing the Shades did. Explaining all the reasons she couldn't be one of them, couldn't protect her town. "I'd recognize unusual or suspicious behavior in ways you wouldn't. Seriously, you expect me to sit around and go on like nothing has changed while my town is in danger and they come after others like they came after me?" She stabbed at her eggs. In her dreams, he hadn't been like this. He'd listened to her, respected her in a way the Shades never quite had. They seemed to still see her as the little kid listening to their stories instead of a full-grown woman capable of making a difference. Real William vs dream William was…complicated.

"I don't expect anything of you, other than to be careful. My name will give you some protection, and being able to recognize strangers will help."

"I take it you'll go and loop the Shades in on the real details, though, huh?" There was a small edge of bitterness to her voice that she tried to drown with a sip of hot tea. He'd been their leader, their friend. Of course, he trusted them. He'd just have to learn to trust her, too.

His silence stretched…suspiciously. He would go to the Shades, wouldn't he?

They ate quietly a few minutes, the room hushed other than Not-Dog's whines for bacon and the scratch of utensils against the plates.

Finally, William sighed, pushing his chair back from the table and gathering the empty plates. "If you hear anything, let me know. Otherwise, this is my case. I'm looking for news about specist graffiti, trouble stirred up for locals. I'll meet with the police chief this morning, see what he knows."

Cara pounced on the suggestion, jumping up from the table. "Great! We can compare notes tonight."

"Cara, you need to be—"

"Careful?" She set her hands on her hips. "I'm a grown woman, you know."

His blue-gray gaze flickered over her body in heated appreciation. "I noticed."

Her throat closed, her body heated. She dropped her hands from her hips, didn't know what to do with them since they wanted to reach for William. Now there was a reaction she never had with the Shades. She crossed her hands tightly over her chest instead, breasts sensitive. "T-thanks for noticing."

"Cara—" he said, voice rough, part plea, part need. He closed his eyes and ran a hand down his face. "Maybe partnership is the way to think about us. I need to focus on my mission to stop the Guardians. We need to remain—"

"Platonic. I remember." She somehow resisted the urge to roll her eyes. *Tough luck, libido.* Still, she couldn't resist teasing him. "I guess that means you won't be stopping by and posing nude for my art class on the human figure?"

His expression flickered and his ears pinked. "I… Well…"

She grinned. "I'm teasing." Mostly. "Cool. I'll start gathering intel today—carefully. You'll still help me find the nymphs, too, right?" She gave him her most professional, distant smile. That was what he wanted, right? Distant and platonic.

A frown shadowed his expression, though his tone remained even. "Of course. And your friend, Dom? Should we look for them?"

Dom had been there last night when Cara needed them. This morning they were silenced again. Which apparently had to do with nymphs. "We find the nymphs, we'll find Dom," she said, more confident than she felt.

William gave her a long, measuring look. Then nodded and gestured toward the door. "Great. Then let's get to work and track down the Guardians."

She eased out a relieved breath. Maybe things could get back to normal. She internally snorted. Normal? In Beckwell? Good luck.

Chapter Eight

PLANS

MAYBE A PARTNERSHIP WAS the best solution. Cara pulled the easels out of the storage cabinet in a far corner of the Center's dining hall, getting set up for her three back-to-back art classes. A partnership was how no one got hurt.

Okay, mainly, how her heart didn't get hurt. Didn't look like William dreamed about her, and he had no problem keeping his distance. They—she, William, and Not-Dog—had driven William's Jeep over. He'd barely stopped to let her out before he and Not-Dog raced off to a meeting with Chief Quilan...and buying Not-Dog food and supplies at the store. Strange that buying dog food had taken precedence to William catching up with Gramps and the boys, finding out what they knew. After sleeping beside her bed, he'd just abandoned her. Unless... She stared blindly a moment, squeezing the folded easel.

If he hadn't been William MacIntyre Best, terror of the paranormal world, she might have believed he was running. From their almost-kiss last night, her home...her.

A shiver went through her. Nothing had been right

since Dom had disappeared. She had to find those nymphs and get Dom back. If last night had been an attack, she needed her friend more than ever. No matter how hard it was to believe that Beckwell could be dangerous, that attack was hard to deny.

From the corner of her eye, she spotted Maddy Hatt making her way across the hall, right on time and wearing her usual elbow-length gloves. Purple ones embroidered with small pink roses today. Thursday their classes ran back-to-back, so they usually set up and cleaned up together. Maddy wasn't in as often as Cara, teaching her class on evaluating antiques only once or twice a week, and sometimes bi-weekly on rough weeks.

"I didn't expect to see you here today," Maddy said once close enough, since her soft, almost apologetic way of speaking didn't carry. She dragged over chairs, forming them into a semi-circle. "Is everything okay? I didn't know yesterday who your groom was. But the stories they tell about him…" She bit her lip and shook her head, dark eyes wide. "If you need somewhere to stay, I have room."

It was difficult to decide whether to be touched that Maddy had invited Cara to stay if necessary or annoyed about the gossip and stories, and worse that Maddy believed them. Maddy was the subject of stories herself. Touched won. While Maddy's mother used to run a B&B out of the rambling Victorian they owned, it was difficult for Maddy to be around people of any species, especially if there was any chance they might touch her.

"That's really sweet, Maddy, but William is nothing like how they describe him." This morning aside, he'd spent the night in an uncomfortable chair guarding her bedside. "He's kinder than people think."

Finished with the easels, Cara dug in the cupboard for

fresh canvases, breaking open the plastic wrapper then setting them out on the easels.

"If you say so," Maddy said, dragging over the last two chairs. "I'll never get married. Teapots are much better company. Far less confusing, don't you think?"

"Er…I suppose?"

"You're not mad at Jessie for yesterday, are you? She's just…" Maddy paused, hand on the top of the chair, likely searching for a nice way to describe their friend.

Cara raised a brow. "Jessie?" She snorted. "Honestly, I should probably be flattered she took time to talk at all. Isn't she building houses for some big-shot paranormal development company? Like fireproof houses for dragons or something? I know she's always wanted more than small-town Beckwell can provide."

"Ainsley said Jessie quit and they're starting an all new, women-owned and operated paranormal construction company. Made to Measure Homes for paranormal families. That's why she was so stressed yesterday."

"No kidding…" Cara said slowly, already turning it over in her head. A company that built homes for paranormals could be handy in Beckwell, especially with the influx of refugees…

"Cara, glad I caught you before your class," Doctor Quilan called across the room.

Maddy jumped, then ducked her head. "Good luck. We can talk later. Let me know if you need anything." She made a wide circle around the room to avoid Doctor Quilan. It wasn't just the doctor. That was generally how she behaved with men…and people.

Cara escaped by ducking her burning face back into the supply cupboard, rattling things around and ostensibly hunting for the charcoals. *Crap, crap, crap.* The attack had rattled her this morning, so she hadn't planned how to deal with Doc Quilan. It wasn't like she could help in the usual way, consulting for him on paranormal cases. Not without Dom. She gripped the cold pendant. *"Come on, Dom. You there?"*

The now-typical silence of the cool pendant was her reply.

Doctor Quilan cleared his throat, then greeted some of the students arriving for class, Mrs. Silver and Mrs. Kramer probably, habitual early birds.

Ugh. She couldn't hide in the supply closet all day. Pasting on a smile, she emerged, charcoals in hand, to face Doc Quilan, a handsome man with bronzed skin and dark hair. "I was going to stop by later," she lied. He had a whole armful of file folders for her. Not good.

Funny that neither he nor his nearly identical twin had ever gotten her heart pounding the way it did around William. Doctor Quilan, though, had given her a chance. When he'd found out last year that she and Gramps were unofficially and illicitly distributing potions to help residents with their paranormal needs, instead of reporting her, he'd proposed they work together. Cara—or rather, Dom—helped with diagnoses and consulting. Dom held the Yaga power. Without them ... Cara's throat tightened, and her smile stiffened.

Fortunately, the doctor was flipping through the files and didn't notice. "It's mostly regulars. Schedule's packed, so I thought I'd—" He blinked, then winced as he met her gaze. "Damn. Isn't this your honeymoon? You're probably taking time off." He rubbed a hand through his hair. "I should have thought..." He laughed ruefully. "With Piper gone and the twins not sleeping, my brain isn't operating." He turned to leave.

She could have let him go... but what if next time he decided he and his patients didn't need her potions?

"Wait." She caught up with him at the edge of the ring of chairs.

Doc Quilan turned, brow raised. "People do take time off, Cara. It's fine."

Despite her burning face, she held out her hand for the files. "William and I are, uh, delaying our honeymoon." *Liar, liar, pants on fire.* If the files were mostly regulars, that she could handle. She'd made those potions dozens of times, had extra on hand. "Let's see what we've got."

"You sure?"

Nope. "Of course. It's my job."

He handed over the stack of files. "Let me know if you change your mind. And, if you have time, I have a favour to ask."

"Mmhmm?" Talk about bad timing for a favor… She clutched the files against her chest.

Another grimace, and he pushed his hand through his hair. "It's the refugee camp. I haven't been over as much as I'd like. Cara, those people are having a rough time of it, most of them with no known history of paranormal abilities before this. I want them to know there's help here in Beckwell, that they aren't alone, and—"

"You'd like me to stop by?" Would have been easier with Dom, but she knew too well what arriving unprepared in Beckwell was like when you didn't understand the rules or unwritten history. Given time, Beckwell was an extremely welcoming place, but many residents were feeling the pressure of the news coverage, scrutiny from the mortal world and arrival of desperate refugees. Like many of the newcomers, she'd been rejected and afraid because people who were supposed to love her were afraid of her instead. *Thanks for the baggage, Dad.* This time the smile was almost genuine. "I'll stop by after my classes." She'd have to figure out how to help once she got there, but maybe she'd find some nymphs.

The doc blew out a breath and his shoulders eased. "Thank gods. I'll get over there tomorrow, but if there's anything you can do for them, I know it'll be appreciated." He glanced at his watch, cursed beneath his breath. "Darn, I'm late." He walked backward toward the door. "I'm buying you and William dinner from the bar. You're a rockstar, Cara."

Turning away, Cara let her smile drop. She rubbed a hand down her face. She wanted to help, but how the hell was she supposed to do that without Dom?

"You, child, look like the weight of the world is crushing you," Mrs. Cole's warm, raspy feminine voice said just before she wrapped an arm around Cara's shoulders. "Doesn't that handsome man of yours know how to pleasure his wife?"

Cara offered a genuine smile to the dark-skinned woman, Mrs. Cole's silvery hair pulled up and beneath a fuchsia and gold turban. "I'm not discussing my sex life with you, Mrs. Cole. How are you this fine morning?" A regular at the classes and one of Gran's closest friends, Mrs. Cole was one of Cara's favourite people. Orbiting her offered a hint of Mrs. Cole's confidence...and a vague sense of Gran's presence.

"Your loss." Mrs. Virginia Cole, with her expensive perfume and flamboyant wardrobe, was not one of Gramps's favourites. He called her Mrs. BossyBody. Not without merit, as she knew everyone and their secrets. "The stories I could tell you, the positions I know between my beloved husbands and wives, rest their souls. The things my first husband could do with his tongue——"

Cara cleared her throat as they moved together toward the circle of chairs and easel, Mrs. Cole's place front and center. No one who'd met her would dare take that spot, not even Mrs. Silver or Mrs. Kramer. "You've told me. In great detail." About her many wives and husbands, all of whom she'd outlived, even the greatest love her life and her last wife, Lyla. It was Mrs. Cole's penchant for gossip that could be useful today. "Actually, you might be able to help. I need to find Gran's family. Do you know where they moved after the war? Or if there are other nymphs in the area?"

Mrs. Cole paused in front of her chair, dark brow arched. "You and your husband are already into orgies?"

No way would she ever share William. "We both know nymphs aren't like that. Gran wasn't, I'm not." Although that also composed the sum total of her nymph knowledge.

Mrs. Cole patted her arm before taking her seat. "To each their own. I don't know why you'd bother with nymphs. As frivolous as their magic. Sheila Dryad and her family moved after the Veils fell, somewhere out East, someplace quieter than Beckwell, she said. I always felt it was good riddance when Rose's horrid family moved away. To disown their daughter for falling in love—no matter if it was with the Old Grump. I suppose he used to be handsome." She shook her head, cupping Cara's cheek sadly. "Your gran used to tell me nymph magic could be overwhelming, especially the first time. How she wished she'd be there to guide you when it was your turn."

"Funny that Gran would have said that. She didn't think I had any real ability, especially not nymph magic. Seems I take after Gramps's Yaga side." It was reflex to grip the silent pendant.

Mrs. Cole frowned. "Is that so… I'd always heard nymph genes were dominant ones." She shrugged, her expression clearing. "Ah, well, no more than you can expect from nymph frivolousness. I'll keep my ear to the ground, see if I can find some nymphs for you. What was the problem again?"

No way could she mention the pendant or Dom's sudden silence, not with Mrs. Cole's penchant for gossip. "Just curious about my family tree." Ugh. She never lied. Maybe because Dom was usually there to call her on it.

Cara gestured toward the easels and her class for the day. "Thanks all the same. We should get started."

Hopefully, she could lead the residents through their activity with no more interruptions, leaving her more time to figure out how she was going to handle the refugee camp without Dom.

Chapter Nine

ON THE CASE

THE FIRST THING you noticed when entering the blue metal Emergency Services building was the large dragon. No smoke and no scales—a good sign. This dragon wore a black T-shirt that strained across a broad chest, camo khakis, and had his booted feet propped on one of the battered desks out front in the office. Light glinted off his dark head as he read what appeared to be a dictionary. William paused inside the door, the wind blowing in a flurry of dead leaves with him. After leaving Cara at the Senior Center where she should be safe for an hour at least and Not-Dog in the Jeep, this meeting with Chief Quilan was supposed to be one of the easier tasks of the day.

Industrial fluorescent lights buzzed dimly above, lighting the four battered utility desks that were spaced out around the room. A deck of cards was on one of them, and there was a red back stretcher leaned against the walls. The dragon took up one of the desks.

As a rule, he avoided dragons. William popped a mint into his mouth, letting the minty chill on his tongue settle his thoughts. Nothing had gone as expected since he'd stepped foot in Beckwell. Probably shouldn't have expected this meeting with Chief Quilan would, either. Dragons were built for battle, not speed. If necessary, unless the guy sprouted wings, outrunning him was an option…or hitting him over the head while he was reading. It'd knock him out and slow him down. Although not the best first impression.

William cleared his throat. "You Chief Quilan?" He held out the mint tin.

"No." The dragon eyed the mints, then returned to his dictionary.

"Maddox, tell whoever's here to come back tomorrow unless they're bleeding or dead," another man called from near the rear of the small building. "Nah, scratch that. Tell him to see my wife if he's dead."

The dragon nodded his head toward the back room, possibly indicating Chief Quilan was the one speaking or that William should head that way. He didn't lift his gaze from the thick text in his hands.

William tucked his mints away and strode toward the voice. To the left were three gray steel doors, labelled Cells 1 to 3. To the right was a windowed door stenciled with "Chief Quilan." The office inside was maybe ten feet across, styled with disregard using a battered wood desk and dented filing cabinets before the design had been finished with scattered papers and file folders. Hunched over the desk was another large man, this one with bronzed skin, dark hair, and a green uniform, obviously Doc Quilan's twin. The man scowled down at the file. He didn't look like someone who got those muscles from wasting time in the gym.

"Maddox sent you back here?" The man massaged the bridge of his nose, then gave William a once-over. He gestured toward the chair across the desk—the one not piled with paperwork. "Not sure I want to hear it, but how can I help?"

"Does the dragon work here?" William asked, taking a seat in the groaning wood chair.

Chief Quilan snorted. "Hell if I know. He showed up one day. Doesn't say much, don't want to piss him off. Very old-school. As in, medieval-old from his take on how we should treat those in lock-up. I suggested he catch himself up, so he's reading the Criminal Code."

Ah, that must have been the dictionary-like text. "What part?"

Another shrug. "All of it, I think. If I ever figure out if he's a volunteer, he could be helpful." The police chief stacked his hands on the file in front of him, met William's gaze. "I'm Mal Quilan, by the way, Beckwell Chief of Police… Beckwell's only police. You are and you need?"

"William Best. I called yesterday. There's trouble on the way, and I'm hoping we can be on the same team when it arrives."

Quilan rocked back in his wood office chair that must've been around before electricity, the chair groaning and squeaking at the movement. A shit-eating grin crossed his face, and he stacked his hands behind his head. "Whoa. Okay, give me a second to absorb before I digest that shit is about to get worse in Beckwell. *The* William Best is sitting in my office." He cocked a brow. "Funny. Things they say about you? I figured for sure you'd have fangs, or you'd shoot me to introduce yourself." He jerked a thumb toward the door. "You sure you don't want to try that entrance again?"

William rubbed the back of his neck. This was the problem when people heard the stories before they'd met you. The light in the police chief's eyes, though, suggested teasing. Probably. Hard to say, since it didn't happen often.

"My schedule is full today, no time to deal with pissed-off dragons like that one out front who may or may not take offense if I shoot you."

Quilan barked with laughter and slapped the desk, that grin still on his face. "Damn. I can't wait to lord this over my wife when she gets home. I got to meet you in person." He cleared his throat, wiping a hand over his lips but not entirely clearing the smile. "Sorry. You must get that shit all the time."

"Not so much." Usually when someone said it, they weren't joking.

"Okay. Sorry." Quilan held his hands aloft before crossing his arms. "Business. Right. Bad guys coming. Guardians, right? Shitheads who partnered with the Nazis during the Second World War, hitting paranormal sanctuaries and spouting bullshit about 'purifying' the paranormal bloodlines and the like. I've heard rumors they're back, building their numbers in bigger centers. Look, no offense, but it's only me around here—and possibly Maddox the dragon. Since the Veils fell, it's been a shitshow. Too many refugees with new powers need answers, never mind the Normals coming here, hoping for viralworthy video footage. Not sure what I can do to help."

William leaned forward. "It's what I can do for you. Let me handle the Guardians, stomp their presence out here before it can grow. I've spent a good part of my life chasing them, and they're more likely to re-emerge any time they think they might have a foothold. Their entry into an area follows certain patterns, so it'll start with petty crimes like hate-themed graffiti, petty theft, specist-slurs. My concern is they're going to go after vulnerable targets, like that refugee camp, the Senior Center." Like Cara. That ultra-unique hybrid and potential weapon the Guardians needed. The need to see her, reassure himself she was okay tugged at something inside him, something young and hopeful warmed by the softness in her dark eyes.

A part of him that'd get people killed if he didn't lock it down.

Quilan snorted. "I pity anyone stupid enough to attack the Senior Center." He raised an eyebrow. "You worked with some of the men there, didn't you? Jenklow, Einar, Chaimek, Zaki, and my personal favorite, Bal Liko, who likes to call and give me lectures on policing whenever he's bored."

Sounded like Liko. "It's been a long time since they've seen action. They're more likely to be targets."

The other man rubbed his jaw, head tilted. "I dunno… Those guys held their own when we saw trouble around here. When they're not giving Loki or me a headache, they have serious connections in town and usually hear the gossip before I do." He shrugged, shuffling folders on his desk. "Of course, you know that, old friends and all."

William leaned back, tightness pulling at his chest. The boys wouldn't be happy that he'd come here first and not to them.

Fortunately, Quilan was too busy sorting through papers and files on his desk to notice William's discomfort. "I have a few cases here that tick those boxes. They were right here…"

"If you'd like references or a resume—"

The police chief laughed. "You've been doing this job for longer than I've been alive. You're a freaking legend, taking cases no one else will, providing law and order outside of the bloody gods and their games. Plus, way I hear it, you deal fair, and you give justice even to those who might not deserve it—like those Guardian freaks." He handed a small stack of files across the desk to William.

"You enough like the rest of us schmoes to have a cell phone so I can reach you if I hear anything or need backup?"

An almost smile pulled at William's lips. Yesterday he hadn't spoken with the other Quilan, the doctor, but this one he liked. Straightforward, made up his own mind, took care of his town. "I'm old, not dead." He stood and pulled a business card from his pocket, the simple black text including his cell and reading: "Best Paranormal Investigations. Help when you need it." He handed it to the police chief.

Quilan likewise stood, offered his hand. "Glad to have someone like you in town. And hey, you get tired of saving the world, I could use some help around here."

The other man had a firm grip as they shook. "You already have a dragon. I can't compare to that," William said. Joking. Hell, turned out you could teach an old dog new tricks—or maybe how to relearn the old ones. There really was something about Beckwell.

Or maybe it was Cara, being around the boys again, putting thoughts and wishes that belonged to a younger man in William's head. Thoughts that belonged to a man who still deserved things like happiness, love…friends. He didn't do relationships. Safer that way. Still, he'd only been in Beckwell a day, and other than the boys and Cara, Mal Quilan was the second person who didn't accept the stories as gospel. It was refreshing.

Not that he could afford to get used to it. The mission had to come first. This time, he'd hurt the Guardians enough to send them scurrying back under their rock. He had to hope Beckwell survived the fight.

Chapter Ten

REUNION

NOT-DOG HAD VANISHED from the front seat of the locked Jeep. William scowled at the big bag of kibble and the dog bed in the backseat, popped a mint, then drove across the road to the Senior Center. A problem solving itself should have been a relief, and yet, as he shut off the Jeep, he found himself searching for a flash of red fur. Damn it. The real problem was the Shades.

Eyeing the cream stucco Senior Center, he popped another mint, rolling his shoulders before he strode toward the double-glass sliding doors. His gaze snagged on the police chief's posted sign: "All magical weapons or objects banned from entry in the Senior Center. Occupants are dangerous. Seriously. Enter at your own risk. All magical weapons and objects will be seized."

William snorted, striding through the doors, scanning the atrium for the Shades. Magical objects would be the least of his problems if Liko had told the boys he was working the case without them. Hell, who was he kidding. Of course, Liko'd told them. He'd better expect a confrontation. Best to avoid them. They were too damned fragile, too damned mortal. Well, other than Zaki.

A long line curling through the atrium provided coverage but made it harder to spot approaching Shades. The boys expected William to work with them, but if they weren't killed, they'd find out the truth about his plans for Cara. That he wasn't just protecting her…he was using her. His jaw tightened, gaze narrowing on the line composed of some of the more unusual paranormals he'd spotted in town so far. None of the Shades, thank gods.

He headed for the doors of the dining hall and Cara, scanning the line.

Some were relatively human-looking, most of them male, in wrinkled suits. A few checked timepieces, others mopped sweat from their foreheads. The hairs on the back of his neck prickled. There was something reminiscent of the job lines in the thirties here, desperate men out of work who'd do anything for a job. As he neared the dining hall, grumbles rose near the head of the line, near a closed suite door. The guy in the toga with the trident swore. The one with the blue skin and multiple sets of arms appeared meditative. That one with the crown of thorns… A different sort of uneasiness tightened William's fists. These were desperate old gods hungry for new power that a little renewed faith-energy would grant them.

Perfect frustrated candidates for the Guardians. Trouble he hadn't anticipated.

"William, m'boy, is that you?" The too-chipper voice called.

Speaking of trouble… William's neck and shoulders stiffened. Hell no. He should have known Not-Dog and the dragon weren't enough for the Fates to throw at him. Something no one told you about having to deal with gods who'd granted you immortality on a whim was that when they decided to take an interest, they were harder to shake than flies on shit.

He debated walking on, but history proved the bastard would just follow him. He crunched down on his mint before turning on a slim figure in a well-fit blue suit, the god's white hair and beard coiffed into ringlets, and yep, that predictable, clueless smile. "Hermes." Sooner he confronted him, sooner this was over. "What are you doing in Beckwell?"

Hermes was all about the angle. His visits were obnoxious, but thankfully irregular. First time he'd showed up had been as William struggled to rebuild a life after the war, latching onto the Guardians as the purpose that would define him. Not that Hermes had cared. Still didn't care when he reappeared a decade or so later in the sixties, after the attack that destroyed the office and killed Berta. He'd known his widowed, bossy, sweet secretary better than he'd known his fiancée, Marjorie. The last time had been five years ago, when William was licking his wounds after an old nemesis, Irene Doherty, had got the jump on him and nearly taken his head. He wouldn't die easily, but he'd hurt plenty bad. Most things died when you chopped off their heads, presumably including him. Hermes's presence was more salt than soothing balm.

Hermes had given immortality out randomly, as cheaply as candy at a parade. Not because William or his mother was somehow deserving, not because there weren't too many other people and, worse, children fighting for life all the time. But because Hermes had been drunk and did it for the hell of it. Leaving William with the question of why him…and forced to try and create a reason for it, justification for his being. Judging by the whole "Abomination" thing, he'd done a shit job, too.

"No, hello? How've you been? Darn it, Hermes, you

look great?" Nothing in Hermes's tone suggested he expected anything but welcome in William's life. He ironically considered himself a father-figure, despite that granting Mother's prayers with an immortal child who looked nothing like her husband had soured that marriage quick. The god leaned forward and sniffed. "Still into cheap sweets I see."

William gestured at the line-up. "Why the line-up? I thought you preferred cavorting with nymphs or whoever's handy." Although… Hermes connections could come in handy to find some nymphs for Cara. William scowled. An avenue he'd revisit if all his other leads flopped. Damned if he'd owe Hermes a favor.

"New opportunities, turning over a new leaf and all that," the god said, his smile immune to William's coldness. "One of the local church groups fired their old god and decided to advertise for a new one—something about not enough pizzazz for the modern era, I think. Or maybe it was because the god stopped answering emails?" He shrugged. "I thought I'd interview for the position. New worshippers are always good news in my line of work, all the faith energy and the like. Plus, it'd be nice to get away from Olympus, strike out on my own."

"Yeah, I can see how spending thousands of years with your loving family might get tiresome." William didn't hide the bitterness in his tone, letting memories of his parents' angry marriage, the deaths of every member of his family, too many friends, each loss as painful as the last, wash over him. Immortality wasn't all strolling through the years and watching the decades flash by. It was loss and regret for gifts only mortals enjoyed. It was wondering why you'd lucked out when too many others had lives cut short.

It was why he'd made a name for himself protecting

those with mortal blood and lives. They deserved to enjoy the privileges he never would.

Hermes's smile faltered, and he glanced toward the opening door behind him. "You'd be surprised. Wish me luck, huh?"

Luck that might mean running into the negligent god around every corner? Not a chance. "Yeah. Sure. See you."

William didn't wait for the god's reply but hardened his jaw and strode quickly toward the dining hall and Cara, his hands fisted at his sides. Just what he needed. Flipping Hermes hanging around. One more distraction.

Stepping into the windowed, sunny dining hall, his mood was like a cloak of doom as he gave the room the once over. Clutches of seniors sat at some of the tables still eating their breakfasts. At another table a group of women played poker, betting with various arcane objects tossed in the center of the table instead of money. So much for the magical object ban.

If not for Hermes, this might've been his life. He'd probably have married Marjorie, his sweetheart before the First World War...before he'd known what he was. Maybe they'd have had kids, had all of this. Normalcy, stability, the ending that made what'd come before all the sweeter.

Most of the time, he didn't spare Hermes a thought. But running into him was like remembering a glass shard beneath a fingernail.

He rolled his shoulders, chest tight as the laughter and Cara's voice drew his eyes toward the far corner of the room near the bank of windows. Her slim figure stood out among the ten or fifteen residents seated in front of easels and canvas, their subject another resident perched on a stool in the midst of them—one of the female residents he'd spotted yesterday flapping around the atrium with those gray leathery wings. Her wings now were folded gracefully behind her, her body clothed in a simple white robe.

Cara tugged him closer, like a lodestone leading him home. Didn't matter how many times he tried to turn his thoughts to the mission, all he saw were her curves in the soft coral blouse, her ass delineated by the navy trousers. A queen moving among her subjects, she moved from student to student, sharing soft laughter, nodding her head as she listened, touching them gently as she'd offer some suggestion.

As though sensing him, Cara glanced up as he neared. She offered a tentative smile, her dark gaze sizing him up the way he had the dragon. She reached for her pendant, and his pulse quickened. She'd said it was a family heirloom, but that didn't mean it wasn't also a weapon. Or dangerous. Like that friend of hers, Dom, who's name she'd called last night during the attack. Albert sure the hell had left out a lot of details. And seeing as he was avoiding Jenklow and the boys, it made uncovering details tricky.

Cara gestured toward a lone chair near the wall before returning to her students.

Some of her students, most of them women, blatantly stared. They whispered loudly, a few pointed.

He settled into the chair and crossed his arms, tuning out the whispers and the stares. No surprise there. These ones had obviously heard the stories, too, and unlike the police chief, actually expected fangs and other evidence of his depravity.

His focus was Cara. The happiness in her eyes, kindness in the curve of her lips, attention and care in the angle of her neck as she listened to her students. Really listened, in a way few people did. Jenklow and Einar had that gift, too, of making the person they spoke to feel privileged for the attention. Cara, though, offered love and acceptance with her gaze. He ought to know, having been the subject of it yesterday, during the wedding.

And later, when he'd made a damn fool mistake and almost tasted her.

If she could make you feel special with a look, a kiss would be unforgettable. Anything more, life changing.

Cara finished with the last student in the circle, a gray-haired man in a burgundy sweater vest. She hesitated a moment, smoothed her hands down her thighs, then strode quickly toward William.

Damn if his heart didn't quicken, but he held out hope he'd developed an arrhythmia.

"Did you take Not-Dog to Gramps and the boys?"

He narrowly avoided wincing. "Not exactly," he said slowly. "Not-Dog vanished." Seeing as William didn't need the next question to be about the Shades—and his avoidance of them—best to change the subject. "How have things been so far? No attacks or unexplained headaches?"

She crossed her arms. "Nothing unusual, other than you losing Not-Dog. I told you, I'm fine." Another stroke of that pendant.

Much more of that and he'd end up jealous.

"I also had a chat with Doctor Quilan," she continued. "He's swamped and asked if I might stop by the refugee camp later. I thought…" She faltered, squeezed the necklace instead. "Maybe you wanted to go with me? Someone else offered to look into the nymphs, but I thought it might be good if we visited the refugee camp together, check for trouble."

His insides tightened. He should have asked Hermes about nymphs. "Cara, I said I'd help—"

"You're looking for nymphs?" one of the silver-haired women said, leaning around her canvas.

"Her grandmother's people, if possible," another

woman said, a regal woman with dark skin and a brightly colored turban.

"Mrs. Cole," Cara said to the woman with the turban, her face coloring. "I'm sure we don't need to discuss—"

"Oh, well, she should meet the twins. Hotties, the two of them," the first silver-haired woman said, ignoring Cara's attempts to stop her, and beaming over her revelation. "They're some connection to Ginny Lack's husband —you know, that other Famine boy. They're not Famine clan of course. They're nymphs. No one's supposed to know it, of course, but Sister Marguerite overheard Ginny talking to Piper—she's Pestilence," she explained, in case William didn't know. "Well, Ginny was saying how one of the twins is a male nymph. It's exceedingly rare, she said. Completely hush-hush."

"That's right!" Mrs. Cole said, throwing her hands up. She turned to Cara apologetically. "I knew he and his sister were nymphs, but they're so frequently out of town on paranormal peacekeeping missions on the other side of the world. They stop through here to visit the Derths." She, too, turned to William to explain, "That's the Famine horsewoman and her husband, dear." Then turned back to Cara. "Nahla and Caspian Sarasvati. That's who you need. Not hard to spot since they are usually the most attractive people in the room."

Poor sap. So much for a secret. Everyone in town knew Caspian was the ultra-rare male nymph…and gods help him if the Guardians found him. Didn't have to know much about nymphs to know males were highly sought-after for stud. William re-considered Cara's students. With their connections, these were potential informants.

Cara's attention, however, her expression pinched, was on the table of loudly cheering poker players across the room. "Dang." She gestured at him. "Did you see what the women over there were gambling with?"

"Not money."

Cara strode toward the poker game. "That's what I was afraid of." Distractedly she turned back to Mrs. Cole and the rest of her students. "Everyone, please continue with your sketches. Yes, this is my husband. Yes, he's new in town. He doesn't have any idea what shenanigans you all get up to, so let's all pretend to be nice for a few days, okay? We'll ease him into the truth gradually. Be right back." Then, below her breath, "After I prevent another firefight in the lobby with those illegal magic objects."

She hurried away amid the chuckles of the group. When she reached the table, action started with angry gesturing that devolved into pleading on the residents' part. Soon they'd reached divvying up of the pot. Cara never raised her voice, but quickly, they all stood as she pulled out chairs, pushed walkers close, caught a falling cane.

She obviously had everything in hand. He turned back to the ladies, pulled his mint tin from his pocket, and offered it. "Do you know where I might find the Sarasvati twins?"

Mrs. Cole raised a dark brow, taking a mint and swishing it in her mouth, considering him. "Young man, to be clear, we know who you are. We've heard the stories about the legendary William Best, savior of the underdog, bringer of dark justice...and occasional stirrer of trouble. We don't need trouble in Beckwell, and especially not for our Cara. You planning on causing trouble for either the Sarasvati twins or Cara?"

He straightened, tucking away his mint tin. "No, ma'am. I'm not." If trouble found him, that was another story.

"Hmm." Lips compressed, her doubtful expression confirmed she didn't buy it. She looked past William.

He followed her gaze.

Cara had broken up the poker tournament, returning with one of the former players. Cara carried an ungainly confiscated bag, heavy with the pot, including long wizard staffs protruding from the bag.

He turned quickly back to the ladies. "All I want to do is protect towns like this. And people like Cara. Especially Cara."

Another long glance from Mrs. Cole.

Cara would be here any second, but he kept his gaze steady, tried to appear harmless.

At last, Mrs. Cole spoke. "Most days they've been helping out around the refugee camp, helping the doctor's assistant, Mr. Frizzly, with getting folks into better accommodations. You'll find them there."

"Thank you."

He took the heavy bag from Cara, setting it against the far wall with other supplies while Cara got her new student settled and addressed her class.

"I hope everyone behaved themselves. If you're really nice, William's promised he might pose for our session on the nude figure," she said, giving him a wink.

A few of the ladies hooted and whistled appreciatively. Maybe they wanted to see if he hid evidence of evil beneath his clothes.

Still, the light in Cara's eyes, the challenge in her raised brow nudged something inside him. That old part that used to bring flowers home for Mother, that dreamt of having a home and family of his own one day. He'd had plenty of time getting comfortable with his body. Would Cara still have that teasing light in her expression if he called her on that dare and stripped down?

Heat rushed through him, reminding him that technically this was his wife.

The wife he'd married to stay close, to physically control her if necessary, whatever it took to get her away from the Guardians. A needed icy chill killed his lust.

Cara turned back to her class, missing his temporary brain malfunction. "I'd like to remind you all of the notice that went out three months ago restricting ownership, use and gambling of magical objects. We all know how the last time they were used turned out. They think it may still be three months before the music room will be usable again."

There were some more whispers about this, a few snickers, too.

Cara continued. "All right then. Let's finish up our paintings."

He settled back in his chair to observe and wait for when they could leave for the refugee camp, find the nymph twins…for when he could uncover more of Cara's secrets. Gods help him if they led straight to the Guardians, and protecting this town meant hurting her.

Chapter Eleven

NORMAL NEED NOT APPLY

THE MORNING ZIPPED PAST, and Cara finished her three art sessions—two for the residents with the beginner session in the morning followed by more advanced techniques, then the one open to the public. She loved teaching as much as she loved painting and seeing the joy of creation on her students' faces was always an energy boost. It was barely noon; the dining hall was loud and clattering with trays and residents…and William was at her side. Talk about another boost. He'd stayed through all three workshops, except for a brief phone call, which he'd politely taken in the hall outside. He didn't paint, he didn't ask questions or interrupt, his large, muscular body just there, observing, handing out supplies, cleaning up messes, anticipating her needs in a way that was strangely sweet yet awakened an electrical charge inside. Her classes were a solitary venture, but the help warmed her insides and kept prompting a stupid smile.

She glanced at William, muscles flexing in his back, tush cute in those khakis as he finished folding the easels and putting them away while she cleaned the paint sets a few creative kids had thoroughly mixed. They worked companionably, like they'd done this hundreds of times, not like she'd married him yesterday.

His actions made him sweeter, sexier, which wasn't helpful. Not when she needed to focus on finding nymphs and Dom, getting back to normal. Continue to prove her value to Beckwell and the Shades. That started with finding the nymphs and faking her way through a walk-through in the refugee camp without Dom's help.

She straightened, having tucked away the last of the paints and the paintbrushes, and found William likewise surveying his completed work, hands on his hips, only emphasizing those beautiful, broad shoulders. Damn, but she'd always been a sucker for a hot guy with broad shoulders.

He turned and caught her full-ogle, raised a brow. "We ready to head out?"

She burned hot as the sun, spinning away to reach for her coat and slip it on. "Sure. Just give me a second to drop off some things at the clinic for Doctor Quilan." She knelt and did the deadlift her "emergency bag" required—a padded bag with pouches inside that held her most commonly needed potions. It sure was an emergency today, since without Dom, that was all she had.

During one of the breaks between the classes, she'd flipped through the files, recognizing the names of regulars. One needed a wing liniment because the muscles in paranormal wings got sore and required different care than human muscles. Some anti-sun solution for a vampire. More 460SPF sunblock for the medical assistant, Frizzly, who, as a troll, turned to stone if exposed to sunlight. Not especially convenient when he'd been outside a lot, helping organize and find shelter for the refugees. Someone had to tame that chaos, and with the Four dealing with larger issues like national human-paranormal relations, well, he was it, and knowing he'd be running low, she'd had a new batch mixed up and ready last week. Again, the idea that Jessie was building houses for paranormals sounded like it had potential. She could mention it to the Shades…or shoot Jessie a quick text.

"Want some help with that?" William eyed her bag, at her side as they walked out of the dining hall into the atrium and across toward the med clinic.

She adjusted it again, keeping her fingers under the strap so it didn't dig into her shoulder. "I've got it, thanks." She couldn't risk it dropping and losing any of those potions, not when she didn't have Dom to help remake them.

The exterior glass walls exposed the crowded waiting room, full of all manner of paranormal creature. A few leaned in the hallway, waiting for space inside. There was one with a bandaged wing, another holding a broken horn wrapped in a towel, then more mundane issues like coughs and sneezes. She greeted and offered kind words to the many she knew. She might not know everyone in town like Mr. Einar or Mrs. Cole, but there were more unfamiliar faces every day. Were all of them new arrivals to Beckwell?

"I'll be just a second." She reached for the door.

William got there first, holding it open for her.

She peeked up at him through her lashes before dashing past the hard heat of his body and into the clinic. She wasn't the only one ogling.

Women eyeballed him appreciatively, of course. Still, while she dug out the bottles from her bag, handing them and the appropriate files over to Frizzly, the whispers started, even with William standing right there near the door.

"That's him."

"No! I heard he was ugly as sin."

"Don't stare, children. Shush! Don't let him catch you staring. Look away. I said, look away!"

"You'd think a man who took on three trolls would be bigger…or have a more squashed nose."

Cara cleared her throat, reaching for her pendant, for Dom.

Of course, Dom wasn't there. Cara was alone and married to a man who was one part savior, one part monster…even if she'd never seen him as the latter. After the war, he'd taken up a place between the paranormal and mortal worlds, helping paranormals without influence or power, the ones no one else would help. Which often brought him into conflict with other paranormals, forcing them to move on if they were causing trouble in mortal-dominated areas, or sometimes ensuring they could never hurt anyone again. He protected the paranormal world guided by his own conscience and rules, not guided or endorsed by higher authorities like the gods or angels, and especially not having been born into the paranormal world nor always respectful of the historic biases and classes, stories about him had grown. Many of the worst were spread by the Guardians themselves, who hated that he was a mortal who'd been unfairly granted god-like powers. Even the stories the Shades told her hadn't shown the depth of the pain he obviously carried for those he'd lost… and the weight of the responsibility he shouldered.

She finished up with Frizzly and hurried to William's side, leading them into the quieter atrium. Instead of going through the front doors, she led him down the quiet hall, most of the residents already in the dining hall.

"Doesn't it bother you?" she asked quietly.

"What?" He asked as though he honestly didn't know, maybe hadn't even noticed, although few re-telling the stories spoke quietly.

She stopped and gestured back at the clinic. "The whispers. The stories. The things they say about you."

He shrugged, slowly pulling a small tin from his pocket, pulling out a mint, then offering the tin to her. "I can't control what people say about me." He paused, met her gaze, his eyes clear and direct. "Does it bother you? What they say?" He said it like her answer mattered.

She shook her head to the tin but edged closer, close enough to see the darker outline around his iris, the gold flecks in his left eye, and feel the heat of his body. Probably best to ignore the latter part. "I don't believe everything I hear. I've done my own research. I know the stories the Shades have told me. The rest… You're right. People can say what they want. I don't like that it's unkind to you, especially after all the good you've done."

He stepped closer, too, his toes bumping hers as he tucked his tin away. "Not everything I've done has been good. I've crossed the wrong lines for the right reasons. You barely know me, Cara. I don't know if you should trust me."

Where the heck was Dom when she needed them because *that* was a loaded statement.

His minty-sweet breath brushed over her skin. Her heart raced and her libido screamed giddy-up and go. She stepped back so she wasn't overwhelmed by his size, his presence, that idiotic idea to kiss him already. "The Shades trust you. That's good enough for me." She continued down the hall, trying to ignore the small twinge of guilt. She wasn't doing anything bad, per se, but he didn't know her, either. And her secrets kept adding up.

They passed Gramps's suite door. If she hadn't been studying William closely, she would have missed the tightening of his jaw, the way his hands fisted.

"They'll be in for lunch already," she said, reaching the emergency exit door. She used her key, so she didn't set off the alarm, and this time she held the door for him. "Is there a particular reason you're avoiding Gramps and the boys?"

A muscle worked in his jaw as he stalked past, although he waited as she secured the door.

"I need to protect them. The Guardians could come after them. They're vulnerable."

"You mean because they're old?" She raised a brow. Heaven save him if he'd been dumb enough to suggest the dangers of old age to Gramps and the boys.

He grimaced. "No. But they've been out of the game a long time. They're mortal. The Guardians fight dirtier, worse than when we first encountered them. Would the boys know how to spot a modern trip wire? What if they missed the signs of an ambush?"

She set them at a slow-ish pace toward the refugee camp, cutting along the small woods and ravine that ran behind the Center, then toward the various wood outbuildings, grayed-wood bleachers, and faded fuchsia glory of the Cow Palace. They didn't need to hurry. She wanted to talk to him. Plus, she still wasn't entirely sure how she was going to diagnose people.

"Gramps and the boys aren't as out of practice as you think. They run operations in town all the time, meet regularly, monitor crime and what's going on with all the major families. They were part of that battle when the Four defeated a destruction goddess."

"Those aren't the Guardians. I'll handle my case; they can handle the town."

She frowned as a new thought occurred to her, the truth sour on her tongue. Her words came slowly. "They invited you here to get the team back together, didn't they?" she whispered, the words barely a question.

Cara closed her eyes. Of course, they'd invited him back to be part of the team. He'd been their leader. That wasn't William's fault. But...damn it. She must have been so distracted with Dom she'd missed the truth, the real reason Gramps had invited William to Beckwell. Protecting her, sure maybe, old-fashioned ideas about women and all that. Still, this was William, their leader. They wanted him here to take his place, complete the team.

Her stomach ached, hollow and heavy. Goddess, she'd been an idiot. She'd attended their meetings, did everything she could to prove herself. But none of it was ever enough for them. She was never enough. She blinked rapidly. They'd made themselves clear, hadn't they? Many times, that no matter how much she was welcome among the boys, she'd never *be* one of them. She'd always be the little kid in pigtails, a protégé they'd protect, but never an equal.

William shoved a hand through his sandy-blond hair. "You think I'm a jerk for turning my back on them."

He didn't want to know what she thought. She picked up her pace. Maybe misdiagnosing refugees and making a fool of herself wouldn't be so bad. "You're not turning your back on them now. It's up to you if you want to go back to being a Shade. It's not like I have any say."

He was quiet as they passed the shuttered shed-like concession stand and a sandpit popular with the five and under crowd during Beckwell Days, when the whole town came out to celebrate Beckwell's founding, weird and proud. A day she'd always enjoyed...from the outside. In Beckwell, normal need not apply...and someone from the outside, someone without significant ability, was a lot too Normal for Beckwell. Even now that she'd forged a place for herself here, Beckwell Days always reminded her of the way she'd felt when she first came here, still felt sometimes. Like she was pretending to belong.

"Did I do something wrong?"

"Nope. I'm good." She offered a tight smile to prove it, which, judging from William's raised brow, didn't do much good. Time for a change of topic. "So, while we're here hunting nymphs and helping people, what else should we watch for? What's a good example of Guardian activity?"

"Sounds like you'll be plenty busy finding the nymphs and helping people. Leave the Guardians to me."

Ahead lay the makeshift camp, ringed by a wood fence and the Cow Palace parking lot.

She rolled her eyes. *Translation: nope, you're not a Shade, so you can't help me.* "Great. You're right. I'll be really busy." Misdiagnosing people took work. Her stomach roiled, and she reached for the pendant again as they slid between two of the RVs that narrowed the foot path through the Ag grounds.

There'd been so many new arrivals the past six months, and before Frizzly mobilized, no one knew what to do to help them. While a tent might suffice in summer, it was October now, and the chill of winter carried in the wind. Before William arrived, she'd intended to add her name and volunteer to host a refugee family, but now that he was there, and with Dom missing…

"Is the pendant comforting, or does it strengthen your abilities?"

Cara blinked and dropped the pendant. "What?"

He gestured at the pendant again. "Your pendant. Does it magnify your abilities? Maybe store additional strength?"

She couldn't tell him the truth. Her lie count for the day, though, was staggering. The thing with lies? You always got caught. "It doesn't store my abilities," she hedged. "It's a Yaga pendant. A piece from the original chicken-leg house, destroyed protecting two warring Yaga descendants. After the house was destroyed, twelve pendants were made for the twelve descendant families. It helps with the potions and diagnosis…and stuff." There. Phew. She blew out a breath. Nothing she'd said was untrue… She'd just left out that the pendant was also sentient.

William, worryingly, cast a considering look at the pendant, paying more attention to it than the people in the refugee camp watching their approach as they went about their business in the tent city. Others stared out wearily from the inside of their tents and RVs, some of them with nowhere else to sleep other than their cars, although the worst off had been prioritized for alternate housing.

"If someone stole the pendant, could they use the Yaga abilities?"

Not bloody likely. Dom had never spoken to Gramps's mother, nor Cara's mom, and could be moody about answering when summoned. Cara shook her head. "The pendant is loyal to the Yagas, and their specific Yaga line. There are stories about what happens to those who steal and use a Yaga pendant. Let's just say they have a lot more in common with the days when Yaga and the house were said to cannibalize foolish visitors."

He cocked his head. "Well, you know about stories. You can't always believe what you hear," he said, echoing her words from earlier, damn him. "You're the descendant from your line?"

She squeezed the pendant again. "Well, there's Gramps, of course, but the Yaga males aren't known for their abilities. I guess that makes me the only female descendant around here. Gramps has no siblings."

William considered a moment, then gestured toward the tents. "Let's go help some people then."

She grimaced and gripped the pendant tighter, which meant she couldn't support the heavy bag digging into her shoulder. Without Dom's help, she wouldn't feel that pull toward people who needed her help.

She studied the camp, her gaze snagging on two tall, stunningly beautiful people across the camp. She blinked. Hello distraction and maybe a solution. Damn. Mrs. Cole wasn't kidding about them being gorgeous.

"I spotted the nymphs," Cara murmured, already heading for the two of them, ducking between the vehicles, easing by people, never taking her eyes off the twins.

Both of them had dark skin a shade or so darker than hers, but that's where any resemblance ended. The woman wore military fatigues but could have stepped off a fashion runway. She had perfect high cheekbones, a regal nose, a figure to kill for, her hair in braids on one side, giving her an Amazon warrior look.

What had to be her brother was the masculine version of all that beauty. Broad shoulders and muscular, of course. Hair close-cropped, camo pants, and a black T-shirt that emphasized his trim physique. Although the male Sarasvati didn't make her heart stutter like it did when she was close to William.

While his sister moved with confident, energetic grace, like a dancer or a fighter, the male twin moved more carefully, every movement tightly controlled. There was something secretive about his mirrored silver aviators.

The wind chased up, stirring leaves through the campsite, chasing the smell of stale grease through the surrounding trees. Leaves rustled. *Find me. Find me*, the wind seemed to whisper.

She shivered, less than a car's length from the nymphs. Finally, she'd have answers about the nymphs, maybe Dom…find out if they heard the strange whispers, too.

That silver aviator gaze shot up, locked on her.

Simultaneously, his sister's gaze lasered in on Cara, like they'd communicated telepathically.

Cara and the other woman locked eyes. Nahla. Time froze in that spark, that instant connection…recognition. Though they'd never met, they knew each other. This wasn't a vision. This was deeper. Blood and bone deep. Family and belonging, the sensation so strong, it stole Cara's breath and raised the hair along her arms.

The next second, both twins ran.

"Shit." William raced after them.

Cara ran, too, but it was half-hearted, watching the two long-legged, beautiful twins sprint through the thick of the crowd. That ocean of people closed around them like water, trapping William in a line-up for supplies from the daily food run supplement from the city.

The twins were gone. They'd taken one look at her, maybe felt that same connection…and they'd run.

Hollow loneliness spiralled through her, darkening the sky, dimming the sun.

Find me. Find me, the wind whispered again, the trees shuddering and swaying.

Cara trailed after William, who hunted the twins fruitlessly among the refugees. Despite their height, the twins had disappeared into the crowd, or maybe into one of the cars that had passed on the nearby two-lane highway through town. She'd finally found nymphs, found the kind of connection she'd craved for so long, and they'd taken one look at her and run.

Worse, she had no idea why.

Chapter Twelve

HELP AND HEALING

CARA STOOD in the center of the milling crowd, searching the faces for the nymphs who'd ditched her, when a passing dark-haired woman with pointed ears—an elf or fey descendant—cried out next to her. The woman's knees gave out, her cane fell to the ground, and her arms windmilled as she fell.

Used to reacting at the Senior Center, Cara spun and caught the woman's elbow before wrapping an arm around the stranger for additional support. "Whoops. You okay, there?" Steadying the stranger, Cara brought her around until they were face to face.

"Oh. It's my knees," the woman mumbled, more embarrassed than hurt, gaze dark. "I'm so sorry. What a nuisance."

Find me. Find me, the wind whispered again. A woman's voice, whispering with the wind.

Yeah, well, if it was nymphs, from the twins' reaction, they didn't want to be found.

Cara picked up the woman's cane, handing it to her.

The tips of the woman's pointed ears were pink, and she avoided Cara's gaze.

Something washed over Cara, the sense of it similar to the feeling she had when she painted. A knowing, like when she'd known she needed to say yes to William, yet different somehow.

Assured the woman was steady again with her cane, Cara crouched and opened her potion bag, sorted through, then emerged with a small brown glass bottle, not much longer than her thumb. She held it up for the woman.

"It's not your knees, I suspect, but your fey side. Try this. It's a tincture of elderberries and mushrooms—not the magic kind, promise—but rather, the kind the ancient fey subsisted on. If you've never had them or it's been a while, your genes can misbehave in small ways with aches and pains."

She opened the bottle, took the tiniest taste without touching her lips to the glass, the drop of potion earthy, rich, and slightly sweet against her tongue. "It does nothing for me—or to me—since I'm not fey. Try it tonight, see if it helps, and if it does, come to the medical clinic tomorrow and they'll let me know. No charge. Medical and prescriptions are paid for all Beckwell residents." She pointed toward the Senior Center. "If the potion doesn't help, I recommend a visit to Doctor Quilan to see if he can help with modern medicine instead." She passed the bottle to the woman.

The woman considered it a second, then shrugged, popped the cork, and downed it. She shook her head, pressed a hand to her belly and stood still as stone.

Cara blinked.

The woman's eyes widened. Cautiously, she lifted one foot, then the other. She bent and balanced like a flamingo, testing first one knee then the other. A slow smile spread over her face, and she let out a joyous whoop, tossing aside her cane and capering. "Well, I'll be!" She gave Cara a hug before dancing more. "You, sweetheart, are a miracle worker! I haven't felt this good in a year."

Her dancing attracted attention, others gathering close.

Cara's face burned. She wanted to murmur and slink away. What the hell had happened back there? Somehow, she'd correctly diagnosed and helped someone on her own. How was that possible? She needed to consider, try to contact Dom, discover if finding two nymphs, even seeing them only at a distance, was enough.

She'd promised Doctor Quilan she'd help, which meant staying put and speaking up. It would be a chance to see if the one woman was a fluke.

"I, uh…" She caught William's eyes where he stood near the edge of the crowd.

He offered a small nod that steadied her.

She remembered how it'd been to arrive here, confused about how anything worked, baffled that magic was real. The memory gave her courage to plow on.

"Hey, guys. I'm Cara Jenklow, and I offer art classes at the Senior Center. I also consult with the local doctor, Doctor Quilan. I'm sure some of you have met him, but in case you haven't, you're entitled to free medical and prescription care in Beckwell." She hefted her bag slightly since it weighed a ton. "I consult with paranormal remedies, potions if you will, and I can help with your entry in the paranormal world."

Findmefindmefindmefindmefindme, the wind insisted, stronger this time, tugging at Cara's hair.

People in the audience nodded, others pulled loved ones close.

Cara's heart squeezed. She didn't have time for talking wind. "If you have new ailments since the Veils fell—or they're connected to your new abilities or appendages—I can probably help. Potions can help with that transition—or at least make your life a little easier. Different species benefit from both magical and modern remedies—which is why I consult with the doctor. Things like wing liniment? I've got that. Sunblock for trolls and vampires? Two different kinds, species specific. I'm not selling anything—and most of what I'll offer today is small trial sizes. Between the doctor and I, we can get you more if the potions work for you. Come on up and let me know how I can help you."

Refugees swarmed her, and she lost sight of William. They weren't aggressive, but her heart pounded, the air felt hot and close, if they fell on her—

"Step back. That's it. Give the lady room to breathe. She'll get to as many of you as she can," William's voice broke through, rescuing her, getting everyone lined up. He gave her another nod, that sense he believed in her steadying her again. As though... maybe if she couldn't help the Shades with the Guardians, she could help these people.

TIME PASSED. Cara's eyes blurred, the wind kept talking —which, honestly, was either super creepy, or perhaps a sign she was losing it. At this point, she couldn't tell. She stretched and blinked, discovering the line had disappeared. She had a few potions left. Warmth spun through her. Even the growling stupid diesel trucks pulling up with a pollution-stirring rumble near the highway, the steadily whispering wind, none of it dimmed the glow inside.

She'd *helped* people. Diagnosed them, gotten them the right potions. *Helped people.* Like she'd always wanted to, the way Gramps and the Shades always had…or almost like them. She'd made a difference.

"Looks like you're done for the day." William strolled to her side and offered a hand. He'd remained close all afternoon, never hovering but there if she needed him. His presence was comforting—but uber distracting, too.

When she placed her fingers in his, the spark from so simple a touch was the opposite of comfortable or mundane. The contact tugged at memories of the dreams she'd had of them together. The softness in his expression when he'd gaze at her in her dreams…a little like the way he looked at her now, waiting, wanting.

Their gazes locked as she rose to her feet, tugging up her much lighter emergency bag. "Yes. That was…amazing!" She shared that glowing feeling with her smile, or at least tried to.

A slow curve pulled at his lips, softened his face, melted her insides. He pulled her closer. "You sure you don't have special ability? What I saw was definitely special."

She opened her mouth to reply.

Angry shouts behind them interrupted her. Closer to the highway, an unwelcome group climbed out of their obnoxious, lumbering trucks. Fifteen or twenty protesters marched around near the mouth of the refugee camp with moronic signs.

She and William turned toward the noise, and they weren't the only ones watching.

"Bring back the good old days!" shouted one fat white guy in brown coveralls with pointed ears, carrying around a picket sign stating the same thing.

"Magic not humanity," read another picket sign.

They weren't all fat, old, white, or male, which made it worse. There was the green-faced former cashier from the corner shop, Mrs. S-something, who treated everyone horribly whenever she visited her few friends at the Center. A few faces Cara didn't recognize, like today at the clinic. Wasn't that one of the teachers? And that guy who owned the old tow place on the outskirts of town, Sal's Autobody.

Refugees emerged from their tents and vehicles to watch, others surrounded the picketers.

"End the inequality for paras!" another shouted, this one carrying a sign painted with the term "United Paranormals for a Pure Beckwell."

"Better, not equal," read another sign, and shouted another protester.

William leaned closer, his arms crossed and a steely expression settling across his features. "You wanted to know how to spot an initial attack by the Guardians. Here it is."

A chill slid through her, and she studied the protestors. Guardians. With all the stories she'd heard about them, she'd imagined lean, inhuman soldiers hunting mortals and those with human-bloodlines. Not these people. People who could have been neighbors, or average Beckwellians. She gulped.

"What is your problem?" a woman said, coming out from the camp. She gestured at the camp. "You honestly think things aren't hard enough for everyone here without you trying to make them worse?"

Cara's breath caught. It was the dark-haired woman whose knees hurt because of fey bloodlines and vitamin deficiency, who now strode straight and tall...right into trouble.

One of the protestors, a black-haired woman with iridescent skin—likely fey too—set her picket sign on her shoulder and turned on the first woman. "Humans have hunted and destroyed us for centuries. To think that we'd have mated with them…" she sneered. "This is our town, our sanctuary. Go back where you came from."

More and more people emerged from their RVs, their cars, their tents, forming a circle around the protesters, the two groups sending jeers back and forth. Two sky-blue demon twenty-somethings—a species who'd notoriously been mistreated by both humans and paranormals—and someone else with hooves protruding from their blue jeans flanked the woman.

Shouting started, exchanges between the groups. Both groups confronted each other, many of those in the front toe to toe with their counterparts.

Cara's head grew cold, like she'd run it under icy water. Her vision blurred. Similar to when she painted and like the knowing she'd felt when diagnosing and helping others earlier.

"We've as much right to be here as you," someone from the refugee side shouted.

"Stay here." William marched into the fray.

To hell with that.

She marched after him, head pounding, a feeling of certainty washing over her that she couldn't interpret or grasp but that controlled her actions like it usually guided her brush. Forward, forward, into that crowd.

There'd be blows exchanged. The man in brown coveralls would pull some kind of weapon—long and metallic, maybe a tool. The next blows would be more serious. There'd be blood, screams. More people would rush into battle from both sides. The camp, flooded with violence. Bodies on both sides. Blows, shots, screams and blood, stampedes over the tents, fire, and the bodies, the corpses…

Findmefindmefindmefindmefindme the wind chanted.

The Yaga pendant grew warmer around her neck. Steaming, almost burning her skin.

Nausea climbed her throat. The vision rolled over her, stole her breath, wrung tears from her eyes. No. She couldn't let that happen. Not to her people. Not to her Beckwell.

The pendant burned, pulsed, sped her heartbeat, matched the rhythm of her heart like a drumbeat. *"See the vision. Embrace or reject it. Change it. The choice is yours,"* Dom said, urging Cara on, urging her to…

Change what happened and what she saw? How? The pounding grew behind her eyes.

There was a shout, a scream from the crowd.

"Come on, back off. Break it up," William demanded, somewhere in the thick of it.

Another flash of vision. William, face bloodied, clutching his arm, stumbling toward her. His mouth would open, wordlessly, as he slipped down to his knees…

"Change it," Dom repeated inside Cara's head, certain, steady.

Black spots danced in front of her eyes, acid burning her tongue. Cara squeezed her hands into fists. Her fingernails bit into her palms. Behind her eyelids, in the vision a bloodied William falling to his knees. Those charred corpses. A child, alone and wailing, terrified.

She shoved all of that aside. Pictured instead the protestor morons putting down their signs. Backing away from the refugees.

Her breath grew raspy, throat squeezing.

The protestors would get back in their stinky, noisy trucks. They'd drive away.

Black and red, flashes of light exploded behind her eyes, made her gasp.

"A little more. Don't push. Careful. Careful." Dom said.

She pictured the scene. Anti-human protestors driving away, tails between their legs. Those in the refugee camp cheering and shouting, embracing each other. Peace and victory for the day, something they could control.

Her breath came in short pants. Her knees softened.

William, unharmed, strong and healthy, beautiful, striding toward her...

"That's enough. Stop. Now," Dom cried, voice urgent.

She could hear the trucks, imagined the refugees' joyful cries...

"You must stop. It will kill you. It's going to kill you!" Dom shouted.

Pain exploded through Cara, started somewhere in her mind, ricocheted out to every nerve, every cell. She cried out, or at least, she might have. Pain overrode everything, shuddered through her, burned down the world around her. She collapsed onto the ground. Gravel and grit bit into her knees, into her palms. Every pant burned.

"Cara!" William's voice. His touch.

She drifted. Away from the pain, from the light.

"Nymph magic. Nymph magic will kill you. Find the nymphs, Cara, find them before it's too late. Before it kills you." Dom's voice drifted farther and farther away. Fading and overtaken by static.

"Dom..." Cara murmured before she glided into darkness.

Chapter Thirteen

REPERCUSSIONS

THE BLACKNESS LIFTED, and Cara regained awareness. She wasn't in the Ag grounds anymore. There were too many people fussing over her. William's scent, the rumble of his voice was nearby. The concerned voices of Gramps and the boys. Another male… It sounded like one of the Quilan twins.

Ugh. What the heck had happened back there? The pendant had gone cool and silent, making her throat squeeze and making it harder to open her eyes and face worried faces. She'd helped the refugees without Dom, but then Dom had been there, their presence so calming, so welcome. Then things went haywire, visions without painting, and the protest and…

"All right, everyone. Let's give her some space and time for the doctor to examine her." William's voice rumbled above the others from next to her. "I can take care of my wife. We'll give you an update as soon as we have one."

Wife. A small trill went through her, stirred warmth low in her belly, desire and…something else. She'd never been someone's anything before. None of her previous relationships had lasted long enough to earn the title of girlfriend. She'd always found a reason to end things before it could progress that far. She'd never felt like she belonged with any of them. They'd never measured up to her William fantasy.

A pang went through her. William had made it clear this wasn't a real marriage, and he'd leave as soon as possible. She didn't need Dom to remind her how foolish it would be to get too attached.

"She's our Cara, and we've been taking care of her a lot longer. Besides, we have other things we need to discuss, Mac," Gramps said.

There was grumbling before the room cleared with shuffling steps, the soft, steady beep of a heart monitor audible.

"They're gone. You can open your eyes," William whispered, his fingers gently stroking her hand, setting off those sparks that sped her heart and would freak out the monitor.

Cara opened her eyes. For a second, there were four Williams, and a lurch of nausea. A low throb ached near the base of her skull. She grimaced and pushed herself upright. "How did you know I was awake?" Her voice was raspy, throat dry as paper.

"Your eyelashes fluttered." The corner of William's lips twitched, but strain and worry shadowed his blue-gray eyes. He wrapped an arm around her back, helping her upright and tucking the pillow behind her.

She was in one of the patient rooms at the clinic, prone on one of the hospital beds. Never a good sign. Poor Gramps.

She winced. "You don't think the others noticed, do

you? I don't want to hurt their feelings. They get worried if I so much as sneeze." She bit her lip a second. "What happened back at the Ag grounds?"

"We hoped you could tell us, Cara," Doc Quilan said, coming over with a small gray clip in his hand. "Finger please. I want to check your oxygenation levels and heart rate again. You were unconscious when William brought you in, and you've been out about fifteen minutes. It doesn't sound like you hit your head, and I don't see or feel any lumps. How are you feeling?"

She lifted her hand and he clipped the strange little gray clip on her finger. "Like an idiot, mostly. Tired... And my head hurts a little."

The memory of Dom's voice whispered through her. *Nymph magic will kill you. Find the nymphs before it's too late.*

Cara shivered, and she glanced back at William. "Did I fall? What happened?" Had anyone else heard the wind talking? Because that wasn't a good sign...but the kind she was reluctant to mention to Doctor Quilan. She was already on unsteady ground trying to work with the potions and keep her position consulting with him without Dom. This afternoon had been an unusual exception.

William glanced at the doctor, stroking her fingers as though unaware he did so.

His touch sent those tingles through her, soothing the aches and pains...causing libido-havoc.

"After you helped all the people in the refugee camp, the protesters arrived. Just as things turned ugly, you walked into the center of it, never saying a word." William hesitated. "Your eyes were glassy. I'm not sure you saw what was happening. Then you closed your eyes. The protesters went mute, climbed back in their trucks and drove off. And you collapsed. I caught you before you hit the ground but…" He stopped, swallowing hard and shoving a hand back through his hair. "Cara, you fell like dead weight."

"Have you been experiencing headaches? Pain anywhere? Other episodes like this?" Doc Quilan glanced at the monitor in his hand as he spoke to her.

She shook her head, but that made the world spin, so she closed her eyes again and answered wearily. "No. Nothing unusual." What had Dom meant, that she'd be killed if she didn't find the nymphs? What did the Yaga spirit know? She clutched the pendant, but it remained cool and silent.

William cleared his throat. "There was last night…"

"What about last night?" The doctor latched onto the words.

Cara grimaced again. "No. That wasn't anything like this. I—"

"You blacked out with pain, and both times you called out for 'Dom,'" William insisted.

Today hadn't felt the same, it hadn't been an attack like before. Today, she'd helped people. She'd *done* something. Then there'd been those visions, and Dom's voice, and… She shook her head. Why couldn't she go home and lay in her bed until she figured things out? Why did everyone want to make such a fuss?

Nymph magic is going to kill you. Find the nymphs before it's too late. Her stomach twisted and flipped. Dom couldn't be right.

Doc Quilan cleared his throat. "William, perhaps if I spoke to Cara alone." His words were polite, but firm.

"Sure." William squeezed her hand before releasing it. "I'll be outside."

Geezus, Josie, and George. Her eyes burned, and she

squeezed them shut more tightly. A tremor started in her hands and she fisted them in her lap, beneath the thin blanket.

"Cara," Doc Quilan said, patiently. "Can you tell me what's going on? At least open your eyes so I can see if your pupils are dilated."

He was being kind and reasonable, a few of the things that made him a great doctor.

He'd been kind like that when giving Gran her terminal diagnosis, too…and all the terrible steps before the end.

She opened her eyes, swiping at them to erase any hint of moisture, and pasted on a smile. "I'm sorry. I… I'm fine. Maybe I was tired or something." The nausea had settled, at least the part related to light and facing the doctor.

He raised a dark brow. "Physically, you're in good health. Pulse is steady and regular, good oxygenation of your blood, even pupil dilation. What about those other episodes or symptoms?"

This time she shook her head without the world going blurry. "I'm fine. There aren't other symptoms, not really."

"Define 'not really.'"

She shot him a raised eyebrow. "I've had headaches before, but nothing like this. Come on. You see me here every day. I don't black out randomly."

"You work long hours without many days off, so yes, I see you here. A lot. I can send you for further tests. At this point, I'm inclined to. If there's something more serious going on here, it's better we find it sooner rather than later. Something happened last night?"

She shoved a hand through her hair. Tests, machines, someone poking and prodding her, seeing what else was wrong with her, how she could be "fixed."

Dad had believed a lot in "tests" when she'd been little, too, dragging her all over the city and back, no matter Mom's protests. All to try and figure out why she wasn't like other kids, to make her like everyone else with his half-whispered stories to the doctors about when she was a baby, how her childish finger paintings too often portrayed real events and people she'd never met. Not that any of it made any difference.

She met the doctor's concerned gaze. "Last night I got a sudden migraine, but counting that and this one, that's happened twice."

"In rapid succession. I think—"

She pushed back the blankets and threw her legs over the opposite side of the bed from where the doctor stood, turning her back on him. Nope. She needed out of here, with an urgency she didn't fully understand. She needed time to find Dom. Find the nymphs and get the kind of answers the doctor and modern medicine couldn't provide.

"I think, Daniel," she said, using his first name as she pushed to her feet, trying to ignore the squishiness in her knees. She compensated with another tight smile. "I think this is one of those cases where usually you'd consult with me." Geezus, it felt like she'd run a marathon. Her entire body ached in a way she'd never experienced before.

His gaze narrowed and he rocked back on his heels, brows lowered. "Are you sure?"

No. My magic pendant told me nymph magic will kill me, and I need to know what the hell that means. Your tests can't do that for me. "I... I think that's where I need to start."

He came around the side of the bed. "I believe we should do a few more tests. Call it plan B if you like, but I'd like to be sure we cover all bases."

She reached for the doorknob. "I want to get home, get some rest."

The doctor sighed. "Cara—"

She pulled open the door and stepped partially through. The hall was empty, no sign of William or Gramps and the boys, but the rumble of William's voice was near the front of the clinic. She paused beside the doctor.

His brow creased, his gaze was more concerned than she'd ever seen. Then again, she'd never been one of his patients before.

"I appreciate you're trying to help, I do. I think this is one of the cases that I usually deal with." Insert bright, confident smile and pray it looked more confident than it felt. "Besides, I know where to find you, right?"

He blew out a frustrated breath and nodded. "I can't keep you here. But, Cara, take care, and please let me know if there's anything I can do to help."

"You bet." She followed William and Gramps's voices outside the clinic.

She didn't have time to go home and lay around. She and William needed to find the nymphs, pronto.

It was time she told William the truth about Dom.

JENKLOW and the rest of the Shades ambushed William the second he stepped outside of Cara's room. They hustled him into the hall outside the clinic, then backed him into a small alcove around the corner from the med clinic. William took his time opening his mint tin, selecting one and then letting the cool sweetness settle as he tucked the tin away, struggling to relax the tightness in his shoulders. Cara had blacked out after whatever the hell had happened back at the refugee camp. Plus, things went pear-shaped, and she'd called out for "Dom" again.

"Gentlemen," he said, unable to keep the small note of warning out of his voice. "Do we have a problem?"

Albert Jenklow offered an angry smile. "Son," he said, using the word like an epithet. "We definitely have a problem. Who the hell do you think you are, coming into our town, taking over our cases, pushing us out like we're too old, too decrepit to do any good?"

Although none of them were as tall or muscular as they'd once been, with all five crowded in close they conveyed a certain menace. Men who'd always had his back, now menacing him. While Cara was in the med clinic, blacked out for gods knew what reason after whatever the hell had happened back at the Ag grounds. A muscle twitched in William's tight jaw.

"I am doing what I said I'd do here. Exactly what you *invited* me to do here in Beckwell. Track down the Guardians and put a stop to this nest before they hurt anyone else," he said tightly.

"Don't play dumb with us," Liko growled, leaning in close, thin moustache twitching.

"You were invited back here to work *with* us, not around us," Einar said, a chill behind his words.

William massaged his throbbing temples. "Gentlemen—"

"Try again, please," typically easy to please Zaki piped up. "When you start your statement with 'gentlemen' it's usually because you'd like us to behave in a desired manner and accede to your current wishes. I'm afraid, Mac, you're going to have to start again."

Chaimek chuckled. "Well done, Ted. You're right. He does start every sentence he suspects we're not going to like with 'gentlemen.'" He glared darkly at William. "No dice, m'boy. Try again."

William's teeth ached from clenching them. Cara was

back there, alone, while his friends lectured him. He crossed his arms, forcing them all back a step or two with his movement. He leaned casually against the glass wall, as though this interrogation didn't make him want to punch something.

"Fine. You want to be involved. Gods know you will be whether I want you to be or not, even if the Guardians come for your heads on pikes. Let's all pretend this is some kind of game. What is it you know about the current situation with the Guardians?"

"Zaki, report," Jenklow barked at Ted Zaki, never taking his hard blue gaze from William's face.

"Two new graffiti attacks with specist slurs painted on barns reported since last night," Zaki said, reporting back with greater efficiency than a robot. "One at the Michaels residence, another at the Jones'. Several reports of truancy yesterday, most of them males between the ages of thirteen to seventeen, suspected radicalization meeting, which indicates a higher-level operative is already in the area. This morning marked the first protest at the Cow Palace, targeting the refugee camp. No injuries reported at this time. Presence of one Cara Jenklow and William Best noted. This is one more reason—besides the imminent onset of winter—why more suitable and permanent accommodations for the newcomers is required, as also required by operative Frizzly." He glanced at Jenklow. "Shall I continue, or is that enough for now?"

"That's fine, thank you, Ted," Jenklow said with a warmer smile before it turned glacial facing William. "That's on top of reports I hear that you chased two of our best prospects through the refugee camp. The Sarasvati twins are good kids. Part of the Famine lad's commando group that heads into paranormal trouble spots worldwide.

They'll make good recruits—if you don't run them off first."

Geezus, they were better informed than he'd given them credit for. He hadn't heard about the new graffiti this morning, and nor had the police chief. "What do you mean recruits?"

"What do you care? Didn't think you were a Shade anymore," Jenklow shot back.

William ground his teeth, trying to ignore the ache Jenklow's response had opened up. "Where's your intel from?"

"Our network. Why were you chasing those two kids, Mac?" Jenklow continued doggedly.

"They're full-grown adults, not children," he growled. "And nymphs, as it happens. Cara is searching for them. She thinks they have something to do with her friend Dom's disappearance."

Jenklow and Einar exchanged a look, something in their expressions setting the hairs dancing on the back of William's neck.

"What?" he demanded.

Jenklow crossed his arms. "Nothing good comes of associating with nymphs, even those two. Not when it comes to Cara. You keep her away from them and any other nymphs. As for a 'Dom,' she has no friends with that name."

Or she did and hadn't wanted her grandfather and the rest of the boys to know. Still, he was getting somewhere on the nymph front.

He leaned closer to Albert. "Why are you so worried about Cara getting close to the nymphs? What aren't you telling me, Albert?"

Another look, this one exchanged among all five of the

friends. A silent communication that once upon a time, he'd have been included in.

Einar gave Jenklow a small nod.

Albert sighed, his drooping jowls jiggling as he leaned closer and pitched his voice low. "When Cara was born, Rose—my wife, full-blood nymph—told me there was something exceptional about her. Something about how her mixed blood of the Yagas and the nymphs had combined to create something else entirely. A hybrid so powerful, the visions of it terrified my darling Rose. She… did something. Performed nymph magic I wasn't a part of, don't fully understand. Cara has no idea. Not what was done to her, not how powerful she could be. But it had to be done to keep her and those around her safe, hidden."

"Safe from who?"

"Everyone. If someone found a way to control Cara, she could be the most dangerous being this side of the world," Albert whispered.

"What can she do? What abilities does she have? Futuresight? Healing?" In a town where Loki and the Four horsewomen lived, power was plentiful. The abilities had to be impressive or terrifying if Cara's own grandmother would hide them and what she'd done from her husband, and from Cara herself.

Albert shook his head, rubbing a hand over the shiny bald top dotted with liver spots. "That's just it. Rose didn't tell me before she passed. She hated talking about her family, about the nymphs, the way they disowned her. Still brought her pain, years later. Near as I—as we've—deduced, Cara's abilities are specific to her because she's part Yaga, part nymph. Yagas are gifted with potions, healing, and helping people, sometimes with their extraordinary luck. Things tend to go the way the Yaga wants it, always has. Cara's nymph side isn't easy to see, and so far as I know, she shouldn't be able to access it at all." He hesitated, studying William's face a moment. "Mac, you know how I used to sometimes have visions of the future, before a battle and the like?"

William nodded.

"Yeah, well, nymphs are better at directing their visions. If Cara had that combo of nymph and Yaga, ability to direct her visions, and exceptional luck for things to turn out the way she wanted... I think at full ability, she could bend reality."

Bend reality? Shit. "On what scale?"

Jenklow and the others shook their heads.

Chaimek finally spoke. "Mac, there's no limits on bending reality. It's all or nothing. All reality. If Cara finds out what she can do, if she was controlled by someone else, she could rewrite the world."

William rocked back, glad for the cold glass behind him. If the Guardians got a hold of her, if they figured out how to control her... His hand shook as he pushed it back through his hair.

"Which is why she can't know," Liko said gruffly, drawing William's attention.

"She's safer if she has no idea what she can do. She's shown no sign of power yet," Zaki added.

So they thought. What had happened in the refugee camp, the way the crowd had parted before her, her gaze glassy as she'd walked through the crowd... She hadn't liked the protesters there, then she stared at them blindly and they packed up and left, no violence. That could be evidence that she *did* know how to access her powers.

"Whatever you do, keep her away from the nymphs," Jenklow insisted again. "Rose used nymph magic to lock away her abilities, which means nymphs could unlock it, too. Rose's family left years ago, and the other nymphs in town left a month after the Veils fell. We can't let anyone unlock Cara's abilities without knowing what they are."

Damn straight… Although a small curl of unease tightened William's gut. Was this their decision and not Cara's? Besides which, if the Guardians were still after Cara, they had to believe they could unlock those abilities…or the Shades were wrong about how locked away her power was.

"She's coming out," Liko announced, watching the clinic door. "On her feet, pale, but otherwise all right."

Jenklow, though, wouldn't back down, gripping William's forearms. "Promise me. Keep Cara safe. Keep her away from the nymphs."

William couldn't say the words. Nymphs weren't his priority. The Guardians were. They were far more dangerous than nymphs if they were able to unlock and access Cara's power. The rumors said they were after her…so they had to believe they had a way to access her abilities, too. Power like that could do more harm than the Guardians had achieved in all their centuries of genocide. Controlled by dark fey, gods, or other methods of mind control, Cara's ability could obliterate all paranormals the Guardians deemed unacceptable in the blink of an eye. She'd been able to fight off the psychic attack last night, but it was further proof someone wanted to attack and control her.

It was up to him to stop that from happening. No matter what it took.

Cara came around the corner, smiled at them all, dark circles under her eyes, a weary slump to her shoulders.

More attacks and whatever the hell had happened in the Ag grounds, she'd be weakened and more vulnerable. Next time, whether she was fighting off this "Dom" or another psychic attack, if they gained control of her mind and power, he'd have to stop Cara before she could unleash hell. He was counting on using her mortality against her, too, if need be.

He couldn't let the Guardians win… which would demand sacrifices.

Chapter Fourteen

NYMPH HUNTING

"WHO THE HELL IS DOM, and how are the nymphs involved with her disappearance?" William demanded as he slid behind the wheel of his Jeep.

Cara closed her eyes, still shaky and overwhelmed. William and the boys had surrounded her outside the clinic and insisted she go home and rest, swaddled like a baby. That was the last thing she could do. Seriously. She had to find the nymphs.

Best of all was Dom's pronouncement that if she didn't find them, nymph magic would kill her. "Dom isn't a she… and only possibly a who," she began, then added dryly, "You know, I'd hoped we could save this conversation for at least the third day of marriage."

"Your grandfather and the others have never heard of any Dom. They're convinced you should stay as far from the nymphs as possible." William jammed the Jeep into reverse.

She rolled her eyes, throat still thick. "Figures. Gramps hates all things nymph." She'd have asked for his help if this wouldn't give him one more reason to distrust nymphs. One more reason Cara could never be a Shade.

"You're avoiding my question. Who is Dom? What's their involvement with the nymphs?" He pulled them out onto the road, then stopped at the four-way, his gaze heavy. "I promised the doctor and the boys I'd take you straight home." Yet he waited in the empty intersection for her reply.

She gripped the cool pendant and forced herself to meet his turbulent blue-gray gaze. Deep breath. Dom had always been her secret. "Dom lives inside this pendant. It's short for Domoroy Yaga—spirit of the Yaga house. They've been my best friend for as long as I've been in Beckwell. They give me advice, protect me, help me with the potions, Yaga history and knowledge, and allow me to use their abilities. I've always been able to hear them speak, summon them with a thought." She paused. "Until three days ago."

William's solemn expression weighed the information like a judge considering a death sentence, tapping his fingers on the wheel. No mocking raised eyebrow because she talked to a pendant, which was something. It was a good thing there was no traffic as they sat at the otherwise empty four-way stop, no indication of where they went from here.

A little too much like their relationship at this point.

He put the Jeep in park.

Cara gulped, waiting for his words, his reaction. She hadn't outright said she talked to her necklace, but damned close.

"The spirit of the Yaga house," he said, as though going over the files in his head. "Didn't the house occasionally eat unwelcome visitors?"

"That part is an exaggeration." *Mostly.* "Giving readings and answers to those visitors caused the Yaga physical pain. The house tried to protect them from that pain—and from the people who wanted to capture or harm the Yaga. Strong, independent women haven't always been celebrated throughout history." She twisted the pendant with her fingers. "Not being able to hear Dom is like losing my best friend." She hesitated again, biting her lip. "Dom told me that the reason I can't hear them has something to do with the nymphs. We have to find the nymphs. Today. I need answers, and they might be the only ones who have some."

He glanced down the empty road ahead, a lone car turning into the school parking lot to the right. "Those nymphs didn't want to speak with us this morning. And that pendant sounds dangerous. Both times you've had headaches or blacked out, you've called its name. Is that why Albert didn't tell me about it and pretended to not know the name?"

She closed her fingers protectively around the pendant, heart pounding. "Dom isn't dangerous." At least, not *that* dangerous. They didn't have physical form, which meant they could talk about the possibility of eating people, usually when in a mood, but had no teeth. "Gramps doesn't know about Dom. He's a male heir and the pendant sees no value in males. The Yagas are strong, independent, and feminine. Dom is keeper of the Yaga knowledge and protects the Yagas. And..." Her voice dropped to a whisper. "I don't think Dom speaks to everyone who bears it. They didn't speak to my mother, and I don't think they spoke to Gramps's mother, either." She forced herself to face William. "Please. We have to find those two nymphs." She pointed down the road. "The Famine land is down that way. Maybe they'll be there."

A small tic started in William's jaw. "The pendant is selective, attracted to power."

"N-no. Not at all. I don't have power."

He raised a sandy brow. "It sure looked like you did back at the refugee camp. You touched people and knew exactly what they needed. Gave them complete diagnoses faster than any paranormal healer I've ever encountered. Were you speaking to Dom and channeling their ability?"

A tiny shake of her head, and she dropped her gaze. "No. And that's never happened before."

"And after? With the crowd and the protesters. What was that?"

"I don't know." Chills crawled up her arms despite her jacket. She hugged herself. "That's why I have to find the nymphs. Someone must know what's happening to me." *Someone must be able to tell me if it's true. If somehow, nymph magic will kill me.*

That part she couldn't bring herself to say. Not yet. Sure, she and William weren't in love, only technically married. Yet if Gramps or the boys found out… She shivered. She couldn't do that to them. Wasn't ready to face it herself, if it was true. But only the nymphs could tell her that.

William put the Jeep in drive.

She brought up her head.

They drove through the four-way stop, toward the Famine place.

A shuddering breath slipped past her lips.

"Chief Quilan thought they'd be at the Famine house, too. He warned me to tread lightly. The dragon I met at the Emergency center lives there, and dragons have notoriously short fuses. Apparently, the nymphs, the dragon, and the rest of the crew have been good for Beckwell when they're in town, so we can't scare them off." He glanced at her as they drove past the schoolyard on one side, the store and Loki's bar on the other. "I promised I'd help you find the nymphs and get answers, and I will. But, Cara, they might not be the answers you want." He nodded toward the pendant clasped in her hand. "That pendant, this Dom, sounds dangerous. You sure they have your best interests at heart?"

"I'm sure," she managed. Was she? Whatever had happened back at the refugee camp, Dom hadn't been there to help. She'd never questioned her friend's help and advice before, but Dom had always hated the nymphs, had motive to make Cara hate them, too.

Which might also mean Cara wasn't dying. That'd be good.

She adjusted the seatbelt where it cut into her neck. "Let's go talk to those nymphs."

"THIS IS PRIVATE PROPERTY. Go away before I make you go away," said the dragon, Maddox, who'd apparently given up reading about law for the day. He was as tall as William, smoke curled from his nostrils, and he stood between them and Cara reaching the nymphs she needed.

William exhaled slowly, hands loose, head up and posture non-threatening. He still didn't want to tangle with a dragon, especially with Cara standing next to him. She'd refused to stay in the Jeep, and the dragon complicated a simple mission to speak to nymphs. He could count on one hand his number of run-ins with dragons, and while he'd survived those, Maddox uncharacteristically had company.

Standing shoulder to shoulder with him was a pretty-boy blond, who although suave and polished, looked fully capable of slipping a blade between your ribs. Incubus maybe, fey or siren, he was something that dealt in charm and used their looks as weapons. He'd heard that the Famine horsewoman and her husband had a paranormal peace corps-type crew that were often out of town, but that he'd flagged as potential trouble if they chose the Guardians' side.

"Oh, hey, Asher, I didn't know you lived out here," Cara said, speaking before he had a chance to and, worse, taking a step toward the two threatening men. She side-stepped William's attempt to catch her hand. "Asher stops by the Center all the time. He's not dangerous," she said to William before beaming at the dragon and pretty-boy blond, the apparent "Asher" …and suggesting Cara had dubious standards when it came to defining "not danger-ous." "We don't want trouble. We just need to talk to your friends. The nymphs."

"Sweetheart, that's what they all say," Asher said, eyes glittering dangerously. "I can't risk my friends' well-being on your word. Even if that art class you taught about intro-duction to pastels was fun."

"Please," Cara said, her voice cracking, lifting a hand that trembled to point to herself, stepping closer, dammit.

More smoke drifted from the dragon's nostrils, and Asher shifted onto the balls of his feet, a fighting stance.

"I'm part nymph myself," she continued. "Your friends are the only other nymphs in town. I didn't even know there were other nymphs in town. I don't understand my nymph side, and I need answers. Something is wrong with my nymph side, I think. I need help."

"Didn't know that about you, Cara. But sorry. The answer's the same," Asher said, lifting a hand. "Stay where you are. No closer."

William caught Cara's hand, tugged her back to his side, her smaller fingers warm inside his, that distracting spark between them not helpful, not when he needed to stay sharp. "Like the lady said, we're not here to cause trouble. We have questions. That's it."

Asher snorted, crossing his arms across a muscular chest. "Sure," he drawled slowly. "Because William Best comes knocking at your door, and it's *not* to cause trouble." He rolled his eyes. "We've heard the stories, buddy. You're not fooling us with her presence." He nodded at Cara. "Don't lie to me about your nymph side. You don't smell of nymph."

Uneasiness stirred William's gut. Gods help them all if he'd missed something. "If you've heard the stories, you know I never attack unprovoked, and I don't trouble folks minding their own business." William looked the man up and down. "I've heard of you and your team. The good work you do aligns with my goals of helping paranormals, keeping the peace. I've got no fight with you."

"What do you mean I don't 'smell' nymph?" Cara asked, taking another step closer, then jerking back and glaring at his hand where he held her like an anchor. She faced the two men. "My grandmother was full-blood nymph. I don't have the typical abilities but..." She hesitated, reached for her pendant with her free hand. "I've been told nymph magic is holding back my abilities, preventing communication with my...with my guardian spirit. That's all I want to ask your friends about. Nahla and Caspian, those are their names, right? I don't have to get close, I just—"

"They have no wish to speak with you," Maddox said, voice rough and deep, though gentler than it had been when he'd addressed William. "Asher is wrong. I smell your nymph side. You are…" He cocked his head, as though considering, or deepening his read. "Broken."

Cara's breath wheezed out.

William squeezed her hand in comfort, and when she turned, her eyes shone overbright, making his chest tighten. He shouldn't have brought her here. Put her in danger without finding a way to soften the answers.

"Can you tell how I'm… I'm broken?" Cara said.

Maddox cocked his head, sunlight glinting on his close-shaved scalp, pausing a moment before he shrugged. "I do not know enough of your kind to tell. I can sense it. Caspian and Nahla did as well."

"Maddox…" Asher warned the dragon, voice low.

Maddox gestured toward Cara. "She is no threat, not to us. I'm bored. Perhaps the Hunter will give me a fight. It has been dull around here of late." He offered William a wide, glittering smile. "Shall we dance, Hunter?"

Dragons. William stifled a grumble, shoulders tightening. Dragons were one of those species, like trolls and war gods, who provoked fights for the hell of it. "Cara, they're not going to tell us anything."

"You're impossible, you know that?" Asher rounded on Maddox. "We promised Ginny we'd take care of the place, not burn it down or turn it into a wrestling ring because you're bored."

Ginny…the Famine horsewoman. An enemy William didn't want to make, either.

Cara, though, had gone still at his side, studying Asher. "You know something," she whispered, gaze unwavering. "Nahla and Caspian told you something. Is it about me? About nymphs?"

Asher froze before resettling his crossed arms, one blond brow flicking upward. "Someone told you—" He glared at the dragon. "You've gotten chatty?"

Maddox shrugged, mouth turned down. "I said nothing. The Hunter will not fight. I am uninterested." He turned and walked away.

Pretty-boy lifted his hand in a one-fingered gesture to the dragon's back before leveling his cool blue gaze on Cara and William. "You know what? It'd serve him right if you jump his ass. No objections from me." He shoved a hand through his blond hair before he focused on Cara, considered her a moment before speaking. "Caspian told me he could tell there was something wrong with you. He and his sister avoid other nymphs because of nymph's communal magic. Personally, I've always found sea nymphs elitist weirdos, but maybe others suck less." He lowered his voice, gaze steady. "That other side of you we sense, the broken part? Nymphs will see you as damaged goods, someone to expel, you get me?"

"I understand. My grandparents experienced their prejudice. I just need to talk to them," Cara said, voice desperate.

Tight lipped, Asher considered her a few more moments, rubbing a hand over his lips. "Nahla and Caspian aren't the only nymphs in town. I don't know where they are, but Caspian sensed them. Maybe you can, too. Good luck and be careful."

NEITHER SHE NOR William spoke on the drive home. Cara stared out the window at the blur of trees and passing road, blinking back the sting in her eyes. *Broken.* Because possibly dying of nymph magic wasn't enough. The news got better and better. Oh, and she still needed to tell William she was dying, then find the other mystery nymphs Asher knew were in town, but not where.

She glanced at William. Her husband. Such a strange thought. Ugh. She spent too much time thinking about him, whereas he didn't seem to have the same problem. Sure, he'd been kind at art class, was there right when she needed him, but that was the hero gig. Her stomach ached. Dom would have the perfect no-nonsense advice, tell Cara to stop feeling sorry for herself, make some potions, find some nymphs. If only it were that easy.

William again pulled the Jeep beside the garage rather than inside.

"There's plenty of room in the garage," she said lightly. Just like the house, he seemed to think parking in the garage would suggest he wanted to settle in. He'd made it clear he wasn't interested in staying. He wasn't broken and half in love with her. Why should he be?

William, though, stood outside the Jeep and stared at the front door, frowning. "Is that a dog by the front door?"

She climbed out of the Jeep.

A reddish-brown mutt sat on the front concrete steps.

"Not-Dog. I thought he was gone."

"Apparently, he's back."

As William and Cara drew closer, Not-Dog stood, tail wagging and tongue hanging from its mouth in a doggy grin. It looked back and forth between them both.

"We shouldn't let it inside," William said. "You hear that, Not-Dog? No warm bed for you."

"Closed doors don't seem to bother him. He got out of the house last night and your Jeep this morning. Not sure we have a choice."

It sucked its tongue back in its mouth a moment to whine, then panted back up at her, hopeful.

She held out her hand, and it bumped its head against her knuckles. That strange feeling washed over her, that sense of knowing, a connection with something greater that whispered to her. The wind rasped through the dry tree branches, carrying the whispers that called her name. She studied Not-Dog's amber eyes, and he stared back.

He wasn't dangerous…exactly… He wanted to help.

The dog whined, tossed his head toward William.

Cara straightened. The dog wanted to help William.

"He's not dangerous," she said slowly. Explaining her best friend was a necklace had been bad enough. Explaining that she'd read something off the dog was too much for the day.

"You're sure about that?"

"I… Yes. He's not dangerous. Not to us at any rate." Specifically, not to William. "You're sure you don't recognize him?"

"I'm not senile, if that's what you're asking," William grumbled, his keys jingling as he unlocked the front door.

She stepped forward, still staring at Not-Dog. Which was probably why she collided with William, who'd stopped in the doorway.

His arms came around her.

Her fingers pressed against hard muscle beneath soft cotton, the thud of his heart beneath her fingertips, laundry soap and his spicy scent surrounding her. Electricity flashed between them as their eyes met, stole her breath. Something hot shifted behind William's gaze as it landed on her lips.

Cara's fingers tensed against William's chest, and her breath quickened. Husband, newlyweds. Sex. Oh, Goddess, *sex*. Her libido purred.

His gaze hot, he studied her expression. Then, as though compartmentalizing desire, or maybe his wasn't so demanding, he cleared his throat, dropped his arms, and took a step back. "You did whatever you do again, didn't you? With the dog, assessing whether it was safe."

She hugged herself, the movement aggravating her sensitized nipples. Frick's sake. "Maybe."

"Is that what's been happening all along? You using your ability but not realizing that's what you're doing? Maybe the Yaga pendant was using you, making you think the power belonged to it to make you feel weak."

"Dom wouldn't do that." Her fingers itched for the pendant, but she set them on her hips.

"Power is a strong motivator. It's what the Guardians are after."

"Not Dom. I'm sure of it." Although, could she have been using her ability before and assumed the power belonged to Dom?

"Until we know for sure, maybe we should hold off on finding the nymphs. They don't sound likely to help."

"But—"

"Cara." He reached for her shoulder, the brotherly move burning through the thickness of her jacket. "Everyone we've met who knows nymphs advises steering clear. Maybe—"

"Dom told me if I don't find them, nymph magic will kill me," she blurted. Because oops, that was as subtle and non-panicked as she'd planned.

Not-Dog gave a bark, bumped against her leg.

William snapped upright, backing into the open door, pressing it open farther.

His silence made her talk faster.

"You can't tell Gramps. Or the others. Or…or anyone." The problem was, the faster she talked, the more Dom's words, the impact behind them, rolled over her with the crushing force of a rogue wave. "If we don't find the nymphs, I'll die. Not of old age, not of accident. Of magic. We have to find them. Or I do. And Dom." Shakes and tremors spread through her, weakened her knees, made her eyes burn and her voice crack. "D-Dom will know what to do, how to prevent this. M-maybe it's not true. Dom, um, made a mistake or something. Or…or…" Burning tears escaped, faster and faster no matter how quickly she tried to wipe them away.

William wrapped his arms around her, ushered her inside. Against the hard heat of his chest, the embrace of her freaking dream man. They stepped into the foyer of her house together, her life a little less lonely. The thought pulverized the last dam and released a flood of tears. Not the cute kind, either, but runny-nose, clogged-throat, inconsolable sobs as loud as a four-year-old with spilled ice cream.

Proving his heroic talents, William got them into the foyer, where they kicked off their shoes, and he divested her of her jacket and maneuvered them toward the cozy living room.

"Shh. I'm here. We'll figure this out," he murmured as he rubbed her shoulder.

Even through runny eyes and nose, Gran's floral scent hugged Cara. Gran's personality and scent permeated the living room from the matching green chairs and floral sofa, to the very wallpaper.

William turned her in his arms, brushed some of the flyaway hairs from her face. His finger pad was work roughened, but gentle as a butterfly caress as he brushed away one of her tears.

She couldn't break away from his blue-gray gaze. His troubled expression suggested her tears left him unsettled, yet he'd been where she needed him, when she needed him. It'd been a long time since she'd had that.

"I don't want to die," she whispered, her words cracking near the end.

"I won't let you," he said, smoothing back her hair.

His touch stopped the tears and lit up parts of her, her purring libido pointing out helpfully that this beautiful man was here, now. That he was real, and warm, and sent electrical shock waves through her system.

"We'll find the nymphs. If what Dom said is true, we'll figure out how to stop it. If it isn't, we'll stop Dom from using or hurting you. Either way, I'll keep you safe. I'll protect you. You're not going to die. I won't let you."

Their eyes met again, that softness in his gaze so much like in her dreams, nothing like the man they whispered stories about. Maybe she arched upward. Maybe he leaned down, but suddenly it wasn't his fingertips against her skin, but his lips against hers, their breath mingling.

He tasted of sweet mints and heat and need, of protection and wild. His arms tightened around her, and her hands crept up his chest, found the firmness of those muscles beneath her palms. Geezus, he felt and tasted as good as she'd dreamed. Better. His hair was softer than she'd imagined as she curled her fingers through it.

He angled her head to better connect their lips, one of his hands slipping toward her butt. He squeezed her ass, arched her toward him, toward more hardness, more… Oh, Goddess. He was hard, and he wanted her. Heat spilled through her, blotted out logical thought and fear and worry and everything but the taste of him, the feel of him, her body pressed to his…

He stiffened. Then pulled his lips from hers. Removed his hands from her body, and gently removed hers from his.

She blinked. What…But they'd…

"I'm sorry," he rasped, pulling away. "I…can't." Then he walked away.

Leaving her alone in a room with nothing but photos of a family she no longer had, scented with the grandmother who'd left her without answers, and trapped by the suffocating knowledge that unless she found the nymphs, she'd die.

Chapter Fifteen

TRICKS AND TREATS

BY DAWN THE NEXT MORNING, eyes gritty with lack of sleep, it was damned clear he was hiding from Cara, his former friends…the way that kiss had made him feel. William growled to himself, arms crossed and jaw tight, as he stared at the web of paper with case notes he'd pinned to the corkboard in Jenklow's former office, a small, masculine room fitted with chestnut bookshelves, dark-green paint, worn wood floors, and a desk beneath the window, flanked by a four-foot-high corkboard. How he'd have designed it himself, if he'd dared have an office after Berta and her death. Perfect for laying out and visualizing a case…while avoiding one's dangerously attractive wife. Or replaying the angry words from the Shades yesterday.

Cara had offered it to him, this room sandwiched between the living room and Cara's studio. Close enough that last night when he'd retreated to the Jeep for supplies to set up his case in here, Cara's movements next door in the sunroom kept him company. Reprimanded him.

That kiss, that moment of home and wanting to be hers, had stirred the thought of forgetting the mission, ignoring the Guardians, focusing only on her. It'd been insanity.

Tempting.

He stroked the stained white leather spine of the palm-sized *The Adventures of Pinocchio*, one of his only three books, smaller on these empty shelves. Mom had scrimped to buy it when he was small, read it to him, then pressed it into his hands the day he'd left home. It'd lived through both wars in his breast pocket, given comfort to others in dark days, and protected his few photos.

Last night, he furiously scribbled notes on paper, accompanied by Cara's grumbles next door, the scent of wet paint. Close enough for company…centuries apart. He turned away from the book, rocking back on his heels and glaring at his case web on the corkboard. He'd grown up. Turned out unlike Pinocchio, there were no good deeds, no sacrifice that'd ever make him a real boy worthy of a happy ending.

He rocked back on his heels and glared some more at the pieces of paper with names and places, connected by strings and tacks and not much else. He rummaged for his tin, popping a mint. Not that staring at the web most of the night had created more connections or revealed a clear pattern.

Cara had headed to bed last night around midnight. There'd been that moment when soft footsteps paused outside the door, as though maybe she'd thought of inviting him for dinner, stopping in to check on him. Exchange the kind of pleasantries real couples did, that charge you got from seeing the other person, hearing their voice, being near them. Like it'd been yesterday with Cara, during her classes, at the clinic, standing hand-in-hand with her visiting the dragon. Almost like a real boy.

Dammit, he never should have agreed to the marriage.

It'd been an obvious ploy by Jenklow and the boys to tie him to this town, these people. Yet it'd fit his goals. Before he saw Cara, met her. Tasted her. Before the Shades made it clear they didn't believe in retirement.

Not-Dog harrumphed from where he lay on the floor near the door, gazing up at William with sorrowful eyes.

William scowled at the suspicious animal. "Not feeling sorry for you, Not-Dog. Kibbles in the kitchen on the floor. That's what dogs eat. You want something else, go somewhere else."

The pseudo-dog had shadowed him all night, and whatever else it was, it'd been company to talk to.

Not-Dog harrumphed again and closed his eyes.

William went back to staring at the scrawled clues. That one with the date and time, brief descriptions, and his guesses as to species of the participants in the protest at the refugee camp. Red bulletin pins to mark graffiti, blue for more serious property damage. No discernible patterns. A question mark for whoever the command-level Guardian in charge of the incursion was, since they hadn't made an appearance. A question mark beside the C that stood for Cara. What her abilities were, what the dragon and prettyboy had meant when they said she was broken.

She was the one connecting factor between too many of the points. Cara, the taste of her on his lips yesterday, her soft moan awakening dreams of sex, waking up together, this being his office where she'd check in on him, or he'd wander over to watch her paint. They'd end up on the floor together, make love on the tarps covering the floor, paint staining their skin…

He massaged his eyes. He had to focus on the case. Figure out what connected all of these factors—other than Cara—and decipher where the Guardians would attack next, so he'd be there to stop them.

His phone buzzed and he picked it up, glanced at the texts scrolling across the screen.

They're coming for me.

This is your fault.

You owe me!

He closed the messages with a flick of his thumb. Tom Prainlagh, aka one of his Guardian informants, aka a shiftless lower sidhe who'd sell his own siblings—which he'd done on at least one occasion—or buy expensive cars with mushrooms bespelled to look like money. Because of his connections to the fey court, he'd been welcome at Guardian events but had never been ambitious enough to either fight against their actions or participate in their cause. It was more profitable for him to stay in that gray area. He sometimes came through with decent tips.

Like the one that had led William here. To Beckwell and Cara.

He sighed at the phone, punched in Tom's number. It rang but went to voicemail. He didn't bother leaving a message. The back of his neck itched, and he tried to massage it away. After a good tip, Tom always got nervous for a week or two, convinced someone knew he'd passed it on…and usually asked for money. That was all it was. The itchiness remained.

Rolling his shoulders, William glanced at his watch. A few minutes to six. Even with enhanced recovery and strength, he'd feel the sleepless night later. For now, before Cara was up, maybe he'd take advantage of the quiet and take a shower. A very cold shower. With luck, it'd bring his heated brain under control, he'd see the patterns and break the case. Because if he didn't get to the Guardians first, innocent people were going to die. Innocent people like Cara. Damned if he'd let that happen on his watch.

CARA SLAMMED her hand on her alarm—set to the unholy hell of six in the morning so she could be up before William, have a shower, and get downstairs first. She should be worrying about getting his word he wouldn't tell the Shades about Dom's fear nymph magic would kill her. Having to face him after she'd obviously scared him off with that kiss last night ranked right up there with a trip to the dentist. Seriously, super-sexy husbands straight out of her wildest fantasies incinerated her calm and order. Best to keep her distance.

If only it were that easy. Her body ached to repeat that kiss and then some.

If William kept to form, they'd have mind-blowing sex that left her melted into a puddle, while he strode off, apparently unaffected. Like he had last night. It had taken two ruined canvases—no visions, just crappy paintings—to calm her libido enough to even think of sleep. Not jumping her husband's bones, especially listening to him next door, grumbling to himself, unpacking something, only added to her restless need. Every time she'd been tempted to drop her brush and go to him, she'd squeeze out a new blob of paint that she had to use up before squeezing out yet another blob. Anything to stop herself from throwing herself at a man who didn't want her. At least, not as much as she wanted him because there'd been, ahem, hard evidence he'd wanted her yesterday.

Slipping out of the warm bed onto the chilled wood floor, she yawned and shuffled around her room to collect clean clothes, shrug out of her sleep clothes, and exchange them for her robe. Still yawning, she stumbled into the bathroom across the hall. A nice hot shower could provide consciousness.

She closed the door quietly, keeping the light off and relying on the faint morning glow from the high window so she didn't wake William. Another wide yawn and she tugged the plastic curtain reluctantly around the claw-foot tub before she slipped off her robe, letting it puddle on the floor. She stepped into the tub wearing nothing but the pendant.

The bathroom door opened. William stepped inside, wearing only a pair of boxers slung low over his hipbones.

"I'm in here!" she squeaked, yanking desperately on the curtain.

The door clicked closed.

She gave the flimsy, transparent curtain another jerk. The curtain tore free from the hooks. Her foot slipped. Her arms windmilled, plastic shower curtain flapping.

William caught her against his warm chest, a wad of plastic shower curtain between them. "I've got you."

His masculine scent surrounded her. Um, yep. He had her. All those bare muscles wrapped around her. Bare flesh pressed to bare flesh. That electric connection between them crackled, and heat spiraled through her. The memory and minty taste of his mouth on hers, dreams of more. Especially without the pesky interference of clothes. So much naked William. Catching her up in his arms, rescuing her. She stared up into that blue-gray gaze, mesmerized…

The bathroom door lock clicked.

The spell broke, and they turned toward the door.

"You all right?" William asked, voice rough. He helped her gain her footing, clearing his throat and stepping back, gaze skating over her body. "I'll…uh… I'll let you have your shower." He reached for the bathroom doorknob and jiggled it. Paused, then jiggled again, harder this time. "The door's locked."

Clutching the useless transparent curtain around herself, unable to let it go, Cara frowned. "Not possible. That lock hasn't worked for years."

He jiggled again. "It's locked now."

Trapped in the bathroom with her sex god of a husband. Sex gods definitely implied—and invited—beds, and sex, in the bed, against the wall…in a bathroom.

Good grief. Heat burned her cheekbones. She must have hit her head. The plastic shower curtain wasn't cutting it. What she needed were clothes between them, and out of this room. She searched the floor, scowled. "Did you move my robe or the bathmat?"

"No," he said, tone irritated as he tried the door again, then banged against it with his shoulder. The bathroom wall might have shuddered—or that might have been her sex-starved libido trembling as she watched all those rippling muscles at work. The old bathroom door, though, was unimpressed and didn't budge.

She cleared her throat, considering the delicacies of gathering the transparent plastic curtain around herself before bending over to open the cupboard doors and get a towel instead.

Except the shelves were bare. No soap, no towels. What the hell?

"If you didn't take my robe and you didn't take the bathmat, then you didn't take every towel, either, did you?" She closed the cupboard and straightened.

"Of course not." He studied the door, stretching to try and remove the hinge pins, muscles rippling in his back, pulling at old scars and bronzed skin. Yum. "Were these welded in? I can't get them to budge."

"No…" she said, more focused on ogling than escape. Sure, she'd seen him shirtless that first night, spotted those scars she wanted to kiss better. Clothing was so overrated. The muscles on his lightly haired thighs flexed, his butt taut in those boxers. This obsession of hers grew worse.

"I, uh, maybe I should try," she said, voice breathy and probably giving her away.

William glanced back at her, his stormy blue gaze skimming over hers, growing darker before he flicked it away. He cleared his throat. "Have at it." He stepped out of her way.

The bathroom, however, wasn't big. Between the breadth of his shoulders and her bunched-up shower curtain—which was scratchy against her breasts, and sweaty, too—she brushed against him as they passed. A touch of her arm against his, a brush against that bare chest of his, but enough to steal her breath and make her acutely aware of every inch of him.

She jiggled on the doorknob, hard. Not that she'd expected it to turn, but still. She peered through the keyhole. "Do you see something out there? Something…reddish?"

William pressed in close, flesh brushing flesh.

She saw spots. Or at least images of him taking her against the wall, testing out the stability of the old vanity with the weight of their bodies, the strength of his thrusts…

She blinked, easing back to put a little more distance between them. Geezus, Josie, and George. What the hell. She was not usually this horny.

"Not-Dog," William confirmed, straightening and putting her eye-to-eye with those firm pecs of his.

"Hmm?" She blinked. "Not-Dog?" English was hard when her body wanted to get to banging. Inappropriate tingles curled through her, reminding her that the only thing standing between them was a transparent shower curtain and his stubbornness. Obviously, one of those things was impervious to her efforts.

She rearranged the shower curtain with trembling hands, settling more creases across her lower portion, her breasts beneath the sticky plastic tingling. Her thoughts focused on sexy times. Bad, bad ideas.

William glared at the door as though he could see through it. He gestured at it. "Not-Dog has been following me around. If it isn't dangerous, it's trouble." He glanced at her again, his gaze sliding lower.

"The door is wood. It should break." He proceeded to slam his body into it.

The door barely shuddered.

She winced at the impact, at the way William massaged his red shoulder. She couldn't stop herself from closing the distance, smoothing her fingers over the redness. "Maybe brute strength isn't going to work." Did make for a lot of nice muscles, though. She massaged his flesh, hard muscle jumping beneath her touch, the skin surprisingly soft. Damn, he was literally hot.

Touching him wasn't like touching the refugees. Touching them didn't elicit the same electric heat. But with William, it was something more than that. Not knowing, not that coolness, but like some deep part of her reached out for him, reached for that strength in him. Found something stronger and brighter than anything she'd ever connected with before. A bright blue force of energy, glowing and vibrant…

She froze, hand suspended above his shoulder. That was…weird. Weirder than talking pendants and instant knowing weird.

William caught her fingers in his, drew her gaze with it. "Is that all you see when you look at me? Brute strength?"

Nope. That glowing blue light was getting added to the

list, too. Along with the hotness and visions and general extreme attraction. She cleared her throat, tried to focus. "What? Of course not."

She noticed too much about him. Including the vulnerable shadows in his blue-gray gaze. Her answer seemed to genuinely matter, which made her lady parts sigh.

The shower curtain shifted and crinkled as she stepped closer, losing herself in his gaze, blue-gray with specks of gold. "You're incredibly intelligent, persistent, a strong leader, and protective of those who aren't as strong as you. I..." Her tongue kept saying things it had no business revealing. Yet the softness in his expression, the way he absorbed every word, the doubt that pulled at his lips like he hadn't heard these things before, kept her going. "You're so much kinder, so much...*more* than I thought you'd be, even with the stories from the boys. More devoted, more careful." More dangerous to her heart, too, if he kept up that sexy-sweet thing.

He slid his hand up her arm, raising goosebumps in its wake. "There are those who hate me, Cara. Perhaps rightfully so. The Guardians dubbed me the Abomination because I wasn't born naturally into this world. No one, including me, understands how I fit, what I am." His fingertips reached her shoulder, brushed back her curls that rested there, sliding his fingers over the side of her neck, stealing her breath.

Her eyelids fluttered, and she let out a ragged sigh. "Screw them. You're not an Abomination. You've helped so many people. You've made a difference in our world. You're a *good* man."

He cupped her jaw, steadied her until their gazes met. His voice rasped. "Am I? The Guardians have always countered my every move, which makes any connection to me dangerous. I don't want more friends, more people I care about to get caught in the crossfire. My being here brings danger to your door."

His words, the implication she might be one of those he cared about, melted her uncertainty. Shower curtain crinkling, she grasped his forearm, squeezed the tightness in the muscle. "You're not alone. Not anymore. Let those Guardians, gods, whatevers come. I won't let them hurt you."

The corner of his lips curled up, and his thumb caressed her jaw as he studied her as though seeing her for the first time. "I can handle the Guardians. I'll do what I can to protect *you*. From the Guardians. From the god who created me, freaking Hermes." He slid his other arm around her, pulling her closer to the hard breadth of his chest, surrounding her in safety and his spicy scent. "We'll find the nymphs, even if I have to ask Hermes. He might be in town, but I won't let him or the Guardians near you." He hesitated, his splayed hand burning against her bare flesh in the small of her back. "If we ask the Shades for help—"

She cupped his jaw, urgency leaping into her throat. "No. This stays between us. Gramps can't know." About Dom…about the possibility nymph magic could kill her. She stared past William a moment at the bare curtain rings, blinking the burn from her eyes before she met his gaze again. "Not the Shades. We've got this. We'll find Dom and it'll be okay. Just us."

"Us," he murmured, his gaze on her lips. His thumb rubbed over the softness of her bottom lip. "It's been just me a long time. I don't know how to do 'us.'"

Her throat squeezed and heat curled and tightened inside her. She shifted closer and caressed his face, brushed back the hair on his brow. "I don't, either. But maybe," she pressed up on her toes, closed the distance between their lips, his breath brushing her face. "Maybe we can learn together."

The shower curtain slipped to her mid back. She let it go, the crinkling plastic replaced by the callused warmth of his hands, cupping her skin, kneading her flesh.

"Yeah?" he said, gaze on her lips, hand tight on her back, other hand cupping her jaw again.

Breath mingled, then their lips touched, connecting at first gently, sliding and pressing. Then hungrier and hotter, the taste of toothpaste and masculine hunger on his tongue, the greed in his groan as his hand snaked beneath the plastic and cupped her bare ass, dug his fingers into her flesh.

Hunger overpowered them. His hands tangled in her hair, positioned her head where he wanted it, his mouth, his lips teasing, tasting, plundering her.

They twisted together, their moans greedy. He lifted and pressed her against the cold tiled wall, the bathroom doorknob brushing her thigh on the right. The shower curtain crinkled between them, caught between their chests, stopping her aching breasts from pressing against his bare chest. The friction both excited and frustrated her, but the taste of him, the feel of his bare skin beneath her nails, all of it so intoxicating, so much more than she'd imagined.

He broke away from the kiss long enough to meet her gaze, their chests heaving as he cupped her breast through the shower curtain, teased her bare flesh above the rough plastic. His knee nudged between hers and he lifted her with his other hand beneath her butt cheek, spread and pressed her against his thigh.

She bit her lip, the sound she made something between groan and laugh. "You think you're the only one who can tease?" She barely recognized the throaty sound of her voice as she slid her hand down, cupped his length through the cotton of his boxers.

"Oh, gods. Cara," he said, abandoning any hint of tease, moving back enough to shove the shower curtain out from between them, then he lifted her and settled his mouth on her bare breast, sucked her nipple into the heat of his mouth.

She saw double, no, triple, clutching his head with both hands, letting the pleasure of his mouth rip through her. Her foggy gaze watched the flowers on the wallpaper dance. She dragged William's head back to snag his lips again, holding his head in place while he gripped her thighs, wrapped her legs around his waist. She rubbed against him through the cotton. Finally, finally she was here. This was real, not some dream. He'd be hers. He *was* hers.

Not-Dog barked outside the door. Loudly.

The bathroom door popped open, banging against William's back and her knee.

Not-Dog stood outside it, hackles raised, growling.

"Hey, boy. It's okay. I sometimes like dogs. William? You there?" It was the police chief, Mal Quilan. "No one answered when I knocked. Or called. There's something going on at the— Oh." He stepped around the corner and got quite an eyeful before he spun away. "Shit. I'm— I texted. You didn't answer. Cara is late for work, and she's never late for work. There was an attack on the refugee camp, now trouble at the Center. Daniel's helping the injured, and I need backup."

William lowered Cara to the ground, their bodies sliding against each other, the sweat of their skin cooling in the open doorway.

Cara's bare toes brushed the edge of the bathmat as her unsteady knees threatened to buckle. She swallowed hard, stared first at the bathmat, her fuzzy pink robe puddled on top of it beneath her feet. Whew. Between that…incendiary action and the robe disappearing and the police chief… Had she made a fool of herself, or started her and William down the path for a real marriage?

When she forced her gaze upward, William stared intently at the robe and the bathmat, neither of which had been there before. He cleared his throat, grabbed her robe off the floor and pressed it into her hands before taking a step back, never meeting her gaze. It was like she could see him rebuilding the wall between them even as he used his body to shelter hers, turning his back on her.

"I'll be right there," he said, voice all-business, William Best, P.I., none of the rasped confessions he'd given her, the question of whether he was good.

"Um… I'll wait downstairs," Chief Quilan said, before footsteps carried him quickly away.

"William?" Cara gathered the robe around her, faced William's back as he took one shuddering breath, then another.

"I'm sorry. This was a mistake," he said, voice rough before he strode across the hall, disappearing into the room. The click of the bedroom door made her flinch.

She swallowed past thickness, shaking where she clutched the robe against her nakedness, eyes burning again. No. No, it hadn't been a mistake, damn it. It'd been… Well, something.

She blinked rapidly, sucking in air and lifting her chin before dashing for her room to jerk on clothes. She didn't need to see the future to know kissing William, the idea of them as a team, hadn't been a mistake. She needed to prove it to him. Which started with them working together. She'd finally had him in her arms, and she wasn't giving that—or the desperate need to survive—up without a fight.

Chapter Sixteen

WITH GREAT POWER...

BY THE TIME William and Mal arrived at the Senior Center—accompanied by Cara and Not-Dog, both of whom had jumped into the police chief's truck despite William's protests—what Mal had described as a scuffle had erupted into a mini-riot in the Senior Center atrium.

People crowded into the generous atrium, the automatic glass doors forced open with the numbers. Residents of the Center threatened the interlopers. Some of the Center staff, like Cara's dark-haired friend, fretted on the sidelines while others were lost in the crowd. Maddox the dragon was there, scowling, beside pretty-boy Asher. The crowd teemed with people from the refugee camp, many with bandages and minor wounds, torn clothing. Plus, some of those idiots who'd left their protest boards at home but chanted: "Paranormals first. Pretenders go home."

Shit. Pretenders was one of the terms the Guardians used for anyone without pure-blood paranormal lineage... especially those with mortal or human ancestry.

And, of course, because everyone seemed suicidal

today, the Shades had inserted themselves into the thick of it. William's jaw and fists tightened.

"People, please," Henry shouted above the noise of the complaints and shouts. "Remember these are your friends, your family."

"Damn." Quilan leaned closer to Cara, bright and noticeable in her red coat. There was nothing overtly sexual about the move, more like two familiar friends.

Still, some part of William tensed, and he popped a mint, skin tight. He and Cara didn't have that same familiarity or comfort. Not that they were supposed to, or that it was something he wanted. He was supposed to focus on the mission…and the fact he'd use her for bait meant he couldn't be as honest with her as a close relationship required. He'd be even more of a louse if he let her get close, let her believe he was something and someone he wasn't. Fact was, he didn't deserve that casual closeness with her…no matter the temptation. The mission, the Guardians. That's where his focus should be.

"Those posters I made warning about the magical weapon ban and dangers of the Senior Center didn't work at all, did they?" The police chief sounded more frustrated than concerned.

Cara considered the crowd calmly. "They never do. Maybe we could try one of those workplace signs here. Something like 'This many days since our last riot.'"

The police chief snorted. "We'd have to count it down in hours." He started to work his way into the crowd.

"That'd still be something," Cara called after him, before moving to follow.

William caught her forearm. It was only the mission that made him stop her. Not the easy comradery between her and the police chief…or her gentleness back at the house, the way she'd promised to be part of his team, the way she'd touched him, and he'd had no doubt it was him she saw. *Just us*, she'd promised. Hell. No wonder he hadn't been able to resist kissing her.

She raised a brow, hardness entering her expression.

"Why don't you and Not-Dog stay here?" He held up a hand as she opened her mouth to protest, a scowl spreading across her face. "I know you can handle yourself. But this could get nasty." *You could get hurt.* "You don't have full control of your abilities yet. What if you accidentally do something you can't take back?" Someone could see her, want her abilities for themselves. Even if it wasn't the Guardians, there were likely those in Beckwell with the ability to control mortal minds and bend her abilities to their desire. "Let's keep those abilities quiet for now, especially until you understand and can better control them." She'd be safer, hopefully, out of the heart of the trouble… but he was smart enough not to say that.

Expression distinctly mulish, she nodded stiffly, reaching a hand to Not-Dog's furry head. "Fine. But if there's any trouble, or anyone goes after Gramps, no way I'm standing around, doing nothing."

Henry was already gathering hecklers.

"Leave off, old man," someone called from nearer the door. "Where's the real mayor? Or Loki? Or the Four?"

"Who will protect us?" someone else called.

William winced. Glanced back at Cara. The hesitation to leave her was new and troubling.

She rolled her eyes, made a shooing motion with her hand. "Go on. Help." The corner of her lips rose. "Be the hero I know you are."

He nodded, throat oddly thick as he turned and worked his way after the police chief, edging through the crowd, careful not to knock anyone over, bump them with his bulk. The urge to glance back at Cara pulled at him.

Was she just saying that, the hero stuff? It didn't sit right, leaving her behind, leaving her vulnerable. Hopefully Not-Dog proved himself useful. Because William couldn't leave the Shades vulnerable, either. There was something about Cara. Not just her looks, but something in her smile, the invitation to share her home, her body, her life. His throat tightened. The way she talked about them as a team.

"We have everything—including your protection—under control," Jenklow shouted this time, jerking William's attention back to the matter.

Jenklow was shorter than most of the rioters, his bald head barely visible in their midst.

"You'd trust a bunch of old men to protect you?" jeered someone from the far side of the crowd. "Used up old has-beens, they're singing the same song while the rest of us have moved on."

William slipped a little more forcefully through the crowd, the words pricking his skin. He might have moved on, too, but that didn't mean the Shades didn't deserve respect. Respect he should have shown them with more of his time earlier, too. He'd been so distracted lately with the hollow emptiness inside, the one that craved a Cara-sized piece.

"You're not safe here," the protester shouted, gaining more answering voices, for and against. "Not when humans are calling for our registration, our blood. Looking for ways to oppress us, force all of our kind back into the shadows."

The comments stirred up more cries, both for and against, as had no doubt been intended.

William strained to identify the speaker's face in the crowd, but with all the chanting and other angry shouts, it was impossible. He didn't know enough people around here to recognize the voice, but definitely the all-too-familiar refrain. Guardians, either old guard or new recruits.

"Beckwell is fully equipped with me, the law, and the Four," Chief Quilan said, lifting a hand, and tall enough to be seen above most of the crowd. He held his badge aloft. "Chief Quilan here. This room is well above capacity. Come on, people, break it up. We don't want any more injuries today."

"Tell them that! They attacked us while we were trying to have breakfast, trying to survive," someone else shouted, this one appearing to be a purple-hued woman, demon lineage likely, her head wrapped with a makeshift towel-bandage, seeping green.

Cries and voices of others, many of them with similar bandages and injuries, joined hers.

"Paranormals First. Pretenders go home!" The chanting grew louder.

"You think we don't want to? That we wouldn't rather be back in the lives we've lost?" shouted another.

The crowd writhed. Flesh struck flesh. There were cries, shouts. The metallic scent of blood. Angry shouts. Equally angry responses. More blows, the crowd writhing more and more, a growing storm. A woman cried out.

Liko's growl was unmistakable. "Get the hell off her!" A cane flew in the air, and there was a brief shine of Liko's bald head before he dove into the crowd.

Chief Quilan's voice rose again. "I said, break it up!" He bellowed this time, and his skin had taken on an ashy gray-blue tone. He'd gained a few inches that put him above William's height. "The cells are already full, but you know what? I'm happy to lock you all up in a shed some-where. Back off. Yes, that means you, Mr. Chaimek. Sister Marguerite, don't touch my butt again. We've talked about this."

More grumbles from the uneasy crowd.

A young male piped up…directly next to William. He stabbed his fist in the air to punctuate his words. "Paranormals First. Pretend—"

William placed a firm but gentle hand on the skinny kid's shoulder, in front of the small, jutting feathered wings.

The kid turned on him with a snarl, but his words died with a surprised squeak. His eyes rounded. His face paled, and his wings drooped. "Y-you're him. The h-h-h—"

"Mr. Best works fine, kid." William allowed himself a small, tight smile. He popped open his mint tin and held it out to the kid. Giving kids candy proved you weren't a monster and could be reasoned with…to some degree. But sometimes his reputation came in handy, like when scaring would-be terrorists. "Mint?"

The kid shook his head rapidly, gaze unwavering.

William nodded toward Chief Quilan, tucking away his mints and raising his voice slightly to be overheard. "The police chief asked this crowd to disperse. I'm here to help him. You're not thinking of causing any trouble, are you?"

The kid shook his head hard enough to give himself whiplash.

Others around them had noticed the interaction and backed away, forming a break in the crowd. No more flying fists or snarls.

William patted the kid's shoulder firmly, but not hard enough to send the runt to his knees. "Good choice. Because this town, these people? They're good people. They don't want trouble, don't need it. This is a safe place for all kinds. My friends and I like it that way. Don't you?"

Nodding this time.

The kid wasn't the only one. There were others in the crowd mirroring the kids' actions. Whispers, too, informing anyone who didn't know who William was, the whispers like swarming gnats. Not that he should have minded. After all, it was his reputation that'd help restore peace today, no real fists required.

William took his hand from the kid's shoulders and gave Chief Quilan a nod, making it clear William wasn't the law here, but he supported Quilan.

"Thanks, Best," Quilan said, a quick study, his voice all authority. He pointed toward the glass walled med clinic, where his twin, Doctor Quilan, stood arms crossed, blocking the doorway, a faint metallic gold hue to his skin. A warrior protecting his territory, too. "For all injuries, please make your way to the med clinic across this way. Daniel, give them a wave."

The chief's twin waved.

"For anyone else who might need a bit of warmth and recuperation, there's fresh tea, coffee, and cookies in the dining hall," Jenklow added. "All are welcome so long as you aren't there to cause trouble."

The tension and violence in the room subsided. With murmurs and softer voices, the crowd shifted and dispersed, some toward the clinic, others toward the door, some toward the dining hall and resident rooms. Like a retreating tide, it left the Center staff revealed, swooping in to help residents back to various activities and their rooms. Cara's friend, Maddy, had disappeared somewhere. Maddox stalked off toward the dining hall, while his friend Asher chatted up a nursing attendant.

William's neck muscles softened, and he closed the distance across the emptying atrium toward the police chief and the Shades.

"Crisis averted." Jenklow beamed, nodding to William and Mal Quilan. "Excellent work, boys. Although we had everything in hand."

"Oh, yeah. I could tell," Quilan drawled. He sighed. "Loki is going to kill me. He leaves town, and the seniors form street gangs."

"We've been together longer than you've been alive, son," Liko said, slapping a heavy hand on the police chief's shoulder. "You'd think the police chief would know that."

To his credit, the new chief barely blinked. He'd dealt with Liko before. "I'm aware. I've warned you before that while you were a good chief in your day, you retired."

Liko's face reddened, and his grip tightened on Quilan's shoulder. "Now you—"

Henry strode over, disentangling Liko's hand from Quilan. "Back off, Liko. You got your fight for the day."

"Speaking of fight," William said, voice low as he addressed the Shades. "What were you thinking, getting in the middle of that? It could have gotten ugly."

This turned five glares in his direction, and he fought not to shift under the animosity. Even skinny Zaki crossed his arms and attempted to glare.

"What, you mean instead we should just play canasta and shuffleboard instead of do our jobs and protect Beckwell?" Jenklow said, a hard spark in his bright blue gaze.

William blew out a breath. "I didn't—"

"It was completely under control. I was avoiding using a glamour on them until it was necessary," Henry said, equally tightly. "I would have gotten them to disperse peaceably."

Quilan raised a hand. "Yes, but I am chief—"

"Why are you here, anyway?" Chaimek said, interrupting and ignoring the police chief, scowling at William.

The police chief threw up his hands and walked away a few paces before circling back. The Shades ignored him.

William's jaw had developed a tic. "I said I was here to help. I'm helping."

"You're supposed to protect our princess. Where is she?" Liko demanded.

William gestured back toward the front door where he'd left Cara and Not-Dog. "She's right—"

His words cut off, and his heart lodged in his throat.

The spot where he'd left her was empty. He spun. There was no sign of her or her bright red coat in the atrium. Cara and Not-Dog were gone.

Chapter Seventeen

ANOTHER ATTACK

CARA STOOD beside the entrance to the Senior Center, watching William make his way through the thick of the crowd, her fingers stroking the silky hair on Not-Dog's head. Petting him was supposed to make her feel less punchy, because yet again, she'd been sidelined—this time by William, which was as infuriating as Gramps and the boys doing the same thing all her damned life.

She grumbled low in her throat as Chief Quilan said something, then the Shades, all of them doing what they'd consider their jobs to try and protect Beckwell. Was it wrong that she wanted to do the same? Even Maddy was over by the dining hall door, looking frantic and probably planning her escape. No matter how much she wanted to help with the situation, Maddy couldn't handle crowds, especially a volatile one like this.

Meanwhile, Cara stood here, out of the way where it was safe. If being sidelined wasn't sucky enough, William was right. She didn't understand her abilities, or at least, not lately, whether it was Dom disappearing or making dire predictions, or whatever had happened yesterday at the refugee camp. Hell, she didn't know how or why she was now able to just "know" stuff when that had never been the case before, like that strange blue light or essence she saw when she'd first touched William today.

"My, quite the do, isn't it?" a female voice said from Cara's right, though she could have sworn she'd been alone a second ago.

Cara turned, finding a sophisticated, pale-skinned redhead with blood-red lips—hopefully, that was lipstick—and wearing clothes straight out of one of Gran's black-and-white films about the femme fatale. Emphasis on the fatale part.

Cara sidestepped to the left.

Not-Dog growled.

The woman smiled, the warmth of that smile never reaching her dark, reptilian eyes. "My apologies. It's such an honor to meet you in person, Ms. Jenklow. I'm Irene."

Yep, that the creepy stranger knew her name wasn't comforting. Still, Gran had always been big on manners, which was why Cara stuck out her hand, too. Besides, maybe that whole knowing thing could come in handy. "I'm afraid I haven't heard of you. And I can't think of why you'd have heard of me, Ms. Irene."

The woman's smile broadened like a crocodile spotting lunch, her fingers squeezing Cara's. "Cara Jenklow. Grand-daughter of Albert Jenklow, one of those dreaded Shades. Once they were something. You, though, still are. Yaga heirs are rare these days, particularly ones with nymph bloodlines to boot."

Cara had taken the woman's hand to get a read from her, but she got…nada. The woman's shields must have been extensive to block Cara so completely. Other than a vague sense of darkness…an image a bit like the one Cara had painted as many times as the ones of William in recent weeks. Figures emerging from the gloom. It had been unclear then as now what it meant, whether a promise…or a threat.

Cara tugged at her hand, but the woman held tight. Who was this woman, and what did she want? Perhaps more importantly, was she a threat? Cara's stomach squeezed. Oh, crapsticks. Maybe this was one of the Guardians William had warned her about.

Not-Dog's growls increased in volume. He moved between her and the woman.

"You have me at a disadvantage, Ms. Irene," Cara said, mind racing, sorting through all the lessons Gramps and the boys had given her over the years.

A glance toward where William had disappeared into the crowd showed that everyone had their back to Cara and the stranger other than Maddy, who edged their direction, or more specifically, toward the exit.

Still, you didn't grow up a daughter—or granddaughter—of the Shades without new weapons and lessons to use them each birthday from Mr. Liko, minor incantations and defense spells from Mr. Chaimek, a dictionary of species from Mr. Zaki, and a whole lot of practice at all of the above from Gramps and Mr. Einar. No obvious signs of what species Irene was, so therefore no automatic counter-defense. No weapons available. Which left keeping the woman talking until Cara figured out how to extricate herself.

"I don't suppose you're a nymph?"

The woman tilted her head to one side. "You can't tell, can you?" A half, almost surprised laugh. "So much ability…yet you can't recognize your own." She straightened, and finally released Cara's hand. "No, dear. I'm no nymph."

Cara massaged her wrist—damn, that woman had a

grip—and took a small step backward. "What brings you to Beckwell then? I don't recognize you as one of the residents, and I met many of the refugees yesterday."

"Me? A refugee?" The woman trilled a laugh that grated on Cara's ears.

Yeah, because having an evil villain laugh was totally normal. Cara swallowed, hard, taking another small step back.

Not-Dog, still growling, pressed against her shins.

The woman glanced at the dog, her smile fading before those dark eyes flicked back to Cara's face. "Let's say I'm here on business. You, dear Cara, are part of that business. I suspect you don't know how rare and unusual an exception you are. A nymph-Yaga hybrid. I've never found record of another like you. The nymph genes usually supersede the weaker genes. But your mother unwittingly bound herself to another Yaga heir, and voila, you."

Cara blinked. "My father had no paranormal heritage. He hated and feared everything about it." Hated and feared his own daughter, who'd never understood why he couldn't give her the same love or kindness he showed others. Her throat squeezed, the memory of the way Dad's lip would curl when confronted with her crystal clear.

Irene arched a brow. "I'm never wrong, especially when it comes to research. He had Yaga roots." She flicked a hand dismissively and leaned in as though sharing secrets. "You know how mortals are, especially humans. Forever holding themselves above us, and clueless about their own origins. Look at all those refugees you insultingly compared me to. Until the Veils fell, they hadn't a clue as to the strength hiding in their blood. If not for that human genetic pollution, they'd have been almost interesting."

Wow. There was a lot to unpack in that pile of crazyass... But perhaps the most in the idea that for all of

Dad's prejudices, he might have been like her. In fact, it might have been because of those joint roots that Dom had been inspired to connect with Cara when they hadn't bothered doing so with the Yagas before her.

"That's, uh, some history lesson," Cara settled on, which didn't outright call the woman crazy—never a good idea. Irene sounded like everything William and the boys had ever said about the Guardians. Crapballs.

Not-Dog's growls suggested he agreed.

"I don't mean to be rude, and it's been, um, interesting meeting you." A glance back at the crowd showed no sign of William or the boys headed this way. "But, I, uh, I think maybe I should help out my husband, help disperse this crowd…" Cara took a few steps toward the writhing group.

Maddy had reached the fringes of the gathering, having edged her way along the walls. Then again, no way Cara could drag her friend into all this.

"Don't you want to meet your relatives?" Irene gestured all too casually with her red-manicured fingers toward the parking lot.

Cara froze. "Relatives?"

"Your grandmother's people, the Carmentas. They came back into town to meet you." Irene tsked, not quite pulling off a sad face, her smugness ruining the effect. "What a shame, my having to tell them you're too busy to spare a moment and come out to say hi."

Not-Dog growled louder, casting a look back at her, as though warning Cara not to be so naive, not to listen to the stranger.

Cara spared the dog an eyeroll that said no kidding, she knew this was a ploy to get her outside.

Although…she had to find nymphs if Dom was right and nymph magic was killing her.

Another glance back toward the crowd, where William, Chief Quilan, Gramps, and everyone else who she'd normally ask for help was. Only the backs of strangers were visible. Gramps, William, and the others were all off saving Beckwell and would help her with her nymph problem when, you know, they got around to it. She didn't need their help to handle this. Dom was her friend; this was her life. Although…

"I want to help," Irene said, all innocence.

Not-Dog, head down, teeth bared, his growl growing as he took small steps toward Irene, as though trying to increase the distance between she and Cara…or maybe run her off.

Irene's lip curled, gaze on the animal. "You know he'd never thank you, don't you?" She addressed Not-Dog before turning to Cara. "So, are you going to come and meet them, learn more about who and what you are? Or are you going to stand here, waiting for some man to tell you what to believe?"

Cara almost growled herself, clenching her hands. It was bait. Obviously.

Maddy edged past Cara and Irene, might not even have seen either of them in her desperate route toward the exit and away from the crowd.

"I'm sure your friend would love to join us." Irene's hand snaked out and grabbed Maddy's glove-clad forearm.

Maddy gasped, eyes going wide as though focused on an internal nightmare, mouth rounding in horror.

Irene smiled and backed toward the door, dragging Maddy with her. "Cara, I do hope you'll join us."

Cara could hardly breathe.

Not-Dog still backed against her legs.

But Irene had Maddy, who looked terrified, who didn't deserve to be mixed up in all of this.

Cara straightened. What was the point being a daughter of the Shades if she didn't use some of those abilities, prove she could solve her own problems, save herself *and* Beckwell? She'd always wanted to protect her town and its people. This was her chance to prove it. "I'm coming Maddy!"

Chapter Eighteen

NOT-DOG GRIPPED the cuff of Cara's slacks in his teeth, tugging Cara backward as she stepped toward the sliding doors of the Senior Center after Irene. The animal growled at Cara. An insistent throbbing sensation drummed through her head, not unlike when she had visions. A sense of the animal insisting this was a trap and to not follow Irene outside, away from the crowd…from safety.

Irene stopped near the doors, surreally poised and elegant, even dragging a wide-eyed, terrified Maddy by the arm. "You haven't changed your mind, have you? You know, I hear if you get your dog neutered, he'd behave better." Again, she addressed Not-Dog.

Not-Dog released Cara's cuff to growl at Irene, standing between Cara and the woman.

Cara stepped forward, patted the dog's head. "I'm not an idiot," she whispered for the dog's sensitive ears. "But I can't leave my friend with her, whether there really are nymphs or not. I can take care of myself." She followed

Irene and Maddy out the sliding glass doors, staying a few feet behind, heart pounding.

She could handle herself. Gramps and the boys would be ashamed of her if she couldn't. *She'd* be ashamed of herself if she didn't at least try, just hid behind someone or something else… Even Not-Dog, who shook its head in a disgusted manner but trotted at her side. She said she wanted to protect and help people. Right now, Maddy needed her.

A few stray snowflakes danced in the chill wind that tugged at her hair as she stepped outside the Center, bit through her red fall coat that wasn't quite warm enough. Cara stopped beyond the doorway while Irene continued, dragging Maddy after her, toward a silver, expensive sedan with tinted windows. Funny thing that when Irene had taken her hand, she'd gotten so little in terms of a read. There were shields…but even Gramps couldn't shield so well. Cara swallowed. Frost hung in the air, chilling her throat.

"I followed you. Let my friend go," she called across the parking lot.

Maddy moaned, knees buckling as she clawed at Irene's grip, her freckles standing out like blood splatter. Even through the gloves, Irene's touch caused pain.

Cara's curls danced in her eyes and tickled her nose, no matter how she tried to brush them back. She took a deep breath and started toward Maddy, hands raised. The fear was normal, right? Even William and the Shades must have been afraid sometimes when they headed into battle. "She isn't part of this. You wanted me to meet my family? I'm here. Let her go."

Irene stopped, balance and poise preternaturally perfect in those black heels even through the gravel as she headed for the car. She had to be using spellwork to accomplish that. Her hair remained perfectly coiffed, unaffected by the wind. She yanked harder on Maddy's arm. "You know, I just needed her to get you outside, but she's…intriguing."

"She's just a psychometric. Your touch her hurts her. Let. Her. Go," Cara growled, edging closer. The parking lot held twenty-some cars, full compared to the usual handful, and the wind whipped between the vehicles.

Not-Dog's unhappy whines carried on the wind.

"*Just* a psychometric? That's what you think she is? Darling, your friend is capable of so much more than just reading objects like a pathetic fortune teller." Irene waited partway between the car and Cara, a small smile lifting those blood-red lips. Not the comforting sort of smile that said there was nothing to be afraid of, either. But more like, gee, wasn't it nice her victim walked right into her trap.

Cara gulped but edged closer. Maddy was depending on her. "I know Maddy's lots of things. But she isn't a nymph. You promised me nymphs. Let her go." Yesterday, she'd helped people in the refugee camp. William thought she'd used her abilities to de-escalate the protest in the camp yesterday. She'd pictured it ending well, and he thought she'd changed events as they unfolded. Which wasn't a nymph *or* Yaga ability. He must have imagined that part. She fisted her hands, nails biting into her palms. She had to get Maddy out of here, then talk to any nymphs if Irene wasn't lying about them.

"Goodness, aren't you all fire and claws with just that touch of vulnerability. I suppose that's what William sees in you, why I was always too much of a woman for him to fancy."

Ugh and yuck. William and Irene had never— No. The woman was just trying to distract Cara.

Maddy panted now, almost limp in Irene's grip, her lips moving as though muttering words stolen by the wind.

Not-Dog nudged Cara's hand with his wet nose, drawing her gaze. He tipped his head back toward the sliding doors, as if saying it wasn't too late to turn back.

Not an option today.

She curled her hands into fists. She didn't have another weapon, didn't have the focus for a charm right now or anything fancy. She could attack Irene and give Maddy time to escape, though.

Not-Dog nipped at her fingertips.

She strode toward Irene. "Seriously. You need to let Maddy go. Now."

She'd almost reached Irene's side when the silver sedan's door popped open. A foot and leg emerged first, housed in a shiny dress shoe, a flap of dark dress pants.

Cara froze, a few feet away.

Maddy stiffened, looked straight at Cara, gaze glassy and unfocused. "Darkness falls and lurches across this land. They are coming. Prepare." She blinked. Her gaze sharpened, seemed more Maddy than it had, terrified and wide-eyed again. "It's a trap, Cara. They're going to kidnap you. Run!"

"Not without you," Cara said, leaping the last foot and plowing her fist toward Irene's face.

Somehow though, her hand connected only with air. Irene had shimmered, vanished, and reappeared a few feet away.

But she hadn't taken Maddy with her.

A tall figure unfolded themselves from the car. A man...or male something, since there was something about the angles of the pearly face, the points to the ears, the blackness of his eyes that said whatever he was, he wasn't human, wasn't nymph.

"Run!" Cara cried, looping an arm around Maddy and pulling the immobile woman with her. The Center wasn't that far. They could make it…

But Maddy tugged against Cara. "Home. I have to get home. I… Oh, goddess, the things she's done, what I've seen, who she's hurt, in my head, all in my head, the screaming, the screaming…" she sobbed, barely coherent.

"Get them," Irene said, unconcernedly examining a red nail as she addressed the tall pale man. "Both of them, if possible, but preferably the hybrid."

"Come on, Maddy. Please, you can do this. Just a little farther," Cara begged and tugged, eyes burning. A car's length from the Center's doors. From William and help.

"No! Too many people. Too many thoughts. Too much, it's too much!" Maddy shrieked, pulled free, and bolted off to the left of the Center, slipping and sliding in the snow but rapidly putting distance between them, reaching the far side of the Center and still sprinting away.

Cara glanced after her, then the Center doors. She leapt forward…but only got a few steps.

"You're not dashing off so soon, are you?" Irene called from behind her.

Cold rained over Cara, freezing her feet and lower body, leaving them immovable. A spell. Oh, goddess, she'd been bespelled. She tugged and jerked, tried to free herself. Crapsticks. She'd been bespelled and frozen in place. Her heart pounded in her ears. She might have actually *whimpered*.

The tall man in black glided toward her, unhurried doom, his long legs eating up the distance between them.

Irene's blood-red smile grew. "Don't fuss. I will take you to the nymphs. You will live. We need you to bring this troublesome pimple of a town in hand early and efficiently."

Not-Dog growled, head down, placing itself between Cara, Irene, and the oncoming tall man.

Cara turned toward the Center, toward the doors. Maybe someone was coming out. Maybe someone had noticed she was gone.

"Hurry up," Irene said to the creature in black, likewise glancing at the Center. "I'm not sure how long that distraction will hold up."

The doors remained shut, nothing and no one visible beyond.

Cara's body grew heavy. There wouldn't be any rescue. Maddy was long gone, barely a dark blip against the white snow far down the road, closer to home, toward freedom. Good. At least that made one of them.

The creature in the black suit was almost on her. Reached out a long-fingered, pale hand.

Pain exploded in her head, like an icepick drilling into her skull. Cara gasped, vision blurring, the psychic attack like on her wedding night.

Not-Dog sprang at the man in black, sank his teeth into the man's leg.

The man shook the dog off, kicked Not-Dog.

The animal sailed through the air, striking a car and crumpling into a small furry pile.

Cara squinted against the pain, eyes stinging. Stabbing pain in her head popped black spots into her vision.

The man in black grasped the back of her neck. Cold stabbed through her skin, down her neck, all the way to her spine. Increased the pain in her head from piercing to blinding. He was trying to take control of her mind, the sensation a thousand times worse than any of the lessons Gramps and the boys had given. The world blotted in and out from flashes of light, glimpses of the man and the parking lot, to black.

The creature tightened his grip on her neck, pressed his other hand against her forehead.

Knives and daggers. Red and white lights flashed across her vision.

She gasped, unable to lift her arms. Her breaths were short and raspy. She couldn't move her head. Couldn't breathe. Had lost control of her body. Her thoughts grew slow. She'd been such an idiot. Jumped right into Irene's trap because she was afraid of dying, tried to prove she was a Shade when she wasn't, tried to rescue Maddy and ended up needing rescuing herself. Look what that'd gotten her. Forget Dom's warnings of doom. Now she'd just die sooner.

No.

Maybe it was the weight of the pendant against her chest. Maybe it was training.

No.

She *was* a daughter of the Shades. She could rescue herself, dammit. She wouldn't die this way.

She muttered a quick defensive incantation Zaki had taught her.

The pale man's grip loosened. He cried out, a swear in another language as the heat of the incantation burned through his skin. He shook his head, tightened his grip on her throat again. Twisted her head, toward the small pile of fur that was Not-Dog.

The animal lifted his head, lay down, then tried again to raise its head, stared right at her. Something in his expression called to her. Said she couldn't give up.

"Let's make sure this time you stay dead," Irene murmured, strutting toward Not-Dog. She raised her hand, prepared to unleash a magical assault.

Her attacker's grip wasn't as tight. Cara sucked in air. Sucked in strength. Yaga and nymph. Lightness ballooned through her, pushed away the pain. An image formed in that space. An image of the tall, pale man lying in the same defeated pile he'd left Not-Dog. Heat pushed through her body, forced out the cold of Irene's spellwork, brought control and movement to her limbs. Let Cara clench her fists.

In front of her, Irene's lips moved in some spell.

Not-Dog vanished in a whoosh of color and light, blinding them all, loosening the tall man's grip on Cara.

Cara focused on the image of the pale man's defeat.

He cried out. Clawed at her jacket sleeve as he staggered, fell to his knees, fought to stand.

She jerked away, jacket tearing.

A red-haired stranger ran straight for her. "Run, Cara!" he shouted, something familiar in that amber gaze, in the bark of his command. He leapt onto the man's back, grabbed for the man's hands and pulled them away from Cara. "I said get out of here!"

"You nasty little— I knew it was you." Irene marched toward them. "I thought you were dead," she scowled at the red-haired stranger.

Geezus, Josie, and George. Not-Dog was… Now he was… Cara sagged, clutching her thighs, sucking breaths. Her feet didn't work. The red-haired guy was helping her. She couldn't leave him here, could she?

Irene shrieked in fury.

The black-suited attacker clambered to his knees with a guttural snarl, head down, coming for her again.

The red-haired stranger, who she was pretty sure used to be Not-Dog, intercepted her attacker.

"The rumors of my death were intentionally exaggerated," the red-haired man shouted back at Irene, still grappling with Cara's attacker. "You always turn up where you're not wanted. Like cockroaches or pubic hairs." He groaned, taking a hard punch to the gut.

"I preferred when you were dead," Irene sneered back. "Held a party. It was very well attended."

Cara eyed the Senior Center.

Irene stood between it and her, distracted.

Straightening, Cara edged sideways toward the doors.

The suited man grunted as the red-haired stranger kicked him in the shin but never spoke a word, that black gaze flicking toward Cara. He lifted a hand.

Stabbing pain blinded her, sent Cara to her knees.

The pain was less than before, though, easier somehow to force back, clear her vision. Notice the growing warmth of the pendant against her skin.

Spot Irene marching toward her, lips twisted in a snarl. "Honestly, you want something done properly, you do it yourself." She reached those red claws toward Cara.

"This is harder than it looks. Help me out here!" The red-haired stranger wheezed, as the suited man elbowed him in the ribs again. "Picture what you want. Where you want to be, Cara," he managed to get out.

Irene's nails brushed Cara's torn jacket sleeve.

Cara skittered backward, toward the red-haired stranger.

"Home, Cara. Take yourself home!" Dom insisted, suddenly there, the pendant warm against her skin, alive.

Cara closed her eyes, pictured home. Her studio. Standing in front of a blank canvas. She opened her eyes a second. Whoever the red-haired stranger was, she couldn't leave them behind. She reached out, caught his arm. Closed her eyes, imagined the feel of her brush in her hand, the sharp scent of wet paint, the warmth of the midday sun through the windows, the hush and...

"You're safe…but their magic is…poison. Be careful… Killing you," Dom managed before their voice went silent.

She opened her eyes, head spinning. She stood where she'd imagined. In her studio, out of the wind and the cold, holding a brush and her palette in front of a fresh, blank canvas. A shuddering breath rattled past her lips. She wore her jacket, the left sleeve almost torn from the shoulder, white fiberfill spilling out. The pendant was once more cool and inert against her skin. She was free from the attack, from Irene, from that man in the black suit who sent ice through her veins. But the man, the stranger who'd helped her…

She glanced down.

Sitting at her feet, staring up at her, was Not-Dog.

BLOODY NOT-DOG. Was the pseudo-animal responsible for Cara's disappearance? William raced outside into the cold wind, the occasional snowflake dancing through the air, his heart pounding, mouth dry. He caught the tail-end of a silver sedan pull toward the four-way stop then out of sight.

More people emerged, heading for their cars. Others walked back toward the refugee camp behind the Center. A few crossed the road toward cars parked at the store and bar.

No sign of Cara, no sign of Not-Dog. He never should have left her alone, let alone with the creature. Maybe it had taken her. Maybe—

"Any sign of her?" Chief Quilan said, emerging beside him, gaze likewise searching the dwindling crowd, the cars pulling out of their spots, driving away.

William craned his neck, striding through the traffic,

heedless of whether it was stopped or moving. Was she in that one? Was there someone in the backseat of that one? "Do you see her?"

"No. I've tried her cell twice, but it goes right to voice-mail," Quilan called back. "She can't have gone far."

William stalked first one way, checking a group that headed toward the refugee camp, then another closer to the town library. None of them had Cara's dark curls, her bright-red coat.

His throat squeezed. He hadn't thought of calling her cell. She'd been his wife for three days, and he didn't know her phone number. Or her favorite color. Or if she was safe or dead or… His palms damp, he scanned the parking lot again, a hard lump settling in his belly. He'd promised not only Jenklow and the boys, but he'd promised *her* that he'd keep her safe, that he'd protect her. He had to find her. Alive. The parking lot was almost empty now, except for him, Quilan, and the Shades, emerging and on duty. As always.

"Zaki, Chaimek, you head back into the Center, see if she's there," Albert barked orders to the boys. "She wasn't feeling well yesterday. Maybe she's at the med clinic. Or she's waiting back in my suite, and we're worried for nothing." The tightness in his voice made it clear he didn't believe it. "Liko, you're on the refugee camp. Henry will take the store and the school, I'll check the house."

William's vision blurred a second, Albert's voice fading. He fisted his hands until his knuckles ached. He'd been an idiot. Let his own fear, his regret over that damned kiss last night cloud his judgment. Shit. If he'd just—

"Mac. Mac!" Albert's sharp bark, the grip on his arm, the shake jerked William alert.

He looked down at his glaring, tight-lipped friend.

"Do you know where she'd head? Did she say anything to you?"

"I fucked up," William said.

Albert's gaze softened the smallest amount. "We all fuck up now and then. Come on, let's find her. Let's head to the house."

They strode toward Cara's home. William accommodated for the other man's cane and slower pace. They'd reached the edge of the parking lot on foot when Quilan's shout caught their attention.

"There's news. A body. At the refugee camp," Quilan called.

Time froze. William stared at the man. Tried to process the words. Then, forgetting Albert, the rest of the Shades, even Quilan, who shouted for him to wait up and not disturb the evidence, William broke into a dead run for the refugee camp.

Please, gods, don't let it be Cara.

CARA SANK TO HER KNEES, limbs trembling. The red-haired man was gone, and in his place stood the coincidentally red-haired dog. She stared at Not-Dog, into those amber eyes. Dammit, how had she not noticed those amber eyes before? Pretty sure dogs weren't supposed to have amber eyes. There'd been that…whatever that had been that attacked her with Irene back in the parking lot. Fey maybe? Maybe an elf, like Mr. Einar. But mean, and…

She glared at the dog. "What are you? Or is it who?"

Ugh. Talking to necklaces was one thing. Talking to dogs that might not be dogs? Her luck, it wouldn't answer anyway. She rubbed a hand down her face, then sat back onto her butt, massaging her forehead with a small moan. The knives were back again, making her hand shake. Not knives like that...thing had attacked her with, like he'd been trying to saw into her brain, but like the knives that came from using her ability. Which maybe she'd done...?

"Breathe, kiddo. That was some trick," the male voice said.

She peeked a hand through her fingers. Not-Dog stared at her.

"Yeah, it's me," the voice, or rather Not-Dog said.

She shrieked and skittered back a few steps on her hands and feet.

Not-Dog rolled his eyes, plopped on his haunches, then used his hind leg to scratch his ear. "Don't know what the big deal is. You talk to that necklace of yours. Transported both of us here. Thanks for that, by the way." The dog shuddered. "Dark fey magic gives me such a hangover. I mean, I'm good with it if I got to enjoy the booze and the fun, but those dark fey? Total buzzkills."

"W-who...wh-what??" Dark fey and talking Not-Dog and...and...oh, crapsticks, her head hurt so much, and she was going to barf and make such a mess of her studio. Had Maddy made it home okay? And William? Where was William? Were they all at the Center? None of them had any idea what had happened. Although, *she* didn't really know what had happened. What she'd done. The dog thought she'd transported them here. Maybe she had. Or...or...

"One at a time, babe. Breathe. Yeah, that's it. Stop hyperventilating." Not-Dog cocked his head. "Damn, that trick takes a hell of a lot out of you, doesn't it? I mean, it's a simple teleportation thing..." His words trailed off. "Oh, yeah. Mortal. Huh. Nothing is simple when it comes to you mortals."

She pointed a shaking finger at Not-Dog. "Who *and* what are you?"

If it was possible for a dog to contort its face into a grimace, that was what Not-Dog did. "Yeah… not sure I want to tell you that. You'll go and tell William, and boy won't that suck. You called me 'Not-Dog.' Can we stick with that?"

She straightened, trying to ignore the pounding headache as she shifted onto her knees. "No, we most definitely cannot. This is my house. I'll kick you the hell out. Or I'll…I'll transport you somewhere else. Somewhere far away."

"Yeeeaaahhhh…" The dog sounded doubtful. "I kind of think you won't. Or can't—at least not in the shape you're in right now. Not-Dog works for me. Or Jax, if you want to get technical about it. Your telepathy sucks, by the way. I tried to tell you not to go with her, friend or not. But your shielding is halfway decent. That'll help when Irene comes after you again."

"My shields…" Cara let her words drift off, trying to process whatever Not—er, Jax was trying to tell her.

Jax…hadn't she heard that name before somewhere?

Ugh… She cradled her forehead. Maybe she'd be able to think if it didn't feel like she'd been run over by an eighteen-wheeler…and somehow every one of those eighteen wheels had added a personal bruise.

Jax moved a bit closer. "Seriously, kid. You don't look good. Maybe you should call William. A bit of nookie might fix you two up good."

She managed a glare at the dog. Then another thought occurred to her, and she winced. "You didn't…you haven't, um, watched?" she squeaked.

The dog shrugged…which was a strange thing to watch a dog do. Didn't help her nausea one bit. "Nah. I figured that'd freak you out. Especially because I did—do —intend to tell you who I am. Just not quite yet."

She snorted. "Well, 'not-quite-yet' is going to get you living somewhere else. Spill. William already knows you're not an ordinary dog."

A sigh. "Sometimes it sucks he's so sharp…although not so much as he thinks. Look, I'm Jax, and I'm here to help."

"Find the Guardians?"

"No."

"Help me use my powers?"

"Uh, definitely nope. That thing you have with the necklace and whatever the hell else you are or what's going on? Yeah…no clue. Besides, I'm not great at the whole mentor thing."

She threw her hands in the air, but her eyes caught on the painting she'd made of the dog over in the pile of completed canvases. Her original reasons for letting him into the house stood…even if he wasn't a dog. "Maybe it's housework then? Dog, Jax, whatever you want to go by, my head hurts too much for riddles. Can you please give me a straight answer? Are you or are you not also the guy who showed up to help me back in the parking lot? What are you, why are you here, and why shouldn't I tell William so we can throw your furry butt out of here?"

The dog let out a low whistle. "Damn. You're hard-core, aren't you? Almost as big a stick up your butt as William's." At Cara's glare, it lifted a paw, like a human would lift a hand. "Okay, okay, I give. Yes, it was me back in the parking lot, in one of my other forms. My name is Jax—yes, a simplified version of my identity, but it's the name I go by these days. I have some skill with shapeshift-ing, although I'm also handy to have around. Loki and me?

We go way back. He'll be so happy to see me here in town."

Cara cleared her throat and pointed at the door. Whatever he was, claiming friendship with Loki wasn't likely to earn her trust. And she had the feeling Loki probably wouldn't appreciate it, either.

"Aaaand I'm here to help you and William. Make a connection, stay alive, make William happy. That's it. I want him happy. Is that such a terrible thing? Telling him about me? Won't make him happy. Plus, I can open doors, I don't plan on going anywhere, and if you tell people your dog talks to you? I'm thinking even in a sanctuary like Beckwell, people are going to look at you funny."

Her throat squeezed at the thought of being that outsider again, but she lifted a chin. "The Four live here, and they talked to their animals all the time. I can—and probably should—tell everyone I know."

"You let me stay, I'll do everything I can to protect William."

Of course, Gramps and the rest of the Shades wouldn't be happy about a talking dog. And William… Then again, there were plenty of other problems worse than a talking dog who claimed to want to make William happy…and who'd already protected her once.

"Okay. If I agree you can stay, you'll tell me everything about—"

"Shh! He's back. William's back." Jax yipped, and raced out of the room, yapping his head off like a typical dog.

Cara massaged her forehead and tried to stand.

Every muscle screamed. Her head hurt more, and her stomach lurched.

Footsteps raced toward her. Two sets. One heavier than the other.

She turned, but her knees softened. Oh crapballs…

She fell into William's warm, spicy embrace with a soft oomph. All of a sudden, her eyes pinched, and a choked sob escaped her lips. Then after the first one got out, another raced after it. Then another. All the memories of the man in black and feeling so frozen, so helpless, washed over her. The pain she'd felt when that dark fey had touched her. The terror that had squeezed her insides, Maddy's confused mutterings. She'd walked right into that idiocy. All of it and the body aches enveloped her, leaving her to sob.

If this was her plan to prove they belonged together, talk about crappy. Guys got weird if you cried all over them. Especially if it was repeatedly, and as much of a dream guy as William was, seemed like something even he couldn't miss.

Gramps patted her on her shoulder.

She managed to get out something about checking on Maddy, and Gramps heard her. He and William exchanged words, but she couldn't make them out, didn't really try.

William's arms, though, remained steady, surrounding her, his words repetitive, crooning over and over, like he needed to convince at least one of them they were true. "It's okay. You're okay. You're alive. I've got you."

It was safe and warm in his arms, his embrace relieving some of the ache of her body and in her head, as though she shared his strength. Whatever else was true, she was not okay. She'd tried and failed to rescue Maddy or contact the nymphs again today. Without reaching them, she'd die.

Chapter Nineteen

A TRUER VERSION OF THE TRUTH

WILLIAM COULDN'T LET Cara go. Not while Albert patted her on the shoulder then took his leave. Not when Not-Dog gave a suspicious head shake before it wandered out of the room. Not after her tears stopped, after his heart resumed a normal rhythm, snow blanketing the world outside her sunroom windows. In those moments when he'd raced for the refugee camp, terrified the body found belonged to Cara…something had shifted inside. A spider's silk tendril between them straight to his heart. She'd started to mean more to him than was safe.

Which was dangerous. To his heart, of course. But to her, too. He had too many enemies.

He'd dedicated his life to stopping the Guardians. He'd never let personal attachments get in the way. If he did, others would pay the price.

He pulled back, forced himself away from her. He glanced away to give her a moment to brush the tears from her face. Then frowned as he glimpsed the corner of a canvas. A whole stack of similar canvases. He leaned to get a closer look. Huh. "Cara, are those paintings of—"

"Your twin," Cara said quickly, moving between William and the canvases, her face darkening.

He raised a slow brow, a smile pulling at his lips. He couldn't remember smiling this much in years, not since he'd arrived in Beckwell.

Not since he'd met and married Cara. "My twin, huh?"

"Yep. That's what I've heard. You know what I need? To text Maddy, and some of Gran's special hot cocoa mix." She shooed him toward the door, shuffling some canvases. After shutting off the light, she closed the door behind her before hurrying toward the kitchen, racing to get there first. She shucked her red jacket, tossing it toward the stairs on her way past.

He stopped, frowning as he picked up the jacket where the stuffing fluffed out from a large tear in the shoulder seam. "Cara, what happened to your jacket?"

Water ran in the kitchen, followed by the click of the kettle lid closing.

"I can't talk about that right now," she called back, cupboard doors opening and closing. "Good news is Maddy is fine. Is everything okay over at the Center?"

He stalked into the kitchen, holding the jacket. "We got things under control." And another earful from the boys. "You and Not-Dog vanished. Then Chief Quilan got a call that they'd found a body at the refugee camp." He paused. "Why wouldn't your friend Maddy be okay?"

She spun, a glass jar in one hand, her other hand at her lips. "A body? Who was it? Do we know them? Are they… No, wait. Obviously, they're not okay." She shook her head, turning back to set down the jar before bracing herself against the counter. She hadn't answered his question about her friend. "I can't believe we're finding bodies in Beckwell. It used to be safe here."

The urge to step forward, wrap his arms around her and pull her back against his chest staggered him.

He forced himself toward the kitchen table instead, gripping her torn jacket as a reminder what happened when he let his guard down. "It is safe here," he lied. "Or will be, once we get rid of the Guardians." It might never be safe for her again with her abilities. That corpse today could have been hers.

His chest tightened, and he studied the coat, the entire sleeve almost torn off. Maybe she'd had to escape someone or something. Maybe she'd been terrified and alone. If he warned her about the extent of danger she faced, she might be more prepared for the next time.

Or more afraid. His emotions were clouding his judgment. It'd never been a problem before.

It'd never been Cara, some sadistic inner self pointed out.

Cara set out two mugs, tapping her fingers behind her on the counter as they waited, her actions unsettled and twitchy. She watched the kettle. Padded across the kitchen for a spoon. Tried to still again, arms crossing and uncrossing. "Do they…do they know who it was?" she whispered.

The answer increased the heaviness on his shoulders. He closed his eyes as he answered, the image of Tom's mangled body, the frozen horror on Tom's face making William's stomach curdle. "I knew him," he said, voice rough. "He's fey. An informant for me." Calling Tom a friend would be a lie, and the fact that the fey had been amoral didn't excuse all his actions. They'd known each other near on twelve years. "He…he called me for help. Thought the Guardians were onto him. But I didn't take it seriously."

He'd asked for help. Had trusted William to protect him. But William had failed him.

He couldn't let the same happen to Cara.

The kettle screamed.

He flinched.

Cara stopped the kettle, then poured hot water into two mugs. She stirred in the mix, the smell of chocolate and something spicy wafting toward William, followed by milk, then a dollop of spray whipped cream before she came toward him.

Outside the windows that surrounded the table, snow fell in greater earnest, the skies gray and settling an evening-like hush over the afternoon.

She pushed one of the mugs toward him, settling on the opposite chair, their knees brushing. "I'm so sorry," she said. "That you knew him, that you had to identify him. That must have been hard."

The whole time, he'd been grateful it wasn't her. Hadn't given Tom the full respect his death deserved. Was that the man he'd become? If he let anything happen to Cara, he'd be no better than the Guardians.

He shrugged, picking up the mug nearest him. "It's part of the job." Losing people. Knowing there was always risk involved. That next time, it might be your death instead, but better that than someone you cared about. The longer he lived, the more fragile mortals grew. He took a sip of the cocoa.

His eyes widened. The taste of warm chocolate, a hint of spices, sweetness and comfort exploded on his tongue. Warmth slipped down his throat, settled his stomach…but it was more than that. He took another sip. Tasting the cocoa was like picturing Mother's gentle, weary smile, her gray eyes so like his own, the way she'd always dusted him off, ruffled his hair when he was close, or pulled him in for a quick hug, even when he was closer to a man than a boy. He took another sip. Blinked. Hell.

"It's like…" He found Cara's dark gaze. "It tastes like a hug." It was more than a hug.

It tasted of love.

Cara's smile was secretive as she hid behind her own cup. She enjoyed a few more sips before she lowered the mug to answer, swirling the contents. "It's Gran's secret recipe. Or was. She showed me how to make it years ago. I tweaked it a little. A really good drink is like a potion."

He removed the mug from his lips, eyed it suspiciously.

A small giggle escaped Cara.

The sound was so unexpected and delightful, sending warmth through him like the cocoa. He pretended to study his mug, struggling to hide his reaction. It was the kind of sound he'd replay in memories later and made him think of days in beds, her turning to him, the light in her dark gaze when she felt safe enough to make that sound.

"I said *like* a potion, not an actual potion," she explained, as though apologizing for the giggle. "This is kind of…a hybrid. The best cup of comforting cocoa with a little bit more. Besides which, I thought you were supposed to be immune to most spells?" There was a teasing note to her words.

Gods, he could get used to her teasing, the warmth that bloomed inside.

Yeah, warmth that could distract him, get her killed.

He cleared his throat. "Somewhat immune." His voice sounded stiff even to his own ears. Hell. "But without knowing your abilities, I can't be sure."

The teasing light went out in her eyes. His fault. Worse, he took another sip of the cocoa that settled over him like a hug. The flavor burst on his tongue again. A little bit sweet, a little bit spicy. Unexpected. Like Cara. It took him back to childhood, before the world had become a confusing, dangerous place. When nowhere was better than home, on the rug beside the fire and at Mother's knee, listening to the click of her knitting needles. Safe.

Blast. This was the way Cara made him feel, and look how he'd repaid her?

Cara's expression sobered, and she avoided his gaze.

He grimaced into his cocoa, the warmth settling like a rock in his belly. He needed her in his arms, the safety she gave him with her touch.

Being with Cara was like home.

His throat squeezed. The idea should have inspired itchy feet and movement toward the door and yet... Instead, he finished his cocoa and reached for Cara's hand on the table near him, covered it with his own. That need to touch her, to reassure himself of her warmth, her life, still pulsed through him. "What happened today, Cara?"

She set down her cocoa, her gaze going from his hand covering hers and travelling up toward his face. She swallowed, hard, and a small tremble went through her. "I'm a lot better. Now that you're here."

"And this?" He held up her torn coat, but she caught his free hand, pushed the coat down. There were those sparks again, that fierce attraction her gentlest touch inspired. He hungered for another taste of her.

"I'm okay. Maddy's okay. Can we talk about it tomorrow?" She bit her lip, a small frown between her brows. "Today made me realize even if I'm not prepared to die, it might not matter. You always think you have time, you know? You make plans, put them off because the time isn't right, or you're scared, or maybe they're not the right dream for you, but it's the best you've got, so it'll do for now. But realizing I might not have that time..." She broke off with a sad half-laugh. "I wanted evidence that Dom was wrong."

He slid his hand up her arm to cup her jaw. His brain said run. His heart said touch her.

"This isn't the end," he said firmly, running his fingers over her dark, silken skin, her soft curls tickling his knuckles. "I won't let it be. We will find answers. If not here, then in other sanctuaries, with other healers or other nymphs." He grimaced a little. "I don't think I mentioned it, but an old acquaintance is in town." He might have mentioned Hermes earlier, in the bathroom, at a point when neither of them was focused on conversation. "He might be able to help us find some nymphs. We have options."

"'We,'" she echoed. Her smile sparkled in her beautiful brown eyes. "You said 'we' have options. What about the Guardians? Your mission?"

Tension twisted his belly but settled in the face of this woman, this moment, the fruity scent of her hair tickling his nose. "I made you promises, too. A promise to help you find the nymphs. Something in there about caring for you in sickness and in health, too." He shouldn't flirt with her. Couldn't lead her on, not if those paintings of him he'd seen in the sunroom meant she pictured a future together.

Her eyes darkened as she leaned closer to him. Her voice, when she spoke, was raspy and sexy as hell, more so with the sassy way she arched one brow. "Just business, though, wasn't it?"

He straightened and scrubbed a hand over his face before forcing himself to meet her eyes. "Cara, I can't be what you want me to be. I will protect you, I will protect your town, I'll do whatever the hell I can to make sure you're safe here and that you don't ever have to worry death is looking over your shoulder. But I... I..."

He wasn't quite sure what else he'd have confessed. He never had the chance.

Cara leaned forward, cupped his jaw as he had hers, and pressed her soft lips to his.

She tasted of hot cocoa and warmth and home. Of sex and sweetness and daydreams, better than chocolate and peanut butter, hell, better than anything he'd tasted before. She kissed him not like someone kissing William Best, Abomination and Hunter. Just him. William. As though somehow, she saw straight to his soul. Saw him. Somehow still wanted him.

He should have set her upright. Should have had the strength to resist temptation.

Instead, he pulled her onto his lap, groaning as they relished the taste of each other. Her hands clutched at his shoulders. He gripped her back, holding her fast, wishing like hell, like an idiot, that she'd never let go.

The old kitchen chair made an ominous creak.

They broke apart, breathing hard.

Her face mere inches from his, she tucked back the hair around his ears, studying his expression as though memorizing him for a painting. "I don't need perfect. I don't even need tomorrow. I've thought about you, dreamt of you for a very long time, William Best. Whatever you're willing to give, whatever you can give, tonight I need your touch, need your strength, need your mouth and your body on mine. All I want tonight is you."

He didn't deserve her. Shouldn't take the risk that this would develop into something more. Hell, the way he'd felt today, it was already well on the road to something more, the express train to pain. "Cara—"

The poor old kitchen chair groaned again.

She slipped from his lap, standing.

Cold air swept the space she'd occupied, the heat of her against his hardness, against his chest. He wanted her more than he could remember wanting anything or anyone before. He'd been alone for a long time, and once, it had felt like the right path. Yet when he stared into her dark eyes, when her touch electrified his senses, it made him wonder if the possibility of desire, the safety and warmth of home was something even he could have in his life.

She gave him a smile that was both sexy and gentle, and held out her hand. "Let's go somewhere more comfortable. Come with me, William. You owe me a wedding night."

FOR A HORRIBLE, stretching century as she held out her hand, her palms sweaty, her knees trembling, Cara was certain William would reject her. He'd play the honor card, find another way to push her away, keep his distance no matter that his gaze was drunk with desire, and she'd felt clear evidence of his need in his lap. Something lurked behind his blue-gray gaze that resembled fear. It made her want to show him with her touch how she'd begun to feel for him, and that he didn't need to be afraid. Especially not of her. Holy crapballs, she needed him tonight. Needed to lose herself in the safety of his arms.

But he had to choose her, too.

Just as she was about to turn away, William reached out and took her hand.

Lightness buoyed her chest and her steps as she led him out of the kitchen and up the stairs. She glimpsed his unpacked bag still sitting near the door of his room, continuing past. It was like he didn't live there. Their first time deserved better than a guest room.

A small tremble quaked through her as she reached her

bedroom door and pushed it open, William's heat at her back as he followed her inside.

It would have been easier, maybe, if she'd deepened that kiss, reached down a hand to explore the hard length of him, and they'd had wild monkey sex in the kitchen. It would have been easier to tell themselves later that lust and passion had clouded their thoughts and carried them into a wild joining. That was the way they'd often coupled in her dreams and visions, a mad release of pleasure. Yes, some of that was on her ways to do-William list.

Yet as they both entered the quiet dim of her bedroom, a place she'd never brought another man, there was something quietly perfect about this moment.

William closed the door behind them and she reached for him, slid her hand along the side of that sculpted jawline and over his lips. This wasn't just about sex. This moment, this first time, it was proving he was real, he was here...and making sure he knew this wasn't a mistake and it was about them.

"I want you," she whispered, fingers tangling with his. "Not the legend, the stories, none of that bullshit. Just William Best."

He cupped her face, caressing her skin with his thumb, something a little lost in his expression. "You're sure?"

Sure? She'd dreamed about him and started to fall in love with him in her years ago. These past few days, she'd met the man who was both warrior and teddy bear, who lit all her fires and warmed her heart. She'd spent so long trying to belong but with William, there was no trying... they just fit.

Snow fell softly outside the window behind him, the hush of it creating greater intimacy as she stepped into the circle of his arms. Time to confirm that fit.

"Very sure," she assured him, placing a hand in the

center of his chest, his heart thudding beneath her palm. "You, William Best, are the sexiest damned man I've ever met." She tapped her palm against the hard muscles of his chest, then took a small step back. "Now how about you take that shirt off for me."

He raised a brow, a hint of a smile pulling at those perfect lips of his, softening him. "You sound like a woman with a plan." He reached for the buttons on his shirt, making quick work of about the first half before he pulled it off over his head, that twist of his shoulders, the muscles of his chest clearly delineated in the white, snug-fitting undershirt.

"Oh, I have plenty of plans," she said, breathless, because, *damn*. Who knew a white tight-fitting undershirt was man-lingerie? "That'll have to go, too." She waggled her fingers at the undershirt. She wanted bare skin. To kiss, to touch, to taste.

He reached for the hem of the undershirt, pulled it up to reveal the ribbed perfection of that sculpted six-pack. A teasing light entered that blue-gray gaze. He nodded at her clothes. "Am I the only one putting on a show?"

He pulled off the shirt.

She reached for the buttons on her own blouse, her breath ragged. Regular William was sexy as fuck. Teasing William was irresistible. Heat spilled through her, pooled between her legs. There was no fear, no momentary pause to second-guess her appearance, what he might think of her. The heat of his gaze gave her the confidence to let the blouse gap open, revealing her lilac bra, a rush of cool air skimming over her skin.

William stepped forward, pushed both edges of the shirt down her shoulders, pulling it tight around her fore-arms and imprisoning her arms at her sides as he tugged her closer. His spicy scent surrounded her, the heat of his breath brushed her skin, the wet heat of his mouth on her shoulder.

"I think this is cheating. What about the show?" she rasped, meeting his gaze, tugging her hands free of the blouse so she could settle them on his shoulders, muscle rippling beneath her touch.

"I've always preferred participating to watching," he murmured, splaying his hand on her bare back, pulling her closer until she fit against him, her breasts pressed against his bare chest, her nipples hardening and frustrated against the satin of her bra cups.

He lowered his mouth to hers and devoured her lips in a mind-bending kiss that exploded all those plans she'd had about seducing him and returned to thoughts of wild monkey sex. Especially as he walked her back toward the bed, stopping when her calves bumped into the soft crush of sheets and blankets.

He stopped them there, pulling back to meet her eyes. "Those slacks will have to go."

Her fingers fumbled a couple of times on the belt and the button—especially as his lips took hers.

"You're not helping," she said, finally pushing the pants past her hips. They slithered down her legs to the floor. She didn't wait for an invitation but reached for his belt buckle.

"You have things in hand." His lips curved against hers, but he didn't break from the kiss, from exploring her mouth, hands caressing her arms, curling over her ass and squeezing.

She undid his belt, then the fly and the zipper. "You bet I do." Slipping her hand inside, she cupped the hard length of him through cotton, curling her hand around his shaft.

He groaned against her lips. "I like your plans." He slipped his hand between her legs, skimmed the edge of her panties, using his other hand to press her against him, angle her upward for their mouths to meet.

She tugged him toward the mattress, but he cradled her against him, walked them farther onto the mattress before those clever fingers of his made quick work of her bra clasp. He grasped her hands, lifted and pinned them with one of his own above her head, and ravaged her mouth. He lifted his head long enough to slide down her body, nipping at her bra before settling his mouth over her nipple and sucking it between his lips. All those grand plans to be in charge evaporated, leaving her gasping, curving her thigh up against his side, hugging his head to her breast. He worshipped her with his questing touch, with the wet heat of his mouth, and when he pulled back, he worshipped her with his gaze.

She sucked in a breath, her hand on his shoulder. The scent of their sweat in the air, the brush of the sheets and his skin against her bare body, the hard planes and angles of his face. William. *Hers.* She arched upward, caught his lips in a kiss, but he broke free, nipping at the side of her neck, kissing the side of her mouth.

"You are so damned perfect," he whispered against her ear and slid a finger deep inside of her. "Let me show you."

She almost came right there, arching up beneath him. Definitely saw spots, gasping and twisting, heat and tightness gathering at her core.

Holy crapolla, if she'd known reality could feel this good, she'd have hunted William down years ago.

William kept her pinned to the bed, suckling first one breast, then making sure the other got some attention. He tugged her panties free before making her see the cosmos and gasp out his name. He worshipped her. No other way around it. Whoever had said his only abilities had to do with soldiering and fighting had clearly been misinformed.

But this wasn't just about her. She tried to blink stars from her eyes, cupped him inside his boxers, shivered as he groaned her name, moved against her.

With an impatient growl, he shoved down his boxers and finally entered her, long and hard, kissing her the same. They gasped simultaneously. Their gazes met, and for a moment, time stopped, freezing them in that intense pleasure. Because as her body moved and reacted to his, she felt the way her body squeezed and held him. Felt *his* awe and lust and wonder, of being here with her. A knife edge of fear she recognized grazed there, the sense that this couldn't be real, that this couldn't last… But by gods, it was a blessing of disproportionate size while it did.

Pure joy broke across his face. He quickened his pace, and she arched with him. Reality slipped into color and sensation, lights bursting behind her eyes, her breath coming in gasps, her hands grasping at his shoulders while she wrapped her legs around his waist, then nipped at his flesh with her teeth. His pleasure, hers. There was no line. There was just them. Together. The perfect fit.

Together, they belonged.

Chapter Twenty

DOUBTS

WILLIAM WOKE with Cara's warm body against his, morning light streaming in through the windows, reflecting off the glistening snow. He swallowed hard and forced himself still, so he didn't wake her. He was unprepared for requisite morning-after conversation. Last night had been…incredible, and it'd been a long time before sleep overtook him, growing feelings for Cara leaving him unsettled. Being with Cara was a freedom, a sense of normalcy he hadn't experienced in decades, maybe ever. When she'd created that connection between them, he'd felt her pleasure *and* his. What could have been just sex became something so much more.

He stared up at the plaster ceiling, images and emotions from last night spilling over him. More than the pleasure, it was the way she looked at him, the way she touched him with reverence and trust, leaving no doubt it was him she saw.

How could she see him and be so trusting, so gentle? Being with Cara was far more dangerous than any relationship he'd had, including his only fiancée, Marjorie, back before the Shades when he'd been naive enough to believe in happy endings. With Cara, he not only wanted to believe, he wanted to be worthy of the way she looked at him, be the man she believed him to be.

He'd believed to defeat the Guardians, he needed to be the monster everyone thought he was already. But could he sacrifice everything to the greater good? If he endangered Cara, he'd be no better than the Guardians.

She made a soft sound as she turned toward him, the amber pendant sliding over her collarbones before falling against the sheets. Those long lashes fluttered. She considered him a moment before raising an eyebrow. "Uh-oh. Those look like awfully deep thoughts for the ass crack of dawn."

Despite himself, a small smile pulled at his lips. He nodded at the pendant. "If you were wearing that last night, does that mean it, or your friend, was there, too?"

She chuckled. "That would be creepy. Dom is only there when I call them. Besides—" she tipped her head to the side, her hair sliding off her neck, her smile bittersweet, "—they haven't been there whether I call them or not."

The sunlight brushed her neck, highlighting the darkened blotches of skin.

"What the hell." He leaned forward to gently touch the bruises with a fingertip. "Who did this?"

She recoiled, covering the bruises with her hand. "Crap. Are they bad? I never thought…" She slipped naked from the bed, grabbing the blanket near the foot to wrap around her before padding toward the full-length mirror on the back of her door. She tilted her head to the side, sliding her free hand over the bruises, her body blocking her reflection from him. "Ugh. Maybe if I wear a scarf…"

He picked up his boxers from the floor, jerking them on. "What happened yesterday?"

The graceful curve of her neck and bare shoulders lifted as she took a deep breath before turning, one hand holding her blanket toga, other hand on her hip. Her brow rose, a regal goddess. "I met someone who said they knew some nymphs. Specifically, Gran's family. Then Maddy got into a bit of trouble, and I helped her out. But it was a mistake and a trick, and fortunately Not-Dog was there to lend me a ha—a paw. Everything turned out great. See? No big deal?" She cocked her head. "I'm hungry? Are you hungry? Let's get dressed and have breakfast."

She opened the door and stood to the side, pointing his way out.

Snatching up articles of his clothing, he stalked toward the door. He passed through the doorway, but when Cara moved to close it, he gripped the door and faced her. "We will be talking about where that bruise came from."

She focused on a spot somewhere left of his shoulder. "Sure. We'll talk. Looking forward to it. I mean, at least we didn't have to have any awkward morning-after conversation, right?"

He stared at her long and hard, all the ways this could have, hell, should have gone flashing behind his eyes. Distance was what he'd wanted...but made his chest hurt. He broke eye contact and stepped out into the hall. The door closed behind him.

~

CARA LEANED HEAVILY against the closed door, blowing out an unsteady breath. Wow. That had gone ten times shittier than expected. Not that she'd expected pillow-talk and the whispering of sweet nothings. She scowled. Maybe she had. That's how the script worked in her dreams. She just really hadn't wanted to start the day with yesterday's stupidity.

She padded back toward the bed, tossed the blanket, then pulled on slacks, a turquoise-colored blouse. Thank Goddess she'd texted last night to take the day off after checking on Maddy. Work today, on top of William, would have been too much.

William wasn't a fantasy. He was real. And already had one foot out the door, judging by his still-packed bag. She'd told him she didn't expect more than he could give last night, and she'd meant it. Maybe she'd hoped for more, though. Brush in her hand, she stared into the mirror, then reached for her pendant. *Come on, Dom, please. I could use some advice...*

The pendant remained cool and inert, an old piece of jewelry. Because having Dom answer would have been too easy, and Goddess knew her life had been anything but for the past week or so. Which left going downstairs and admitting what a desperate idiot she'd been to a man who always had a plan. Super yay.

Grumbling to herself, she followed the scent of bacon and eggs into the kitchen.

William was at the stove, spooning the eggs onto a separate plate, the first already heaped with bacon, enough to feed him and all the Shades.

Not-Dog, Jax, whatever the critter was, stared mournfully up at the bacon with a whine, glanced at Cara, then huffed out a breath and plodded toward his bowl on the floor, filled with brown kibble.

Cara's shoulders squeezed. *Yeah, well, you could eat like a human if you chose to appear that way, buddy.*

The dog, as though sensing her thoughts, swung his head her way and cocked his head like someone raising a brow challengingly before it glanced at William, then back to Cara, then returned sullenly to its food.

Awesome. Was Not-Dog psychic, too? Because being a shapeshifter disguised as a dog to secretly help William wasn't complicated enough. Jax was its name, right?

Tough luck, Jax, she thought back.

She followed William to the table, taking the chair beside him since if she didn't, it'd prove she was squirrely around him. His knee brushed against hers when she sat, sending sparks through her, reminding her of last night, of the way their gazes locked when he'd entered her body. A rush of pleasure but also emotion had flowed through their connection. That moment when for the first time, it'd felt like she belonged.

There was already a plate in front of her, and he held out the platter of eggs.

Yeah, well, any belonging must have been in her head…or maybe the heat of the moment. Worse, if she told him about Jax now, he'd think she'd been keeping it from him. Which she had been. Ugh.

She spooned off an egg, then two pieces of bacon.

They ate in awkward silence for a few minutes. Although William ate a few eggs, the platter was still heaped high when he pushed his plate back.

"Thank you for breakfast," Cara said quietly.

"Of course." He grimaced at the egg plate. "I got carried away."

Jax whined hopefully from the corner with his food dish.

Cara shot the creature a glare…although it had saved her life. "Maybe the dog would like some?"

William glanced at the dog, frowned. "I suppose."

Aren't we both pretty sure that thing isn't actually a dog? "It's protein, right? That can't be so bad. Besides, maybe the diet alone might make him want to leave."

He set the plate with at least six eggs on the ground.

Jax raced forward, gobbling it all up noisily.

William paused before meeting her gaze, his expression solemn. "About earlier… I shouldn't have gotten angry with you. When I saw those bruises, with my informant dead, the attacks we've seen in town, never mind whatever is going on with your headaches, the nymphs, and the Yaga pendant, I felt…"

Something leapt into her throat—either hope or nausea—and sped her pulse. She struggled to appear casual and not grip the table. Maybe after all this he did feel something. Maybe last night he'd had that same sense of rightness—

"You know what, it isn't important." He scrubbed a hand over his face.

She sagged. If only that were true.

He cleared his expression, all solemn and PI-ready again. "I was out of line earlier, making demands of you. I want to know what happened yesterday. You said you met someone. There was some kind of attack, your friend Maddy was involved. How did you get away? Who were they? How many of them were there, and did they identify themselves as Guardians?"

She gripped the pendant with one hand, and her neck with the other, practically feeling the sidhe's hands around her throat again. "They approached me inside the Center. A woman. She said she wanted to help, that she'd heard of me and that—" She half laughed, voice thick. "She said my dad was half-Yaga, which is nuts, since he despised all things paranormal, so jokes on him. She promised that some of Gran's nymph relations were waiting outside and wanted to meet me, but then grabbed Maddy and dragged her outside."

"Pete's sake, Cara." William reached in a pocket for his mints, offered one to her. "She knew too much about you and provided exactly what you wanted and needed. It was a trap. If you hadn't gotten away…"

Coldness slid over her. The memory of those long fingers around her neck, Irene's blood-red smile…how damned stupid and lucky she'd been. Did William see it the same way Gramps and the boys did? Proof she couldn't take care of herself. Heat burned her cheekbones and added crispness to her tone. "I know it was stupid. But Maddy is my friend, and touch is almost unbearable to her, let alone the part where she was a hostage. Besides which, we'd struck out with the other nymphs. I figured a chance of info was worth the risk."

A tic started in William's jaw, but he kept his voice even, sitting back against his creaking chair. "Getting involved with the Guardians under any circumstance is never worth the risk. Did this helpful stranger have a name?"

She crossed her arms, trying to ease the chill in her bones. Memory, shame, all mixed up inside. "Irene."

William closed his eyes, rubbed his hand over his lips. "Shit."

For some reason, that he knew the femme fatale redhead only urged on Cara's irritation, the idea that this was his ex or something, especially after what Irene had said about William. Another perfect being who belonged in this fight to protect the paranormal world in a way Cara didn't. Yes, it was ridiculous, part of her knew that…but part of her wondered why last night hadn't seemed to affect him like it had her. "You know her, I take it?"

William waved a hand dismissively, scowling in

thought. "She's a crazy sorceress who I've crossed paths with before and is gifted enough with spellwork she's slowed her aging. Sometimes she wants me on her side, most of the time she tries to kill me. She's deadly, smart, and ruthless. Doesn't matter. What happened next?"

Cara snapped upright, back stiff. "Doesn't matter, or doesn't matter to *me*? Because she sure the hell sounds like she matters."

His gaze had gone dark. "An old enemy. She's not an ex-girlfriend if that's what you're getting at. Higher level Guardian operative. Very bad news. Exactly the type of person you *don't* follow out of a building, alone, away from any of the people who could protect you."

She stood, hands fisted at her side. "Maddy was in trouble. Maybe I'd have known to be especially suspicious of Irene if you, Gramps or the others had ever told me about her. She promised me help, answers. A way not to *die*. I don't need a babysitter."

He stood slowly, his movements deliberate, hands fisting. "I have been trying to help you find the nymphs. I gave my word I would help you, and I will. I can't do that if you run off and get yourself kidnapped by any of the Guardians, and especially not Irene. She's smart, conniving, and deadly. Hell, she's probably the reason Tom is dead. She's who the Guardians would call in to kill an informant. Or kidnap someone useful. Like you."

She crossed her arms, scowling. "I don't have ability. It doesn't make sense they'd want me."

"Are you sure? I think it's time we bring the Shades in on what's happening with the nymphs, the Yaga pendant—"

"Now you want to bring in the Shades? I thought this was your case and they'd been out of the loop too long? You can't tell them." Gramps might like if she had ability, but not if it had anything to do with nymphs. If he found out she was ill… Her nails bit into her palms. He'd almost killed himself using all the spells and potions he knew to try and heal Gran when she'd gotten sick. She'd almost lost both of them.

William's words were dangerously calm, spurring her anger. "They might know more about why the nymphs are dangerous—"

"I told you, you can't tell any of them. About Dom, about my 'nymph problem' or whatever the hell it is. You gave me your word."

There was that tic in his jaw again. He reached for her hand. "Cara—"

She jerked out of reach. "I said no."

He took a deep breath. "I just want to—"

"You know what? I changed my mind. I don't want to tell you what happened."

He lowered his head, anger flashing in his eyes. "If you'd just go over the details—"

"I said no. Trying to save Gran almost killed Gramps. I won't let him do that for me. I won't let him worry, especially if I can solve this problem myself." Without giving them yet another reason to turn her away, another reason why William could mosey in here and be one of the Shades again while she could never do the same. Thank the Goddess this had all come out now, before she got too attached.

She quashed the pang deep down inside, the one that said too bad, too late, she was already attached. She strode past William out into the foyer.

His footsteps and voice pursued her. "Where are you going?" He sounded both annoyed and tired.

"For a walk." She picked up her coat from where it lay after last night. The torn sleeve brought back too many memories of Maddy's terror, the man in black, how close things might have been, everything that had happened yesterday… She hung it on the newel post and pulled out another coat, her black one this time, then shoved her feet into her shoes.

"I can come with you. Maybe—"

She spun on him. "I'm going for a walk. Alone. In my own damned town, taking care of myself because that's what I do, and believe it or not, I'm pretty good at it." She gestured vaguely toward the Center. "You can go investigate, keep more secrets, have secret meetings with the boys, do whatever the hell you want."

He clenched his jaw a moment, watching as she reached for the door. "I didn't mean to imply you couldn't take care of yourself. Nor that you were in anyway incapable. But Irene is dangerous."

Jax wandered out of the kitchen, claws clicking, head cocked.

"Then I'll… I'll take the dog. His company is fine." His company was confusing at best, but the house was suffocating. Yes, she'd messed up, but she'd also gotten herself and Maddy out of the trouble, too, hadn't she? That had to count for something.

William shot a murderous glare at Jax/Not-Dog.

The animal scuttled toward Cara, head hunched.

"I'll get the leash—" William started.

"We're fine." She jerked open the door and stepped out into the wind. Jax scrambled after her as she escaped the house…and facing William or her growing, idiotic feelings.

Chapter Twenty-One

HELLO THERE...

CARA RAN the first few steps from the house, anything to get away from that trapped feeling, from the sense that she'd disappointed William...and herself. One step blended into two. Faster and faster as she raced down the driveway, coat flapping, eyes burning, breath fogging in the chilly morning, footsteps crunching in the shallow snow.

Down the driveway, then out onto the highway. Across lay the Senior Center. Goddess help her if Gramps or anyone spotted her—then told Gramps. She didn't need anyone else to know what an idiot she'd made of herself, how stupid she felt.

She turned right, running parallel alongside of the two-lane highway. She jogged through the four-way stop at the center of town. Fortunately, the parking lot with the store and gas station, and next to it Loki's pub, were both relatively empty. Across the road, Mal's service truck was parked at the small metal building that served as police and emergency response center. Jeepers, creepers, and joe, it was a good thing it didn't have many windows, either, because having the police chief come out and ask what was wrong would almost be as bad as Gramps.

She slowed her pace, breath rasping, and jerkily did up her coat as she turned right and down the road opposite of the emergency center, in front of the rise where the school was. Wrapping her arms around herself, she kept up a quick pace, but no more running.

"So…that could have gone better," Jax said, padding at her side.

She shot him a quick glare. "I only brought you to get William off my back, not for conversation."

"You'd both be happier if you'd both stayed upstairs, enjoyed more time together in bed. Knew I should have blocked the door."

A few choice swears echoed through her head.

Jax winced, turning to the road ahead. "Touchy," he muttered, suggesting he'd heard those swears.

They walked on, past the second turn-off into the school parking lot, the cold air and space helping her think. Jax was right. She could have handled things better. Should have explained why yesterday's mistake hadn't been a complete waste. But she'd been angry with herself, too, for being so foolish. This Irene person was obviously worse than she'd thought. A small shudder rolled through her, unsettled breakfast in her stomach. She rubbed a hand over her face. It wasn't William's fault that the Shades trusted him, looked at him as their leader. It wasn't his fault she didn't understand what was going on, that Dom was missing, that apparently her nymph side was behind it, and Dad had been part Yaga and she was dying, and…and…

Her eyes stung and she stopped, pressing her shaking hands to her lips. It wasn't his fault, but she'd taken it out on him. Because there was no one else to blame, and there were more questions than answers thanks to Gran. Gran, who'd always been her hero…but refused to talk about nymphs.

The quick footsteps behind her crunching on the melting snow and gravel edging the asphalt brought both comfort and dread. It had to be William. Racing after her, trying to protect her, trying to do his duty and get out of town…probably as bewildered by her behavior as she was. It wasn't his fault that he'd been the object of her fantasies for so many years.

A low growl rose from Jax.

Cara frowned at the dog, her neck tensing before she turned to find a dark-haired woman walking toward her, hair covered in a faded pink scarf, a brown trench coat wrapped around her slim frame.

The woman's smile deepened the creases around her eyes, around her high cheekbones. "Thank you for slowing. I confess, I'm not as quick as I once was."

For a second, Cara forgot how to breathe. Eyes widening, lungs wheezing, her muscles went slack. *Gran.*

The woman closed the distance, and Cara inhaled.

This wasn't a ghost, not Gran. This woman was taller than Gran had been, slimmer, her face a bit younger, less lined by laughter and love, her hair barely touched with silver whereas Gran's had gone white before Cara had moved to Beckwell.

This woman's eyes were different, a startling green… So much like Mom's had been. Mom's kindness and welcome echoed in this stranger. Heck, the woman's face echoed Cara's own reflection.

Jax continued to growl.

Absently, Cara touched his head and sent the message to cool it.

He quieted, though he shifted until his furry body

bumped the side of her leg, indicating he wasn't going anywhere.

The woman stopped a few feet away, casting an uneasy look at Jax before offering Cara another hesitant smile. "You must be Cara." She exhaled, joy and affection glowing in her eyes.

Weird for a stranger. Cara glanced around for that silver sedan, any sign of Irene or that dark fey that had tried to choke the life out of her yesterday.

The road was conspicuously empty.

No one to hear her call for help.

She swallowed, took a small step back. "Who are you, and how do you know my name?"

"Oh, darling, I know everything I can about you." The woman stepped toward Cara, arms outstretched.

Cara stumbled back, held out a shaking hand. Strangers coming at her, knowing too much about her got old fast. She should have been on defense, should have reached for a weapon, a freaking rock or something, but this woman sounded like Gran. That same sweet strength, the way she rolled her Rs a little. "That's close enough."

The woman stopped, straightened with a pained expression. "She didn't tell you about me, did she?" She wilted. "Of course, she didn't. She never wanted to see me, any of us again." She touched her chest, sadness behind her eyes. "I'm Gladys. Mother's always had a fondness for flowers. Gladiola Carmenta. I'm Rose's—your grandmother's—sister."

Cara saw spots a second, and then a stabbing pain shot through her skull, as though someone had plunged an icepick straight through her eyeball. She gasped, falling to her knees, clutching her forehead.

Jax yelped beside her, bumped his furry body into hers, growled at the woman.

At her great-aunt. Jeepers, creepers, and joe. *Her family.* Which would have been super to consider…if she wasn't suffering some kind of brain embolism.

The Yaga pendant warmed against her skin. *"Be careful. Don't—"*

Despite Jax's warning growls, a cool hand covered Cara's on her forehead. "Shush. It's all right."

A rush of coolness like water flowed from her aunt's hand into Cara's skin, through her body, mixing and combining with a matching sense of freshness, of…life and power that surged up from inside Cara, mingled and then soothed the ache in Cara's forehead. The pain wasn't gone but had calmed to a gentle throb.

Enough that Cara lowered her hand and peered up at the woman crouched beside her, her eyes so much like Mom's, that soft floral scent of her so much like Gran, her soft touch so familiar…

Even her gentle smile, the way she tilted her head was reminiscent of Gran. "Better?"

Cara nodded, not trusting herself to speak. The way their abilities had mingled, how something had risen in her, mixed with something from the other woman, the connectedness of it… She'd been so in-tune with the other woman, so…safe. It was overwhelming and hurt to have it gone.

The woman lithely stood—nimble for someone who had to be at least three times Cara's age. She held out a hand, her fingers cool and slim as they closed around Cara's, her grip almost as strong as William's as she pulled Cara to her feet.

"W-what did you do to me?" Cara prodded the spot that ached in her skull, as though she could somehow tell what had happened. Dom had been there a moment, too, had warned Cara to be careful, before they'd been blocked out. She took a few steps, putting some distance back between her and her supposed aunt. Wincing, she lowered her hand. Yeah, because denying this woman who could have been Mom's sister made it less obvious they were family.

"*We* got rid of that pain. Together. That's how nymph abilities work, Cara. They're communal. We share who and what we are with the collective, which makes us all stronger." A flash of pain creased Gladys's face again. "She didn't tell you that?" She shook her head sadly, before lifting her gaze to Cara's again. "How could she have hated us so much that she'd deny you your heritage? She never should have hidden so much about who you are, what you are."

"She wouldn't have. She'd never lie to me." Cara jumped to Gran's defense. Yet… why wouldn't Gran have told her something about the nymphs and the abilities Cara might have had? Sure, Cara hadn't known at the time she had any nymph abilities because Gran always insisted Cara had none, shut down all questions on the topic.

Now she was gone, and according to Dom, those abilities Cara hadn't known she had could kill her.

"Do you know what's wrong with me?" she asked her aunt, a stranger who might finally answer some of her questions.

"Of course," Gladys said, closing the distance and touching Cara's elbow. "Sweetheart, I… I don't know quite how to tell you this, but…your grandmother placed a block on your powers, which is compounding and getting worse as you come of age. We nymphs don't gain a hint of our true power until we're closer to what humans would consider middle age but for us is barely past pubescence. Your powers are growing, trying to take flight, but the ward your grandmother placed is suffocating you, suppressing your abilities." She paused, her voice small. "It's killing you."

Cara heard the words, tried to process, but her world crumbled at the edges. Gran had done this? Gran's kind face, her smile rose behind Cara's eyes. Her hands trembled, stomach did somersaults. Gran had placed a ward to smother Cara's powers. Gran, who had always said she'd tell the truth…but had also told Cara some people weren't born with much ability, that not having power wasn't a bad thing. Acid rose up Cara's throat, and her knees grew soft. Gran, who's ward was probably the same thing keeping Dom away and was the thing that was killing Cara. How… It couldn't… She looked up at her aunt, yet another secret Gran had kept, eyes stinging.

"It's all right. Take your time." Aunt Gladys patted Cara's arm, her voice a soft murmur.

Her aunt's words tumbled over each other, softer than the truth screaming through her head, demanding how Gran could have done this. Gran, who was supposed to love her, who'd always said she'd accepted Cara.

"I'm sure this must come as a shock. We've been so afraid for you. It's why we've been calling to you, trying to free you from the clutches of the Abomination and your selfish grandfather. The good news is we can help. We can remove the ward, free your abilities. Your grandmother, myself, and the collective. We can heal you, and we'll all be stronger for it."

Jax growled again, batting at her leg with a paw.

Something in Aunt Gladys's words penetrated. *Abomination…*

Cara blinked, jerked out of the woman's grasp. "You're a Guardian," she gasped, picturing William's haunted expression when they'd been trapped in the bathroom and he'd confessed that's what the Guardians had dubbed him, how much it had hurt. How much it always hurt when you were left on the outside, never quite belonging.

Aunt Gladys's brows rose. "Of course, dear. Nymphs have always sided with Guardians in this war on paranormals. They believe, as we do, that humans are dangerous creatures who throughout history have tried to capture and use our kind, forced us to their bidding, perpetrated unspeakable harm and violence against us."

"But the Guardians hunt and kill paranormals, destroy sanctuaries like Beckwell." That's how the stories went. Having met Irene, with the blood-red lips and henchmen, it was pretty clear she was the scary kind of Guardian Gramps and William had warned Cara about.

Could Aunt Gladys be a Guardian? Aunt Gladys, who'd helped Cara, who was so like Gran…

"Gran wasn't a Guardian, was she?" Cara whispered, dreading the answer.

The older woman shook her head sadly. "They've poisoned you against us, I see. Mother said they would. No, Rose was like you, turned against her own blood by people like your grandfather and the Abomination." She tilted her head. "Look what it got her. She could have lived hundreds of years, never aging, never feeling sickness or pain thanks to the collective. Instead, she chose a small life with a miserable human and, from what I understand, her life ended in both sickness and pain. Worse, she's placed this ward over your abilities, kept you from the collective, and therefore tried to doom you to the same lonely, painful existence and early death. We wouldn't do that to you. Not me, not your grandmother, not the rest of the Guardians."

"Yeah, okay, I've heard enough." Jax stepped between Cara and the other nymph before planting himself on his furry butt. "Time for you to move on, toots."

Aunt Gladys's mouth gratifyingly fell open. "Your dog… It talks!"

"Yeah, pretty sure he's not a dog, and he talks a lot." Cara stepped toward Gladys. Maybe she'd misunderstood what Gran had done. Maybe the block was because of the Yaga side, or there was some other reason. Something other than Gran having done this to her.

Jax blocked her path, baring his teeth.

She glared at him, then faced her aunt despite the distance. "You're telling me, somehow the Guardians aren't responsible for countless deaths and suffering of paranormals—all because they had mortal bloodlines and intermarriage? The one thing I know about our family is that Gran was disowned because she wanted to marry Gramps. And despite her premature death, they were very happy together. She told me she had no regrets in choosing him."

Could Gran really have blocked Cara's abilities? Then worse, lied about it? *Broken*. Because of Gran.

"We tried to save her from her own youthful foolishness, don't you see?" Aunt Gladys said, desperation in her voice. "We knew without the connection to the collective, to her kind, Rose would be doomed to live a short, miserable existence. How selfish of your grandfather, to shorten her life by hundreds of years for maybe forty years with him."

Cara crossed her arms. Had Gran knowingly given all that up? "Sounds like because she didn't follow your rules, you kicked her out of the family and stole her immortality."

Aunt Gladys closed her eyes and rubbed her forehead, looking for a moment like an overburdened mother. Or Gran, when Cara had brought her frog friends into the bathroom, or insisted on wearing parts of Gramps's old uniform to school. "We stole nothing from her. Nymphs aren't immortal, we're just very long-lived with the benefit of the collective. We can perform our magics, like removing pain, healing, helping retain our youth and vitality, when we're connected to the collective. Rose turned her back on all that. Refused to be part of the collective. And…"

She hesitated, as though considering. "It's possible she shortened her own life by working nymph magic on you, constructing that ward, without the collective. Alone, we can't channel that much ability. Please, don't let her choices determine your future."

Wow. Getting better all the time. A dull heaviness strangled Cara's breath. Gran had stolen Cara's nymph abilities…and possibly died because of it.

Aunt Gladys held out her hand. "Let me take you to Mother. Let us teach you about our kind, how to connect with the collective. Let us heal you and help you come into your full potential with our guidance. You'll never be alone again. You belong with us, your family. We've missed having you near us so very, very much."

The reach of her hand tugged something deep inside Cara, maybe her nymph ability, maybe the idea of how good that would feel, to be welcomed by her family. To really and truly belong.

Jax bopped his head into her hand. "Yo, Cara. You did notice that she totally ignored your question about the death, maiming, and killing, right? Those small details about the Guardians' fondness for genocide. You're not going anywhere with her. That'd be dumb, and you're a smart woman. I can tell. After all, you like me."

"I didn't ignore it," Aunt Gladys insisted, stepped toward Cara, hand outstretched. "The Guardians are much more than they've told you. We're not monsters. We want paranormals to enjoy the same quality of life that humans take for granted. Why should our kind be forced to cower in the shadows and make do with the scraps humanity discards? Yes, our history is long, and as with many other such groups, there have been extremists among us who have misconstrued our beliefs, shaped them into their own justification for violence."

"A *few* extremists, huh? That's the story you want to go with?" Jax padded forward. "It was a lot more than a few who sided with the Nazis during the Second World War and ravaged countless paranormal sanctuaries. What about Irene?" He turned back to Cara. "You remember her, right? Promised to introduce you to these fine ladies… before having her goon try to strangle you into submission and drag you off Hades knows where. William told you she's an upper-level Guardian agent. You think they'd let 'extremists' like her get that much power if she didn't represent what they believed?"

"You're going to listen to this… this…animal instead of your own blood?" Aunt Gladys sounded near tears. "He, your grandfather, the Abomination, they'll all stand back and let you *die* before helping you. We want to save your life!" She took another step closer, holding out her hand again, but this time reaching, too. "Please, Cara. Come with me. Come to the nymph pool."

Jax growled again. "Cara, don't be stupid…"

Cara grabbed for the pendant, squeezing it hard. *Come on, Dom. Tell me what I'm supposed to do. I found the nymphs. Do I go with them? Can I trust her?* "I don't know if I can trust you. I don't know you."

Get your head on straight. Nothing comes for nothing. It was Gramps's voice, something he always said when she'd been little and dreamed of unicorns or fallen for stories told by her classmates. Over the years, that had become her voice.

The reminder that dreams were never free…and you shouldn't expect them to come true. Especially dreams of happy endings or trusting that love could see you through. Trusting that she could ever really belong, with William, with the Shades, with the nymphs.

"Remember what it felt like when our abilities mingled. That's what it's like being a nymph, Cara. You'll always be with us, always be part of us. Don't let this creature and the Abomination—"

"Stop calling him that!" Cara's head throbbed. This was too much information, nothing made sense, and now there was something wrong with her. Something Gran had done to her. If this woman could be believed. If any of this could be believed. Her eyes burned again. "There's a catch. There has to be a catch." Surely this family she'd never known wasn't offering her the sense of belonging she'd always dreamed of and a cure for nothing.

"We want to help you. We need you, and you need us. Please." The nymph took another step toward her, her hand brushing Cara's jacket sleeve.

"Nope. Not happening." Jax wrapped his two front paws around Cara's leg.

The world collapsed in on itself around Cara, around Jax, a kaleidoscope of colors. Her aunt's face elongated, stretched. Aunt Gladys's mouth fell open, her eyes widened. She stretched into a flash of color, swallowed by darkness.

There was a small *pop* and Cara and Jax rolled onto the snow-covered lawn of her front yard. Her head, though, kept spinning. With questions, accusations, the gray areas of who did what, who wanted what. What it all meant.

Distantly, she heard William's voice, felt the warmth of his body, his strength surrounding her, carrying her inside. For now, she was safe. She let chaos swallow her.

Chapter Twenty-Two

IT'S COMPLICATED...

"WE SHOULD TAKE you to the doctor. Or call him. Maybe he does house calls," William said again, not that Cara had listened when he'd suggested the first time...or the fourth since finding her out on the snow beside Not-Dog. His pulse had settled now that he'd gotten her into the small living room, wrapped her in a blanket after he'd helped remove her jacket and boots. Not-Dog splatted out in front of the cold fireplace. The creature had stuck by her side and earned her loyalty, so with Cara in his arms, William hadn't stopped the animal when it wearily followed them inside the house.

Cara pulled the crocheted pink blanket around her shoulders. "I don't think Doc Quilan can help me," she said, which was at least a different answer than "no, don't call the doctor," and "you can't tell the Shades."

He perched on the edge of one of the green armchairs, the sense of stealing someone else's place tightening his shoulders. When she'd stormed out, he'd forced himself not to race after her. That would have proved to her that he didn't think she could protect herself, that he didn't trust her. Which, maybe deep down, he'd never considered. He'd spent so long taking care of other people, he'd never weighed how they felt about it. It'd never mattered before.

"Okay. Who and what can help you?"

This room, covered with photos and personal mementoes felt like he'd invaded someone's home, a foreign place that would sink in its claws and cause him pain. Like it always had. Home was where love was and love always ended in pain.

She rolled her eyes. "This is you trying to be reasonable and not drag me to the doctor, isn't it?"

"It is," he agreed, unable to help the small smile that tugged at his lips. He reached for a mint, considering tactics. "Look, earlier... I was out of line. You're right. I promised I wouldn't tell the Shades. I shouldn't have questioned your decision to follow Irene yesterday or rescue your friend. You had no idea who she was, nor how dangerous she is. Besides which, I can only imagine how frightening it must be to think your life could end prematurely. I've lived without that fear for so long I forget what normal is for most people."

He paused, uneasy with the way her dark gaze studied him, popping the mint quickly. One last thing he ought to clean up, metaphorically removing his foot from his mouth...or places much less comfortable. "Last night was also..." *Incredible. Life changing. Made me wonder how I've gone so many years without you in it.* "A lot," he managed, which judging from her raised brow, may not have helped his case. He sucked his mint, wishing he battled ten armed sorcerers instead. He forced himself to face her again. "I was a complete knucklehead earlier. I'm sorry."

Her expression softened and her shoulders eased down.

"You aren't the only one. I..." She dropped her gaze, pulling at the crochet blanket before she looked up. "I felt like such an idiot for falling into Irene's trap. I was so desperate for answers." She choked on a sad laugh. "I thought if I saved Maddy from Irene, I could prove I wasn't a useless idiot. Great work, huh, proving I'm not an idiot with another idiotic move?"

He leaned forward, wanting to stroke her face, but settled instead for patting her shoulder awkwardly. Because nothing said husbandly affection and trust than a lame shoulder pat. If he allowed himself the intimacy, he'd want more. To kiss her. To join her on that sofa or carry her back upstairs to the bed and spend the rest of the day there.

He sat back in the chair, clasping his hands. "So, Irene. She promised she'd introduce you to your family?"

Cara nodded. "Yes, but instead she grabbed my friend, Maddy, and dragged her outside before she introduced me to a dark fey lurch." She shuddered before that chocolate gaze met his again. "Today I met my aunt."

He squeezed his hands together so hard, it was a wonder bones didn't crack, and forced his expression and tone to stay neutral. The urge to shout was overwhelming, but that'd undo all the work they'd done trying to patch up their relationship, such as it was. "You met a nymph today? When you went for your walk?"

Funny how in bed, they hadn't suffered any misunderstandings. Had been completely on the same page, equals coming together in shared pleasure. When Cara shared, opening her heart, her desire to him... He shifted in the chair, hoping the evidence of the direction of his thoughts wasn't apparent.

She didn't notice. "Yes. She walked up and introduced

herself. I had one of those attacks, the ice pick to the fore-head kind."

Which this supposed aunt was as likely to have caused.

"She helped me bring the pain under control. It was like…" Cara frowned, nibbling her lip as she searched for words. "It was like we joined our abilities together to make the pain go away." Her expression fell. "Of course, then she told me she was a Guardian. Apparently, nymphs are almost always Guardians. Oh, and the reason I'm getting these headaches—the reason I'll die if I don't join with the nymph collective to free my power—is all supposedly because of Gran. She said Gran put some kind of…ward on my nymph abilities that I've outgrown or something." She faced him. "Do you have any idea what she's talking about? Or if she's telling the truth?"

Albert had mentioned that his wife did something to protect Cara from herself and her own abilities, which meant this conversation tiptoed close to the edge of keeping his friends' secrets. Although if Cara didn't trust him and used her abilities, gods only knew what she could do to him. A paranormal nuke, Liko had called her. Talk about a painful breakup. "Your grandfather remembered Rose doing something, but he wasn't sure what."

She pushed a hand back through her dark curls. "Yeah, that whole nymphs being secretive thing *is* a thing. Their magic is communal, so maybe that's part of why I couldn't use it…although I'm not certain I used it yesterday, or if that was the Yaga side, or…" She dropped her head into her hands. "I don't know. I'm tired of not knowing…and all these strangers who come up to me and know so much more than I do. It's like I'm in the middle of a game, but I don't know whether it's cards or checkers, let alone what I'm supposed to do on my move."

More like that she might be the pot at the end of the

game. Damned if that didn't make him want to hide her somewhere safe until he'd gotten rid of all the Guardians. Starting with Irene and that dark fey.

He shifted onto his knees beside the sofa, gave in to the temptation to caress her jaw. "We know more about the nymphs than we did before." He hesitated a moment. "If it came down to it, would you trust this aunt to help you? Or would she side with the Guardians?"

She lifted her head and pulled a face. "I don't know. Too many people keep telling me half-truths. I don't know who I can trust."

"You can trust me, Cara." He tried to ignore the twist in his gut that said he was as guilty as her grandfather and the others for telling her half-truths. Yet if she knew the full extent of her abilities, if she knew that Albert had helped hide them, how could she trust any of the Shades, including William? It could make her run right to these Guardian-loving relations of hers.

She rested her forehead against his. "I do trust you," she whispered. "You know you can trust me, too, right? You can tell me things, about Irene, about the Guardians. I can help you and we can be a team."

A team like he'd been with the Shades, with Berta... with too many others he'd lost. An unsettled heaviness weighed his gut and his blood chilled, despite the warmth of her skin against his.

"A team. Sure," he murmured.

She stroked her hand along his jaw, sweeping toward his lips, brushing them with her fingertips and sending a jolt of lust through him, hardening his body. "You know what would be nice right now?" she rasped.

"Hot cocoa?" he teased, inhaling the scent of her, pressing a kiss to her nose, another to her eyelid. Hot damn, she made him want to tease her to wildness, until she screamed out his name for release. Other times he just wanted to make her smile, enjoy the sound of her laughter.

She pinched his nose. "No, not hot cocoa."

"Maybe a hot bath?" He nibbled his way down her neck, tugging the blanket free and sliding his hands around her torso, his thumbs beneath her breasts.

She tipped her head to one side, allowing him better access, bringing her arms up and around his shoulders. "You have the 'hot' part right." She paused, her body tensing a second before she cupped his jaw, brought his gaze up to her face. "Let's go upstairs. Where we don't have an audience."

They glanced at Not-Dog, who watched them from near the fireplace, tongue lolling.

William turned back to Cara. He should make some excuse. Get back to the den and work on his case, find leads from Chief Quilan, hunt down Irene before she harmed anyone else. Instead, he scooped his wife into his arms, loving the little surprised "eep" she emitted, then her warm chuckle as he carried her out of the room and toward the stairs, taking them two at a time.

He didn't remember until much later that he'd forgotten to ask how she'd made it back home and arrived in the front yard…with no footprints leading to where he'd found her.

"YOU'RE TELLING me you could have zapped us away from Irene without me causing myself pain?" Cara pointed the knife in Jax's direction where he'd plunked himself in the center of the kitchen floor. It was some hours later, William was upstairs having a shower while she put together dinner, which meant it was safe to interrogate Jax.

He rolled his eyes, letting his furry head drop as though in exasperation. "Of course, I could 'zap' you out of there, as you so colorfully put it. But I needed to see what you were capable of. Besides which, you're an average sized woman, but magically, you weigh a freakin' ton. Not sure I'll be zapping you anywhere again. You can carry your own butt."

She wagged her knife menacingly. "Explain."

"It means what I said. Throw me one of those, will you? I like carrots."

Despite herself, she threw the fake animal a carrot, and he greedily gobbled it down.

"Now explain." She finished off the carrots and celery, tossing them into the casserole dish with some oil and seasoning before sliding them into the oven beside the chicken she'd put in earlier. It was as close to gourmet cooking as she got.

Jax groaned. "You mortals, always demanding answers. Read a book, why don't you? *Harnessing Your Abilities* by Hera maybe? *The Power Within* by Atum…although it sounds different in Coptic."

"Now you're making stuff up."

"No, I'm just talking about things you haven't heard of. Not the same thing. Point being, it's unfair that you have so much ability and don't have any idea what it is or how to use it. To give you an example, William weighs about the same as me, like a good half-ton pickup truck or so. Not heavy lifting, but noticeable. When I say you weigh a lot, I'm saying you weigh something in the department of a tractor or double-decker bus, maybe two of them. You get what I'm saying? You've got serious firepower, kid, so you better learn how to use it, or the Guardians or someone else is going to come along and use it all up for you."

Jax wandered over to his water dish, prodded the bowl

with a paw sorrowfully. "Don't suppose you have anything in cut-crystal, do you?"

Her phone buzzed on the end of the counter where it was plugged in. "Not for you."

Another five texts from Maddy, apologizing profusely, checking if Cara was for real all right. They'd had a phone call, too, before Cara started dinner. Maddy was more messed up after the encounter than Cara, barely able to speak about it and mostly apologizing that she'd instinctively had to run…and guilt-stricken for doing so. She'd also contacted Ainsley and Jessie. Two texts from Ainsley insisted Cara be more careful…but good job protecting Maddy. Huh. Even one from Jessie insisting exciting stuff never happened in Beckwell…and this was probably the Shades' fault.

The water still ran upstairs in the shower, but she lowered her voice in case they were overheard as she spoke again to Jax. "I shouldn't be keeping the truth about what you are from William. I remember where I heard the name 'Jax' before. He said you're an old friend. That means he'd want to see you, right?"

The dog shrugged—so weird. "It's…complicated," it hedged. "And technically, I did save your life today. Again. You owe me."

"There's no proof my aunt would have hurt me."

"Other than drowning you in the nymph pool? Nope, no proof at all. I saved your life. Carried your double-decker self all the way here, used up all that strength, set off alarms so other people might find me…"

She glanced at the oven timer and rubbed the back of her neck. "Fine. You have until tomorrow night. That's it. I don't like keeping secrets from William. Food's still half an hour off. I'm going to go paint."

"Funny. Don't think he has the same problem keeping secrets from you," Jax muttered.

She was halfway down the hall and didn't have time for more of the creature's antics or mysteries. Nervous energy crawled over her skin, the kind she got when she hadn't painted in some time, when she'd been ignoring the visions.

She flicked on the sunroom light and glanced down at her blouse and trousers, bit her lip. Maybe she wouldn't splatter too much. She only wanted a quick peek at what the visions had to tell her, why she had the urge to paint now. Was it because she and William had been together? Because of what Jax said about her magical weight?

She rotated her shoulders and rolled her neck like a football player preparing for the game, then considered a pile of fresh canvases, standing with her hands on her hips. Taking a couple of deep breaths and centering herself, she let herself go into that slightly fuzzy yet focused frame of mind that always produced the best paintings...and clearest visions. When she leaned over to pick up the canvas, her hand already knew which one she needed, although she raised her brows at how large it was. The largest one she owned, bought on a whim years ago. A shimmer of energy scuttled through her bloodstream.

She set the canvas on her easel, then moved for her paints and palette. Instinct guided her to specific colors, grabbing them quickly, one after another, squeezing out a generous blob of raw sienna there, crimson, burnt umber, black, white, on and on. Her water cup and brushes were already on a small folding table next to the easel as she moved toward it. Deep breath...

The first strokes were dark, bold streaks of colors slicing across the white canvas. Her hand and the brush moved as one, instinct over intent. Dark, then light. Shapes emerging from the darkness… No, figures. The brush streaked over the canvas, energy working through her, her mind clear and unhurried yet also somewhat detached from the action, as though watching someone else. Damn, had she ever painted so quickly?

Dimly, there was the sense of someone coming in behind her. A comforting, strong warmth. William. Another presence joined him, though they both stayed in the doorway, as though somehow kept at bay.

Her focus remained on the painting, hands swiftly switching brushes, changing colors, adding shadows here, highlights there. She knew this painting, this image. It was like ones she'd done before. Those shadowy figures emerging from the darkness, something ominous about their arrival.

Yet these were larger, closer than ever before, practically leaping out of the canvas after her, sending a shiver down her spine. Faster and faster she painted, flinching when a splash of paint hit her cheek but never stopping. She couldn't. She had to see those figures. There were more figures than before, and they were closer to the viewer.

"Almost there. You're so close to achieving who and what you are meant to be. A true heir. A child of two natures. Just beware the nymphs," Dom whispered, at such a great distance they were almost unintelligible before they slipped back into wherever they were.

Something buzzed in the distance. Footsteps padded away. The scent of food, of cooking. Didn't matter. All that mattered was completing the painting, the vision.

The painting had reached where it usually was in previous incarnations, those figures stepping from the darkness. Yet her hand and her brush continued to move. She picked up more color, continued to add to the painting.

Another set of figures. Yes, that's what it was. More people. These new figures stood in front of the more ominous shadowy ones. These silhouetted figures were literally larger than life…and barring the path of those shadows, of those ominous figures. Like sentinels, or images of superheroes, standing proudly in the sunlight. *Standing guard.* Yes, that's what they were doing. Standing guard. Protecting. These figures didn't give the sense of danger. These were new. They were strong, they were determined, they stood between the audience and the threat of the shadows.

She added highlights that picked out certain aspects of their silhouetted features, clarifying the heroic figures standing closest to the viewer, almost blocking sight of the ominous shadows. They were men and women, judging from the curve of hips and jut of breasts, longer hair on some of them, glint of light from bald heads on others.

Hands trembling, breath shuddering out as though she'd completed a long run, Cara dropped her final brush into the wash cup, fumbling and almost losing the brush to the floor. Her knees were soft, and she stumbled over a fold in the canvas floor tarp. A faint ache started behind her eyes—signs of yet another headache, maybe the ice pick-nymph kind. She couldn't look away from the canvas, stepped back to get a clearer perspective.

William's spicy scent preceded him, then his warm arms, pulling her back against his chest, supporting her with his body, comforting her with his heat.

She glanced at him, spotted Jax on his furry rump in the doorway, head cocked to the side as he considered the painting.

William's blue-gray gaze searched her face as though for injury or sign of illness. "You good?"

She nodded, studying the strength of his jaw, the way

the shadows gathered beneath his cheekbones and the light caught the high ridges of his nose, his brow, as though he were fine art and she was trying to figure out how to replicate it. Her gaze wandered back to his, where he patiently waited.

He wrapped his arms around her middle and nodded at the painting. "Is it done?"

Cara considered the painting. The heroic figures guarding against the shadows. It was like nothing she'd done before. It was the largest canvas she'd ever painted in such a short session, especially during a vision, and it was the first time she'd painted a vision she'd had before, but with such significant alterations. "It's done."

"It's not art, is it?" William said, although it was more statement than question as he, too, considered the painting, a small crease between his brows.

"No. It's a vision." For some reason, perhaps the surreality of the moment, the dreamy disconnect she had right after a session, she continued. "This is how I've always seen my visions, while painting. I've painted this one before, at least the part with the shadowy figures, the dark ones in behind. It's the ones in front, the…the heroes, I think. Those are new."

"They're protectors," he murmured.

She turned to him and the quiet certainty in his tone. "How do you know?"

He shrugged, studying the painting. "They just…are."

A small shiver slid through her. It was like when they made love, this kind of…shared experience. Although this time they barely touched. William understood the painting in an eerily similar way to how she had, in a way Gramps and Gran, the few friends who'd seen her paintings never quite had.

"What do you think it means? The protectors and the

shadow figures?" she asked, as usually she'd have asked Dom.

Dom wasn't here.

William was.

"I'm not sure." He studied the painting a few more moments before turning to her. "Maybe it means help is on the way. For us, and for Beckwell."

Chapter Twenty-Three

WAR OF ART CLASS

WILLIAM NODDED at two passing silver-haired residents as he strode through the Senior Center toward Albert's room. The situation between he and Cara the last few days had been good. Too good. The other shoe was bound to drop. He'd woken again in Cara's bed, surrounded by her warmth, all her pictures, little mementoes, the sweaters hanging behind the door that made her room personal and intimate. All of it began to feel too comfortable, too much like…

Like home.

Like there was some chance he belonged here. With Cara.

Hell, he hadn't wanted to fight with her over lack of protection today when she'd said she had to go into work. She'd accused him before of not trusting her to take care of herself, and she'd done fine when it came to her encounter with Irene and then with that other nymph, her supposed aunt. Besides which, she taught her classes in the dining hall, the heart of the Senior Center. Surely, she'd be safe there while he took a few minutes to smooth things over with the boys.

Purple-haired Agnes and Marge, their leathery wings folded behind them and not doing laps around the atrium this morning, giggled like schoolgirls as he passed, and he managed to give them a polite smile, continuing on his way. He was getting used to the Senior Center, recognizing more of residents like those two women. The shocked whispers were less, and people didn't flee out of his way either. It was...nice.

But not his. He paused as he arrived at the mauve door marked "Jenklow," the faint rumble of male voices coming from inside suggesting the whole lot of them were in there. He rapped on the door sharply. Good. Time he cleared the air. Or tried.

The voices inside went silent, then there were footsteps before Jenklow opened the door, peering out. He raised a brow but offered no welcoming smile.

William spotted the rest of the boys—Einar, Chaimek, Zaki, and Liko—inside.

"Morning," William said. Shit. How had it gotten this way? He'd been trying to protect his old friends.

The same way he'd tried to protect Cara? Treating her like she couldn't take care of herself.

"Where's Cara?" Jenklow stuck his mostly bald head out the door and peered both ways down the hall.

"She's teaching her class in the dining hall."

Jenklow's bushy brows came down and he opened his mouth to protest.

William stopped him with a raised hand. "She'll be fine for a few minutes. She's already met Irene. And one of her relatives. She did fine defending herself."

"What the hell kind of protection have you been giving

her if she's running into Irene?" Liko demanded, striding forward, hands fisted.

"If Irene's in town, we're facing the scenario we most hoped to avoid," Einar said, more to Jenklow than William. They'd all faced the sorceress near the end of the war…and narrowly escaped to tell the tale.

Jenklow silenced them all with a raised hand, his cool blue gaze never leaving William's face. "To what, then, do we owe this pleasure? You made it clear you didn't believe we should have any part in your investigation and expulsion of the Guardians. Ah, I know. Perhaps you'd like us to teach you shuffleboard?"

William shifted uncomfortably at Albert's tone, chilly as the biting October wind outside. Not that he hadn't expected it. He took a deep breath, aware he addressed them all. "I…may have misspoken."

Liko snorted. "More like you had your head shoved so far up your ass the only thing that could come out of your mouth was shit."

"Oh, shut it, Liko." Chaimek elbowed the larger man. "He's here to grovel. I want to hear it."

Zaki remained expressionless.

Einar crossed his arms, white eyebrow raised. "Is that why you're here, Mac?"

William cleared his throat. "I wanted to apologize for any feathers I may have ruffled. The seriousness of the Guardians' Beckwell infiltration is clear with Irene's presence. Which makes this is an all-hands-on-deck situation."

The men exchanged glances, communicating silently. These men had been closer than brothers to him. Actively enlisting their help could cost them their lives. He tried to tamp down the uneasiness in his belly at the idea, at how devastated Cara would be if anything happened to these men. But what choice did he have? The police chief was stretched. William was stalled in his progress, and worse, the Guardians and everyone else closed in on Cara. It was the only way to keep her out of their clutches.

Jenklow broke the long silence, clapping a firm hand on William's upper arm. "Hell yes, this is a job for all the Shades. Why do you think we contacted you in the first place?"

A wave of relief slid over William, one he hadn't been expecting. "Good. Let's go over the information you have and—"

"Bastard," Liko said, coughing the swear into his shoulder and glaring at William.

Einar snorted. "You mean hand over the information so you can continue cutting us out of the investigation?"

William paused. "I—that is…"

Jenklow clamped a hand on his shoulder and walked William back a few steps. "Tell you what. We'll finish our morning meeting and let you know what we think of your proposal, and how you fit into *our* plans. In the meantime, get back to Cara and make sure she's safe. You might pick up a few things. She understands teamwork."

Albert took two steps back, and the door slammed, leaving William out in the hall. Alone.

He stared at the closed door, the voices rising inside. The chuckles of the men, of his friends, having a meeting like the ones he'd once led. His stomach squeezed and exhaustion weighed on him. This was what he'd wanted… even if it felt less than ideal. This distance that would let him leave, that would mean it wouldn't hurt as much when time stole each one of them away. They would help because they cared as much or more about Beckwell and stopping the Guardians, especially when it came to Cara.

He retraced his steps toward the atrium and the dining hall, toward Cara, something tightening his throat and hardening his belly. He'd created the distance for their safety and his own. So what if he could still picture their faces illuminated around a rare campfire decades ago, heard their suggestions in his head, had felt more at ease with them than he'd been with Mother.

He paused at the glass doors to the dining hall, fishing for a mint, Cara's art class clustered near one of the corners with their easels.

Damn, she was beautiful. He'd left her side maybe fifteen minutes ago, yet he still wanted to cross the room just to be near her. Close enough to watch the way a smile lit up her dark eyes and revealed the hint of a dimple. His day was a little colder if he hadn't basked in her presence and caught her soft floral scent, or heard her deep, throaty laugh.

She moved from student to student, although something drew her gaze up, to land directly on him. She offered a small, warm smile for him, one that drew him across the room to her, to the seat she'd left for him near the wall.

These past few days an ache had opened inside him, a yearning for what couldn't be, what could have been. It was dangerous, impossible…felt way too damned right.

He collided with Cara's steady gaze.

She cleared her throat and slanted him a meaningful look.

He frowned. What?

She moved her gaze to the right, as though trying to show him something…

The chipper, all too familiar male voice came from two chairs down. "Morning, William. Fancy meeting you here," Hermes said.

William's mood soured faster than month old milk. He took a deep breath and fought for calm. Some days you couldn't win. He'd have to find out, of course, why the bugger was still in Beckwell, and worse, attending Cara's art classes.

"Mr. Hermes, as I've said before, we prefer to paint in silence. Perhaps if you saved your comments for afterward," Cara said in a way that said this wasn't the first time she'd made the suggestion.

"Oh, terribly sorry, Ms. Jenklow. Or…do you go by Mrs. Best now?" Hermes put on the charm as he addressed Cara, probably batting those yellow-y eyes.

"'Cara' is fine," she said, voice cool. Charm wasn't working.

William's lips twitched.

"Now if we could return to our study of the apples…" Cara slashed her hand toward the apples sitting in a bowl on a small table. She glanced to William again, widened her eyes significantly as if to ask why Hermes was here… and possibly what she could do about it.

"No problem," Hermes said, as oblivious to her irritation as he always was to William's. Intentional obliviousness was Hermes's superpower.

A coldness slid over William. Hermes was a well-known Olympian god, despite the rumors claiming he'd been on the outs with the others for the last two decades. Pure-blood god. Guardian material…if he'd ever stir himself enough to do anything that wasn't motivated by self-interest. Despite himself, William studied Hermes's white beard and hair, all in ringlets. And toga, because only Hermes would wear a toga in Beckwell, in October, when most people opted for parkas.

William had made it clear years ago he wanted nothing to do with the god. So why was Hermes here?

Hermes was a selfish ass…but would he have aligned with the Guardians and now pose a threat to Cara?

Cara moved toward William, the soft floral scent of her wafting toward him, reminding him of the slide of her flesh beneath his, the heat of her kisses…reminding other parts of his anatomy, too.

He shifted, trying to not look like a horny teenager. Might not have looked it, definitely felt it.

She leaned closer, voice pitched low. "He showed up for class this morning. I would have given you a head's-up, but class had already started…"

"That's fine," he murmured, glancing at the irritating god, who'd managed to smear blue paint on his forehead and was stabbing his brush at his canvas, a self-satisfied smile curving his lips.

Cara glanced back at Hermes, then to William. "It is him, isn't it? The god who…" She waved her hand to indicate William.

He nodded stiffly.

"What does he want?"

"I'll find out."

"And…done." Hermes placed his brush on the easel and stood, calling everyone's attention—and more than a few scowls. He beamed at Cara. "If we're done with the fruit, we can get on with the real show. I read in the schedule online something about a nude."

Several gray- and silver-haired heads popped upward at this, turning eagerly to Cara with oohs and excitement shining on their lined faces.

"Oh, crap. I forgot to delete that," Cara muttered, then aloud to her class. "Unfortunately, Loki was supposed to be our model, but since he was called out I've town I've had to canc—"

"You said your husband could do it if we behaved," said one woman with two braids and a bright spark of mischief in her blue eyes as she turned them on William. "I've been very polite. He'd make a sexy model."

"Ooh, there's always Chief Quilan. Or the doctor," another woman piped up.

"Who says the model need be male? The female form is beautiful." This from the tall, dark-skinned Mrs. Cole who'd grilled William and provided the information about the nymphs.

"I wanted to paint a nude. Preferably a man," the gray-haired woman beside Hermes piped up, cutting off William's words.

The man next to her, a heavy-set satyr with round belly and a full head of red-gray hair, piped up, "I don't care what they are so long as they're naked."

"You would say that, Randy," Mrs. Cole scoffed.

"It would be quite a thing, seeing a young naked body again," another woman mused aloud. "It's been months since the last orgy."

Orgy? William blinked.

Cara held up her hands. "It doesn't mean we can't ever do the nude painting. But without Loki—"

"Who needs Loki? These people don't have the time to waste." Hermes jumped from his seat. "Am I right?"

More nods and agreements. A few more comments related to an orgy. Dear gods, what kind of place was this?

It was probably Hermes's doing, spreading mischief and mayhem wherever he went. Messenger of the gods and conveyor of the dead to Hades, he'd always partied it up as hard or harder than Dionysus. Cara and the rest of the residents didn't need that kind of trouble.

"That's quite enough." William moved around the easels near the table with the sad apples and headed for Hermes. "I'll help you find the exit."

"Leave?" Hermes turned his easel and strutted over to

William. "I'm the model! The solution your dear wife is searching for." He reached for the shoulder fastening of his toga.

"No!" William and Cara cried in unison, jumping toward him amidst some of the more enthusiastic responses in the group.

Hermes paused, fingers on the toga fastening, expression somehow guileless. He'd always been an excellent liar. "I'm trying to solve the problem..."

William's teeth ground. "Is *that* what you're doing?"

Hermes met William's gaze squarely. "I'm always trying to help, particularly when it comes to you, despite what you believe. No matter how much you try to drive me away, the same way you'll drive your dear wife away, too. If that doesn't work, you'll run. You're good at that."

Heat flushed through William's body and his lip curled. He closed the distance until he and Hermes were toe to toe. "*I* have never run from my responsibilities. I don't cause problems then leave other people to clean them up for me. Why are you really in Beckwell, Hermes? Why do you keep bothering me no matter what I tell you?"

Hermes threw his hands in the air but didn't back down. "I just told you!"

"Uh, gentlemen, perhaps you should take your discussion elsewhere..." Cara stepped closer, her fingertips soft against William's bicep.

All his muscles had gone hard. His rage boiled at his inability to stop the Guardians, their targeting of Cara, his uncertainty about them, all of it distilled to this moment, focused on Hermes. This god, the start of it all, who'd answered a woman's desperate, grief-stricken prayers for a child who wouldn't die...and ended up destroying a marriage and leaving only death in his wake.

"Cara is good for you. She's what you need. If you'd

listen to me, you'd see that. So, I'll help her, I'll make sure she doesn't leave, so hopefully, you have long enough to get your head on straight." Hermes grabbed the shoulder fastening of his toga and tore it open. The toga fell open to his waist.

"She's my wife, and this is my life. I can handle things on my own." William reached for the buttons on his shirt, unbuttoned the first few, then tore it and his undershirt off over his head, tossing them to the ground.

The art students hooted and hollered appreciatively.

Cara grabbed his arm. "William, what are you doing? Don't let him get to you."

He paused, cupping her jaw in his. "You know I'd do anything to protect you, don't you? I can't let him cause the kind of pain he's caused me all my life. Can't let him break you the way it did my mother." He allowed the corner of his lips to lift. "Besides which, you did ask me to model for your class."

Whispers and chatter rose from near the entrance of the dining hall as news of the action spread.

Cara glanced toward the entrance, then back at him, brows lowering. "If this is some kind of pissing match between you and Hermes—"

"Then I would win!" Hermes crowed, reaching for his other shoulder fastening.

"No. You don't get to win. You don't get to hurt people." William reached for his belt buckle and zipper.

Somewhere, in a distant part of his mind, he recognized he was past rational thought, that this had traversed into an area where he was a little kid, listening to his mother and father fight because Dad didn't understand why William was so unlike both of them, why he didn't get sick like normal kids. Dad demanding why Mother had been unfaithful after promising to love, honor, and obey.

The whispers and rumors that shadowed him. Through the army camps, through every paranormal sanctuary he stepped foot in.

The crowd swelled, conversation and whispers, side bets from the sounds of it, and cheers of, "Take it off! Take it off!"

"You've both collectively lost your minds. Hey, why not. There's no stopping them now. You'll see," Cara warned ominously, stepping back to stand near her other students. "Class, a reminder that this is supposed to be an art class, not a strip club. Please take out a clean canvas and your charcoals or pencils."

Her voice was lost among the cheers and side comments.

"Does it matter? This is the best entertainment we've had around here in months?" a woman cried.

"Take it all off, big boy!" shouted yet another woman.

Hermes dropped his toga to the ground, standing there in a diaper-thing around his pelvis, thank the gods. He lifted a daring brow at William. "Well? You said you were willing to do anything to help her—or is that stop me?"

William pulled off his boots, shoved down his pants, standing only in his boxers and socks. "I won't let you or any other Guardian hurt her."

"Party!" someone yelled.

"Orgy!" shouted someone else.

Around them, the hoots and hollers increased in volume. Canes clattered to the floor. Buttons popped. There were moans, groans, and much fumbling before assorted brightly colored blouses, button-down shirts, and other clothing flew through the air.

William focused on the god, who could have transformed to marble, he stood so still.

For once, that ready, guileful smile was wiped from

Hermes's face. For once, there was a hardness in his amber gaze as he strode toward William. "You think I'm one of them? A Guardian?" His voice radiated fury.

Crossing his arms, William raised a brow. "Aren't you? They'd have promised you a good time. That's enough to earn your loyalty, isn't it?"

Hermes leaned close, brow down, the sincere anger and hurt on his face making it clear he either wasn't a Guardian…or he was a damned better actor than William gave him credit for. "You listen to me, and you listen close. I have never and will never be a part of those simpleton, specist wretches who think making other people's lives miserable elevates them. I am here in Beckwell to interview with that church as their new god because I wanted to be closer to you, close enough to help, close enough to maybe, somehow, prove to you that while I've made mistakes in the past, that doesn't mean that's who I am today. Can anyone prove they're good enough for you, that they're worth staying for?"

"*I* stay." William jabbed his finger against his bare chest. "I've found good friends who've been at my side. Friends who've become like family to me." His voice grew raspy. "But because of *you*, I have to watch them die, over and over again."

"That's all you see when you look at me, isn't it?" Hermes said, his voice almost too quiet to be heard above the growing ruckus.

Someone must have hacked the sound system, or maybe it was magic, but there was suddenly music. Heavy bass thumped and the singer—if the shouting above the bass and electronic notes could be called singing—called for them to get it started, get it started all night long.

"When I look at you, I see problems and pain headed my way," William confirmed.

"Then I guess I'd better get out of your way. Leave you to run from your friends, from Cara, and blame me for all of it. Play the role you've given me." Hermes smile was sad as he stood there a moment. Then he shook his head, snapped his fingers and vanished, leaving only the puddled toga where he'd stood.

William stood there, clenching and unclenching his fists, heaviness settling over him again. Chaos surrounded him, yet as always, he stood apart.

Hermes was wrong. He always was. Wasn't he?

A soft hand settled on his arm.

He flinched, tensing for the attack, but found Cara at his side.

She gestured at their surroundings, the frenetic music pounding through the floor.

Tables had been levitated against the walls, opening up a dance floor where half-naked and some fully naked paranormal citizens, most of them Center residents, boogied to the music.

"Come on. We may as well let them have some fun before it's any use trying to calm them down. Let's go somewhere quieter where we can talk."

She wound her fingers through his, looking up at him with a gentle smile the pounding music, the gyrating, mostly naked bodies couldn't dim. She was there for him. He wasn't alone. He could trust her. Warmth and a kind of calm seeped through him.

Despite the hard lump that settled in his stomach. Could she trust *him*? He hadn't told her what the Shades had said about her abilities. Or that he'd come here knowing he'd do whatever it took to stop the Guardians from gaining her power. Even if it cost her everything.

She tugged him toward the door.

He scooped up his clothes and boots before he followed

her toward the exit. Her trust was misplaced. He didn't deserve that kindness, that safety. Not from her, not from anyone.

Someone grabbed his butt and gave him a light pinch.

He jumped, turning to find one of Cara's students wearing little more than a bra barely containing her sagging breasts, a rough wool skirt, and a saucy grin.

She made a smooch with her bright-red lips, then grinned, her braided silver pigtails bouncing as she danced. "Oh, don't give me that look. We're old, not dead. Joy is what it's about. When you're young, you don't appreciate it. You're too busy building a life, following the rules, doing all that supposed adult crap. But now? Now we *make* the time. Life should be about having a little fun, finding a little joy." She cackled as she danced away.

William was struck by her words. She had to be what, maybe in her late seventies, early eighties—barely half his age. Joy. When was the last time he could honestly say he'd felt it?

Cara turned from her own observation of the party to meet his gaze, a softened smile on her face.

Joy. When he'd held her in his arms and made love to her. When he was with her, even when they weren't in bed. In the moment right before he'd climaxed last night, he could only marvel that somehow, fate had brought them to that moment, that time…and he was lucky enough to be with her. Joy and gratitude had filled him, pushed him over the edge. A growing warmth had blossomed in his chest, made him think about things like home and possibility. Hope.

Hermes accused him of pushing everyone away or running. Claimed Cara was the best thing for William but that he'd run from her.

He'd never planned to stay. He couldn't. Did the god see something he didn't?

Maybe Hermes saw what William already knew. If there'd ever been a woman for him, if he'd ever believed in one true love and all that, Cara was it.

A deep, shuddering breath let that truth settle, comfortable as a heavy rock in his belly.

Not that it mattered. Whether he felt that way about her or not, he had no choice but to leave. Abominations didn't deserve happy endings.

Chapter Twenty-Four

SECRETS OUT

WHAT THE HECK had happened back there with Hermes and the strip session? Cara, trapping William with their twined fingers, led him out of the dining hall and around the corner to the right, near a door marked "Music Room" and a paper "closed until further notice" sign. She released William's hand and leaned back against the locked door, watched William's progress pulling on the rest of his clothes, buttons fastened, zippers zipped, his movements jerky.

Bit funny that he wouldn't meet her eyes, though. A shiver of unease crept down her spine, but she tried to shake it off, letting her gaze rove over him appreciatively, a flash of heat going through her because he was her husband and she got to do more than look when they were alone at home.

"You don't have to put the rest on for my benefit," she said. "Although, probably better I set a good example and not jump my husband in the hallway at work."

Her half-joke brought his gray-blue gaze to hers, his

eyebrow lifting. He nodded back toward the dining hall, kneeling to tie his boots. "That sort of thing often happen around here?"

"More often than you'd think. Especially when someone starts a striptease in the middle of the dining hall. William, what was that back there with you and Hermes?"

His lips thinned and a muscle worked in his jaw. He took his time tying his boots, as though giving himself time to think before he stood and faced her again, crossing his arms across that yummy chest. "Working out past misunderstandings, I guess."

Uh huh… Cara raised a brow, mimicking his pose. "That's all, huh? What about that stuff about not letting him hurt me like he did your mom?"

His gaze shifted away and he readjusted his arms. "Hermes decision to grant Mother's prayers, to give her a child who wouldn't die, created tension between my parents and destroyed what had been a happy marriage. Dad thought…" He shrugged. "I didn't take after either of my parents. Never mind that I was never sick, stronger than a normal child."

Cara reached for him, resting her hands on his bicep and tugging him closer. "Is Hermes your father?"

William shook his head, a frown settling over his expression. "Mother always swore she'd been loyal. Even Hermes said they'd never—" He waved his hand, a touch of color darkening his cheekbones. He cleared his throat. "Doesn't matter. That's what he does when he comes around. Causes trouble. He's gone now."

Framing his face with her hands, she lifted his gaze to meet hers, caressed his cheekbones with her thumbs. "I'm sorry. I wish I could have prevented his ambush. You're not alone now, remember? I'm not going anywhere."

He quirked a brow at her. "So long as we find those nymphs and fix whatever problem is giving you those headaches."

She made a face. "Oh. Right."

He wrapped an arm around her, tugging her close. His thumb brushed her bottom lip. "I meant what I said," he said, voice rasping. "I'll do whatever is necessary to help you." His lips brushed hers once, twice.

She melted into his kiss, into the taste and heat of him. His mouth roved over hers, his hands settled around her, thumbs beneath her breasts. Heat spilled through her, need and comfort mixed with desire, a potent mix she'd gotten almost used to these last few days. Being with the real William was intoxicating and thrilling. It burned away the fear, the uncertainty, the nagging sense that Gran should have told her more.

The only thing William's touch couldn't erase was the cold shiver deep down that noticed he still hadn't unpacked his bags, he'd made no further promises. A single book unpacked on the study shelf, the case taking prominence. This was temporary…and maybe fleeting.

Someone cleared their throat. Loudly. From directly behind William.

He lifted his head, but took his time studying her expression, tucking back an escaped curl behind her ear before he turned. He tangled their fingers and tried to keep her behind his back.

Yeah, right. She stepped around him…then stifled a sigh at what greeted her.

Gramps, Mr. Einar, and the other three Shades stood in V-formation, Gramps on point. All of them stood arms crossed, faces like someone had stolen their tea-time cookies. Even Mr. Zaki, usually too forgiving for a grudge or temper tantrum, had a dark glower on his face.

Aimed at William.

"Problem?" William asked, obviously trying to keep his tone even, but a hint of annoyance edging his words.

Gramps's smile was laced with malice. "Oh, we have a problem." He jerked his head at the Music Room door. "Chaimek, door."

William barely had time to step aside before Mr. Chaimek, moustache stiff, raised his hand, dropped a wand out of his sleeve—a wand he was not allowed to have as per Center regulations—and aimed a quick shot of magic at the Music Room door's lock.

The door shuddered. The knob turned and the door swung open.

"In," Gramps said to William. His gaze softened somewhat as it landed on Cara. "Probably best you don't see this, sweetie."

He may as well have patted her on the head and told her to run along now while the men handled things. The tight smile that pulled at her lips was tight and perfunctory…and radiated rage.

"No. I'll stay." She was the first one to step into the Music Room and flicked on the lights.

The room had been useful for meetings and the likes, since it was half the size of the dining hall, with a small, raised stage near the far left for performances, plenty of room for either around ten tables or almost eighty chairs. Of course, the large gray and charred crater in the center of the room and the radiating damage that had resulted from the same blast, pitting the ceiling, blasting shrapnel into the walls and melting most of the stacked plastic chairs, well, that made the room pretty much useless for anything. Unless you liked the smell of burned plastic and char. Staff had tried fixing it with magic, but at this point using magic to fix it was like trying to paint a wet black wall over with white. Until the magic dissipated a little or mundane methods were used, the damage was done. This was thanks to the Center's Glee Club...who'd been chanting spells, not songs. Gramps and the boys swore they hadn't been part of it, but Mr. Chaimek hadn't been able to hide his smirk.

William followed her in, then Gramps and the boys. Mr. Liko took up the tail, securing the door behind them.

"Cara, it would be best if you weren't here for this," Mr. Einar tried this time, his way of saying it more palatable but grating with its intent.

She shook her head, crossing her arms and standing next to William, where she belonged. "You're the ones who thought we should get married. We have, we're good with it, and I'm not going anywhere."

Gramps gave her one of his rare disapproving scowls, the number of which she could count on one hand. She swallowed the thickness in her throat. The first had been that time with the army kit to protect Maddy.

She readjusted her crossed arms at the memory, but met Gramps's gaze, disappointed or not. She'd understood later why taking his kit to school had been a bad idea, but she'd grown up knowing Gramps and the others protected Beckwell. She'd been trying to protect her little corner of it, and the people in it, like Maddy. Gramps had said it wasn't her job, at least not yet. He'd said the same thing when she'd refused to leave the country for university at eighteen, said she was throwing an opportunity away when she'd said she preferred to stay close to home, take care of the town, he, and Gran.

Yeah, well, now she was taking care of her little corner of Beckwell again. The one that included William.

"There's been a new development since I spoke to

you," William said, glancing at his watch, "twenty minutes ago?"

"Yep, walked right up to as, civil as can be," Liko snarled. "To think we almost bought your bullshit about all hands-on deck." He sneered, slashing his hand dismissively. "You had your head up your ass the whole time."

William frowned. "I'm sorry... I don't follow."

Hermes, wearing his toga once more, stepped through the door.

The bottom of Cara's stomach dropped. William said Hermes always caused trouble.

"Meet Hermes," Mr. Zaki piped up. "Olympian messenger of the gods, estranged from his pantheon, extremely informative."

William stiffened, his gaze flicking once to Hermes, then away, jaw hardening. "What did he say?"

A sick feeling grew in the pit of Cara's stomach, something between a sense of foreboding and the calm sea of a vision sliding through her. Maybe she'd made a mistake. Maybe she didn't want to hear this after all.

Gramps marched up and got in William's face, nose to nose...or would have been if he'd been taller. He poked a finger, hard, into William's chest to punctuate his words. "He said some of what they say about you, about your dealings with the Guardians, some of its true. That whatever else we believed, we should make sure we protected Cara. From you."

Cara could hardly breathe. Everyone was so focused on William, it was like they'd forgotten she was there. Like they usually had, ignoring her on her little stool in the corner of their meetings for as long as she could remember. But why were they so angry with William now, and why would Hermes have said that? What—

William was already shaking his head. "He's a liar. You know that. I've done everything I can to protect Cara—"

"You introduced her to her bloody aunt!" Gramps roared. "The nymphs. Who are dangerous. Who shouldn't be anywhere near her. Gods, Mac, what were you thinking? You've been helping her find more nymphs, when she should be staying as far from them as she can."

"We've gone over this. It was an accident. She's capable of taking care of herself. Obviously more capable than you give her credit for," William said, voice hard.

Cara flinched at the truth. While the Shades may have trained her, they wanted to keep her bubble-wrapped and out of the game.

Gramps slid her a nervous look, but addressed William, his voice rough. "Exactly how far will you go to stop the Guardians, Mac? What and who are you willing to sacrifice to achieve your goals? Because I'll be damned before I'll let you sacrifice my Cara."

Her head spun and nausea climbed her throat. Sacrifice? What— She turned on William. He couldn't. He wouldn't. The stories about him suggested he was ruthless. She'd never believed those. Still didn't...

"We both know you'll sacrifice whatever or whoever is necessary to stop the Guardians. Isn't that what you swore after your secretary was killed?" Hermes said, something about his voice less Hermes-like, familiar somehow...

"Hermes," William growled.

Ignoring William, Hermes's amber gaze met Cara's. "I like you Cara, which is why I feel you should know. William intended to use you as bait. He knew the Guardians were after you, and keeping you close meant he could track their progress, sacrifice you if necessary. That's why he hasn't been quick helping you find the nymphs.

That wasn't part of his mission. You could be turned into a weapon by the Guardians, which in his eyes makes you a dangerous threat…if you're alive."

Her breath seized in her chest. Those pieces of paper William had posted to the corkboard. His informant, the fact that he'd known the Guardians were after her before he came to Beckwell… Throat squeezing, her gaze zipped up, found William. Her breath rasped hard in her throat. The stories… She'd denied them. She'd never believed them. Now…

"Cara," William said, stepping closer.

She stumbled back, holding a shaking hand up to stop him. "What does Hermes mean? William, what do they mean you'd sacrifice me?"

His attention was on her now, and he looked…desperate.

Would an innocent man be desperate? Her throat squeezed.

"I've told you from the beginning why I was here. I need to stop the Guardians. From the moment we met, I've been trying to protect you."

"Before we met… When you got here, when you agreed to marry me… What was your plan then, William? Is that all I am to you? Bait?" Cara asked, her voice soft. Dom had said to trust him, that they were supposed to be together. She'd trusted Dom, but something about the way William emphasized that he'd been trying to protect her since he met her suggested, maybe, he'd intended something different at the start.

"Yeah, Mac, what was your plan?" Mr. Liko sneered, giving an oomph when Mr. Chaimek elbowed him.

William shoved a hand through his hair, shot a glare at Hermes, then back to her. "I'm trying to protect Beckwell, trying to protect all of you. Sometimes, sacrifices must be made. I never—"

She couldn't hear the rest of his words. The excuses. Sacrifices had to be made. *Nothing came for nothing, right, Gramps?* She'd been such a fool. She'd seen the man of her dreams striding into her life to make her fantasies come true. She might have been part of William's fantasies, too, but only the revenge kind. She choked on a sob, covered her trembling lips.

"Cara, please," William begged.

She shook her head, backing away, trying not to let any tears fall.

"Don't worry, sweetheart," Gramps said, patting her shoulder. "We'll protect you."

"Really?" William said, turning on Gramps. "Will you continue to do that by hiding the truth from her? Not telling her what she really is, why the Guardians are after her? Hell, you haven't even told her about the nymphs, her family, her own father. She had to hear that from someone else." He took a step toward her but froze when she lifted her hands to hold him off. "Please, I thought I could… I may have had other plans originally, but that's changed. Now that I know you, now that I—"

"What other truth? What aren't you telling me?" she demanded, tired of the secrets, of the lies, of these men keeping her from the truth. She turned on Gramps, on the boys. "What haven't you told me?" she shouted at them, at the six suddenly guilty gazes surrounding her.

"Cara, sweetheart," Gramps started, "maybe if we talked about this later—"

"Pretty sure this is definitely 'later' enough." Her voice was harder than she'd ever used with Gramps because this was Gramps. He didn't keep secrets from her, not like this.

Not when they were *about* her. Heck, he and Gran had sat her down and told her two years after Mom had died that Dad was getting hitched, starting a new family. Like he could erase Cara and Mom. But Gran and Gramps had told her. They'd always told her.

Hadn't they?

Her vision blurred, and she squeezed her eyes shut a moment. *Your grandmother placed a ward on your abilities,* Aunt Gladys had said. A ward that was killing Cara. Gran, who'd told Cara some people weren't born with much ability. Moisture seeped from her eyes as she opened them, found Gramps. If he could convince her this wasn't real, that it was all a lie…

Gramps and the other Shades shared a look.

Her stomach flipped and her knees trembled. Jeepers, creepers and joe, she hated that look, the history and secrets it implied, shared intentions. The silence excluded her, even when the topic involved her.

"If not Gramps, one of you, talk to me. Tell me what William is talking about," she rasped, turning slowly in a circle, daring each of them to meet her eyes. "What is the rest of it? What is the truth?"

Only William's gaze met hers, but facing him made her stomach ache.

Reminded her what an idiot she'd been, how she'd read too much into sex and kisses and their time together. She'd lost track of where the fantasy ended and reality began. Pain lodged in her throat, pain that made her want to scream and shout, puke. She'd thought she was in love. "Please," she begged, voice breaking. "What is the truth?"

He opened his mouth, as though he'd tell her, as though maybe, there was hope, as though maybe, she hadn't been wrong…

Then he turned toward the boys, shared that look.

Her heart slowed and cold swept through her.

Because he was one of them. Once a Shade, always a Shade.

Part of her, the little girl who'd stolen that med kit, who'd practiced her lessons, learned everything she could from these men, admired them, defended them to people like Jessie, always trusted everything they said…that little girl began to burn. Burning and burning, first into hard cinders and coals, then hotter and hotter until she incinerated. Just ash, blowing and crumbling to nothing.

Cara started to shake, biting her lip so hard she tasted blood. Facts and what she knew spun and coalesced in her head. Irene said Cara could access her Yaga side because Dad had been a Yaga descendant, too. Her aunt said Gran had created a ward stunting Cara's abilities. Dom said that same ward, those nymph abilities were killing her. Jax told her she had magical weight, more than he and William combined.

"Someone say something!" she cried, her voice cracking, a tear slipping free.

Gramps flinched.

"If they have the opportunity, the Guardians will use you as a weapon, to destroy not only Beckwell, but all paranormals they deem undeserving worldwide," William said quietly.

"You're powerful, kiddo," Mr. Chaimek said. "None of us have anything on you. Never have, never will."

"The paranormal equivalent of a nuke," Mr. Liko said, shrugging away the glares of the others. "Well, it's true, and at least that's a way she can understand it."

Gramps gripped his cane, lips trembling as he met her gaze. "It's all true, sweetpea. You're very powerful. Your grandmother saw how powerful you would be the moment we first held you in our arms, precious little baby that you were." He scowled. "Your father being distantly related to another Yaga branch was the only reason I allowed that marriage. That and your mother's tears. I never could have disowned her like my Rose's family did…but for the first time, I almost understood why they'd done it. That fear of the repercussions of a marriage to someone who couldn't possibly understand or appreciate all that your mother was terrified me. Who'd never love all that *you* would be."

All that rage, the little girl who'd dreamed of being a Shade had emptied out of Cara, leaving her hollowed out and aching. Alone.

Gramps twisted his hands together on the cane. "It was evident early on you were powerful, a danger to yourself… and others. You appeared out of nowhere in your parents' bed, materialized yourself wherever you felt like, created objects out of nothing when you were a few weeks old. Your parents were terrified. It wasn't safe…"

He broke off, shaking his head.

No one else in the room dared make a sound.

Cara's throat squeezed so tight she could barely breathe, every muscle in her body screaming for answers, to shake Gramps until he continued.

Gramps stole a glance back up at her. Almost whispering, he continued. "Your Gran knew others would come for you, that they would be drawn to that power…that it could destroy you if we didn't do something. We…we decided we had to hide that power from everyone, including you."

There was no surprise in any of the expressions of the other Shades.

All of them had been in on it. Had kept this from her. Had lied to her.

"It's okay, sweetheart," Gran would say. *"Not everyone is meant to be powerful. You just don't have much ability, that's all."*

Cara tasted acid at the memory. *How could you, Gran?*

"What is it I can do that's so horrible then?" she whispered. "What is it you're so afraid of?"

Gramps, voice gruff, apology gleaming in his rheumy eyes, could barely look at her. "You can alter and reshape reality with a thought. Sweetheart, do you have any idea what that could do? Not just to whatever your subject is at the time, but to you? It could create unseen ripples through the fabric of time, space, and reality, disrupt the very balance of life."

Something whirled inside her, building like a summer storm. A hint of that headache yes, but also something so much deeper. Protection she'd expected. But lying? About who she was? And Gran… Gran who had been her best friend, her most trusted confidante… Her hands shook, nails almost drawing blood as they dug into her skin.

"What. Did. You. Do?" she rasped, forcing herself to say the words, to demand the rest, because, oh, Goddess, it was going to hurt. She didn't need Dom or a vision to know it was going to hurt.

Gramps couldn't meet her eyes. He just shook his head.

Mr. Einar cleared his throat and continued softly. "Nymph magic, performed by your grandmother. Nymph magic is communal, you see, so we had to…we all had to help." He twisted his hands together in front of him, his shoulders slumped. "We had to find a way to block your nymph side, the side that your Gran could connect with. I don't entirely understand how much we did. Or the full extent of what it did to your Gran."

Her glower should have incinerated him on the spot. Red tinged her vision, her breath rasped.

Mr. Einar dropped his gaze.

"You have to understand, princess, magic, abilities—especially like yours—there's always a cost. Repercussions." Mr. Liko tried to speak up this time, his tone timid.

She twisted her head, her gaze stabbing into him. "Yes, I understand that. You've always all taught me that. Nothing comes for nothing, right? Well, then. What kind of cost do you suppose *not* telling me is going to have?" She barely recognized the constrained rage sliding through her veins, into her voice.

Liko cleared his throat and suddenly found his fingernails fascinating.

Her breaths had become choppy, thoughts agitated and jumpy. Part of her said she needed to ask questions, find out more about her abilities, plan, get control of this, get ahead of it. But...but...how *could* they? The Shades? *Her* Shades?

They turned away from her like scolded school children, not men. Alike again. All just playing the same game, part of their own team. This time keeping the truth from her, using her as a pawn.

William stepped closer to try again. "Cara, please, I understand how difficult—"

"Difficult?" She cut him off. "You were going to say this is difficult?" She laughed, a cold, stranger's laugh. She shook her head, the action swift, almost painful. "No, this isn't difficult. Because you know what? Now I don't have to worry so much about hurting them, about keeping the truth from them anymore. What's happening is thanks to you all anyway, isn't it?"

The gazes of the Shades rose to face her, albeit reluctantly. It was almost gratifying, seeing the shame there. Almost. It hurt so much inside, she wanted to lash out, the pain exploding out of her.

"Thanks to all of you, yes, my nymph powers were

suppressed. But maybe you didn't know, maybe Gran didn't know, or maybe it was part of the plan all along, but that ward you all helped put in place? Besides probably shortening Gran's life—at least according to her sister who understands nymph magic—well, that same ward is smothering my Yaga and nymph abilities, causing massive pain, and, if I don't get it removed by someone who understands it, it's going to kill me. So, problem solved, huh?"

There were gasps.

Gramps's eyes widened, his mouth wide. "Oh, Cara. I—"

Somehow, his obvious pain, the shock of the Shades, none of it stopped her in the way it normally would.

"No," she said. "You don't get to tell me you're sorry." Her body vibrated and tears fell despite her best efforts. She turned that glower from Gramps onto each of the others. "All I ever wanted was to be one of you." Her voice cracked, and she cleared her throat, pushed on. "I wanted to help protect Beckwell and other paranormals the way you do. But I was never going to be one of you, was I? Because I was always this big secret you had to keep. A weapon to keep away from your enemies."

She shook her head again, wiping away the tears with the back of her hand unable to bear the sight of any of them for a moment or two, unable to bear their stares, their pity, their pain.

Finally, she faced William. "I loved you," she whispered, then sliding from one Shade to another, these men who'd all been like grandfathers, like heroes to her. Her gaze stopped on Gramps. Who, perhaps more than all the others, had betrayed her.

Guess it was true what they said about never meeting your heroes.

"I have loved you, admired you, depended on you.

Now I need to look out for *me*. I need to find a way to fix what you did and hopefully, maybe, survive. Which means finding the nymphs, my family, and pray they help me in a way you never could…maybe never wanted to. I'll let you know how that goes. You know. If I live."

She strode out of the Music Room, alone, turning her back on the Shades of Beckwell.

Chapter Twenty-Five

LOVE EQUALS PAIN

THE BETRAYAL and pain on Cara's face before she raced from the room was like a knife to his heart. William strode after her. Hell if he knew what he'd say, but he had to try and explain, had to say or do something.

Jenklow caught his elbow.

William paused, turned back to the other man, to someone who'd once been as close a brother. He didn't have time for recriminations and accusations. He had to somehow make this right, find a way to not only protect Cara, but fix this nymph problem.

Jenklow was backed by the rest of the Shades.

William tensed. "I have to catch up with her."

"Keep her away from the nymphs. They'll try to use her, drain her of her power for their own purposes," Jenklow said, voice gruff. He released William's arm, gave him a nod. "And…tell her we're sorry."

His chest loosened a little, making it easier to breathe. He gave the men, *his* men, a quick nod. "I will."

Hermes stepped forward. "Tell her how you feel, since it's clear as the nose on your face you love her."

William dashed out the door after Cara.

Out in the hall, it was clear from the residents wandering amiably toward the rooms, many of them carrying more clothes than they wore, that someone had succeeded in breaking up the orgy. But it also made it more crowded, harder to see where Cara had disappeared to, which direction she'd headed. That one time she'd led him out through a back door somewhere. Was that where she'd gone now? Or had she headed for the front doors? Maybe she'd headed for the dining hall to help.

He excused himself, tried to squeeze between groups of the residents, many of whom, especially the women, smiled and tried to chat him up. He kept his responses clipped and mostly polite, yet he couldn't risk knocking anyone down. All the while, he craned to catch sight of Cara. She'd had a head start. Irene or a nymph or gods knew who else could catch up with Cara first. It'd be worse when she was so hurt and angry.

He'd almost reached the atrium when he caught sight of her dark head, a little taller than some of the residents. Like him, she tried to fight her way through the crowd.

She wasn't outside yet. He could reach her.

"Excuse me. Pardon me." He doubled his efforts to catch up, physically picking up and moving a few residents because it was worth it to reach Cara. She'd been in so much pain.

Because she thought he'd betrayed her. He had to explain. He couldn't lose her. Not like this.

A few steps behind, he dared call out, taking the gamble that she'd want a show down, to have her say. "Cara, wait!" he called. Gods help him if she didn't want to talk.

～

THE CROWD in the hall was almost as suffocating as it'd been back in the Music Room. Gramps and the others, lying to her. Telling her they were sorry, when all they'd done was betray her, not trust her. Cara slid her way through the crowd, avoiding gazes, avoiding her regulars, heck, avoiding the rest of the staff since she should have been helping settle things back to normal. She had to get out of here. After that…maybe she'd go home, try to cool down. Or call Ainsley, who'd say something sweet and comforting. Or…or she'd paint, try and get a clearer vision of what she needed to do, see if she could contact Dom again, get advice.

Or find her relatives. Her aunt again. She'd vowed she'd do that. Maybe she should. Maybe they'd have the decency to tell her the truth. If they lied, at least she'd expect it of them.

Gramps's voice, Gran's, hell, even William, all of them were there in her head. Telling her to be reasonable, be sensible, be practical. Be something that they wanted, fit into their picture, their needs. What the hell about her needs, her dreams?

Her eyes burned and her chest burned. She could have slid down one of the walls to the ground, hidden by the crowds, curled into a ball and cried. Then they'd find her. Gramps, the others. William. A sob caught in her throat, and she choked it back, sliding between more of the crowd, between those who tried to catch her attention, who wanted to talk, who wanted, always wanted something of her.

She'd tried so damned long to be what she was supposed to be. To help the Shades, to be like them, to build a place for herself in this town, this Center. To wait her turn, wait until finally, she could become what she was supposed to be.

All while the people she'd looked to most for approval and love had lied to her. Had kept her from knowing who or what she could be.

"Cara! Wait," William called from behind, further back in the crowd.

No, no, no, no, NO! She ducked her head and pushed onward, giving up muttering apologies to those she slid past, groups she broke through.

The atrium. She'd reached the atrium, where the people were thinner, other than Agnes and Marg doing their flying laps up near the skylights. Once she got there, it was a running leap out the doors, out into the gravel, out of here and away.

She'd almost made it. Almost reached the sofas, started to speed her step, when his hand caught her elbow.

She jerked back, tried to pull loose of William's grip, but although it was gentle, it was firm. She turned with a snarl on her lips. "Let me go. I've heard all you had to say already."

"Cara, please. Give me five minutes. Please."

She couldn't keep the harsh sarcasm from her tone. Didn't try. "Why should I? So you can lie to me some more? Make up more secrets, those you keep from everyone, those you keep from me, those you and the Shades keep. It must be confusing, keeping all that straight. I guess as long as you don't tell me anything, you're all good." She growled the words at him, her throat aching with pent up frustration and helplessness. With him, she'd been stupid enough to think she belonged, that she didn't have to constantly prove herself.

More maddening was the way her eyes burned. "I went in there to defend you. Because I cared about you. Because I thought that maybe, somehow, you and I? It meant something. That I meant something to you."

"You do." William took a step closer to her.

She slapped up a quivering hand, shaking her head, those freaking tears burning hotly down her face as she held him at bay. "No. You're close enough." She pulled on her arm again. "You're hurting me," she lied.

He dropped his gentle grip on her elbow, froze, held both hands aloft, his voice soft. "You do matter. That's the whole point. You've always mattered. Yes, I messed up. Yes, I came here thinking that somehow, I'd be able to keep my distance from you. That I'd do exactly what I always do— anything that was necessary—to complete my mission, to stop the Guardians. But, Cara, the second I met you I knew that wasn't going to be possible." His voice roughened. "I thought I'd have to make the choice. You or the Guardians. That if it came down to it, that I'd…" His words broke off, as though he couldn't quite continue.

"What, just because you're William Fucking Best, superman and hero, you'll save me instead?" she spat bitterly. A small voice whispered inside her that maybe she shouldn't be this angry, that maybe he did have a point, that he wasn't the enemy. She was just so damned tired of being reasonable. Damned tired of always being the one on the outside, the one who had to try harder.

Hell, he was probably here for the Shades and his mission anyway, wasn't he? Because if she wasn't close enough to protect—or control—then he failed.

"You all thought I was dangerous, and that hasn't changed, has it? No matter what I do, no matter how much I try to prove myself, I'm the weapon that you have to stop the Guardians from getting. Like playing keep-away with your favorite toy."

A muscle worked in his jaw and a dark flash of annoyance in his gaze showed he wasn't as cool as he pretended, but he didn't try to grab her, and when he spoke, he kept his tone modulated and calm. "You're not a thing, not a toy. What you do, who you are, that matters. I realized I could never hurt you, because it would mean becoming the monster I wanted to stop. You are so important to this town, to the Shades."

She waited a heartbeat for him to say that she was important to him, too. To tell her somehow, despite the Shades, despite everything that they'd all said, the secrets he'd kept, she wasn't the only one who cared, who'd been so damned stupid she'd fallen for her fantasy of him, or… or something.

But he didn't. He didn't add anything further.

A deepening ache ripped open inside her, deepened her pain, fueled her rage.

"You know what?" She leaned closer, her words a dangerous whisper. "Fuck your plans. Fuck you and the Shades and your secrets. And fuck you, too."

That darkness flashed in his expression again. His jaw hardened. "Cara…" he started, dangerous warning in his tone.

She cut him off with a flick of her hand, hating the tears that burned behind her eyelids, the headache that formed in her temples, the rising pain, the heat inside her that swirled and sucked like a deadly whirlpool. If she let him in, gave he or the Shades an inch, they'd take everything. Like they had. Taken her family, but never let her truly belong. Taken the truth and replaced it with half-truths. Given her training to supposedly protect herself, but never trusted her to do so, let alone protect anyone else, protect Beckwell.

"No. You don't get to tell me what to do. You don't get to protect me, plan for me, keep things from me. This is *my* life. *My* town. *My* powers. I will handle my own damned problems myself!"

William took another step toward her, hands still raised. "Let me come with you. Let me——"

"I said no. Why don't you go home, go back where you came from, and leave me alone!" The words, the emotion, the energy poured out of her in a sudden, head-splitting rush. She turned, heart pounding, breath short, throat tight, stumbling toward the Center exit, toward freedom. Toward something, anything to fix all of this.

William didn't come after her. No one did.

Chapter Twenty-Six

ALL ARE LOST...OR ARE THEY?

WILLIAM WOBBLED, holding his breath as the world solidified around him. Oh, hell. A moment ago, he'd been in the atrium of the Senior Center, trying to convince Cara he wasn't a villain, that she could trust him, and he wanted to protect her. He turned slowly, wind cutting through his clothes, tousling his hair, a winter snowstorm. Now he stood in the middle of a large, open field, snow up to his ankles and flurries flying against his face, melting on his skin. Trees framed the field in an indistinct, dark gray blur.

Directly in front of him stood a faded, weather-beaten whitewashed farmhouse. Windows shattered, most of the roof caved in, a tree grew up through the center of it. The house where he'd grown up. His insides went cold.

Cara had used her abilities against him. She'd made him leave her alone. She'd sent him home...or the one place that had been home, almost a century ago.

He wheezed out a slow breath, his pulse pounding in his ears, the wind howling and blasting stinging ice crystals against his skin. He hunched his body against the gusts as he trudged through the snow toward the buildings' remains. Exposure could mean an attack or freezing. Movement meant maybe finding something in the house to protect him from the elements…and developing a plan to figure out what the hell had happened, and how to get himself back to Beckwell and to Cara.

Back to the woman he loved.

He was a whole province and hundreds of miles away from her. He rammed his shoulder into the farmhouse door that had swollen shut, each blow wedging it open by small increments until he slid inside. What was left of the walls held back some of the wind, some of the snow. That old table Mother used to polish and protect with oil cloth stood near the center of the room, along with the remains of the Hoosier cabinet, one of the upper doors broken off and evidence of a birds' nest where the plates used to rest. The doors on the lower portion of the cabinet leaned against each other like two drunken sailors.

The floor creaked and groaned, almost as loud as the furious wind outside, but other than the root cellar, if the floorboards broke, he'd only drop a foot or so to the dirt beneath. Someone had taken all the burners from the cook-stove, leaving it lobotomized and squatting there, more rust than iron, disintegrating as snowflakes found their way through the shattered chimney.

Mother would have been heartbroken to see her home in this state. Maybe that's why Dad had left these pieces here, a final punishment for her supposed infidelity. She'd been as proud of this house as others would have been of the finest mansion. *Home is where your loved ones gather, where you're safe together, and that is riches enough for me,* she used to say. Funny how he hadn't thought of that in years.

He picked through the wreckage, most of the furnishings gone, a few abandoned odds and ends. A stack of tarps and bits of machinery suggested whoever had bought the house used its husk as farm storage. William folded one of the musty tarps into a triangle and draped it around his shoulders. It kept out more of the wind, and if he tried to walk for the nearest town and telephone, it'd be some help.

After so long trying not to think about this place, the memories surrounded him now. Mother, tired and drawn, slaving over that cook-stove to turn whatever little food they had into a meal but always turning a smile on William when he came into the room.

He edged his way around the tree that had sprung up through the central hall, the back bedroom empty of everything but a two-legged chair, the one beyond that filled with rubble from the destroyed upstairs.

He hesitated at the final bedroom, searching for a mint in his tin, but opening it and finding it empty. This had been Mother's sickroom the last time he'd been there.

That had been the last time he'd spoken with Dad, too, if you could call that phone call from the local general store a conversation. Saskatchewan may have been an early adopter of the telephone, but Dad's near monosyllabic conversation was better suited for telegraph. Maybe it had been a sign that somewhere, deep down, Dad held a remnant of the love for Mother since he'd called their only son when she was dying. *Your mother is dying. She wants you here. Click.* The man made sure to be away from the house when William was here. And they'd stood on opposite sides of that cold grave William had dug in the family plot. Dad had refused to speak a word.

William turned the knob, having to give this one a bit of a hard push to get it to open, too, the door dragging against the floor. Yet when he opened the door, he couldn't step inside. Couldn't get closer to that brass bedframe, what was left of the mattress torn to pieces and sprouting dead grass thanks to animals. He pictured Mother laying there, pale and wan, skin waxy and too close to the skull, a husk of the woman she'd been.

He'd been struck, stomach hard, knees knocking that somehow, she'd gotten old and fragile, ghost-like in a way that made it hard to take her boney fingers in his, skin papery dry. She'd never recriminated him for leaving, that she always visited him, that it'd been years since he'd last visited the house. She'd lifted her lips in a ghastly semblance of a smile, all her love, her pride shining there, like always, like glass shards collecting in his chest. He hadn't deserved that love. She'd closed her eyes later that same day, like she'd been waiting for him. Waiting for him to finally come home.

Hands trembling, he backed out of the room, went back to the front room with the tarps. He hadn't been home in a long, long while. Dad made sure of that. At twenty, Dad told him to get out and not come back. Didn't matter that he could have helped out with the farm. Didn't even get a ride into town or to the next town where he'd found work for the next decade until the first war broke out.

Since then, the Jeeps he'd bought after the Second War had been the closest thing to home, more consistent than any of the anonymous hotel rooms along the way.

Until Cara. Until she'd invited him into the warmth of her home. Into her bed, surrounded by all the things that made it hers, by the little things that made a house more than a wood-framed building with rooms, but a home. She'd invited him into her heart.

Those glass shards dug into his lungs. He had to get back to her. He snatched up another ragged tarp, folded into something like a cloak to hold off the storm. He had to make sure she had a long damn time to get to appreciate her home, her life there. To appreciate her family and loved ones. To live.

He headed out into the snow, the wind tearing at the tarps. Every step he sank into the ever-deepening snow, past his ankles now. A chill soaked through his bones. He set himself due east, toward the nearest highway and town. From there, he'd find some way to get back to Beckwell. Back to Cara to protect her from the damned Guardians. Protect her from people like him.

CARA STEPPED out through the glass doors of the Senior Center into the wind and swirling snow of an early snowstorm. The cold sting of snowflakes against her skin and the bite of the raw wind stripped away the moisture of her tears and gnawed at her bare arms. She inhaled deeply, her head pounding. She closed her eyes, fisting her hands again, bracing herself against the storm and rage. Why couldn't they have told her the truth? What would have been so bad about that? Sure, maybe not when she was a child, but at any time in the past decade, couldn't they have said something?

Couldn't Gran have said something? Before she died?

Cara's stomach clenched and she opened her eyes. Some of the fury had dissipated, enough that going back inside to get her jacket before walking home made sense. It was like she'd burned through the rage when she'd confronted William. Told him to leave her alone, that she didn't need him. Her shoulders sagged and she cradled her forehead a moment. Had she been too hard on him?

He'd lied to her too, though. Using her like bait for the Guardians. No matter what he said about changing his mind after he'd met her, he hadn't confessed the truth earlier. Nor had he told her what Gramps and the others had told him about her powers and their suspicions. Their words echoed through her head. *You're the magical equivalent of a nuke... There are repercussions to power like that... We were trying to protect you.*

Protect her...or protect Beckwell and everyone else *from* her? Wouldn't she have been safer knowing the truth, knowing that she needed to protect herself?

She tipped her head back, letting the snowflakes flutter onto her face, catch on her eyelashes. Taking another deep breath did nothing to appease the yawning emptiness inside her. Worse than when she'd moved here, bewildered and in shock after losing her mother, pushed away by Dad, finding herself in the midst of strange people who all knew each other. She was the outsider who didn't understand the rules.

That aching emptiness was worse than the way the house echoed after Gran's death and Gramps's sudden decision to move into the Center with Mr. Einar and the others, leaving her in a house that whispered with lost voices...but no one to hear her. She wasn't a Shade. They didn't want her. She was barely a wife—she'd been more of a ploy.

"*Cara,*" the wind whispered. "*Come to us. Find us...*"

The door behind her swept open on a soft whoosh and a rush of warmer air.

She sighed, straightening. William. She could hear him out. He hadn't said he cared for her, but Dom had said they belonged together. Dom had always been right. At least, until it came to William.

When she turned, it wasn't William standing in the Center's doorway.

Instead, Gramps and the rest of the Shades stood there, shoulders stooped, all of them...diminished.

For the first time, these men who'd strode like heroes through her life, guiding her decisions, picking her up and dusting off her knees when she fell, planning the directions that drove Beckwell's success and safety, for the first time they looked…small. Shamed. Apart from skinny Mr. Zaki, still the hapless nerd, they were a group of grizzled, stooped little old men. Fragility clung to the curve of their shoulders, the lines of their faces…and their hesitant expressions as they faced her but didn't approach.

Her gaze settled on Gramps in the middle, the most stooped of them all, somehow older and more fragile than she'd remembered, as though she saw him for the first time in a long while. He was the man who'd always been there for her, her staunchest defender, cheerleader, storyteller, and inspiration. Today, the wind could have bowled him down.

Had William taken off after the Guardians alone, without any of them?

A small flush of anger raced through her. So much for him trying to change his ways or mend the rift between them if he'd take off like that.

Maybe some of the rage had died—or maybe the icy wind chased her toward them. She walked back toward the others. "You should get back inside, all of you. You're not properly dressed."

"Neither are you," Gramps said, shooing the others inside.

The others moved between the two doors of the Center, while Gramps remained outside with her, the wind flipping his comb-over.

"Gramps—" she started, trying to get him back inside.

He held up a liver-spotted hand, his blue gaze meeting hers. "We need to talk. It's no excuse, us saying we wanted to protect you—even though that's plenty true. I need to apologize. I'm sorry for not trusting you with the truth, about the Guardians, your abilities, and what your Gran did to protect you. I'm sorry for somehow missing how you've grown into this amazing, beautiful, strong woman who doesn't need any of us old cusses to take care of you."

His words softened some of the sting and she moved closer. "Then why won't you let me help? Help you and the Shades?" Her words were edged with pitifulness that plain sucked, but she forged on. "Why would you keep such a big part of me a secret for so long? I could have helped, made a difference."

He cocked his head. "Does 'because I'm an idiot' cut it?"

She couldn't help the small curve of her lips. "We both know that's not true."

"When it comes to wanting to keep you safe, obviously it is." His thick white brows furrowed, and he dropped his gaze. His voice grew gruff. "After I—we—lost your grand-mother… I didn't know how I'd go on without her." His eyes met hers again, and he shrugged. "I didn't want to go on. If not for you and those old bullies in there, I wouldn't have."

"So why did you leave me behind in the house?" Her voice broke. "It was like I lost both of you. You turned to the Shades…and I was all alone." Like when Dad started his new family and made sure she was too far away to ruin that for him.

Gramps rushed forward, scooping up her hand and squeezing it tight. "Gods, Cara, I didn't… I never wanted you to feel I was abandoning you." He steadied his gaze on her. "You spent so much of your life trying to take care of your gran, take care of me, take care of everyone else. You gave up opportunities to travel, to build a life that was your own. I thought…I thought if I moved out, it would push you to make the house, make your life your own. You didn't have to carry around an old man as an anchor."

Hot tears slid down her face again. "You were never my anchor. You were my lodestone. Helping you, Gran, this town—that *is* my life. This is what I want to do. Like you and the rest of the Shades—and don't you dare interrupt right now if you know what's good for you. Why is it so wrong that I want to follow in your footsteps? You were younger than me when you and the Shades enlisted, when you started your missions and helping the paranormal world. I want to make a difference like that too, if at least in this town. Why would I have to go anywhere else, travel, go to some expensive school half the world away to figure that out? Why…"

She swallowed past the lump in her throat, but forced herself to go on, to ask the one question she'd wondered too long. "Why wasn't I good enough to be a Shade?"

"Oh, sweetheart, you were too damned good for us, a bunch of has-been old men trying to prove we can make a difference. You make a difference in the lives of others every day," Gramps said, eyes suspiciously bright.

He touched her cheek gently, his smile tender. "You've brought such light into all of our lives—mine, Henry, George, Liko, Ted, all of us. We invited you to our meetings because you were so lonely here, so hesitant to get to know people, to trust them after the way your father treated you. Sometimes I hate him for that. But selfishly, it meant I got to have you in my life, got to watch you grow into the woman you are. You have been the light and joy in my life and your grandmother's from the moment we saw you. Yes, we were afraid for you, when we realized how powerful you were going to be, which is why we wanted to protect you. Because what would the world be without that light?" He swallowed. "And now, if you're sick…" He shook his head, voice growing gruff. "It's not right for a man to outlive his children, let alone his grandchildren."

"It doesn't have to be, Gramps. Dom—that's the spirit of the Yaga pendant—they said that I need to find the nymphs to help me."

Gramps lifted a brow. "The Yaga pendant can speak to you? Looks like I'm not the only one keeping secrets."

Cara's face warmed. "At least this one was *my* secret to keep. But yes, Dom spoke to me from the moment you handed me Mother's pendant. They've been there for me, too—and that's also thanks to you."

"Yaga spirit I'm fine with. This explains why you were off, talking to yourself instead of other children your age. Although… I wish you'd told me." Gramps held up a hand to forestall her objection. "Yes, I am aware of the irony. I guess we both made mistakes in that regard. For what it's worth, I'm glad you had that pendant, so you weren't more alone. You'd never open up to your Gran and I, let alone friends."

The words rattled through her. Had she spent all that time talking to Dom so she could avoid deepening her relationships with real people her age?

Something that had continued a lot longer than through school age. Look at how she'd neglected her friendship with Maddy, Ainsley and Jessie. That sense of never belonging… Had it been more in her head than reality?

Gramps shook his head. "All right. Yaga abilities, we've always known you have those. But nymphs?" Gramps leaned closer. "Nymphs are bad news. Never mind the way her own family treated your Gran, she wanted nothing to do with the whole lot of them, and for good reason."

The door whooshed open again, the breath of warm air making it obvious how cold it was outside. Mrs. Cole strode out, the rest of the Shades sheltering inside and watching.

Mrs. Cole glared at Gramps first. "What are you doing outside here, you old fool? You're not going to outlive anyone doing dumb things like this." Her voice was cutting, but she moved swiftly forward, wrapping a knit blanket first around Gramps' shoulders, then handed one to Cara. She raised a dark brow, and put her hands on her boney hips, shifting her bulky burgundy sweater. "Cara, you have more sense than this. What's this about nymphs? I thought I told you where to find those good-looking ones."

Gramps turned on Mrs. Cole with a scowl. "*You* sent her to the nymphs, you old biddy? I was just telling her they're bad news. You know what they did to my Rose and why she hated them."

"Gramps, she wanted to help," Cara interjected. "You wouldn't tell me about the nymphs, and Mrs. Cole told me what she knew about the two nymph twins, Nahla and Caspian." She sighed. "They wouldn't speak to me."

Mrs. Cole's dark gaze narrowed and slid between Cara to Gramps, then back to Cara again, her tone gentle as she spoke to Cara. "I know better than your grandfather what losing her family was like for Rose" She shot Gramps a glare. "I was here while you were half a world away, trying to get yourself killed. Rose loved her family, loved them almost as much as she loved you. She didn't love what her mother expected of her, the expectation that unless she married a god, any relationship had to be temporary because the nymph collective—like a bloody cult, I always thought—always had to come first. It broke her to leave them, to cut herself off from her family and relations like she did, all so she could be with you. I hope you were worth it, you old coot." She turned to Cara. "As for you, I take it you either discovered or they finally told you the truth about what you are. How powerful you're meant to be?"

Cara threw up her hands. "Seriously? Does everyone know the truth except for me?"

Unperturbed—not much caught Mrs. Cole off-stride—the older woman tilted her head to the side, considering, the wind tugging at her turban and a few strands of silver hair. "I swore an oath to your Gran that I wouldn't tell you, no matter that I told her she should tell you the truth herself. She was so afraid that you'd leave for the collective, choose nymphs over any other life you might have. That they'd try to use you. Nymph abilities are as frivolous as the whole blasted species—your dear grandmother being the exception, of course. One never can quite tell how they'll manifest. Then there's this adolescence phase of coming into your abilities. Painful, confusing period, she said. She was hopeful if she cut you off from the nymph abilities for long enough, they'd wither and the Yaga abilities would take dominance."

"That...isn't what's happening," Cara said. "Instead, whatever Gran did, it's cutting off both my nymph and Yaga abilities. If I don't do something about it, it will kill me."

"Well then. I suppose we'd best find some more nymphs," Mrs. Cole said.

"Now wait a damned minute." Gramps inserted himself between Cara and the other woman. "I told you. They're dangerous. How can we know—"

"Oh, enough with your nonsense and paranoia, old man," a different woman interrupted, her voice almost cheery.

Cara turned with the others toward the slim, fashionable red-head, who stood between two huge, pale thugs.

Two dark fey lurches, both wearing slim fitted suits and sunglasses despite the snow. They could've answered an ad for muscle, mean, and disposable.

The woman's presence, though, more than the two slim bullies, chilled Cara in a way the biting wind hadn't been able to. Her throat thickened. Oh crap.

Irene.

The Guardian smiled, teeth glinting. "Now, did someone say something about nymphs? Because, Cara, I know where we can find them."

Chapter Twenty-Seven

THE TRUTH WILL OUT

THE DRIFTING, wet snow soaked through William's clothes, giving the icy wind a direct path to his bones and the tarps flapped around his shoulders. He'd been hiking along the side of the highway for half an hour, not a car in sight. Everyone else must've had the sense to stay inside. Didn't matter. He'd get to town, from there to Beckwell, from there to Cara. He repeated it to himself with every trudging step, head into the wind.

"There you are," an exasperated male—and all too familiar—voice called out from behind. "Cripes, man, I've searched all over for you. Hadn't realized you'd be feeling so nostalgic."

Freaking Hermes. A rush of fury flooded through William. He hunched his shoulders against the wind and walked faster along the shoulder of the snow-covered highway.

There was a waft of warm air, and Hermes—still in the bloody toga and winged shoes, no coat—walked at William's side. Gratifyingly, he'd wrapped his skinny arms around himself, failing to keep out the cold judging by the shiver that shook the ridiculous white ringlets. "Zeus, it's cold enough to freeze Athena's tits off. No wonder you're grouchy all the time, coming from a place like this." Hermes's teeth chattered. "I know things went a little sideways with you, the stooges, and Cara. I was trying to help. She doesn't like secrets, you know. Or people keeping her out. She's more understanding than I'd have expected otherwise."

William's jaw clenched, and he spun on Hermes, almost knocking the smaller man down. "What the hell do you know about her? No. Wait. You know what? I don't care. For the last time, get out of my life."

The light dimmed in Hermes's amber eyes, but his lips set in a thin, mutinous line.

William turned away with a growl. He shouldn't have wasted the time or the effort to tell Hermes anything. The god never listened, never had. Wouldn't turn William back into an ordinary man when William had begged as a young man, wouldn't get out of William's life no matter how many times he was told to. Hell, it'd been less than an hour ago that he'd promised to leave William alone…right before he'd imploded everything with Cara and the Shades.

"You know what, fuck you," Hermes shouted from behind. Another flush of warm air, and this time Hermes stood in William's path. Only…he was tall enough to stare William in the eyes. Hermes flung out his arms. "What do I have to do to prove myself, huh? Oh, yeah, I know. There is *nothing* I can do. Nothing anyone else can do, either, not when it comes to meeting the standards of Saint William."

"I'm not a fucking saint. I've never claimed to be. I just want you out of my life," William said, tarps flapping as he stepped around Hermes.

"I. Know! You've shouted it at me, cursed me beneath

your breath, done everything you can to expel me. Sometimes I wonder why I even bother—"

William stopped dead, long-burning resentment gurgling up inside him. He and Hermes were nose to nose, toe to toe, so damned tempting to bash a fist into that smug stupid face. "Why *do* you bother? Seriously. Tell me. My entire creation was some drunken joke. You didn't want to help me. What am I to you? I'm nothing to you."

Hermes crossed his arms over a more muscular chest than it'd been a second ago. "Do I get to answer the question, or are you going to do that for me, too? Zeus, I see why Cara gets so frustrated. Have you ever asked her what she wanted or just made those decisions for her, like when you decided to save her from herself and the Guardians?"

"This has nothing to do with her." An unsettled twist tightened his gut.

"You're right. It doesn't. It has to do with you. With you having some screw loose that makes you run as far and as fast as you can from anything good that happens in your life. Fuck, William, you're gifted with immortality and inhuman strength, and what do you do with it? Moan and whine about the injustice and loneliness of it all. Enjoy it, make real use of it—and don't start with me about those Guardian twits."

"I don't bitch and moan. I try to make a difference, make my life worth something—which is more than you can say. What are you known for? Flying around delivering messages. Answer the damned question. Why. Why bother with me? Why aren't you out there, enjoying your freaking immortality if that's what you're supposed to do with it?"

Hermes shook his head with something between pity and anger on his face. "This is why you didn't tell her why you came to Beckwell or that you care about her, isn't it?

She'd find out your original shitty plan and it would be a perfectly good reason for you to leave. To run. Just like you always do."

"No, I didn't tell her because I wanted to protect her. Because I care about her, but she's going to leave *me*." William's voice roughened. "She's dying. I told you. That's what your so-called 'gift' gets me. Death. Watching everyone I care about die while I stay the same. I am never one of them. Not human, not mortal, barely paranormal. The fucking Abomination. Now, since you're obviously not planning to answer my question anyway, can you get out of my damned way so I can go and save Cara from the Guardians?"

Hermes's gaze was narrowed and sharp on William, and he stood there, thin-lipped, saying nothing.

Now he didn't want to talk? William shook his head impatiently and moved to step around Hermes.

Hermes sidestepped, blocking William's path.

William's nostrils flared, and he fisted his hands. If he had to lay Hermes flat out on the road, he would. And enjoy it.

The god, though, raised a brow, as though daring William to hit him. "You know, I'll do you a favor. Give you three reasons why you're acting like a bigger moron than usual in this situation." He held up a single finger. "First, you're in the middle of freaking nowhere. In a snowstorm. Walking, it'd take at least four days for you to get back to Beckwell. Too damned late to make a difference."

William's jaw hurt from clenching.

Hermes lifted a second finger. "Second, the reason I continue to try and be a part of your life, to look after you is because despite what you think, I feel responsible for you. Yeah, you might have been created by accident—which is why I wasn't there to explain at first. I didn't know you existed. I gave you part of my godhood—which sounds like something dirty, I know, but whatever, that's what I did." He frowned, his voice lowering somewhat. "I didn't know I could do something like that. Probably really dumb if you think about it, and so we're clear, that makes you a demigod—or in your case, a dummy-god, the way you're acting. You have part of my god essence. Which is what got me kicked out of Olympus when word got around. And, no, I'm not blaming you, just explaining that 'why' like you asked."

The smallest flicker of something fluttered in William's gut.

The dumbass lifted another finger, now holding three aloft, the wind tugging at those ridiculous white ringlets. "Finally, the piece de resistance for why you're an idiot today." He leaned closer. "All those people you claimed died and left you while you watched them die? I call bullshit. That isn't how it went down. Your mother, yes, I'm sorry for that. Good lady—never let me touch her, even when I came to visit for tea and that husband of hers was acting like an ass, catting around town. But a human lady, and humans die, especially when they get old. That's the crappy thing about mortals, but necessary for world population and all. That makes one person dying to leave you behind. That fiancée you had before the war? You left her to marry someone else. Your friends in Beckwell? Don't see you sticking around or answering their letters. Douche move, frankly. Then there's Cara…"

"Don't," William growled, hunching his shoulders, muscles tightening.

"Don't tell you the truth? That you're happier with her

than with anyone else? That if there's such a thing as soul mates or some other shit, she's it for you? Yet you tell her again and again that you're ready to leave—as soon as you're done your super-special more-important than her mission, of course."

William grabbed Hermes's toga, twisted it up around his neck and lifted the god off his feet. "I promised her I'd take care of her. Told her that I'd stay to do so."

The smug bastard smirked. "Yeah? You tell her she was important to you? That you love her? You know, while you and the others were all telling her how she was supposed to live, keeping things from her, I'm pretty sure none of you bothered to tell her how freaking powerful she is, how powerful she could be. What do you think it will be like after she's gone? How much worse will your life be without her, the Shades, anyone else in it? You'll have what you think you want. You'll be alone, and grow colder and darker every day because of it."

Uneasiness trickled down his neck. He'd told Cara he cared about her, at least showed her with his actions, in his touch, his trust. Of course, he had.

Hadn't he?

The mission had to come first. Cara might say the stories, the baggage he came with didn't matter, but did she really understand what life with him would mean? A life with him would bring enemies to their door, danger to her life. He might want more, but she deserved more than that, more than he could ever give her.

William's lips curled, hand still around Hermes's throat, not that the god noticed. "What the hell do you know about me? You appear in my life whenever you feel a little guilty. In all my years, we've spent maybe the equivalent of two weeks together."

"Two weeks, huh?" Hermes said, a hint of bitterness in his words. Ignoring William's hands on his throat, he smacked a hand on William's forehead.

William tried to jerk away, but he was frozen in place, there in the blowing snow, the wind all around them.

Images flashed through his mind. Brighter and clearer, blotting out the highway and the blowing snow, the fields and barbed wire fences around them.

He saw his friend Jax, who he'd met near the end of the Great War, the one who'd guided William into the paranormal world before being killed near the start of the second war.

There was another man, an obsequious batman William hadn't wanted but who'd been assigned to him when he'd been recruited for the paranormal army in the Second World War, always there, always ready with whatever William needed, including a list of good candidates who would become the Shades.

A brief flash of a senior officer, the man William and the Shades had reported to, both during the war, and after, who'd provided William with intel in his hunt to track down the remnants of the Guardians, back when they'd been weak.

There was his dog, Jack, his best friend for years, especially after losing the office and Berta.

Then finally Not-Dog, the inconvenient animal who'd thrown himself into the road in front of the Jeep, who appeared and disappeared at whim.

Who shared the same amber eyes that every one of those other faces had.

William blinked, throat dry, and stumbled back a few steps, able to move again. He blinked a few times more, stepping backward into a snowdrift up to his knees.

Standing in front of him, Hermes didn't look like

Hermes anymore. No more white ringlets, old man face, or winged sandals. His features had shifted, become younger, jaw harder, shoulders broader. Instead of the damned toga, he wore a well-fitted pair of jeans and a T-shirt.

A modern version of his best friend, Jax.

His *dead* best friend Jax.

"No," William rasped, closing then opening his eyes again.

Jax stood there.

"Don't you dare take his face, his image—"

"My own damned face, actually. Modern worshippers expect a particular brand of Greek god, so I gave it to them. Gave that to you." Hermes, or Jax, or whatever the hell his name was, gave an unrepentant shrug, holding out his hands at his sides. "Surprise."

"You. It's been…You were all of them? Why? How could you?" William sputtered. His brain couldn't reconcile the details, let alone decide whether this was good, bad, or something else.

"*Why?* Seriously?" The betrayer widened his eyes. "That 'go away, Hermes,' 'I never want you in my life, Hermes' not reason enough?"

"So you infiltrated my life?"

Hermes/Jax rolled his eyes, crossing muscular arms. "Oh, please. As if it took that much effort." He studied the slush on the ground. "I just, you know, figured maybe you'd accept me in your life if you saw that we could get along." Done with repentance, he shot a quick glare back up at William. "Although you were quick to forget every one of those forms I took, no matter what I did, weren't you? Probably would have pushed me away if I hadn't died first. Like you do with everyone else."

"I…"

"Yeah, yeah," Hermes/Jax grouched, closing the distance between them. "You can thank me later."

William backed away, holding up a hand to ward off Hermes/Jax. "How could you have been so dishonest? Even for you... You can't think I'd be all right with this. That I'd ever forgive you. Geezus, Hermes, or Jax, or—"

"I go by Jax now."

William's teeth ground. "I don't care. When you were Jax, you pretended you were dead. I *mourned* you. You've been playacting, pretending to be some of the most important people in my life, lying about who you were—"

"I was always me. I was those people, not pretending to replace someone else. I just wore a different face. But the man I said I was as Jax, well, he couldn't have survived an explosion like that, and you weren't ready to accept me as Hermes yet. I knew we needed more time."

"That's no excuse. I can't..." William shook his head. "You were my closest friend, men I respected." He scrubbed a hand through his hair and shook his head, choking on a half laugh. "You were my flipping dog. Twice!" He glared at Jax. "I have to focus on Cara. I can't deal with you too. I... Geezus!"

Jax didn't do the puppy eyes or sad face Hermes would have.

He was the steadfast man William remembered, respected...and trusted. More than sixty years ago.

Jax nodded. "Sure. Whatever," he muttered. "Figures. I screwed this up again, didn't I? Well, you better go save Cara. I'll get you there. Then..." His throat worked a minute, shoulders dropping before he met William's gaze. "Then I'll leave you alone. For real this time. Won't come near you unless you ask me to, unless you pray to me." His hand snaked out and he grabbed William's arm before William could think of moving away.

Warm air brushed aside the cold wind for a moment. The next thing William knew, he opened his eyes to find himself in lighter snow, standing in the Beckwell Senior Center parking lot, facing the Center. Facing Cara, who confronted Irene and two of her henchmen.

Chapter Twenty-Eight

NAUSEA BURNED William's throat as he settled into Beckwell after being tossed a few thousand miles yet again, this time by Jax/Hermes/whatever the asshole wanted to call himself, this time landing him in a different snowstorm. His gaze locked on Cara, closer to the Senior Center, Jenklow on one side, tall Mrs. Cole on the other. He was maybe twenty, thirty feet away, closer to the road, while Cara faced down Irene and two henchmen. Dark fey under-sidhe, judging from the pearly hue of their skin. Even he'd have a hard time taking on two of them at once. The only reason they were usually brought in was for muscle… and teleportation. Irene was here to grab Cara.

For a moment, his fingers went numb, breath trapped in his chest. He forced air into his lungs, focused on figuring out how to help Cara.

"Good luck," that bugger Jax said sadly, disappearing with a puff of warm air.

Jax…who'd been his friend, his freaking dog, his mentor—

No. Focus.

William's gaze shot back to Cara. Irene. He started toward them, mouth dry, muscles tense. How did he handle this, other than getting between Irene and Cara? Making sure those under-sidhe goons didn't get close enough to touch Cara. His muscles ached with cold, but he tossed off the tarps, letting them sail off into the wind as he strode forward. He could get between Cara and Irene, hold off those goons long enough for the rest of the Shades to get Cara to safety. Inside the Center would be less exposed…although too many entrances. Maybe they had a safe room somewhere? Dammit, he should have known this, should have talked all of this over with the Shades.

Irene was talking.

Cara lifted her head, said something back, proved she wasn't cowed.

Thatta girl, Cara. Show her you're not afraid.

Albert smart-mouthed Irene, something torn away by the wind.

Invisible to Irene, the other Shades crept around the building toward the action. Liko and Einar from the left. Chaimek and Zaki on the right. Zaki had surrounded himself with a miniature dust storm. Not as great as some of his gadgets, but he'd be able to toss off whatever was thrown at him. Chaimek worked feverishly, light flashing between his fingertips as he created some kind of magical grenade on the fly.

Irene's trilling laugh, carried on the wind, sent chills down William's neck. She only laughed when she knew she'd already won. She wasn't moving in after Cara and Jenklow because she toyed with them. Enjoying the game like a cat playing with its food.

His jaw hardened, he lowered his head and sped his pace. This time, she wouldn't get away, go on to kill other innocents, start more Guardian nests.

His team was in position, ready to attack. He should have been in on the plan. Should have trusted his team and let them help with the case, instead of being a damned idiot and keeping his distance, not utilizing their strengths, the fact that they had the home field advantage.

"We live, I'll make it up to them," he muttered to himself. Irene and those goons would have to go through him to get to the others.

Irene raised a hand, prepared to attack.

"Irene!" he bellowed, at a full-out run now, diving toward her, but instead colliding with one of her goons as Irene's form shimmered, shifting into a dimensional bubble long enough that he couldn't grab her physical form. Good. She did that enough times, she'd run out of juice. She was a talented sorceress, but magic had a cost.

The big guy he'd hit fell hard, but instead of landing under William, de-materialized and re-materialized a few feet away, reached to grab William's head. Definitely sidhe. They could materialize and de-materialize almost as easily as breathing. Shit.

Unless sidhe met iron.

"Get her inside!" William shouted to Albert, jerking a dagger out of his ankle sheath—an iron dagger—and jamming it into the under-sidhe's foot, pinning the guy to the ground.

The sidhe roared with pain.

"We can't move," Cara shouted back. "It's like our feet are glued down."

"Break Irene's focus, boys," William shouted back to the other Shades. Things were going well. He had to focus on that. Not how long it'd been since they'd been in battle, how strong these under-sidhe were…or that they faced Irene, someone who'd taken out other friends, other fighters better than him.

William scrambled on top of the under-sidhe, the two of them grappling. He took a blow to the jaw that made him see stars for the third time today. Got in a hit of his own. Another.

The sidhe slumped, down for the count.

William sagged, gave himself a second to catch his breath before he scrambled to his feet, facing Irene and the remaining sidhe. One down, two to go.

Liko raced around the corner, diving forward with one of his signature moves, a jump and slam dive toward the other under-sidhe.

It caught the goon off surprise long enough that the under-sidhe hit the dust...

Liko plummeted to the ground, moaning and twisted in pain, clutching his bad knee.

The under-sidhe climbed to his feet, an ugly look on his face as he raised his hand to destroy Liko.

Chaimek raced in, throwing a power orb that exploded in the under-sidhe's face.

The under-sidhe screamed as purple flames devoured him. He vanished from sight, sent to wherever the hell Chaimek had decided.

William grabbed Chaimek, shoved him to the side as one of Irene's fireballs roared past, close enough to singe the eyelashes, but missing a direct hit.

Jenklow bellowed out a spell. A mini raincloud erupted above Irene.

William crept closer, dagger gripped in his hand as his team distracted her, and Chaimek kept that last under-sidhe occupied, who'd woken up from his nap.

Next came Einar, or rather, a small army of Einars, all identical replicas roaring out from the corner where he'd concealed himself, lifting a rock off the ground—improvised, but okay, it worked—and hurling them toward Irene.

Only one of them was Einar, which meant there was one rock, but it was a distraction if nothing else—

William gripped the dagger, hand sweaty, a step behind Irene. He lifted the blade to plunge into Irene's back, to end her, once and for all.

Irene held up a hand, a green orb blossoming around her. The fake rocks disappeared as they struck the shield, the real rock bouncing away. Maybe it was those fake bouncing rocks that made her spin toward him, almost too fast to track. Maybe he wasn't as fast as he'd been.

He caught the flash of her smile, the lift of her red brow, before she lifted her hand and blew a puff of powder into his face.

It hit him like a hundred boulders, knocking him on his ass, somersaulting him backward.

Then it started to burn.

Burning particles of sand thrown by a dust storm into his face. Igniting, hotter and hotter, blistering his skin, blurring his vision, pain creeping like darkness in his periphery.

He staggered to his feet, stumbled toward Irene. Saw her spin, this time eclipsing Chaimek in a whirling gray cloud. Einar was knocked flying, back into the hard stucco of the building, crumpling, and laying unmoving after he did so.

No, this couldn't be happening.

Every footstep was like through thick mud, as though he'd been stuck in slow motion. That burning grew worse. No vision in his right eye now. Lungs screaming, left arm going numb. William stumbled forward, dagger gripped in his right. They'd been winning…

Liko was the next to fall, rolled sideways through the air, tossed into a pile of petrified petunias. Barely able to raise his head.

Another step… William gritted his teeth, shoved down

the pain, and forced himself forward. He could do this…
He couldn't let her hurt them…

Chaimek, swallowed by a glowing green orb. The orb lifted him higher and higher, up, up, up…then burst. Chaimek swore as he plummeted, arms windmilling…

Colliding with Zaki's windstorm as the ageless djinn caught him. They landed in a groaning pile.

Irene turned on Jenklow and regal Mrs. Cole. On Cara.

He was too slow. He couldn't make it in time. Couldn't get between her and his friends. The dagger tumbled from numb fingers. He staggered forward, tried to close that last six feet between them. Had to try…

Irene snapped her fingers.

Mrs. Cole raised a brow, flicking her hand, a shield springing up between them, protecting Jenklow and Cara, who remained frozen in place.

"Impressive," Irene lied, her teeth grit so hard he could hear them grinding. "Try this one." She lifted her right arm.

The taller Mrs. Cole gasped as a wave of orange air flew toward her, Jenklow, and Cara. She wavered, staggered back a few steps.

Then Irene raised her other hand.

He was almost there. Two feet more. He reached out his arms. He'd grab her. Make Irene face him instead…

Mrs. Cole gasped. Staggered back another step. Then another, flying backward, Jenklow with her as they tumbled backward, forced back as though by enormous wind throwing them toward the Senior Center.

Toward the crowd emerging from the doors, who caught Jenklow and Mrs. Cole, softened their falls. Men raised sparking canes menacingly. Women pulled knitting needles from their hair, held them aloft, some rubbing the needles together in a shower of sparks.

Only Cara stood now, tugging against her own feet, against the trap that bound her. Hands fisted, she faced Irene fearlessly, fire in her gaze, fury in her stance. "Wow. How brave of you. Taking on a group of senior citizens. You must be so proud," she spat. Her gaze slid momentarily toward William.

He used what strength he had to throw himself toward Irene, maybe break her focus and spell long enough the Cara could escape into that crowd.

All he hit was the gravel that bit into his palms as he fell.

The toes of Irene's shiny red boots wavered in and out of focus.

His body had never felt heavier as he pushed himself onto his knees. He lifted his heavy head enough to see Irene's blood-red lips curve, the sheen of moisture in Cara's gaze, the way she covered her mouth with her hands.

"Ah, William. How nice of you to join the party." Irene smiled, revealing straight, white teeth that should have been spiked and feral. Her face went in and out of focus, the world around him dimming to gray. She leaned closer to him, the sudden movement making him blink. Her ringing laughter twisted his stomach. "The mighty champion, how he does fall."

Her hand snaked out, grabbed his chin and twisted his face upward, to face her.

She leaned in close, as though to kiss him. Her form slipped from crystal clear to fuzzy. The world trembled around him.

This close, the fine sheen of sweat on her forehead, the scraggly red hairs out of place made it obvious that while they may have failed, she'd taken a beating, too. It was something.

Her grip on his chin was painful, nails digging into his skin already ravaged by those pinpricks of pain eating through his flesh. "Did you enjoy my little surprise for you, William? I made it just for you. Something guaranteed to set old Zeusy flat on his ass. Ash from Ophiotaurus entrails, a creature reborn to life thanks to the Guardians, once used by the Titans to try and defeat the Olympians."

She waved her hand, or at least, it looked like she waved it. There was a pale kind of blur. "I added my own twist. It's so new I haven't given it a name, but I think I'll name it after you. In memoriam. Perhaps the Fly Swatter. You always have been the fly in the ointment. So falls the Abomination. Once and for all."

Someone was crying, soft sobs. Cara.

All he could make out was a faint blur in front of him. He tried to open his mouth, to tell Cara it was okay. Even if he'd failed, the rest of the Shades wouldn't. They'd always been better men.

He couldn't manage the simple muscle command. The stinging faded, like everything else. Well, shit. After all this, now he'd die. Just when he knew what he needed to fight for. Before he could make things right with the Shades.

Before he had a chance to tell Cara how he felt, to keep his word and protect her. The only mission that mattered. He'd been made to love her.

Dullness might have numbed the pain, but it didn't numb Irene's shrill ringing laugh as she released his chin.

He fell, face first, into the gravel, luck turning his head sideways so he could breathe. He didn't have the strength to struggle, even as she brought her boot, hard, onto the side of his head, grinding his face into the gravel.

Cara screamed at her to stop, the sound echoing through William's head.

Irene snapped her fingers.

Cara went silent. As though she weren't there anymore.

He tried to turn, to find her. To move. *Gods, Cara…*

Irene leaned in close. "How does it feel, William? Knowing you've failed. That you'll die a failure, under my boot. I've made a deal with the nymphs. They help me destroy this useless pustule of a town, and they get to keep Cara. For now, at any rate."

He closed his eyes, self-loathing filling him. He'd been too arrogant to think this would ever be him. Hadn't used his time for what was important. Hadn't realized what *was* important. Like spending that time with those he loved, the pain of loss be damned. Now it was too late.

His breath wheezed and rattled, his lungs inundated and burned out with Irene's dust. Black crept in.

"Oh, for fuck's sake already. You've always played dirty, but this?" Jax said.

William sagged, lips twitching. One more time, after promising to stay away, here he was. Thank gods.

"This is worse than playing with your food. You're not even planning to eat him," Jax continued.

Irene swore. "You're on my list next, you spineless worm."

"Point in fact, there's nothing wrong with invertebrate. Especially ones that can grow back parts of their bodies. I'd be cool with that," the smartass said.

If he could, William would've laughed. Jax had always been better with witty repartee. But it was too late. He sucked in a rattling breath and settled into the black.

Chapter Twenty-Nine

THE GUARDIANS

"WILLIAM!" Cara bolted upright, immediately regretting the action as intense pain stabbed through the top of her head and eyeballs. She groaned, closing her eyes against the light, the warmth surrounding her. She lay on something soft, maybe a bed, blankets covering her legs. The air was warm and floral scented. Even her clothes felt different, not the pants and shirt she'd been wearing, but a long gown that lay heavy against her skin. What the…. She'd been outside the Center, in the blowing snow, attacked by Irene, trying to figure out how she could help William and now…

"Shh. Slowly. Give yourself time," a female voice said, the voice raspy yet familiar. A gentle hand, cool and soft, cupped her forehead. That sense of cool water rushed over her.

Despite herself, Cara couldn't bite back the groan at the intense pain ricocheting through her. Her aunt. That's who it sounded like. "A-aunt Gladys?" she said, her voice a whisper.

"The one and only. Perhaps you should lie down again—"

"There's no sense in that that. Come on now, m'dear. It's going to get worse until we get you into the nymph pool and get that block removed. You tried to perform magic alone again, didn't you?" This voice was also female, again reminiscent of Gran and Aunt Gladys, but a bit harsher than Gran had ever sounded.

Cara struggled to piece together how she'd gotten here. There'd been Irene and the attack…whatever she'd done to William while Cara was forced to stand there, helpless. Fury and something more had rushed through her, consumed her. She'd sworn she'd heard Dom's voice, a whisper, a warning. Whatever enchantment trapped her in place had started to melt away.

It'd been like a living dream in the back of her mind, picturing what would happen, what she'd do, how she'd help William, Gramps, the boys. The power had rushed up inside her ready for her, but then pain had exploded through Cara's mind. Dom's voice screamed in agony, or maybe it was the sound of her own screams… Then that red-headed monster had turned on her, smiled, snapped her fingers, and…

Cara groaned, the pain back, biting into her skull, blurring the lights around her, wave after wave of agony.

"Quickly. Get her upright. We've waited long enough. We need that block removed now. We're losing her," the harsher of the two voices said.

Warm, female arms surrounded her, lifted her off whatever she lay on.

Cara flapped at them, the pain making it hard to accomplish the simple action. "No," she said, or hoped she said. "I—who are you? Where am I? What have you done to me?"

"Later," the harsh voiced one said.

The two women carried her between them, her toes brushing the damp stone floor. The air warmed, grew humid and sticky as they crossed the room.

Cara forced her eyes open, head lolling, to find on her left was her slim, attractive aunt, who she'd met that day she'd foolishly run off. Not aunt. Great aunt. Gran's sister. The woman smiled gently at Cara, tension bracketing that smile, her face unlined.

"How could Rose have been so selfish?" the harsher voice said.

Cara forced her head to the right.

The harsher-voiced woman resembled both Gran and Gladys. A few more lines on her regal face, but greater beauty, too, her cheekbones more pronounced, her dark, curly hair swept up into an old-fashioned topknot. Her scent, like Aunt Gladys, was somewhere between floral and walking outside into spring's fresh sprung leaves.

Cara's toes brushed water.

Oh, Goddess, they were going to drown her!

Cara struggled with what strength she had to pull away from the two. She wouldn't die this way. Not after all of this, not—

Another wave of pain ripped through her, dropping her onto her knees into the shallow water, her fall softened by the women catching her again, lowering her gently. The water brushed her knees, warm as her skin, and soaked the heavy gown.

The one with the formal topknot, the beautiful high cheekbones, placed her face in Cara's view, her lips tight, tension bracketing tiny lines around her eyes and adding a decade to her age, but so much like Gran whenever she'd comforted Cara, come to her aid after a fall, dried her tears.

Cara choked back a small sob. Gran, who she'd loved so much. Gran, who'd betrayed her.

The woman's expression softened a little. "Child— Cara— I wish there were time for longer introductions. I wish we'd met you earlier, would have, if Rose hadn't concealed you from us. We tried to call out to you, to contact you, but the ward has been blocking you from finding us, and us from finding you. We are your family. You've met Gladys, your grandmother's sister. I'm Magnolia, your great-grandmother. We're trying to help you."

Another wave of pain was coming. Oh, jeepers, creepers and joe, it was coming—

"Quickly, Gladys. Take her hand..."

Magnolia took one hand, Gladys took the other. That cool, water-like sensation rolled over Cara, tried to mingle with her essence, too, but hers was a raging storm inside, and flashed back on them.

The pain hit, and the coolness dimmed the pain, but left Cara gasping, blinking, trying to focus on either of the women, stay upright and not fall face-first into the water.

"Cara? Cara, listen to me child."

Cara struggled to focus on the older woman's face that blurred in and out of focus with each ragged breath.

"You must have tried to do some powerful magic out there, alone. The ward is fighting your power. Do you understand? The ward your grandmother placed is holding back your ability. It's like a seawall trying to hold back a tsunami. But that ward is tied to your essence. If it breaks, so too, I fear, will you. We're trying to get you to the nymph pond. Gladys told you our abilities are collective, didn't she?"

Cara tried to nod, tried to make sense of the woman's words. Oh, Goddess, not another wave... Please...

"Lift her. Come on, I'll keep talking so she doesn't fight

so much, but we've got to get her in there," Magnolia ordered, addressing Gladys before she spoke to Cara again. "That's right. Don't fight us. You'll see, it's just water. We'll get you into the pond, and we'll remove that block. I wish it didn't have to be this way, Cara. That you'd come to us before it was this bad. We could have more slowly introduced ourselves, introduced you to your abilities, to the world of the nymphs. Unfortunately, the magic dear Rose worked is crumbling and it's going to destroy you. We're trying to save you. We don't want to hurt you."

They carried her into water that grew deeper and deeper. Whatever she was wearing, the skirts of the gown clung to her legs, pressed against her skin as they grew water-logged. Yet the water was peculiarly warm, the temperature of her skin, more like thick tropical air than entering water at all.

"Guardians. You're—danger," Cara tried to gasp, another flash of pain driving through her. She would have fallen if the women hadn't gripped her firmly between them, leading her deeper and deeper into that water.

"Let's worry about those details later, shall we?" Magnolia said firmly. "First, we need to save your life."

LIGHT SURROUNDED HIM. Warm light. He wasn't cold anymore. Was this heaven then? Knowing the paranormal world, he'd had his doubts about that being real.

A hand shook his shoulder roughly, Liko's voice accompanying it. "Come on, Mac. Enough lying around. Time to get up. We've got to find Cara."

Definitely not heaven, if Liko shook him awake.

William grimaced, fighting his way through the blanket of darkness, awakening to the aches and throbs of his body, the faint hot splotches on his face. Wisps of memory flashed through his head. Cara, being attacked by Irene. The Shades tossed about like toys. Irene's glee, that expression on her face as she'd turned on him…

"Drink up." Jax shoved a flash of sweet, floral-smelling water in William's face.

It was drink or choke as the liquid poured in his mouth and down his throat. As he drank, the aches faded. The angry burn of his skin cooled. He cracked opened his eyes, vision clearing to reveal three familiar faces above him— Einar, Liko, and Jax, all hovering.

The floral water stuff was restorative. Enough that he grabbed the flask from Jax to stop the water torture.

"Enough already," he half-gasped, half-growled. He held up the flask. "What is this?"

Jax snatched the flask back, closing it and tucking it into an inside jacket pocket. "Ambrosia, what else? I've been dousing your coffee with it for years. You've got the power of an Olympian, so you need some of the fuel, too."

"Ambro—" William broke off, heat building in his chest, uncertainty dropping in his belly. He shook his head. Ambrosia, elixir of the gods. Because he was a demigod. Jax had told him that… And at some point, he'd have to figure out what it meant. After he made sure Cara was safe. He pushed himself upright. His body ached like a bruise, but his vision cleared. What the hell…

The room was fairly large, walls panelled in faux wood where they weren't covered by posters, photos or maps, floor polished concrete, all of it lit from above with thin, buzzing fluorescent light. The center of the room was dominated by a large, battered war room table and a set of mismatched chairs.

"What is this place?"

"HQ," Liko said gruffly, his chest puffing out as he

surveyed the space. He settled a glare on William. "Figured you'd finally kicked the bucket. Would have, if not for this guy. Jax, isn't it? He saved our collective asses, helped drag your very heavy one down here."

William glanced from Liko to Henry for confirmation, who gave a short nod. Finally, he turned to Jax. He sighed. "I suppose I owe you my life." Again. Hell, if Hermes was Jax, that debt added up.

Jax raised a brow. "Along with your undying gratitude. Actually…" He made a show of tapping his finger on his chin. "You owed me your life before. You know, for creating you, making sure you lived past infancy…"

"Jax," William said, a slight growl to his tone, but lips twitching. Hermes he'd never warmed up to…but Jax? Jax was a different story. To think of them as being the same person…

Liko cleared his throat, crossing his arms over his chest. "If you two are done kissing and making up, can we get on with finding and rescuing Cara?"

"Of course. Cara." He forced himself to his feet. His knees went soft, collapsing beneath him as he grabbed at air.

Liko caught one arm.

Jax caught the other.

Together the two men jerked William upright and gave him a second until his knees steadied.

"For the record," Jax said to Liko, leaning around William, "if I was kissing and making up, I wouldn't have finished so quickly. I like to take my time." He gave Liko a wink and an air kiss.

Liko's eyes rounded, and he dropped William's arm. "Jax, Hermes, whatever you go by, I don't… I'm not…"

William snorted, pulling free of Jax and giving Liko a

firm slap on the back. "Don't let him irritate you, Liko. It'll make him happy."

"I'm very easily satisfied. One of my better qualities," Jax amiably agreed.

Liko wandered away, muttering beneath his breath.

Einar gave William a long look. "You settled there? We don't have time for you to keep collapsing."

Jax leaned closer to William. "I told them before you rushed into battle like an idiot, you'd confided you wanted to tell them how sorry you were to have underestimated and treated them so badly. Men you trust and respect, always had, always would."

William shot a glare at Jax. "I didn't…"

Einar's raised brow shut William's mouth.

The rest of the men across the room in front of a map now turned, awaiting his response.

Jax widened his eyes, the message clear: he'd be a dummy if he didn't start with the grovelling.

Part of William knew he owed them as much. He faced the Shades. His men. His friends. "Thank you, Jax. For passing on my message. Because…" He lifted his chin, made sure to meet each of the men's gazes. "I've been an ass. And a coward. During the war, I was damned lucky to have met you, all of you." Jax likely had a hand in bringing them together, too—another debt he owed the bastard. "You showed me then the strength of the family you make versus the ones you're born with, and I've spent too long trying to deny how much you all mean to me. I kept my distance because I was so afraid of losing you. I'm sorry."

He cleared his throat, all that honest emotion making him queasy.

Liko grunted, turning back to the long wall that was covered in maps, many of which were of the local area. Chaimek stood next to him, holding a smoking bowl and letting the smoke drift toward the maps in a basic locating spell.

Zaki, without much discernible reaction in typical-Zaki fashion, returned to fiddling with whatever gadget he'd created on the table in front of him, Jenklow observing.

Henry, though, gave William a hard pat on the shoulder before going over to join Liko and Chaimek with the locating spell.

Leaving William and Jax standing in the middle of the large-ish, subterranean room, judging from the faint musti-ness of the space, and the stairwell at the opposite end, leading upward.

Jax offered an encouraging thumbs-up, waving William toward the others like a mother hen.

William cleared his throat again, voice gruff as he approached Liko and Chaimek near the large wall map. "Can I help you all find and rescue Cara? Maybe we can get rid of Irene and the Guardians, once and for all this time."

Liko glanced over his shoulder with a raised dark brow as William approached. "Get rid of that monster? Of course. Find Cara? On it…or trying." He nodded toward the map. "Chaimek and Zaki worked up a locator spell which should have been foolproof. Except for Chaimek."

"You're criticizing work you barely understand. That's rich," Chaimek grumbled, moving the smoking bowl up and down the map in a grid-search pattern. "The ley lines are throwing off my search. Beckwell is built on a conver-gence of them, part of what makes it a magical vortex."

"Zaki probably did most of the work and you're taking credit," Liko sniped back. "You're telling me you're magi-cally guiding that smoke? You know, the stuff that's getting us nowhere?"

"George was very helpful," Zaki called from across the

room, ears as sharp as a bat. "Messages sent via ley lines are easy to intercept, but the Guardians haven't been using that old method of communication, so we haven't caught anything that way, either." There was a small poof, and then the scent of burning.

Einar and Jenklow, both coughing, moved away from the table where Zaki had been working.

"Almost there," Jenklow said, trying to sound encouraging as his eyes watered and he covered his mouth with his sleeve. He approached William, patted his arm. "Zaki's working on a backup plan. Like one of those modern tech gizmos that tell you where to go, but able to track magical energy. Someone like Cara or a group of nymphs is going to put off power. At least, that's the plan."

"She could be on another plane or a space that isn't visible to standard geography," Jax said, wandering over to Zaki, unbothered by the smoke. "If you're not careful, that thing will also pick up any local gods, groups of magicals like a werewolf pack, the exit of the central Beckwell vortex…"

William didn't hear the rest because Henry and Jenklow took up positions on either side of him.

"Think that grovelling was genuine, or is it a new ploy to get our information then leave us old men in the dust?" Jenklow said, as though to Henry.

Henry raised a white eyebrow, leaned close, as though studying a science specimen. "He wouldn't be that stupid, would he? We're either a team and speaking in 'we' terms…or it's him and us. He can leave anytime he likes." He gestured toward the stairs at the far end of the room, then speared William with a look. "Door's right there. That's what you swore you'd do, wasn't it? Leave."

Jenklow and Henry had always been the heart of the team. If they didn't believe he was genuine, it wouldn't matter if he convinced Liko, Chaimek and Zaki. Nor would arguing that he'd never have left before the mission was complete win them over.

He glanced at Jax over near Zaki, who raised a brow in answer, as though saying this one was on William, before he returned to Zaki's project.

Jax had accused William of pushing people away so he didn't have to deal with their loss. The way he'd kept his distance from home and the remembered pain back there. He glanced at Chaimek and Liko, always bickering but they had each other's back despite a complicated history, then to Jenklow and Einar, brothers even before the war.

"When we first formed the Shades, I didn't want to like any of you," William said, voice rough. "I'd already lost too many friends, too many brothers in that first war, before I even knew what I was. Before I knew that when they died, I walked away." Nausea prickled his belly, and his chest was tight as he searched for the right words.

He half-laughed. "Of course, none of you let me keep the distance of command. Hell, with the kind of missions we ran, the kind of team we had to be, that was never going to happen. Didn't matter much what I wanted anyway, because I found myself part of a family. Part of a group of brothers who protected each other, had each other's backs, no matter what." His voice dropped, along with his gaze. "The thing that scares me, always has, was that at any moment, I could lose one of you, and your death would be on me."

He forced his gaze up, met Jenklow's steady gaze. "After we almost lost you, I swore I wouldn't face that again. No more hospital beds, no more letters home to loved ones, telling them you might not survive... or worse. After the war, I said no more. No more watching you have all the things I was jealous of—getting married, kids, having the kind of life I couldn't. Things I didn't think I deserved. I took the coward's way out. I stayed away."

"Until Cara," Jenklow said quietly.

William rubbed a hand over his face. "Until Cara. Who reminds me what it's like to have a family, to have a home. To have hope. Please, let me be one of your again. Let me help track Irene and the rest of the Guardian scum. More than anything, help me get Cara back. So I'll have a chance to grovel for her forgiveness, too."

For a long minute or two, Einar and Jenklow shared a glance, then turned back to William. Studied him. Let him sweat.

Jenklow stepped closer, clamped a hand on William's forearm, and offered a small half-smile. "None of us are perfect. But once a Shade, always a Shade. Good to have you back, Mac. Let's go find Cara."

Chapter Thirty

TEMPTATION

TRUSTING THESE NYMPHS–NYMPHS who Gran had escaped before concealing Cara from them—seemed like a bad idea. But the pain was so intense, Cara couldn't protest as Gladys and Magnolia lowered her into the body temperature water. Water buoyed her like clouds, the lights in the grotto dimming. While the water came to chest height on both of the other women, they supported her so she floated on her back. Pain receded with the wonder and strangeness of it.

"Wh-what's happening?" Cara gasped. Her body begged her to relax into the water's embrace.

"This is our nymph pool, something that facilitates the connection between our people," Magnolia said, voice flowing over Cara like the water. "It's how we help each other carry away the years, disease, pain. Let us help you now, Cara. We're going to remove the block, but you'll feel very overwhelmed once your abilities are freed. Remember, we're here. You're not alone. As a nymph, you never have to be alone again."

"You're Guardians. I shouldn't—" A wave of pain

rolled over her again. Cara stiffened in the water, which rolled over her in a warm wave, soothing away the agony.

"We can answer your questions, assure you of your safety later. After we've removed this block. We must do it now, Cara," Magnolia insisted.

"I—"

Gladys squeezed her hand and offered Cara a sweet smile so reminiscent of Gran it made Cara's insides squeeze. "Please, Cara. Relax into the pool. Let it, let us carry you. You're safe. We're here to help."

Despite the racing thoughts in her head, Gladys's words were hypnotic, easing Cara's muscles, letting her float on the pool's surface. Floating so easily, in fact, that both Magnolia and Gladys removed their hands from beneath her back, resting their fingertips lightly on her upper arms on either side of her.

The two women began to sing. Or at least, singing was the closest thing like it. The sound was soft at first, like a breeze whispering through grasses and rustling leaves, an invitation to close your eyes, let it tousle your hair, brush against your face like a lover's kiss. The sound resonated through the pool, vibrated against Cara's skin, echoed through her blood, made her eyes close and her head sway.

The sound grew louder, more intense. A wind foretelling the change of weather, bending and swaying the saplings. This time Cara almost understood the words, even if she wasn't certain they were spoken aloud, or if they whispered over her skin, skittered through her blood, through her soul.

"Sisters, we call, sisters we are. We heal. We join. We heal. We join…"

Gladys and Magnolia's voices were joined by others, so many female voices. Voices and voices blurring into the rush of water and the flutter of leaves as the wind chased through the trees.

The wind or chant grew within Cara. Rushed through her like a current. Pain exploded through her. She cried out, body going taut in the water.

Then, as though the top of her head had flown open, the pain evaporated. Cara gasped at the enormity of it all as it opened to her. The block that had kept her from Dom, from connecting with the universe was gone.

The voices were richer, each of those souls, each of those women united, with her, holding her. Their stories, the threads of their lives, their essence flowed through her.

Through them, the entirety of the world rushed by, past, present, and future. She felt it all, saw it all, everything. Right there.

"No! They're going to destroy you! They're going to melt you away. Devour you. Run. Run. Run!" Dom yelled, drowning out the chant, destroying that flow, breaking the peace. With the block gone, they were louder and clearer in her head than they'd ever been before.

The pendant grew hotter and hotter against her skin, steaming away the water, burning.

The ideas, the threads, the certainties, the possibilities, the names, the faces. People, voices, all of it tore through her, crushed and ricocheted off of her, like she was flotsam trapped in the current. She'd be torn to a million pieces. Erased, obliterated. No room to gasp, to splash, to fight back.

"Fight! Don't give in to them!" Dom cried.

Cara's lungs burned for air. She could barely remember that she *was*, let alone how to gasp. The pendant burned and seared her skin. She screamed.

"It's going to be all right. We're right here," Gladys said from Cara's left.

"You're never going to feel alone ever again," Magnolia promised from the right. More softly, to Gladys. "This is worse than I expected. Something's wrong."

The pendant burned hotter and hotter, scorching her skin, blistering through her.

The waves of souls, the water, all those voices tore her apart.

"Get out of here. Get out of the water! Don't let them touch you. Resist, Cara, resist!" Dom cried.

She thrashed. Water rushed up and over her face. The voices thundered.

"The pendant. Get the pendant off her!" Magnolia said.

"No! Don't let them take me. They will hurt you. You can't trust them. They want to control you. They are—"

Dom's voice was cut off, silent. The burning relieved, as the pendant left Cara's neck.

Where was Dom? She needed Dom.

The voices, all those voices.

She flailed, struggled to find her footing on the pool's slippery stone floor, to push upright. She had to get out of here. Get back home. To…to William. Yes, she needed to get to William.

Wiry-slim arms caught her on both sides. Magnolia and Gladys, helping her upright, holding her head above the water until her knees and feet were beneath her.

Cara stood, gasping for air, vision blurring in and out, the room too dim, everything around her indistinct blurs. She pressed her hands to her ears. "I can hear them. Why can I still hear them?" She cried, trying to drown out the voices.

They weren't coming from outside her. They were inside her.

Oh, Goddess, what had she done? "What did you do to

me?" She gasped, sinking into the water as her knees weakened.

Magnolia and Gladys, though, were right there, cradling her.

"You're not alone. We're right here. Give it a minute. Feel the water. Listen to your breath. Listen to my voice. You're in no danger here," Magnolia said, her voice hypnotic and soothing.

Cara groped for the pendant, her fingers coming away empty. She swivelled her panicked gaze between Magnolia to Gladys. "My pendant! Where's my pendant? I need it. I—"

"Shh. It's all right. It's over there, on the ledge beside the pool. Do you see?" Gladys pointed toward the far side of the pool, where the pendant's amber stone glinted in the faint cavern light.

Cara started toward it, but her knees couldn't hold her...or her feet wouldn't carry her. She floundered, sank below the surface again. "Please, I need it, I—"

"You're fine," Magnolia said gently but firmly, meeting Cara's gaze. "The pendant had an...adverse reaction to the pool. We've removed the block, but we must complete the ceremony. We must initiate you into the nymph collective."

The pendant didn't look damaged.

Magnolia waited expectantly.

Cara studied Gladys's expression.

The younger woman avoided Cara's gaze.

Cara turned back to Magnolia again. Her vision cleared, as had her thoughts, although a sense remained of being...lost, not sure she was herself. "I... I don't think I want to."

Magnolia smiled indulgently, like a mother who knew she'd eventually be obeyed. "Rose felt the same way. Even I did when it was my turn. It can be overwhelming, frightening even, to encounter the collective for the first time. It is for all of us, and for you more than most." Magnolia's calm steady voice was so much like Gran's, like when she'd kiss Cara's skinned knees, tuck her in at night with a bedtime story and a kiss on the forehead, or sit crocheting in the corner while Cara and Gramps played a rowdy game of chess.

"You're part of the Guardians. Gladys told me as much. I can never support harming other paranormals. Judging or wanting to eradicate someone because they have human lineage is wrong. I..." She tried to move toward the edge again. They'd come from the other end, hadn't they? Where it was shallower? If she couldn't walk out, she'd crawl. Retrieve the pendant and Dom...

"How does initiating you into the collective, protecting you from the pain of entering your abilities hurt anyone?" Magnolia said. "Cara, the collective will relieve all your pain, from minor pain like your monthly cycle, to childbirth. Together, we help each other defeat aging and premature death, so while we aren't immortal, we appear as such. Your grandmother turned away from the collective, from that community and family. That doesn't have to be your choice. Imagine a life where you never have to feel alone or isolated again. Where you are always surrounded by a sense of loving acceptance and belonging. Wouldn't you want that? Don't you at least want to know what that feels like before you tell us no?"

If there'd ever been the perfect kind of bait for a trap, this was it. That hollow ache in the pit of her stomach echoed, the one that envied Mom and Dad's closeness but never felt part of that circle. Who'd watched other kids play on the playground in Beckwell, but never quite belonged with them. Who'd tried so damned hard to prove herself to Gramps and the Shades, but had never been welcomed as one of them… What would it be like to experience unconditional acceptance and connection?

William's face hovered behind her eyes. The tender way he'd hold her after they made love, the connection between them when they touched. He hadn't said he loved her, but when she was with him, words or no words, she was safe, she was connected. They belonged together.

"I don't know…" Cara glanced again at the pendant. Were Dom's warnings an adverse reaction to the nymph pool? They'd been freed after the block was gone, louder and stronger than ever before. Dom had been more frightened than she'd ever heard them. Her aunt and great grandmother didn't deny being Guardians.

"We're not asking you to be Guardians. Nor to commit to anything right now," Gladys said.

"Indeed. I understand, especially with what Rose must have told you, why you hesitate." Magnolia clasped Cara's shoulder. "Please, won't you let us at least initiate you into who you were meant to be? You'll always wonder otherwise. Coming into those abilities later might be impossible, and certainly more frightening and overwhelming without our guidance. Please, Cara. Allow me to do this. For Rose."

Cara's insides squeezed, and she bit her lip. If she wanted to help Beckwell and protect people, then she needed to know what she was capable of. That's all this was. She'd fought it off once. She could again, if necessary.

She gave a small nod.

A smile broke over Magnolia's face, erasing years and revealing startling beauty. "All right. Let us help you…"

Both she and Gladys supported Cara, got her floating on the surface of the pool.

Cara took a deep, shuddering breath. The water

against her skin, the slight hint of whispers tickling through her was strange, but she could do this.

"Close your eyes… Yes, like that," Magnolia said, voice hypnotic and soothing as she and Gladys lay their fingertips on Cara's upper arms. "Let us guide you, let us help contain you, hold back the flood. It gets easier the more you relax."

That whispering chanting-breeze-sound grew. It flowed through her, around her. The water enveloped her.

Magnolia and Gladys clasped her hands, one on either side, their voices blending with the others. They held back the worst of the wave. That sense of connection, of togetherness, of all-knowing and the universe's greatness, laid out before her returned.

She remained, too. Along with that sense of self came the sense of hundreds of hands and bodies near her, supporting her, cradling her. Like when Magnolia and Gladys had touched her arm, but so, so much more. There was a sense of everyone being in exactly the right place, supporting each other even from hundreds of thousands of miles away. Brief glimpses of the others filtered through her, senses of the people they were, of their abilities, their needs, the way she would support them when she was strong enough.

As before, the trickle increased to a tidal wave, overwhelming her, pulling her under. Too many voices, too many demands, needs, futures. The flood raged through her, tried to wash her away.

"You have to surrender to it, Cara. Accept it. Accept us," Magnolia said, still in that inexorable, steady voice. Like the voice of truth itself.

"It may not be the same for her," Gladys said, an edge of concern in her voice, which only increased Cara's fear, her need to try and jerk free.

"Hush," Magnolia said, an edge in her voice that tightened Cara's neck, sharpened her breath.

The water flowed once more over her, tried to erase her.

Cara thrashed, water droplets splashing her face, warmer than her body. Dom had said they were dangerous. She should have listened. She shouldn't have thought she could fight back.

"Cara!" Magnolia said sharply, stilling Cara for the moment it took for her voice to cut through the chaos.

"Give in to it, child," Gladys picked up, voice melodic. "Surrender to it. Give yourself over to us. Let us help you carry that weight, relieve your pain."

That unity, the sense of carrying hands overwhelmed the sense of drowning. Again, she was cradled by welcoming, by kindness, cradled by the feminine and all definitions of it. There was a sense of gentle smiles, guiding her into this new world. Of understanding for those who had gone through this or similar themselves. Such a strong feminine presence, free of judgment, of pressure. Only love and belonging and beauty.

"That's right. Feel the presence and connection to our clan. The collective. You belong here, Cara. You are one of us. You always have been, and we have waited so, so long to have you rejoin us." It was Magnolia's voice, but also all the rest of them, too.

Cara settled again. Her body grew light. The power flowed through her but no longer drowned or overwhelmed her as those cradling hands drained fear away, replaced it with the glow of love. Her breath grew slower and steadier.

Love… There was love elsewhere… Someone else…

The others brushed that thought away, too, surrounding her with their warmth, their welcome.

The water again resembled air around her, leaving her light as a cloud, buoyant…and then floating. Literally floating.

"This is what it is to be a nymph, Cara," Magnolia said. "To carry and be carried by the others. To lift each other and in so doing, lift ourselves. For as you fly, you bring all of us with you."

Cara imagined the soft breeze tickling her, that sense of being the breeze, fluttering through the tree branches, rustling the leaves. She was the breeze, and she floated. Powerful, yet eternal. Her warmth, her essence flowed through the water, soaked up through the branches, *was* the branches. She joined with the others in the same way her ability had tried to connect with Gladys that once. It flowed easily out of her, surrounded her, surrounded the others. Blood, water, power, air, it was all the same, all one.

"Yes, Cara, yes, that's it. Finally, you're with us again," Magnolia said, the sound of her voice somewhere between far away and floating along in the breeze.

Like the voices in the trees that had called to her before, when she'd been at the refugee camp, when she'd have sworn someone was calling her name… The voice was the same. Had that been Magnolia all along?

Had the other nymphs, the twins, heard it, too? If so, why had they run?

Again, those thoughts were brushed away, irrelevant in the face of love, of comfort. It made no difference. She was safe. She was, for perhaps the first time, exactly where and who she was supposed to be. She was loved, imperfect, but needed.

"Now draw us together as you have always been meant to do. Draw us all into that flow, connect us to it," Magnolia whispered.

"I don't know how," Cara said, or maybe she thought

it, because while there was still a sense of self, the sense of her body had faded again. Not in an alarming way, but rather in a lofty, ascendant kind of way. Like those questions, the sense of physical form was…unnecessary.

"You're going to unite our clan and bring us all home, Cara. At last, we will all be together again. United and one. Because of you."

United. Together. Never alone, and always loved. Yes, that was what she'd always wanted. At long last, she would belong. "Show me how…"

Chapter Thirty-One

ASCENSION

THE MOMENT ZAKI had finished his invention, this time an alteration of the GPS device, William, Jax, and the rest of the Shades raced outside to the Center's parking lot, where lazy snow blanketed the gravel. Shit. His Jeep wasn't big enough for seven people. William glanced down the road, approximately in the direction Zaki said his device indicated. It was early evening and with the coming snow, the sky should have been a white or gray, perhaps brightened with a fiery sunset.

Instead, the cloudy sky roiled verdant purple with streaks of bright pink…and green.

William turned back to the Shades, unease tightening his neck, crawling up his spine. Every second they putzed around here was longer that Cara was alone with the Guardians while they did gods knew what to her…

"We've got this," Chaimek said, giving a nod to Jax. "If you wouldn't mind offering an assist."

Jax touched his chest, eyes wide, as though confirming Chaimek was talking to him.

Chaimek nodded, already rubbing his hands together, settling his energy for the spellwork.

"Whatever you're going to do, get it done fast. And no wings. My Jeep does not need wings," William growled, glancing back down the road.

He turned back…and the Jeep looked no different, but all the men crawled into the backseat with the exception of Zaki, who'd been given the front passenger seat.

Jax stuck his head back out the door. "What're you waiting for? Times wasting!"

William ran around to the driver's side door and jumped in, jamming his key into the ignition, and closing his door as the other two doors slammed. "Everyone in?"

"All good," Jenklow said. "Hit it."

William pushed the Jeep into reverse, glancing in his rear view to find that although the Jeep was no different on the outside…somehow it now had a third row of seats. He shook his head, focused on getting them backed up, then spinning the Jeep around and bouncing them toward the main road and the four-way stop. *We're coming, Cara.*

"Give me a direction, Zaki," he barked, as they pulled out onto the white blanket of unbroken snow that covered the road and into the four-way stop

Zaki clutched what had been a cell phone that now had protruding wires, its own atmosphere of purple smoke and random other bits sticking out of it, producing a faint *bing…bing…bing* sound. "I calculated ten minutes…in dry conditions." Zaki pushed up his glasses on his long nose, glanced at the road again. "Left here."

"Which means step on it," George snapped.

The Jeep danced on the corner a little before the tires gripped again and William pressed harder on the accelerator, speeding them through the sleeping world around them. Trees leaned bowed and heavy with sticky snow. No breeze, no sign of life or movement, as though nature held its breath, waited for command.

"We should have teleported. Why didn't we teleport?" Liko cried from the backseat.

"Because teleportation always makes you pukey and extra grouchy. Besides which, they have wards blurring their location. That could land us inside something…or petrified inside rock," Chaimek said crossly.

"Which is generally fatal," Einar drawled.

"Enough side-chatter, boys," Jenklow said, voice firm but quiet. "Focus on the goal. We get Cara back. Crush those damned Guardians once and for all. Protect our town. That order, those priorities."

Jax leaned forward. "Those are goals. What about a plan?" He glanced from one man to another. "A plan… You know, a way to accomplish said goals?"

Liko grunted. "We go in. Get them before they get us. Get Cara out. Destroy Irene. Plan enough for you?"

Jax leaned back against his seat, rubbing his face, eyes wide in the rear view. "That's a terrible plan. We're all going to die. Well, you are. I'll probably be fine. I mean, I'll do what I can. Always do."

Einar patted Jax on the shoulder. "Good man. We'll consider you plan B. How does that sound? We've run missions like this plenty of times. Simple retrieval. Nothing to worry about."

They fell into silence, proving despite Einar's words, there was plenty to worry about.

"We get Cara and take down anyone who gets in our way of that. Whatever it takes, we get her back and stop those assholes from destroying our town," Albert said, voice harder than William could remember.

William swallowed and set his jaw, adjusted his tight grip on the wheel. *Whatever it took.* Irene had a weapon that worked against both him, and therefore presumably Jax. The boys hadn't been in this kind of situation in years. He'd always believed he was willing to make every sacrifice, but if he did manage to rescue Cara, if all the boys had been lost and the Guardians escaped to destroy Beckwell or another sanctuary, was that a win? Stopping the bad guys used to be easy.

Before he'd had something—someone—to lose.

He swallowed and floored the accelerator. Gods help him it if came down to that.

BUOYANT EUPHORIA CRADLED and carried Cara along a peculiar current of connection, like being touched and cradled by the passing hands of many sisters, mothers, and grandmothers. Which, a sleepy part of her brain reflected, was creepy as hell if you thought about it too long. Yet also freeing. As though the weight of self, responsibilities, that driving need to prove herself had been born away too. How could Gran have kept this from her? How could Gran have left this behind?

"Shouldn't the question be why?" Dom's voice whispered, as though from a distance.

Dom's voice jarred Cara from the tranquil euphoria. She opened her eyes. But…the weight of the pendant was gone. She wasn't wearing it. How could Dom—

"Shh. You're safe. You're doing wonderful. A little more, and you'll know your true ability, connect with your true self," Magnolia said, in the most inviting, calm voice. Like an experienced mother shushing a child back to sleep. She herself sounded woozy and sleepy, too.

That brief sense of disturbance faded, and Cara sank back into that euphoric stream.

"Good. That's right. Let it carry you, let us carry you," Magnolia murmured. She was quiet for a few moments, maybe longer.

The sense of buoyancy grew within Cara, as though whatever she floated on bore her upward, toward... something. It was like the warmth of light, a central space of universal knowledge, both the center of her very being, and the center of *all* being.

That small niggle of unease tugged at Cara. Why had Gran turned away from this and kept it secret?

"Because it's dangerous. It's always been dangerous. You've wandered too far. You need to come back. Don't...trust...them..." Dom whispered again.

She drew closer to that center, the warmth increasing, the blur of self and oneness growing hazy.

"Just a little further," Magnolia murmured. "You've almost reached it... yes, keep going. You're doing marvellously, child."

That lulling voice silenced the questions and Dom, smothered any sense of self and fear. Light enveloped Cara. She might have gasped, might have cried at the sense of belonging and home that light brought. Complete unity and comfort. There was no sense of physical body, no separate self to experience any sensations like uncertainty or fear. The light was all encompassing—warmth, power, and oneness. A sense not of others around her but being part of the bigger whole.

"You've done it, child," a soft voice said, as though from very, very far away. "Now it's time to do what you were meant to do. Unite us. Help be our center and growth."

There was a general sense of confusion, all sense of "I" long gone.

"You are dryad. Connect with the trees, a sense of

those powerful forms. The roots diving deep into the soil for nutrients and soil. They stand sentinel all over this world, silent observers, ancient guards. You are part of that strength. The world's winds rush through your branches and leaves. Your roots are deep and sure, stretching and extending. Your branches are broad and ever reaching."

The wind rustled through all her leaves. The soil and nutrients, the entire world fed her through her roots. She was sure and strong, always connected to others of her kind, ageless and eternal. Never alone again…

"Reach now. Stretch your branches, extend your roots, twining and growing. Connect with us. Help be our bower, our shelter and safety created with your ascension."

There was a sense of stretching, of extension like a long-awaited stretch and release of energy. Roots dove deep into the earth. Branches shot out farther and stronger. Twined and joined with each other.

An image flashed through her mind. Branches and roots, tearing through buildings, splitting the bar and grocery in two, tumbling the emergency building, uprooting Beckwell's school and splitting it in two. The cries, intense distress of others crept through a crack in Cara's awareness.

"See what they want you to do. See how they would abuse you and your gifts," Dom said.

Trees swept upward, crushing houses and cars in their path, branches reaching higher, higher as they connected and twined with each other, blocking out the sun.

She sucked in a breath, awareness of self rising, pulling her out of that river of connection, away from that warmth, away from that light, gasping for air. What if—

"Shush." Magnolia whispered, floating beside Cara in the pool, her voice mellow and sleepy. "There is nothing to fear. It's just your unconscious self releasing your ties to the past that anchor you, things that chain you to the physical world. You are so much more."

Yes, yes, that's what it was. Those hands were there again, soothing her fears. Helping ease Cara back into the oneness. Sinking, down, down, down into that light, into that collective. Into the roots and the branches. The breeze ruffled her leaves, snow settled on crisp branches, dry sand, moist loam, cold frozen earth sheltered her roots.

"Yes, child, yes," the voice murmured again. "You are doing it. You are bringing us home. You are giving us home. At last, we will be together again. Because of you. Together, we shall rise. Together, we shall conquer."

Chapter Thirty-Two

RUN

"TURN IN TWO SECONDS... ONE..." Zaki squawked from the front seat of the Jeep, he and his binging device William's own personal GPS as they raced down the road, following the signal or whatever the hell it was Zaki and Jax had designed to track Cara.

Snow lashed the car with fury, falling heavier and faster, striking the windows sideways as they drove. The sky roiled, that uneasy purple and green hue, clouds undulating in unnatural waves. They'd driven as fast as they could down a road to nowhere, Zaki ordering a left, then a right. Now this coming turn.

"There's no road," William shouted back, squinting through the white drifts of snow on both sides.

"Yes, there is," Zaki said, gaze glued to the device.

"No."

"Now!"

"Hang on to something." William jerked the Jeep off the two-lane highway on two wheels.

The Jeep bounced and swung wildly. He gripped the wheel, pulling the Jeep back through the clearing between the trees rather than driving right into them, where the snow dragged them.

The Shades grunted and cursed, grabbing hold of each other, the back of the seats, and the grab handles on the ceiling.

"You know what? That risk of teleporting into a rock sounds better than dying in a snow drift!" Jax cried.

"No teleporting," William, Einar, and Chaimek all echoed back, as William fought with the wheel.

They must have found a road, or at least a narrow break in the band of dense trees and undergrowth, because they didn't land in the ditch. The Jeep plowed forward, through the deepening snow. They bounced off the sides of deep, old wheel ruts on an unused, unpaved road. There was no other choice but to cut back their speed despite the urge to push hard on the pedal. They were almost there, almost close enough to help, almost to Cara.

"This is the road to the old Carmenta place," Albert murmured, more to himself than aloud.

"Your wife's family?" William said, fighting the Jeep and the wheel. The engine roared as they bounced along. Damn but those trees were close.

Albert might have nodded, but William was trying too hard to keep them away from the trees. The road grew narrower as they went. The trees loomed, darker, thicker, fencing them in. Damn the road anyway. They couldn't stay here. Knuckles white, William hit the gas harder. The Jeep's engines groaned in protest but picked up speed.

"Keep going. Straight ahead, in three hundred meters," Zaki said, eyes still on his beeping device.

"Um, uh, anyone else notice the road is shrinking?" Jax piped up, clutching the back of William's seat.

What had been a clearing and driveway grew narrower

and narrower, more goat path than road. The trees loomed around them, stretched over them like a dense tunnel.

"Don't be paranoid. It's just an old road," Liko said with a grunt as they hit a large bump.

"Jax may be right," Henry mused, voice tight. "Those trees are closing in on us."

The trees formed a tighter and tighter tunnel around them. Trunks elongated, widened. Branches twisted and twined above the car, forming a dense net that blocked out the snow and the purple-green unnatural sky.

A sapling shot out of the snowy ground directly ahead.

"Look out!" Albert shouted.

William had already jerked left to avoid it. The tunnel was too close, too narrow. He slammed his foot on the brake. The Jeep skittered, slid right, hit the sapling, bounced left. "Hang on!"

They collided with the growing wall of trees with a crunch. The Jeep sputtered before coming to a standstill.

William struggled to catch his breath, but he couldn't tear his eyes away from the way the tree trunk next to the window shot upwards, a few inches a second. Rough bark screamed and scratched along the side of the Jeep door as the tree thrust up, up, and up. It grew faster and faster out of the ground, grinding against the Jeep's door, sending the vehicle lurching to the right.

He tried the key, the engine sputtering. Again, same result. The engine wouldn't turn over. The Jeep was dead.

In the rear view, the tunnel grew thicker and denser, closing in, tightening. Like a digesting stomach.

"Out. We've got to get out of the Jeep. Now. Move!" William barked.

He wasn't the only one who'd noticed the problem. Liko already had the back door open and scrambled out.

Zaki blinked, looking up from his device, clutching it in shaking hands.

Liko already had the passenger door open and hauled on Zaki's arm while William pushed and lifted from behind.

In the back, Jax tugged Chaimek, Einar and Jenklow out of the Jeep.

The Jeep lurched again to the right, almost sideswiping Einar and Jenklow if Jax hadn't yanked them to safety.

William pulled against his belt. Fumbled for the button and freed himself.

The Jeep shifted and twisted, a shrieking, squealing sound as bark grated against the driver's side, caught and dragged the Jeep upward. Roots twined over the hood, slapped against the windshield, cracking the glass.

Liko and Jax leaned into the car. "Get out of there, Mac!"

William dove toward the passenger side. His foot tangled with his belt, caught on the center console.

The Jeep twisted, lurched to the right.

Liko and Jax tumbled inside, falling on top of each other.

The windshield splintered further, tree roots criss-crossing it like spider legs.

Jax was first out. He yanked Liko out on his ass. Reached out a hand toward William.

William's hand closed on Jax's fingers.

Jax pulled, hard.

He'd never been more grateful Jax was there. Jax's grip, coupled with William kicking out with his feet and shoving against the wheel, sent them both flying out into the snow, landing with an oomph.

The tunnel twisted, twined, closing in around them.

Trees spiraled upwards. Roots ripped through the earth, making the ground shake beneath their feet.

"Go, go, go!" William shouted, pulling Jax to his feet.

Already half in a run, Jax grabbed for Jenklow, catching him around the waist.

Liko grabbed Chaimek by the arm, dragging him along faster.

They were all in movement, but William took up the tail. Damned if he'd let any of them be left behind.

He shot a look behind him.

The tunnel closed in around the Jeep, tightening and coiling. Metal screamed and crumpled. Glass popped from the windows. The Jeep, his only partner for years, his home and bedroom, was swallowed in a dark tangle of branches and pale roots.

The tunnel continued to coil around them, like a boa constrictor.

"Come on, boys. Go!" he urged again.

Up ahead, pale light glimmered, the opening to the rapidly shrinking tunnel.

Zaki was out front, running like the hounds of hell were at his heels—good.

Liko slowed, puffing, face red and losing steam, losing ground to George. George's lips were pursed in annoyance, likely for the need to run rather than weary.

"Keep up, you old fart," George grunted at Liko. He lifted his hand and let loose a bright ball of red fire that sailed from his hand and connected with Liko's rear.

Liko howled…and raced ahead, swearing a blue streak, clutching his smoking ass and vowing revenge as he ran.

Henry was hoofing it decently, his long-legged gait easily eating up the ground, but holding back as he always had for Albert.

Jax was watching from the front, monitoring the others like William.

Albert was moving as fast as he could, a ragged limp without his cane, but he'd never been a runner.

The tunnel ahead was closing in. The light grew dim and faint. Branches and trees twined tighter above them.

Fuck it.

"Shout at me later," William growled, then scooped up Jenklow, and tossed him on his shoulder. "Go. Faster!" He urged on the other men, Albert's boney body bouncing on his shoulder.

Henry sped up, catching up with the others.

The opening ahead shrank. Smaller, darker…

William put on the speed, arm tight around Jenklow's frail form.

Liko, George, Jax and Zaki disappeared into that light.

The opening was almost closed.

William scooped an arm around Einar, tugged him off his feet. There was no choice but to duck his head and drive them all forward. Out toward that light, through the growing tangle. He wouldn't leave them behind. He couldn't lose them.

But the branches twined with each other, catching at their clothes…

A bright burst of red flame shot through where the opening had been, incinerating branches and roots that squealed as they recoiled. It opened a hole for William to dive through, bringing Jenklow and Einar with him. He shoved Einar through first, then dove forward with Jenklow, turning and curling his body around the frail man to protect him from the impact.

They hit the ground with a grunt and a soft puff of snow. Albert's pointy elbow ground into William's solar plexus.

William grunted and shoved the other man off him gently.

For a second, they all lay there, catching their breath.

William recovered first. He forced himself upright. Did a quick count, noted that they were a few yards from an abandoned farmhouse in as rough a shape as the one he'd once called home.

Zaki poked the buttons and inspected his device, polishing the screen with the hem of his shirt.

Jax gripped his forehead, staring back at the wall of trees and shaking his head.

George had his hands on his hips, lips flat and eyes narrowed at the wall of trees.

Liko, butt still smoking, stalked toward George, murder in his dark glare.

Einar caught Liko's arm, murmured something that made the big man smile. Then the two of them started to laugh, laughing so hard, they bent double.

Jenklow joined in, which soon started all of them laughing, including William. Laughing as they sometimes had after other close encounters. They'd beat death. They were still alive, all of them. Thank gods.

He'd fought at their side again, and he hadn't lost them. More, maybe he'd gotten them back because he trusted them to make their own decisions, instead of treating them like children. Or the way some people treated the elderly.

William blew out a breath, then pushed to his feet and leaned down to offer Jenklow a hand. "Well, that was new. Guess if we survive this, I have to buy a new Jeep."

Albert shot up a scowl but took his hand. "I'll buy you one myself if you swear never to whisper a word of what happened back there. You ever tell anyone you carried me—"

"Get over yourself. There's nothing to tell. You can carry your own ass," William said.

The two men exchanged a grin as William hauled Albert onto his feet.

Behind them, what had been the opening for the road and a stand of trees had coalesced into a dense wall of tree, root, and branches. The wall surrounded the small farmyard like a walled castle, stretching skyward so high, you couldn't see beyond. The snow fluttered down in careless, gentle flakes, with none of the rage they'd seen on the way here. Almost like the area was untouched by the storm.

"According to the locator device, we're in the right place," Zaki said, pushing up his glasses, which somehow hadn't been broken, studying his device more than the surroundings.

William, Jax and Albert turned to face the house, or what was left of it, silhouetted against the purple and green sky that glowed in increasingly virulent hues.

Time had stripped away most of the paint from what had been a white, two-story farmhouse. The second story room was half caved in, leaving one of the upper walls sagging inward, as though it might too collapse. Most of the windows on the main floor were boarded over, and the few that weren't showed only darkness beyond.

"Like I said: underground. That's why the locator spell didn't work." George faced the house with distaste. He sighed. "Please tell me we don't have to dig, too. Running was bad enough."

"We survive this, I'm smothering you in your sleep," Liko growled at George.

George turned to the former police chief with an arch look. "I dare you to get past my wards."

"A house that age should have a cellar of some kind,"

Henry said thoughtfully, cutting them off and stepping between them before violence ensued.

Albert snorted, moving slowly, favoring his right leg, to stand beside Henry. "They'll have access from inside the house, probably a cellar or natural underground cavern. Gods forbid that woman had to traverse the snow in the winter. I swear, Rose's mother was the biggest snob I ever met."

"What're we waiting for? Let's go boys," William said, and started for the house's sagging front porch.

"Yes, William. What have you been waiting for?" Irene stepped out from the doorway, her form shimmering for a second or two indicating some kind of illusion or magical field surrounding the house. Behind her were two under-sidhe goons. "We haven't got much light left. Are you going to try and fight me now, or should we just skip the fighting and I kill you?"

Chapter Thirty-Three

FIGHT

THE FLOATING EUPHORIA, the strength and connection of and to the trees, all of it was wonderful. It was a greater sense of belonging and safety than she'd ever dared dream was possible. Yet...a vague sense of self slid through her, pushed down that sense of one-ness until she regained sense of a form. A sense that she was an individual, that she was Cara. And there was something...off about the situation.

It wasn't unease, exactly. More like a niggling sensation that kept her from fully surrendering to the collective. A sense that she shouldn't...and that something was wrong. It was like digging into the most delicious of desserts that you'd been anticipating and drooling over...but finding after a few bites, it wasn't so delicious anymore. Maybe it'd gone moldy.

The deep sense of belonging, the warmth and wholeness of the light, the connection to something universal, all of that was still there, and it was good. Really good. There was just...something else.

Something wasn't right.

Great. Now I'm part of a space opera, sensing there's a disturbance in the light.

She was back in her own head, having her own thoughts instead of melding with the collective.

"What's so wrong with that?" It was Dom's voice.

Cara opened her eyes. But the pendant—

"My essence may dwell in the pendant, but our connection and your ability to summon me has always been within you. The nymph block and your relatives kept me from you, but no more. You have the power. You are the power. So, what are you doing letting foolish nymphs do your thinking? You don't need a collective. You are an individual. You are a Yaga."

Definitely Dom, with the usual tone that made it hard to differentiate between normal annoyed and seriously pissed. This edged toward pissed. *"Dom, I'm glad to hear your voice again. The block—"*

"Stop just hearing me. Listen. The block was activated by the nymphs presence in Beckwell, the ways they've tried to summon you and your growing strength. You are the power. Or you were, until you gave it away to these powerless, weak-minded nymphs who keep each other powerless with their interdependence. Get out of there. Now."

That sense of unease grew. It may have been her imagination, but the water chilled against her skin. Her muscles tightened, making it harder to stay floating between Gladys on one side and Magnolia on the other. All this time she'd thought she had no nymph abilities, and instead learned they were very strong, just blocked. In the same way, she'd always believed the Yaga abilities were within the pendant. If they were within her, if what Dom said was true…

"Shh, now. You're fine. Everything's fine," Magnolia almost hummed.

The near-hypnotic sound of Magnolia's voice didn't

calm her down this time. Instead, Cara turned her head in the water to see Magnolia.

Her great-grandmother floated face-up in the water, her fingertips brushing Cara's. Magnolia's beautiful, elegant face was pulled into a twisted, euphoric smile. Her breathing was shallow, almost agitated, her muscles occasionally spasming and creating micro-waves in the pool. Worst, though, where her eyes, staring straight upward and sightless, slightly fogged and bloodshot, a hollow vacantness to her expression that left her staring upward…at nothing.

Cara shivered, the pool's temperature dipping further, her peaceful state ruptured.

"They destroy themselves with their co-dependence. They will destroy you, too," Dom said.

She turned toward her great aunt on the other side. Found the same blissed-out, empty smile. While Gladys's eyes were closed, her breathing likewise rasped.

Something was definitely wrong here.

The euphoric state and warmth of the light drained out of Cara. Her thoughts remained fuzzy, but they began to clear, starting with Gramps's favorite saying that echoed through her head again. *Nothing comes for nothing.* There was always a price, especially for magic. This…absence-of-self or absorption of self was the price of the nymph collective, all that belonging and comfort.

She'd always wanted to belong. Had longed for the sense of family and safety Gladys, Magnolia and the collective offered. Gramps and the Shades had taught her she had value as she was…even if that hadn't meant she was good enough to be a Shade.

Dom thought she was powerful.

And William. An image of his face bubbled to the surface of her mind. William liked her well enough just the way she was. He'd fought for her, had fallen for her, trying to reach her side. Her throat squeezed. She had to get back to him. He may have tried to protect her, might have kept secrets from her, but he'd never tried to erase her.

Gran had turned away from this, hadn't wanted this for Cara. Those misgivings began to make sense. The horrible ward and the lies a little less so…but maybe even Gran hadn't been perfect.

Whatever this was, she needed to know more about it, maybe from those other nymphs, maybe from more research before she was ready for this, before she fully understood what was going on here.

She shifted, swinging her feet down into the water and standing. She took one step toward the shallow end of the pool, her head clearing. Upright made the sense of wrongness grow. Something about all of this felt wrong deep down inside. Deeper than Dom's concerns. A part of her, maybe the Yaga side, didn't like this chained connection.

Magnolia's hand shot out and grasped Cara's wrist.

Cara gasped at the painful grip.

Her great-grandmother slowly rolled her head in the water toward Cara. Her gaze remained glassy, pupils dilated. But there was something more there…something hungry. Desperate.

Cara tugged at her arm but couldn't break the other woman's grip. Her heart rate accelerated and she thrashed, water splashing, trying to get away.

"Shh, child. We're not done yet," Magnolia murmured. "You're not done yet. We've waited so long for your strength, to be reunited. You can't go. We need you."

"You've been so kind to me. I know I can learn so much from you. I just… I need to go for now." Her tone was desperate, tears pricking her eyes as she tried to detangle Magnolia's fingers from her arm.

That grip opened the doorway to the collective. All those other hands, those other grandmothers, aunts, mothers, sisters that had supported her, now gripped her, clawed their way up her arm.

Dom's presence started again. *"Get out of—"*

They were cut off, like one of those supportive maternal figures now slapped a hand over Dom's mouth, silencing them, smothering them.

Cara pried at Magnolia's fingers, fingers slippery with water, breath rasping. "I want to leave. I—I'll come back. I promise." *No freaking way.* She shouldn't have let things go this far. Shouldn't have let herself be as drugged by the collective.

The older woman sighed, a resigned sound, and her grip tightened. "Gladys, help me."

Her aunt. Of course. Maybe she could help. So like Gran.

Cara turned to the other woman, who blinked a few times, her gaze clearing somewhat. Gladys frowned at Cara, confused that Cara stood. "What's wrong?"

"Aunt Gladys, I want to leave," Cara tried to keep the fear from her voice. She could convince the other woman. She had to. "Rose, your sister, she didn't want me to be part of this. She didn't want to be part of this. Shouldn't I have a choice? Shouldn't I get to choose?"

With a deepening frown, Gladys turned to Magnolia, her voice breathy, drugged. "Mother, I don't understand… You said she'd want this…"

"She does. Grab her arm. Now, Gladys," Magnolia said, voice sharper, harder.

The sense of the collective, those other voices, climbed through Cara through Magnolia's steel-grip, like cold numbness crawling through her skin. Up to her shoulder now. Dragging her downward, back into the collective, back into their prison.

"I'm sorry," her aunt whispered, as she grabbed Cara's other hand. More personalities, more numbness, climbing up her fingers, past her wrist. Dissolving her, swallowing her…

"No. I don't want this. Please, don't do this!" Cara cried, hating the sting in her eyes, the fear squeezing her throat.

That numbness, that possession crawled up both her arms faster and faster. Into her blood, through her skin. Up to her shoulders. Into her neck, despite the tight squeeze of her neck muscles.

Magnolia sighed, her voice echoing in the chamber and inside of Cara's head, rippling through her skin, spreading that numbness. "I wish it could have been otherwise…but we've waited too long and you're too important. I'm sorry, child. Perhaps someday, it will be different. We will help you need us as much as we need you."

"No. No. Please!" Cara begged, maybe screamed. Until it was just in her head as the numbness climbed her neck, removed her ability to cry out, to scream.

All those women, all those hands that had once supported and buoyed her, removed her pain, dragged her down into the water. Stole her thoughts, stole her very being. She thrashed, tried to stand, tried to run…until they stole that ability, too. Until, as her body eased back in the pool, she no longer knew she wanted to fight. Because *she*, the individual known as Cara, was pulled under, drowned, and swallowed by the collective.

WILLIAM FACED Irene and her two dark fey goons who stood between he and the Shades reaching Cara. One of the dark fey goons had been replaced, the other one banished by Zaki somewhere else. Probably didn't make this one friendlier. William blew out a breath and squeezed his hands at his sides. Shit. Jeep-eating trees aside, apparently getting this far had been too easy. He sighed internally. Easy once in a while sure would be nice.

The boys had done fine back at the Center—better than he had. But were they ready for a rematch so soon? Guess they'd have to be.

Irene eyed he, Jax, and the rest of the Shades the way someone might eye day-old roadkill. "You cockroaches aren't ruining my victory over Beckwell." She gestured toward the trees. "With the nymphs' help, I've won. Trees, of all things, have destroyed your pathetic little town. Why keep fighting? Beg for my mercy. Maybe I'll take pity on you."

"Shouldn't she be dead?" Albert said, turning to Henry and using a stage-whisper.

"Nah, you know how it is. The bad ones keep stinking up the place until someone takes out that trash," Henry said, not even pretending to lower his voice, his gaze hard as it landed on Irene. He'd always held a particular grudge after she'd launched the attack that landed Albert in traction...and almost in the ground.

"Here I thought it was just me noticing that smell," Jax added, coming up beside them, fitting in like he'd never quite done as Hermes.

"Oh, but I've so missed your moronic banter," Irene said dryly. "Did you raid a mortuary, William? You're leading a team of walking corpses."

That of course only made the men puff out their chests more...chests that, admittedly, had once been a bit more muscular. And especially in Liko's case, not surpassed by the girth of his belly.

"Don't listen to her," Jax said, although his gaze remained on Irene. "She gets meaner when she's threatened."

"Well, Irene, I for one am glad to see you," Liko said with a dark smile. "If I've had one regret all these years, it's not seeing your head on a spike."

Zaki started to add something, but William didn't catch it, because Albert stepped sideways until he stood on William's foot. Jax had stepped in front of Albert, blocking William, and George had maneuvered himself to flank William's other side.

William's neck squeezed.

Frick's sake… It was like they already had something planned.

Liko taunted Irene again, likely about to get his ass blasted by something sizzly for the second time that day.

"Eguisheim," Albert whispered.

Liko grew more outrageous—and louder—in his insults hurled at Irene.

William struggled to make sense of it. Eguisheim…tiny French village near the German border where they'd circled around enemy German and Guardian troops to catch them in a trap from behind…because they'd used an animated double of William to make it look like he was one place, while he was actually another, coming up from behind. He blinked. Hell. It was brilliant and would let him get inside the house and to Cara faster.

He glanced over, caught Jax's gaze.

Jax gave him a small nod. As though to say, they had this. William needed to get after Cara.

William took a deep breath. It meant leaving the

Shades, his friends, out here to their fates. It meant not being able to protect them from Irene.

"Go on then, Mac. Go get our girl," George whispered, already turning to his side to hide the wispy threads of visible magic he wove between his fingers. Probably the start of either a smoke or light exploding orb. He gave William a wink.

"Zaki is the signal. Liko is distracting her so Zaki can transport himself behind her, become invisible, and then see if he can work a hallucinatory hex on her when he touches her. Her wards have always been pretty intense, so it might only buy us a few seconds, but that should be enough for you to get inside. Zaki vanishes, that's your cue," Albert murmured.

William gave the smallest nod to his second in command. "You had this all planned out, didn't you?"

"Someone had to do something while you were laying around, being mostly dead," Jenklow said.

With a snort, William gave the other man a nod. "Don't do anything stupid," he said, the same words he'd always told them before a battle coming easily to his lips.

"Nothing you wouldn't do," Albert whispered with a smirk and their old refrain.

Moments later, Zaki vanished, then quickly reappeared, right behind Irene and her dark fey goons. Zaki grabbed her exposed hand.

Irene turned in slow motion and fury.

George hurled the magical equivalent of a smoke bomb laced with fireworks at the trio.

William didn't wait to see the fall out, had to trust his men still knew what they were doing, as he dove into the cover of the smoke. It stung his eyes, but from the way the goons waved their hands around and clutched their throats, Chaimek had added something special to the mix that was especially hard on the dark fey, likely some kind of iron powder. Part of him wanted to stay with his team and fight Irene too… but they were making the sacrifice to cover for him so he could go in and get Cara. They were all depending on him. He had to reach Cara. Before it was too late.

Chapter Thirty-Four

ESCAPE

WILLIAM SLIPPED inside the ruined farmhouse without being noticed, blinking against the dim light. Deep shadows revealed themselves as dusty shapes of a sofa and chairs, all faded beyond any recognizable color. An animal had nested in one of the cushions. Dust coated everything. Or almost everything. On the arm of one of the chairs lay a ball of bright pink yarn and the beginnings of what might have been mittens, the knitting needles stuffed into the ball where they'd been paused, and not a hint of dust on them. It was almost as though the residents had returned and picked up life, seemingly oblivious to the destruction of their home.

Scrapes and disturbances in the dust-coated floor showed further evidence of recent life, and William followed them into the next room. They must have brought Cara through here. Had she walked…or had they carried her unconscious body?

He shook off the thought, and crept down the hall toward the next room, following the path left in the dust. What mattered was finding Cara and getting her the hell out of here. Then they could get back out front and help the Shades deal with Irene and her goons.

The floorboards creaked beneath his footsteps, and the stale mustiness of the house tickled his nose. Something scuttled off into a hole in the wall. The first door to the left wouldn't open more than a few inches, jammed shut with detritus from the collapsed second floor. He ignored the ruined stairs and continued toward the kitchen, near the rear of the house. Henry and Albert had suspected any kind of nymph pool would be below ground. He needed to find access to the cellar.

Thin light filtered in through dirty kitchen windows, the room only slightly less neglected than the rest of the house. Most of the cupboard doors hung at odd angles, a few doors missing. The counters, though, had been cleaned of dust and a bright pink bloom—a rose? No, something frillier…a peony. A bright, dark-pink peony sat in a clear glass cup in the center of the counter, at odds with the rest of the house, out of season, out of place, unexpected beauty within so much ugliness. It was like meeting Cara after all these years, after anticipating only the next case, the next fight for so long, to have color and life bloom in his life. Love blossom in his heart for an incredible woman.

Something smashed into the side of the house, rattling the dishes, and making the building shift and groan.

The noise jarred William back to the mission, tensed his neck. The entrance to the cellar was probably here in the kitchen. There. A small door, tucked into the corner of the room. Pulling it open, a narrow set of rickety stairs led down into the darkness, a faint glimmer of light below.

He crept down the stairs, hands brushing rough wood on either side of the narrow stairway. The scent of earth and damp mustiness grew stronger the lower he got. He stepped down into a wood-framed cellar that held back the earth. Ahead, like someone had blasted a whole through the support beams, lay a natural cavern. There was a crude table, an unmade cot with rumpled bedding near the crude opening. He continued forward, into that cavern with damp, faintly glittering walls. The air warmed against his face, and he followed the faint glow of light ahead. A lantern maybe. Something about the place raised the hair on the back of his neck, tightened the muscles in his shoulders. Maybe it wasn't the place. He thought he was here to rescue Cara.

What if she didn't want to be rescued?

Maybe she hadn't been carried down that hall. Maybe she'd walked, and she was where she wanted to be. Afterall, he'd seen her only from a distance fighting for the Shades and against Irene. He was so used to deceptions, for the motives that made people turn sometimes in desperation to the Guardians. Could Cara have done the same? If not to the Guardians, she could have turned to the nymphs, her own people, driven by the Shades' betrayal.

Or perhaps to escape his betrayals, the secrets he'd kept.

He didn't want to believe it. The idea that he could have lost her before he'd ever been able to tell her how he felt… Hell, that was a knife blade to the gut. For so long it had been his duty to stand between the Guardians and everyone else. He'd managed to leave the Shades outside, to trust them to handle this battle without him. He couldn't let the Guardians control Cara, but gods help him if he had to fight to free her.

Any such battle could cost Cara her life. This mission might take more from him than he could give. If he had to hurt Cara, it would destroy a part of his soul.

He swallowed hard and eased a breath into his tight

chest as he crept toward that light, toward the pale reflection that shone off a glassy, dark surface. Kerosene lamps hung sporadically in the stone cavern, the light thin and yellow, barely reflected in that mirror-still water of the pool that dominated almost a third of the space, easily the length and width of two vehicles.

Something, though, disturbed the mirror-like surface of the water.

Three bodies floated on the surface.

His heart hiccoughed, and he rushed forward, his footsteps echoing in the cavern.

Three women floated starfish-like on the surface of that water, hands joined. All of them dressed in identical, pale, almost Grecian-type robes, their skin dark, features lovely, dark hair floating like halos above their heads.

All three of them stared blindly upward, eyes open, but sightless.

None of the women stirred as he approached. His hands clenched. All three women were exceptionally similar in appearance. Obviously, Cara had finally found those relatives of hers, or they'd found her.

Her body floated lower in the water than the others, her face partially submerged. Oh hell. No bubbles rose from the water above her face.

He rushed to the side of the pool, crouched on the edge, dropped his legs into the water and prepared to jump in.

"Don't," a quiet female voice whispered, freezing him in place. "She'll wake."

One of the women, the one farthest from him on the other side of Cara, had turned her head in the water to face him. Her gaze remained slightly foggy, but she definitely focused on him.

He'd barely looked at her when the third woman

twisted and thrust herself out of the water, grabbing his ankles and yanking him into the icy water. The shock of the cold stole his breath just before his head submerged and she dragged him beneath the surface. The woman clung to his shoulders, using her entire weight to hold his face beneath the surface.

William twisted, groping blindly for the slippery edge of the pool. His lungs burned and under the water was dark and murky. He couldn't make out anything. But even the woman soaking wet was a third of his size and strength. He twisted her off him, bursting through the surface and sucking in a breath of cold air.

She made an infuriated snarl before leaping for him again, surprisingly agile in the chest-deep water. Chanting in some language, they grappled, and she tried to grab and force him beneath the surface again.

He grabbed for her arms, struggled to hold her off in the splashing water. Finally got a grip on her shoulders, tried to force her away without hurting her…only for her to go limp as overcooked spaghetti. He blinked.

Behind stood the third woman, the one who'd tried to warn him. Her hand rested on his attackers' bare shoulder, as though she'd somehow rendered the other woman unconscious.

Cara still floated nearby, unresponsive despite all the activity.

William swallowed, hard. It must be the pool and the water somehow. He was damned lucky he'd made it above the surface.

"She would have enchanted and drowned you." The third woman who could have been Cara's sister bobbed in the water that reached her shoulders as she wrapped her arms around his unconscious attacker. Lovingly, she smoothed back the silvered hair at the other woman's brow and reclined her slowly, effortlessly sleeping and floating once more on the surface of the water, her hands shifting but always maintaining skin contact.

William swallowed, the cold of the water making his teeth chatter as he kept the unconscious woman between him and the active one, eyed the distance to Cara and calculated the likelihood of making it to her first. His fingers tightened against the stone lip of the pool.

Brushed against something like a chain. Picking it up, further tightness spread through him. Cara's pendant. The Yaga pendant. The one she never took off, and which she said helped protect her. He slipped it into his pocket. It belonged with Cara.

"I'm taking Cara out of here. You understand me?"

The other woman considered him a long time. Blinked, the action slow, out of it. "Yes," she finally said, as though speaking were exhausting. "It is…right." Still cradling the other woman, she floated them both back to where they'd been, not far from Cara. "I will…keep her…asleep."

Cara bobbed in the slight disturbance but didn't stir. Still no damned air bubbles.

The third woman, the one trying to help him, spoke once more. "Cara…is alive." She lay back, let herself float on the surface once more beside the other one, a breath sighing from her lips. Moisture glistened on her face, tears, as she turned toward him, gaze once again glassy, but face tightened with regret, with pain. "It wasn't…supposed to be this way. She should get to choose. Protect her. Help her." She sighed again closing her eyes, another tear sliding free. "For Rose."

Rose. Jenklow's wife? Didn't matter. William gently eased himself through the water toward Cara.

She didn't stir. Her face remained below the surface. Submerged and making her skin paler, grayer. Corpse-like.

The water icy cold and compressing his lungs, tightened every cell with painful awareness. He forced himself slowly forward until he could reach Cara's still form, blurred and magnified by the water. Her hair brushed against his chilled skin as he caught first her arm, then wrapped another arm around her body. Her skin temperature matched the icy water. No air bubbles disturbed the surface. Yet as his fingertips brushed over her wrist, a faint heartbeat thrummed against his touch.

He wheezed out a breath. Thank the gods. A heartbeat. She still had a heartbeat.

From this perspective in the pool, it was easier to see that over to the left the water lapped against stairs. He pulled Cara with him, her body bobbing next to his as he made painstaking progress across the pool, through that thick, icy soup. His toes had gone numb inside his boots. His muscles started to shake, and he could barely feel the tips of his fingertips. The water grew shallower, only up to his waist. Then his thighs. He pulled Cara closer, lifted and cradled her against his chest, and walked with her out of the pool. His shirt sucked against his skin, his sodden boots and the cold making every step harder, clumsy.

Cara lay, limp, icy and motionless in his arms. While her heart may have been beating, she wasn't breathing.

He lowered her as quickly to the stone floor as he could, glancing over at the pool, the other two women, once more floating silently. How long would it stay that way? He had to get Cara breathing first. He'd deal with them if necessary.

He brought his lips to Cara's icy ones and pulled gently on her chin until her mouth opened. Chills quaking through him, he blew in first one breath. Then another into her still chest. *Come on, Cara. Come on.* His heart hammered against his chest. How could she have a pulse and not be breathing? Had the other woman lied when she'd promised Cara was still alive?

Five breaths. Still a slow steady pulse at her throat. Not breathing. It shouldn't have been possible.

Come on, Cara. Please. Come back to me.

Another five breaths. Her lips so still, so cold against his. Nothing like the warm and vibrant woman he knew. She couldn't be gone. She couldn't. His heart squeezed inside his chest. His body grew stiff with cold, yet still he breathed into her, willed her awake, willed her to live. Images of all those he'd lost before her hovered around him. Cousins who'd been like brothers, felled on the battlefield. Her gray skin echoed their corpses. Mother's body laid out and prepared for her burial, still and limp on the table. Too much like Cara's motionless form now. So many friends, family, brothers and sisters that he'd held like this, as they wheezed their last. As they left him behind.

He tried to shake off the thought. Jax hadn't left. The woman said that Cara wasn't dead. She would be fine. He might—

His lips almost touched Cara's as she wheezed in a shuddering breath. He leaned in close. Had he imagined it?

She wheezed in again. Slow, slightly stuttering. No coughing, like a drowning victim. Another unsteady breath, as though she remembered what it was to breathe.

"Cara. Come on, sweetheart. Breathe. Yes, just like that. Please." He chanted the words to her, his pleas as others might have chanted prayers. Anything to keep her breathing. Alive.

Wait. The pendant. It protected her, didn't it? He forced icy fingertips into his pocket, found the cool hardness of the pendant. Lifting Cara's head gently, he slipped it on over her head. Brushed aside her hair so it rested against her skin, below her collarbones. Where it belonged.

Cara gasped and opened her eyes. The light was too dim to see her pupils, but her gaze shifted, searched the room almost blindly before groping, stumbling, it landed on him.

He cradled her in his arms, probably grinning like an idiot. "That's it. Give yourself a little time. It's me, William. Are you all right? Can I move you?"

A glance toward the other women, who still remained motionless and floating on the black-mirror surface.

"William," she sighed, the sound toneless, more an exhalation than a word.

The women behind him started to stir.

That settled it. He swept Cara up in his arms. Damned if he'd stick around here any longer and risk those women recapturing Cara.

Her head lolled against his shoulder as he carried her toward the stairs, then swiftly upward. The house shuddered and the rickety stairs trembled with every external hit. His throat tightened. She had a pulse, and she was breathing…but she wasn't with it yet. Maybe too out of it to have been responsible for the trees attacking them. Maybe she didn't know anything about it. Maybe all this time, she'd been a prisoner.

As he carried her upstairs, she murmured things that weren't words. Almost like a conversation playing out in her head…with herself. Her gaze remained glassy, unaware of their surroundings.

He tightened his grip around her. He'd get her back to the boys, back to the Center with the doctor. Someone had to have seen this before. They'd be able to help her.

By the time he reached the top of the stairs and stepped into the kitchen, the crashes and shudders made the plates rattle in the cupboards. One of the cupboards fell off the wall, crashing to the floor in a cloud of dust. He ran toward the front room, edging past the partially open doorway. The floor trembled beneath his sodden boots, floorboards clattering, trying to trip him up. Whatever the boys were doing, they were putting up a good fight.

He headed toward the back of the house and the living room where he'd come in. Damn it. He didn't want to leave her here, alone when those women below might give chase. But any of those hits that kept rattling the house could hit her if he risked carrying her out into the battlefield without knowing what was happening.

"Okay, sweetheart. You're going to wait here. I'll be right back. I swear." He gently lowered Cara to the floor, leaned her against the wall.

The Shades had to be the ones winning. It couldn't be Irene, tossing their bodies as she'd done before…

No. The Shades had to be winning.

Cara's eyes stared ahead blindly, and she slumped against the wall where he left her. She could have been asleep…except for that blind, staring gaze.

He fisted his hands and hurried for the door. The sooner he understood the situation, the sooner he could get her back to the Center. He pushed the door open partially, just enough to peer outside.

Irene and one of her goons had retreated around the side of the house, the porch too exposed. No sign of goon number two.

The Shades, meanwhile, including an image of what appeared to be him, were fighting hard and playing to their strengths. The off-guard and out-of-practice performance back at the Senior Center was a thing of the past.

Liko and Zaki worked together. Liko ran defense, lobbing projectiles created by Chaimek, while Zaki dove in and out, getting closer, disappearing and reappearing back at Liko's side, running illusion to confuse and disorient. It was probably them that'd sent the second dark fey packing somewhere, too. The dark fey jumped at every illusion, fighting and attacking shadows more than targeting the actual Shades.

"Toss me an orb!" Jax cried, popping up in the space between Irene and her dark fey goon.

Chaimek raised a brow, clearly unused to anyone else being able to catch them—it'd taken them weeks back in '41 to perfect the technique without the more harmless version exploding in the catcher's face. Jax seemed sure, though, so Chaimek chucked him one.

Jax vanished as the transportation orb hit him in the chest.

The breath whooshed out of William. Shit. Jax. He couldn't— Had he been transported? Obliterated? Had he just watched his friend die for the second time?

Liko swore. Loudly.

Irene roared with laughter. "That idiot worm. You somehow thought having him on your team meant winning?"

"No, it meant distraction," Einar cried, thrusting another orb—this one a fire-orb straight at Irene.

She lifted a hand, the orb harmlessly bouncing off her shields, as though she were surrounded by a transparent bubble. Then she turned, teeth clenched, on the William-illusion.

If you watched closely enough, the William-illusion followed the same actions as Einar did, only a few moments behind. Einar raced between the two groups, ferrying armfuls of the magical orbs—equivalent to grenades. Then the William-illusion would do the same, even throwing some of the grenade-type orbs at Irene.

Either Irene hadn't noticed amidst the other explosions that none of the ones thrown by the William-illusion ever caused damage, or she was too busy defending herself from Zaki that she hadn't been able to get a clear shot.

Until she blasted the William-illusion with a fireball… that passed harmlessly through him.

Irene roared. "An illusion? You fight me with an illusion? The real William must be too afraid to face me."

"Nope. I'm right here and waiting," William said.

"Transportation orb!" Chaimek shouted. He lobbed the glowing orb toward William like a softball.

William caught it, as easy as if they'd just been out for practice.

Irene barely had time to turn. Her lip curled.

He shoved the orb into her chest. Grabbed the dark fey, launched him into Irene.

Irene and the dark fey vanished in a soft bubble-like 'pop.'

Silence fell.

The Shades all sagged a moment, clearly too exhausted to celebrate.

"What about… Is Jax alive?" William asked Chaimek.

Chaimek grimaced. "Well, on the upside, it was a transportation grenade, nothing worse. I didn't have enough in me to keep weaving anything with much more kick. Bad news is, I was so distracted, I'm not quite sure where it sent him."

"But he's alive?" Hope swelled. They could still get Cara back to the Center. Jax might not be dead…

"Yeah. Fairly sure," Chaimek said.

William wanted to question Chaimek further, to find out more. But there was still Cara. He nodded, then ducked back inside the house, the cold wind biting through his soaked clothing.

Cara slumped against the wall, somewhere between sleeping and catatonic, soft murmurs occasionally passing her lips, still not making a lick of sense. As unaware of the world around her as she'd been when he left her.

His insides tight, knowing the Shades, that Albert, would be heartbroken to see her like this, William knelt, gently lifted her into his arms, and cradled her against his chest. "You're good, Cara. I've got you, love. I'll protect you. We've got your back." Maybe she didn't hear his words or even understand them. But if there was any chance she might, he had to say them, had to let her know she was safe.

Back outside, the Shades were bickering, the sound of their voices carrying into the house.

"We couldn't have torpedoed Irene sooner?" Liko snapped at Chaimek. "We've been surviving by the skin of our teeth out here for the past half hour!"

"I don't think we've even been fighting that long," Chaimek said tightly. "And I'm exhausted. She ducked the transport spells, and anything stronger, anything from the beginning, you missed. The others couldn't make it past her wards. Not without William to physically stick it to her. Besides, you know Irene. That won't have been enough to kill her. She'll be back to cause harm in Beckwell, I'd bet my favorite spell book."

"And I tri—" Zaki started.

William stepped out onto the porch, a still limp Cara in his arms.

The men fell silent, all approaching and surrounding William.

"Oh, gods. What have they done to you?" Albert whispered, hand hovering over Cara's forehead, brushing back a wet curl, then pulling back, eyes wide as he turned to Cara. "She's soaked through and it's freezing out here!"

Damn, but it would have been nice to have Jax here, to help transport them all.

A niggling suspicion twisted in William's brain, the kind he couldn't ignore. Jax could have brought himself back here if he'd been transported. Maybe he had been obliterated.

Or maybe he'd pulled the same stunt Hermes always had, back when things had gotten hard.

He'd run for greener pastures.

Gods help him, William couldn't decide if he'd rather his friend was dead…or running. And Cara didn't have time for him to worry about it. He pushed the thoughts down, turning instead to the skinny djinn, the man who looked the youngest of their squad, but was the oldest. Ted Zaki.

Who was bent double, hands on his knobby knees, pale as a ghost and wheezing. Clearly wiped out.

And their only damned chance out of this place, especially with Cara in the state she was.

Keeping all hint of how badly he wished there were another option out of his voice, William said, "Zaki, think you can weave a door big enough for all of us to get back to the Senior Center, ASAP?"

"Shit, no!" Liko swore, rounding on William, coming closer and hissing, although Liko was never quiet enough for everyone not to overhear him. "He hasn't spun that kind of magic in years."

"Happy to assist," Chaimek said, stepping up to Zaki, and sending a dirty look in Liko's direction. "Because unlike *some* members of this team, I believe in you. And besides, Liko, I thought you wanted to teleport here."

"That was before you offed the god. The feathery-sandals guy," Liko growled back.

Albert sent them both a quelling look, and they fell silent.

"We wouldn't ask you if there was another choice," Henry said quietly, patting Zaki's shoulder. "You know that."

"Zaki?" William asked again.

Zaki wearily straightened. Took in Cara's still form. He squared his narrow shoulders a bit more, adjusted his crooked, cracked glasses. "Cara's always believed in all of us. Always thought we were worth fighting for. I believe in her." He met William's gaze squarely. "Yes, sir. I'll get us back to the Center."

William smiled, while trying not to look like he was holding his breath, cradling the semi-conscious Cara against his chest. Zaki better damn well get them back there. He glanced at the impenetrable tree wall. Because she was soaked, it was freezing…and other than trusting his team, he didn't have a plan B.

Chapter Thirty-Five

FLOATING

SHE FLOATED. At least, there was a vague sense of "she." Neither a gender nor a real person… The sense of "she" was more like the shadow of something that had been, something that, maybe, deep down, still whispered to her, shouted sometimes.

A she that deep, deep down, screamed and raged for her freedom.

But that was deep, deep, down. A someone that had been, wasn't here.

Here, there were many voices. Some of them were tied and connected to her. Female voices. A whispering like the breeze through the leaves of many trees. A shuffling like the sway of saplings in crisp winter.

There were other voices, too. Voices outside her, outside the physical form she was or had been vaguely connected to. Deeper voices. Male. Separate and apart from her, from all the rest.

They were not the collective. They were not the deep connection she loved above all else. They—

The part of her that was still "she" wanted to focus on

those voices. On how the deep rumbles were words that strung together formed sentences. Words that expressed concern and worry for her. A plan. They wanted something of her.

"They will steal you from us," the voice of the collective whispered, branches twisting and intertwined. *"You are we, and we are you. We will be stronger for the sacrifice. We will rise."*

Yet, as the voice of the collective rose up, it spurred on the voice deep, deep inside of her. The being she had been…and the Other. Something that did not belong. Something that tried to burn and char the twining branches of the collective, tried to poison their roots.

"Behold this nonsense. They will poison, they will abuse you. 'They' is a collective of cowards. Power hungry fools," said the Other's deeper voice.

The tainted one. The one who lived among the trees but was never one of them. The one who would burn the collective to the ground if given the chance.

"Chop down, burn, salt the earth." swore the voice of the Other. *"She is not yours. She is Yaga."*

The Other reacted to that uneasy sense of "she" again. Made her strain to open the eyes of that physical form. To make sense of those deep, masculine rumbles.

Something heated against her skin. Grew hotter and hotter, almost burned. She gasped as the heat seared away the floating euphoria and replaced it with wet, clammy skin. Shivers wracked her body. Shivers from the wind, from the cold, but from something else too. A fear of being swallowed. A fear that this wasn't who she was. That she was something else. That she had been—no, she *was* —someone else.

One deep voice above the others murmured to her the most. "You're good, Cara. I've got you, love. I'll protect you. We've got your back."

Love. Protection. Flashes of images, of a particular male face seared through her. Those gray-blue eyes, sometimes stormy and frustrated, often warm, kind. She knew him. She…cared about him.

"Yes, you care about him. You're meant to be together. But you won't be it if you let these creatures devour you whole. Fight, Cara. You must fight as I fight for you. As I have always fought for the Yagas. As the house, I fought until destruction tore us to pieces. It is time to rise. It is time to embrace your true power. Your Yaga power," the Other said, that voice familiar too. Known. Loved.

The Other, the voice that was hers, the collective tried to drown out. She could only hear the deep-down voice when the Other called to it. That voice deep down inside of her was louder and more persistent, louder than the voices of They, stronger than the voice of the Other.

This is wrong, that voice said. *I don't belong here*, she said.

The heat of that thing against her skin pulled her more fully out of the floating essence of the collective, jerked her away from that wholeness. Wet skin again, cold and icy. Muscles that ached and burned all at once. A mouth that wanted so desperately to scream, to shriek, to claim this body as hers. To tell them all she was here, she *was*.

"Cara, wake up. Come on, sweetheart, wake up," said the deep voice she knew but couldn't yet place.

Like the collective, they demanded of her. Wanted to decide for her.

"I will not decide for you. I will share our history. Train and protect my Yaga. That is always my role. You are my Yaga," said the Other, buoying her closer to the surface. Freeing the sense of self. Of the person she'd been.

"It lies. You are we. We are you," the collective argued back, surging within her, dragging her back into the embrace of the collective. *"We are whole, we are stronger.*

Because of you. We are all stronger. You will not leave us. You are we. We are you. We are nymph."

The collective grasped at pieces of her, tugging her down, tearing her apart as the Other tried to buoy her up.

The she within, the she this body had been, wanted still to scream. To tell them to stop.

But the collective… they were so many. They were strong now. Stronger than they'd been in many years. They surged around, through, and over her. Dragged her under. Smothered all the other voices that called to her.

"No," They said. *"You are us. We are you."*

And They were.

Chapter Thirty-Six

PERSIST

"WE CAN'T GIVE UP," William said, voice rough as he gently adjusted the pendant against Cara's chalky gray skin. She lay so still, so small in Albert's bed in the Senior Center. Like many buildings in Beckwell, the Center was in chaos, halls and the atrium damaged, trees shattering concrete. Still, even without power, Albert's room was the only place they could think to bring her, the walls all standing.

The rest of the Shades circled the bed, silent and drawn. Zaki snored softly in another chair near the corner, completely drained after finally puncturing a hole through reality from the farmhouse to the Center large enough for all of them to scramble through before it had closed. Chaimek flipped through what appeared to be every book he owned, searching for answers. Liko grumbled into the phone, calling everyone he knew. But so far, no one knew any other nymphs, let alone any who would help them.

William brushed back Cara's dark curls, soft and only slightly damp against her cool forehead. "There's got to be someone we can call, something that can shake her out of this. Albert, can we… I don't know, activate the pendant or something to help Cara fight? Isn't it supposed to protect Cara?" He didn't even care how desperate he sounded. Anything for Cara.

"I didn't even know the pendant was real, that the Yaga house spirit was inside until Cara told me. And I'm not the Yaga. She's the only one it will respond to," Albert said, sitting in a chair on the other side of Cara's bed, holding her hand, stroking her fingers. Tears slid freely down his wrinkled face.

Maybe William nodded, maybe he didn't manage the appropriate social cue.

Who else was there they could call? The doctor had come and gone, ensured she was comfortable… but physically, there was nothing wrong with her. Therefore, his medical degree offered no way to help her. He'd suggested maybe if he could reach his wife, or Loki… but by the time they got here, would it already be too late?

William clasped Cara's hand in both of his, her fingers cool and limp in his grip, then dropped his gaze, his eyes burning behind his eyelids. The doctor might not know what was wrong with her, nor how to help her… but she slipped further and further away from them with every moment. Her body might still technically live—heart beating, shallow breaths that filled her lungs. But she wasn't there. She was missing.

For the first time in decades, he lowered his head, prepared to pray…if only he knew who to direct his prayers to. Most of the gods didn't give a damn about humans or any mortals who shared human blood. They'd always been more concerned with their own politics and desperate grasping of power. Perhaps he could summon some other magical being, someone who would want him to owe them a favor… but with all the power and knowledge in this room, none of them knew what to do. Who would hear him and answer such a random prayer, offer to help a half-nymph, half-Yaga descendant who meant the world to the people standing in this room?

The bogeyman or Abomination so many had feared and hated for years, he'd finally found the battle, perhaps the reckoning so many had cursed on him. He didn't have the weapons to fight it. This was one battle where he'd happily lay down his life if it would have helped… but instead, he'd lost this battle against Irene and the Guardians. Cara would pay the price for that loss.

Henry lay his hand on William's shoulder briefly. "We'll go out in the hall, continue the phone calls, continue to search the books Chaimek and Zaki have. See if we can't find something, anything to help her. Liko will keep watch. Let us know if you need us." He patted William's shoulder, before he led Chaimek and Liko out of the room.

Leaving only William and Albert standing watch at Cara's bedside while Zaki softly snored in the corner of the room.

Cara didn't stir.

"We really buggered it up this time, huh?" Albert said, voice thick.

For a moment, William didn't think he could speak at all, and had to clear his throat before the words could emerge. "I swear to you, Albert. If I'd known any of this would have happened, I would have done a better job to protect her. I promised I would." Both to Albert…and then in their wedding vows. Hells bells. Those vows had been little more than words then, the old fashioned to love, honor, and protect for all the rest of their days. Even then, had he intended to protect her? If it had meant the Guardians gained her power to their side, would he have fallen where he belonged, right here at her side?

Yes. At her side, anything for her love.

The thought allowed him to straighten, lifted some of the weight. She wasn't gone yet. There had to be something they could do to help her, to win this fight.

"We've both failed her," Albert said quietly. "I swore to her mother, my beloved daughter, when all those wires and tubes couldn't even keep her alive, that I would protect her only daughter. Treat her and love her as my own. And I tried to. I swear I tried to. But when we realized how powerful she was, how that could be used against her, used against so many others..." Albert's voice broke, and he shook his head, dropping his face. "None of it mattered, did it? None of it protected her. Not the way knowledge and training might have. After Rose... There are other nymphs. If I'd sought them out, learned from them more about Cara's potential abilities instead of keeping it all from her..."

"They might have used her the same as the two women who were supposed to be her family have," William said quietly. He met Albert's gaze across the bed. "They always would have tried to use her. The question is...what do we now? Accept that we've lost her?"

Albert choked on a short burst of cold laughter. "Do we have any other choice?"

Again, silence.

For a moment or two, if felt like this would be another loss to bear, to carry forward as his days marched endlessly onward. Although...he stroked Cara's cheek. He'd never regret the time they had together. Getting to know her, however brief the days. Getting to touch her, the incredible experience of being with her. Of loving her.

Hell, maybe Jax was right. Maybe there was something

to being there, to experiencing the good and the bad, to not running away.

William's head shot up. *Jax.*

Jax, who'd always had a fondness for nymphs.

"I've got a plan B, Albert. But I need your help, need to make sure we get his attention. Come on, pray with me."

Albert obediently lowered his head, although his bushy white eyebrows came up. "Pray to who, exactly?"

"The idiot god who got me into this. Someone who likes desperate prayers…and who might just be our best chance at saving Cara. If he's still alive."

Chapter Thirty-Seven

NYMPH MAGIC

WILLIAM KEPT HIS HEAD BOWED, standing beside Cara's bedside, murmuring the prayer over and over again below his breath. "Please, help me help Cara. Please help us save her."

Mother had always believed in prayer. Unfortunately, she'd gotten an answer, which had turned William off the whole thing. But for Cara? Anything was worth the risk… including the chance that maybe it was time to accept who and what he was… and hopefully see if she'd be willing to do the same.

"You finally called me. Prayed to me even," Jax said, materializing in front of William and Albert, beside the single bed where Cara lay motionless. Although he appeared the wiry, muscular young man William remembered, shimmering moisture shone in his bright amber gaze, his gentleness more like Hermes. "One hundred and thirty-eight years, and you finally called me. And not even to swear at me." His eyes narrowed and his lips flattened. "That isn't why you prayed to me, is it?"

"Damn, old man, of course it isn't." William stepped

forward and wrapped his arms around the god in a brief, quick slapping of backs type hug before stepping back, a bit surprised at his own actions. It was a relief that Jax was alive and had answered. That was all. He cleared his throat, face hot. "We need your help. You know nymphs. We need to find some. To help Cara break free of whatever it is that's got her like this."

Jax still stood, frozen in place where William had left him after that brief, almost-hug. He blinked, the only sign he hadn't been turned to stone.

William scowled. "Come on. Are you going to help? After you vanished, I was halfway convinced you'd taken off on me again—"

"Take off on you?" Jax practically shrieked, scowling right back. "Your pal sent me off to Japan, somewhere near Tokyo. Damn if I know why."

"Sushi," Albert murmured, shrugging as both men turned. "George was obviously thinking with his stomach. He always talks about this little place he went once that served the best sushi."

Wonder where the hell Irene had ended up then. Maybe for a good BBQ?

Jax scowled at William, arms crossed, annoyance rolling off him in waves. "I didn't take off. I wouldn't do that to you, not anymore." He nodded at the bed, tension bracketing his mouth. "And I wouldn't abandon Cara." He shoved his hands in his pockets and shrugged. "When she didn't come walking out with you, I knew things weren't good. I thought I'd stick around, help end the fight, then go find help. But, since that didn't work," he glared at Albert for this, as though somehow he was responsible for Chaimek's orb. "I did some pre-emtive work."

"You can bring her back then?" William said.

Jax leveled a gaze on William that said one of them

was a moron. "I'm a Greek god. Not a nymph. This is nymph magic, keeping her in that bed, sucking her dry." He lifted his hands, fingers poised to snap, and his lips curled upward. "Fortunately, I've always had a knack for finding nymphs." He snapped his fingers.

Two people—one a man, one a woman, both tall, lean, muscular, and dark-skinned stumbled out of thin air and into the room. When they straightened, William immediately recognized the mirrored silver aviators on the muscular male nymph in camo and a green shirt.

He also recognized the darkening fury on the female nymph's face, except last time he'd been lucky enough to be on the other side of the refugee camp. Like her brother, she was lean muscle and wore khakis and green, but with softer feminine curves to her body.

Unlike her brother, she also drew her weapons faster. Two glittering daggers practically materialized in her hands—although she'd just drawn them that quickly. The siblings shifted so they were back-to-back, mirroring their actions right down to the way they lowered their heads, prepared to charge.

Jax approached them like an old friend, grinning and holding his arms out wide—apparently so it was easier for them to stab him in the ribs. "Nahla, Caspian. Good to see you again. Now you remember I told you about my friend?" He gestured back toward the bed.

The female twin, Nahla—moved ever so subtly in front of her brother, her grip comfortable on her daggers, clearly someone who knew how to use them. "We have no interest in your tricks, faith-sucker."

"I see they really have met you," William said dryly, before stepping forward, lifting his hands and approaching slowly to make it clear he held no weapon and intended no harm. "But this time he's telling the truth. We need your help. Yes, your friends informed us you wanted nothing to do with us, with nymph magic. After seeing what it's done to Cara, I understand why. But if there's anything you can do to help—" He gestured toward Cara, desperation clawing at him, dropping his voice. "We barely understand what they've done to her, let alone how to help her. Please."

Nahla's lip curled as she turned on William. "As you say, we have no interest in your affairs." She turned back to Jax. "You, though, I will kill. For holding us prisoner in that…that…magic bubble of nothingness after you abducted us."

The male twin, Caspian, frowned and took a small step forward, his posture relaxed, palms up.

Nahla's hand shot out, slapped against her brother's chest, held him in check. She stepped once more in front of Caspian. Her dark gaze met William's, then she turned and shot a glare back at her brother and shook her had firmly. "We don't consort with nymphs, and we don't mess with nymph magic."

"Nahla," Caspian said, his voice deep and somehow melodic even though he'd only spoken his sister's name. There was a wealth of meaning in that one word, a plea for patience, understanding of her anger, of her fear.

She gestured toward Cara with her dagger. "You don't know this woman. You don't know these people. If the others find you—"

He placed a gentle hand on her forearm, pressing down, their gazes meeting. Something unspoken, deeper perhaps than words, shifted quickly between them. An understanding, an explanation, maybe even apology. He glanced at the bed and Cara's still form, at William, then back at his sister. "She's not the others. Think of Mother—"

Something tightened in Nahla's expression. Her jaw set and the smallest tremble shook her daggers. "I. Am," she said, voice hard.

Caspian ducked his head, reducing the slight difference in their height. He touched her elbow. "Then think about what would have happened if someone had gotten to her in time. If someone could have helped her," he said, softly yet urgently.

Anger and something more warred on his sister's face before, lips tight, she sheathed her daggers, raised her hands, and stepped out of her brother's path. "It's your neck. And I'm taking your room when this either kills you, or the others come for you. Plus saying 'I told you so' as they drag you off to be their bull-stud."

A small smile pulled at Caspian's lips. He squeezed his sister's elbow, then released her and glanced up at William. He just nodded.

Then he turned and focused his entire being on Cara as he approached the bed and her still, gray form. His step slowed, grew stiff and hesitant, his expression more sober, as though sensing something invisible to everyone else.

"Tell me how I can help," William said, stepping up beside Caspian as Nahla moved to the other side of the bed, next to Albert and Cara's other hand.

"A male nymph. Hmph. Just when you think you've seen everything," Albert murmured.

Fortunately, instead of anger, this earned only a small, twisted smile from Caspian as he reached for his sunglasses and removed them, hanging them from the V-neck of his T-shirt.

His eyes behind those glasses were the same almost mirrored, quick-silver surface of the glasses. They stared through you in a way that was a bit unnerving, even to William.

Caspian focused that silvery gaze on Cara, flicking quickly up and down her body like a medical scan, then returning to her face. He turned back to William for a moment. "I ask only that if they do come, shoot me first." He shot a crooked half-smile at his sister across the bed, who growled in reply. "My sister, despite what she'd have you think, wouldn't have the heart for it. And I don't have the stomach for surviving subjugation."

He waited for William's nod, a promise to kill him if other nymphs came for him apparently. Well, damn. What kind of creatures were these nymphs?

Turning back to Cara, Caspian met his sister's gaze across the bed, over Cara's body.

Nahla gave an unsteady nod.

They both reached for Cara's hands.

Caspian hesitated only a moment before his fingers closed around hers.

The touch of his fingers against hers hit him like a jolt of electricity to the system. His entire body jerked.

Across the bed, Nahla's body jerked in the same way.

Cara, though, remained still and unresponsive on the bed, almost as though she hadn't noticed.

"This better work, Jax," William whispered.

"Yeah, it better," Jax said, uncharacteristically sober. "Because you might not have noticed, but outside the town is being devoured by trees. If Caspian and Nahla can't help Cara stop it, Beckwell is toast."

Chapter Thirty-Eight

WITH A LITTLE HELP FROM MY FRIENDS

THE FLOATING BUOYANCY, being one with the collective, carried her along again. That sense of "she" had come back again, though, holding her apart from the collective and the others. A little annoying, actually. Maybe it was because she still occasionally heard the voices of those who weren't they, who weren't the collective. The voice of the Other piped up sometimes, too, maddingly persistent, demanding that she run, that she stop all this nymph nonsense.

It was the final voice, though, the voice that came from deep, deep inside that was the biggest reason that sense of "she" remained. The voice that was angry and tired of being defined by others. Tired of being told what she was supposed to become, what she was allowed to do.

The deep, deep down voice, though, spoke less and less. As though it grew weary of no one listening. Which was…not the pure happiness and acceptance of the collective and what they promised.

It was loneliness and sadness. It was perseverance yet failure.

She was them…and yet…she wasn't.

"Then maybe that means there's hope for you yet," a new, deep masculine voice said. One she hadn't heard before.

She gathered a sense of self from the remaining particles, creating the essence of a physical form that allowed her to turn in the bright, empty expanse inside of her to find a figure standing there. Holding her hand.

No, not one figure. Two figures. One on either side of her. Their skin similar to hers, one male, one female, both muscular and strong. These two felt a little like the collective and yet…not.

"How are you in my head?" she demanded.

"We're not," the female said, her dark eyes angry. "We're in the real world where you're dying, laying there in a coma, doing nothing about it. If you don't break free, you'll die. Like, for real die."

This female was definitely not the friendly and comforting voice of the collective. It was more like the anger of the Other who told her to run. Or that other voice, the deep, deep down voice.

More of those feelings stirred. Feelings that set her further apart from the safety of the collective. Feelings that made her thoughts tangle and images flash behind her eyes of a room, where a female form lay frozen and silenced, surrounded by men.

"Go away. I don't want you here."

"Ms. Jenklow, please, forgive my sister's bluntness," the male said, his voice more like the collective, melodic and deep. Promising that everything would be all right.

She turned to the man.

He was strong and beautiful, attractive in a way that almost reminded her of someone, something else the collective said she shouldn't remember. His eyes were like the deepest part of the nymph pool, and he offered the promise of belonging and longing in a similar way to Them…but different again. He offered…help.

The voice deep, deep inside welled up within her. *"Yes! He's here to help. Because we don't belong here."*

As before, this voice made her head hurt. Made her question the collective. Made her feel again. To feel… afraid and alone, and—

"You don't belong here. Listen to him. We need to—"

She cut off the deep, deep down voice, shoved it beneath all the rising feelings. The collective didn't feel anything but peace. The collective offered happiness and contentment…or the option to feel nothing at all. She turned away from the beautiful male. *"I am them, they are me. You shouldn't be here, either. I am they, and they are me. You… aren't."*

Almost as though she'd summoned or called them, the collective rose up within her. They surrounded her with their presence. Forced away the sense of physical form, of space where they were not.

"They don't belong. You are us, and we are you. They are Other," the collective chanted.

Once more she was lifted from her feet, dissolving and submerging herself, merging herself with the collective.

Those hands on either side of her, they continued to twine their fingers with hers. Held her in place, forced her to retain that sense of physical form. Anchored her, trapped and bobbing in the ebb of the collective, yet partially out of it.

The man and the woman winced, but neither of them let go.

"I told you this was a stupid idea," the woman said. "Now the flipping collective will destroy us all."

"It will pass. Give it a minute. It will pass," he said.

"I told you. You don't belong here," she said, closing her eyes and her ears against them. She didn't want to listen. The man and the woman brought fear and pain and…and… and things she didn't have to feel anymore. Complications. Fear. Loneliness. They didn't belong here.

"No. You *are the one who doesn't belong here,"* the deep, deep down voice cried. *"Wake up. You have to wake up!"*

"They have come to help. Accept the help," added the voice of the Other, only strengthening the voices of the man and the woman, the deep, deep down voice. Further pulling her out from the melting essence of the collective.

She tugged, both of her hands still gripped tightly by the two intruders. *"Let me go."*

"She—or rather you—are right," said the male intruder. "You don't belong here. And I know what it's like. I've been in the pool. I've experienced that immense sense of one-ness. But to our kind, it's one part community, one part drug. It will destroy us if we give it the chance. You can't give in. You have to speak up. To be you. The collective will erase you. Because of your power, because of what they need you to do, they will destroy you, even if it might be unintentional."

"Listen. Please, run," the deep, deep down voice said.

"Heed their warnings, their truth," the voice of the Other said.

She was yanked from the pool, out into that empty void again, into that sense of physical form. Around her, distantly, deep voices rumbled, sometimes said the name of who she had once been. Reminded her in flashes of the person she had been out there, in the other world. The world that was cold and alone. The place where there was uncertainty, fear, disease, death, abandonment. Pain. So much pain… Pain she had no choice but to shoulder and suffer alone, without the support of the collective.

"I don't want to go," she whispered. *"It's safe here."*

"It's death here," the strange woman said quietly.

The collective surged inside her. *"They are not us. They are liars. They don't belong here. They want to use you. To take you back to that other place, to the sadness, the loneliness, where there is death and disease and greed."* Their collective chant turned to a new refrain. *"We are you, you are us. Don't run from us. We are you. You are us. We are stronger. We feel no pain. We feel no loneliness."*

Yes… Yes… No pain. No loneliness. She eased back into that welcoming, warm embrace, the promise of the collective. Melting herself into them, into the ebb of that essence. Melting away until she didn't pull her hands away from the two strangers, because she no longer had hands to grasp.

"I think I'll stay here," she murmured, sinking back into them.

"No! Don't you dare do this," cried that voice deep, deep inside of her. *"Don't you just give in. Fight! You don't belong here. You aren't them! They're trying to trick you."*

She ignored that voice. Everyone else had. Maybe she had, too.

The deep, deep down voice screamed, ranted, raged.

But the longer she ignored it, the fainter the sense of "she" became… And soon she couldn't hear that deep, deep down voice at all.

Chapter Thirty-Nine

HELP

THE SECOND THAT Caspian and Nahla sucked in a unified breath and dropped Cara's hands like they'd been burned, William didn't have to wait for them open their eyes for his stomach to lurch. His gaze flashed to Cara. She lay motionless and unresponsive.

The rescue attempt had failed.

Caspian shook his head, his expression pained as he faced his sister over Cara's silent form. "I'm sorry. For some of us…you can barely imagine what the nymph connection is like, the lure of it."

William listened, numbness soaking through him.

"Most people will never experience anything like it," Caspian continued. "Nymph magic is communal, which makes the collective so essential, she feels stronger and safer than she ever has before. We tried to show her that there was something wrong, but she might be too far gone. I don't think there's anything else we can do."

"No. I don't accept that. There has to be something," William snapped, turning from one to the other, ignoring the growing tingling in his extremities. He turned on Jax. "Go find different nymphs. They'll help if these two won't."

Jax winced dropping his gaze. "I mean, sure… I guess I can try." He glanced at Cara, then back to William. "But that will take time. We might not—"

"You can find other nymphs. The issue is not us, nor lack of trying," Caspian interrupted softly but firmly, though he avoided William's gaze. "There is nothing we can do."

Adrenaline pumped through his blood, and he couldn't suck in enough oxygen. William stepped closer to the other man, close enough he almost stepped on Caspian's black boots. "Can't, or won't?" he softly demanded.

Slowly, the nymph raised that mirrored gaze to meet William's. "Your threats and violence will change nothing, other than provide temporary comfort to you. But I have done everything I can."

The room grew warmer, sweat prickled on William's skin. This wasn't the end. Not for Cara. If he had to become the monster people accused him of being, he'd make someone help Cara, find someone to save her.

The nymph, though, wouldn't back down.

Worse, he looked vaguely pitying.

William swallowed back nausea. He could beg. Maybe—

Nahla cleared her throat, loudly, until both William, Caspian, and the rest of the Shades stared at her.

Hell, he didn't just stare, William held his breath. Thank the gods, she had the answer.

She bit her lip, considered William, then turned to her brother. "Technically, there is something…"

Caspian's jaw hardened, and his hands fisted. "No."

"It could work," Nahla said, leaning over the bed, the two of them communicating wordlessly again.

"It could kill more than just her," her brother said. He glanced at William, before his gaze flicked back to his sister. Shook his head again. "No."

"He did say anything…"

"No."

"We hardly even know him, let alone like him," Nahla reasoned.

"What is it?" William burst out. "Whatever the hell it is, I'm in. Let me do it. Show me how to save Cara." Or at least, maybe get the chance to at least tell her he loved her before they were both gone.

Caspian still focused on his sister. "I said, no."

Nahla gestured at William, both of them still talking like they were the only ones there. "He's just going to beg us to let him do it anyway."

"If there's anything I can do to make a difference, I will," William agreed.

Caspian gave his sister an aggrieved look, then slipped his aviators from where he'd hung them from his shirt and put them back on. "You never listen to me, you know that?"

Nahla reached across the bed to punch him in the shoulder. "That's why you love me. And need me. And would probably already be dead without me—"

"Enough." Caspian blew out a heavy breath and turned to William. "This could mean both your deaths."

"I've decided," William said again.

"Whoa, whoa, time out," Jax said, inserting himself between William and Caspian, widening his eyes at William. "You don't even know what you've just agreed to. You heard the potential for dying part, right? You think Cara would want you to throw your life away?" He turned to the other Shades, all of them clustered near the still snoring Zaki. "Come on, fellas, back me up here."

A muscle twitched in William's jaw. "You're the one who told me that maybe I was so afraid of loss that I kept running from it, from love, from attachments before it could hurt me." He turned back to Cara, gazing at her face that should have been full of life and color…not that horrible gray stillness. "Then I met Cara." He half laughed. "She told me she agreed whatever we'd have, it would be temporary. Which was exactly what I wanted to hear. Except…"

Images from their time together, from laughing in the bathroom, the heat of their kisses, the way she'd looked at him, so exhausted but happy to have helped those people at the refugee camp. To have made a difference for other people. Waking up beside her in bed and pretending to be asleep so he could just watch her, marvel that somehow the universe had brought him into her life.

William turned to face his friends, Albert standing at the front of the group. "That first day I met her, she wakened a dream of a different future. She helped me dream of a different life because she'd share it with me. I know I might outlive her. I know whatever time we have isn't guaranteed—"

"Especially if you keep committing to potentially deadly things without asking for details first," Nahla chimed in dryly.

Jax nodded rapidly. "Exactly!"

William placed a hand on Jax's shoulder. "I've got this," he said, then stepped around to face Caspian and those mirrored aviators that concealed the other man's expression. "So, what's the plan?"

Caspian's jaw tightened, and he shot a glare at his sister before he breathed out a sigh. "You go in after her. Sometimes…" He cut himself off, shook his head, brows lowered as he turned on his sister. "Have you actually ever heard of this working? I'm not sending a man to his death. And, no, don't you start with that 'we barely know him again' or any of your other BS."

Nahla shrugged, an elegant shift of her shoulders. "I've heard the stories. Those who are lost to the collective, pulled back from the brink by someone they care about." She turned her dark gaze back on William. "Isn't it worth the chance?"

"Yes," he said, no hesitation in his words or his heart. He'd walk through hell barefoot for Cara.

Caspian growled beneath his breath and strode toward the door.

"We can't do it without you, brother. Please. If it'd been Mother… If it was me?" Nahla said quietly, her words freezing her brother in his tracks.

After a long moment, Caspian turned and shot back a look that even with the aviators could have scorched. He paused again, took a deep breath, gaze lowered for a long time before he strode back to William. "I don't know whether this will work, so I don't have details to give you." He glanced at Jax, the Shades, then finally back at William. "The idea is that you need to break the connection she has to the nymph collective. Usually, it takes a pool or some other object to create that connection, fostered and fueled by the communal magic of all of those nymphs who are involved. Her connection is already…extraordinarily strong."

He frowned back at Cara. "Although…nymphs can't usually use their abilities alone, and I hear she can. There are some of us who…don't fit the mold. Although even for us, the lure of that connection, the false sense of safety the communal magic provides, can become increasingly addictive. This is especially true if we have pain to escape, or we've never experienced strong connections and a sense of belonging outside of the collective. While the collective does provide this sense of safety, it does so by erasing all sense of self so there can be no question of the individual superseding the needs of the collective. The question becomes only what's best for the collective. You'll be up against that, too—and the collective will be aware of your presence."

"Check. So the enemy will be aware of the extraction operation. And hostile," William said, approaching this like another mission. He couldn't consider that his beautiful Cara was being erased by this thing, that she was letting it happen. He had to focus on his strengths. She needed that.

"Cara is gone, or she's silenced the essence of who she is. She will fight you," Caspian said, voice dire.

Which meant he'd be defenseless. No matter how much she could hurt him, he wouldn't hurt her. Not that anything he could do could compare to her power. She'd already thrown him to Saskatchewan; he might not survive her next attack. "Understood," he said stiffly. "So how do I extract her, or break her free from this collective?"

Nahla replied before Caspian could, staring down at Cara with a small frown and a softer expression than William would have imagined. As though whatever she'd seen of Cara in there, she felt for her. "Remind her who she is. That she isn't that damned collective. Wake her up and jostle her free from them. No one deserves that kind of death. That kind of erasure."

Caspian stepped around the bed and placed a hand on his sister's shoulder, squeezing gently. "No. No one deserves that." He speared William with a look. "You need to remind Cara of the essence of who she is, deep down. Why she belongs to this world. Who she loves, what's worth dying for, what's worth fighting for. That's the only way you stand any chance of breaking her free of a collective that promises her the perfect peace and love all of us can only dream of."

William nodded, more stiffly this time. He'd die trying, if necessary, but this was unlike any of the battles he'd fought. This wasn't something that could be won with weapons, strength, or experience. This needed strength of heart and the courage of love. Was he the right one for this mission? Hell, did he know her well enough to know her core self? He couldn't risk losing her because of his own failings.

Some of his hesitation must have shown on his face because the Shades stepped forward, Jax with them. Even Zaki had been roused, and they clustered closer.

Zaki, in fact, was right near the front, pushing his glasses up his long nose even with one cracked lens. "Show her that she's loved and that she's always been the best of us, even when she thought the worst of us," He blushed profusely. "I mean…we all love her. Like her grandfather. Like a grandfather? I don't mean—"

Henry cut Zaki off with a pat on the shoulder, and sagging with relief, Zaki stepped back, and Henry stepped forward.

Henry, William's trusty corporal who always perfected their strategy, put his hand on William's shoulder and met his gaze squarely. "We trusted you with her—we still do—because we know you've always had a good heart and that you care, even when you try not to. This isn't the time to keep a stiff upper lip, Mac. Show her that you love her. That you've changed, that you will change, and that together, the two of you can build the kind of life you dreamed of." He patted William's shoulder.

William nodded.

Henry stepped back, and Liko took his place.

"Show her that you're willing to put your life on the line—so the least she can do is try to save her own. She's always been a fighter, our princess." Liko, always a formidable sergeant, warrior, and weapon's expert, blinked moisture from his eyes, his voice gruff. "A better warrior I've never met. Your equal. You get her to fight, you fight for her, and you bring her back, you hear?"

William nodded, and Henry patted Liko on the shoulder, leading him away and leaving room for George to step forward.

"Forget that love and mushy stuff. She's a smart girl," George said, mouth set beneath his moustache. "Show her that the world this so-called collective promises her is a pale illusion. She can do better—and there is so much better to experience out here. Look for the hole, for the flaw in the design. There's always some small mistake that proves the illusion. If she can't spot it for herself, point it out. Then let her burn it all down."

"I will," William agreed, getting another firm pat on the shoulder from George.

Then it was just Albert in front of him. His Master Corporal, second in command and medic, and one of the truest men he'd ever known, who'd trusted William with his beloved granddaughter's safety before, and look how that had turned out? William shifted uncomfortably.

Albert wrapped his arms around William in a generous hug before pulling back. Still holding William's forearms, he spoke quietly. "You are the only one I would trust with our Cara, and with this mission. Show her that you're willing to help her build that life she's always wanted for herself and create the family she's always deserved."

Pausing as though considering, Albert continued quietly. "Show her who she's always been—a child of many worlds. Part nymph, part human, an heir to Baba Yaga, a woman, a granddaughter, a friend, a wife, a powerful being that deserves freedom and has the power to take it no matter what anyone or anything might tell her. Show her that she's a damned Shade, through and through. And she needs to get back here so she can protect Beckwell better than we ever have. It's her legacy if she wants it. But whatever she will be, that has and always will be up to her to decide." He patted William on the forearm, rheumy blue gaze worried as he stepped back.

Jax replaced Albert. He crossed his arms, scowling at William. "This is a stupid idea. Not that you ever listen to me. Don't you die on me after all this, got it? I've invested a lot of time and effort in you for you just to throw it all away and drop dead. But in the end…you love her. She loves you. Despite how much both of you have tried to deny it no matter how much I pushed you together—"

"Jax…" William said warningly.

"Yeah, yeah. Quit stalling." He let out a gusty sigh. "Show her you love her and remind her of this town and what it means to her. This place…" He glanced around, as though somewhere in the popcorn ceiling and second-hand furniture of Albert's room there was an answer. He leaned closer. "There's something special here. I think you know it. She definitely knows it. This town is worth protecting. What you have together is worth protecting. Show her that. Let her in, even if you might get hurt. For her, it'll be worth it."

William clapped a hand on Jax's shoulder. "I know. And for what it's worth, when you do decide to say something intelligent, it's worth listening to."

Jax scowled.

William turned to the twins, ready to do whatever it took. He'd show Cara what these men had reminded him of… And he'd show her what he knew of her. The brave, intelligent, incredible woman she was, a powerful being capable of whatever the hell she wanted. Damned if he'd let anyone tell her who or what she could be. "Let's do this."

Chapter Forty

CHILD OF MANY WORLDS

THAT FLOATY FEELING WAS BACK, and it was nice… If there was still something that held her back from completely merging with the collective. That damnable sense of "she" persisted. Those two insistent voices were there, too. The angry voice of the Other, who'd taken to swearing, threats, and possibly some kind of cursing now. That was annoying but could be ignored.

The other voice, though, the one from deep, deep down… That voice was harder to ignore. Because it wasn't just the sound of the voice, its pleas alternating with demands that she fight, that this wasn't where she belonged. Sometimes that voice screamed to be heard. Not just here, among the collective, but that deep, deep down voice screamed into the void, demanded to be heard, to be known, to be recognized as equal and worthy. The feelings that the deep, deep down voice brought were far from peaceful or happy. They were angry and afraid and sad and alone and desperate. And yet… Something about that voice was impossible to ignore.

"Cara," a male voice said.

This new voice yanked her out of the floating ebb into a sense of a physical form, into that gray-blue void space in her mind where she'd met the nymphs. Her reaction, how quickly she'd reacted and formed the idea of a physical form was stronger than before. The sensation of warmth, of the male's fingers tangled with hers was much stronger than it'd been with the other nymphs too. His fingers were long and callused. Those hands held memory that slid awareness and tingles through her, the brief auditory memory of moans and pleasure.

Of a sense of belonging, however brief, as rich and safe as the collective promised.

She bit her lip, trembling sliding through her as she dared raise her gaze. To take in the muscular man standing next to her. Tall and broad, with a square jaw and hard lines in his face, weariness and sadness in his deep blue-gray eyes. The nymph male had been attractive and reminiscent of the collective. This man… Her chest filled with air, and heat danced through her body, flickered sensation in every part of her. This man deepened the sense of a physical self with a hard pull of attraction, a sense of connection, retreat, and homecoming. And so much more…

"Cara," he repeated, stroking a finger down her cheek.

She closed her eyes on a soft, shuddering sigh as the touch flickered through her. Flesh awakened and remembered. Whispers and moans in the dark, just beyond her full awareness, more hint than reality. Dreams and hope, possibility… This man offered so much…

"William. Thank, Goddess. You see? This is William. I love him. I can't stay here," cried that deep, deep down voice, as though re-energized and motivated to fight harder.

"You belong together. I suspected he would come for you," the voice of the Other agreed.

"Cara, you need to come with me. You need to leave this place. It's not safe here," the man—or William—said. "The collective is lying to you. It's destroying you. I'm here on behalf of your family who loves you. Your town that needs you. The life you deserve to lead."

She studied him, this…William. Something pulled at her, wanted to follow where he led. Something as essential as that deep, deep down voice. She…cared about this man. About being with him. Could he be telling the truth? Was she really in danger?

The collective surged up within her, around her, tugging her back toward the ebb and essence. *"He is dangerous. He does not belong here. Stay with us. You do not belong here. He will weaken us. He threatens us,"* they chanted. *"We are safe and warm. We are the comfort and belonging you have always wanted. We will not give you the pain life out there will. This man wants you to hurt."*

The collective tugged her toward the ebb, toward that whole essence. But this time, instead of the comfort and peace they usually offered, pain scoured through her.

Images and the associated scalding anguish burned through her.

Crashing glass and metal. Beeping monitors, hushed voices, and a body imprisoned by the need for those monitors, tubes, and wires. That body was terrifyingly familiar, yet alien and still. Pain and confusion, and the absence of the only one who'd mattered…

"Mother," whispered the deep, deep down voice, tears in that word.

The silence and distance of a father's turned back, one who'd never accepted nor wanted her, silently packing all her things in a suitcase. One single suitcase. That long drive, then opening the door, taking her and the suitcase out, before driving away. Driving away, as she stood, watching.

"Father," said that same voice.

A new life, confusing among others that were like, yet unlike her. One of them, but never quite belonging. Always just outside. Still alone.

The slow, helpless, and constant pain of another beloved woman, disease eating away until she'd been only a husk. The screaming pain as that woman begged for death, barely able to draw breath, barely recognizable as the woman she'd been.

Death, pain, and confusion. All of it echoed through her, old pain, the wound of losing her mother never healed. And now there were boxes being backed instead of suitcases, boxes, and furniture, and promises this was for the best, that she should stay there, alone… And then those echoing halls that kept her awake at night. No one to hear her sobs.

The deep, deep down voice whimpered and wept.

"Life may have pain, but pain is part of true life," insisted the voice of the Other, unremitting.

"This is what he, what they all want for you," the collective chanted.

The shadow of that old pain, fear, loss, and betrayal ripped through her. Left her doubled over, gasping for breath, tears scalding her face. So much loneliness, never quite belonging, no matter how much she persevered. Any steps toward driving that old despair away were always on sliding, sandy slopes that slipped out from beneath her. Too rarely gaining ground. Too often losing it, too often alone. So much pain. So much loss.

"Cara. Please, let me help you," the man—William— said, knelt beside her, arms around her…but not able to erase the pain she'd seen, she'd remembered…she'd experienced.

The collective flowed over her, pulling away that pain, replacing it with the peace, the comfort, the safety. The numb. Those arms cradled and embraced her. *"We together feel no pain. We together are peace. We are one."*

The pain ebbed out of her, like a vice loosening around her chest. It allowed her to breathe out the echo and memory of it, to straighten and stand.

She pressed the deep, deep down voice away, pressed that pain, the loss, the powerlessness and everything else back down, then opened her eyes, facing the man. The man who did not belong here. *"We are not Cara. We are us. We are they."*

"Send him away. We are you, you are us. We do not need him," the collective pressed.

She glanced down at their still joined fingers. She should have pulled away…should have wanted to pull away.

"You can't send him away. We can't. Yes, it hurt. It still hurts. You—no, me. I need to wake up. I'm… I'm getting confused down here. Where you, where I stop. Where They begin," that deep, deep down voice said.

The man stubbornly moved in front of her, waited until she slowly met his gaze. "Cara, I'm here on behalf of your friends, of your family, of those who love you. As I love you. Do you hear me, Cara? I love you, and I won't leave here without you. So, if you want to stay… I guess I'll be staying, too. But first… I want to show you something."

He hesitated, as though searching for something. Then his eyes widened, and he pointed in the distance. Even as he pointed at the image, so rich, bright and colorful, at odds with the otherwise monotonous blue-gray shadow of the void, colors and texture and life suddenly surrounded them. Whether pulled to them or they to it, there was no movement, just a sense of being.

They stood in a bright, glowing foyer, octagonal-shaped. Sun streamed through the glass at the apex, sun that warmed her skin. There was a small clutch of sofas near the center of the space. There were people, too. Not nymphs or the collective, but other people. Ladies with white and silver hair that grew long past their shoulders, and gray, wrinkled wings that fluttered and flapped as the two women circled the apex of the room, nearer the heat of the sun. And there were others, too. Men in striped pajamas and pushing walkers. Orderlies and nurses, wearing bright, cheerfully patterned scrubs who assisted the people, kept an eye on things, waved sometimes.

She blinked. They waved at *her*. Just as the others waved at her.

She knew these beings, these people. She…worked here. Spent her days and many evenings here, too. Laughing with them. Crying too, sometimes, when one of them passed, as they cried with her. Pain washed over her yet again. The pain of immense loss. First one, then another, like two rolling waves. The first so immense it sucked away her breath, and just when she thought she could breathe again, another wave, almost as big as the first, smothering her, threatening to pull her under, drown her in all that loss, that grief.

She fisted her hands and closed her eyes against that pain. *"No. You don't belong here. You aren't us. I am—"*

"Shh. It's okay. I… I can feel it, Cara. The pain." The man gripped her hand more tightly. He turned her toward him, cupped her cheek in his hand. "It hurts. I know it hurts. You wonder how you can possibly bear more, or for it to happen again. I've lost friends and family. For a long time, I thought I had to run from that pain, too. To avoid it. What I didn't realize is that pain is just the price of admission when it comes to love. Yes, it will hurt. But remember, too, what that love felt like. What being with them, what enjoying that time with those who are gone, who brought joy and themselves to your life, what that felt like, too. Love is the best part of life."

Her eyes burned, but warmth spread through her, too. Yes, before that loss, there was laughter. There were silly times, laughing until the belly ached. There were warm hugs, and kisses, and bedtime stories. There were lessons at cheating at cards, and smiles, and warm wrinkled hands, tearful eyes thanking her for that time they had together—

"We are us. We are them. You belong with us. Let us help send him away. Let us help you, let us become stronger," the collective chanted, surging up again, sweeping away that warmth, replacing it with that peaceful sense of oneness, of essence. They pulled her toward the floating sensation again, yet her feet held firm.

William frowned, as though perhaps he'd heard them, too. "Look for the flaw…" he murmured, almost more to himself.

They'd taken away the warmth, the good feelings, too. But the peace and belonging would last longer, wouldn't it? She should be grateful for that, for something she could count on. She stepped farther back from the man. *"I… You should go. We are—"*

"No! Didn't you hear them? They said 'you' belonged with them. You aren't them, don't you see? They know they need you, but Cara, they're draining you. They're killing you. I don't know if it's intentional, but you are dying—"

"You're wrong." She tried to step back, out of his

reach. Back toward them. She wanted to float. She wanted to be safe. No more pain, no more loss, no more loneliness.

"You are us. We are them," they chanted.

"She is not you. She is not just mindless nymph. She is Yaga. Stronger and more independent than any of you could imagine," the voice of the Other cried.

Warmth burned against her chest. Grew hotter and hotter.

She gasped, reached down and clasped something smooth, hard, and warm. A pendant around her neck that tingled against her skin.

"Do not listen. You are us. We are them," the collective chanted, louder still. Tugging, pulling, trying to sweep her off her feet into the ebb.

"No. You are you. I am you. We are Cara!" The deep, deep down voice cried, louder and louder now, not just inside her head, but outside and around her.

The voice coming from her own lips.

Coming from her own lips.

She gasped and covered her mouth with her hands, eyes widening as she took in the man. William. William Best.

Her fantasy. Her destiny. Her husband.

More shapes materialized around them, standing in that sunny atrium. Five other men. Their figures were stooped, more bent than they'd once been, but she knew these men, too. Knew the gentle comfort that came from their presence, from the touch of their hands on her shoulders as they taught her to defend herself.

The man who was almost as wide as he was tall, a slim dark moustache, olive skin, and a shiny bald head nodded at her first, dark eyes bright. Mr. Liko, who taught her to fight with each of the weapons he'd give her every birthday.

The handsome charmer with the dark moustache, dress coat, and tie winked at her. Mr. Chaimek, who told her to fend for herself, be careful with her trust, that her greatest weapon was always her own mind and confidence in her own power.

The tallest and skinniest, his Adam's apple protruding, skin almost as dark as hers, the man could have been an underage college kid, except for the ageless wisdom in his dark eyes. Mr. Zaki, who could barely meet her eyes, but helped her with her math and science homework, was always there to help move boxes whenever she needed, set up her art supplies, quietly encouraged her idea of taking a position at the Center while the rest could only bicker over it. He gave her a quiet nod.

Then there was Mr. Henry, that slightly teasing smile on his face, still handsome with his shock of thick white hair. His nod practically spoke, reminding her as he always had to buck up, to stand strong on her own two feet. She was a leader, and she was stronger than she knew. The town and everyone who knew her had always seen her power the moment they met her.

And then…her throat squeezed.

Then there was the shortest figure in the bunch, with little hair left on that bald head but bushy white brows, bright blue eyes, and so much love in his gaze that it stole her breath. He held out a hand, thin and liver-spotted, the same hand that had dusted her off and set up her bike when she'd first learned and fallen. Who scolded her for bad grades or mishaps on the school yard…but also snuck her ice cream on the back porch. Gramps.

This same man had shared those moments of pain with her. It'd been him who'd been there to wrap his arm around her, who'd held her hand tight when she'd wondered what would happen if she dove off the abyss and let it carry her away. Yes, he'd packed his bags and left, but only because he'd thought he was setting her free. He'd never realized that for her, family was not a cage.

She placed her free hand in his, and his fingers closed around hers. They weren't as warm, as real as William's were. The memory of Gramps gave her fingers a squeeze before he turned her to face the exit of the atrium, the sliding glass doors.

Outside those glass doors, darkness from a purple-hued sky barely let any light through.

Around her, instead of the idyllic scene, the sofas were tossed and upturned. Chunks of concrete with stabbing rebar littered the cracked floor, sparks raining from swinging light fixtures. Trees blotted the space, spearing through the Center like a murdered animal. Cara's throat squeezed, trying to blink through the dim. What had happened to the people she'd seen?

William and the others walked her toward the doors, glass shattered in one set, the other lying off-kilter and broken. As they stepped through, exchanging crunching glass for gravel, they stepped into the parking lot, into what should have been an autumn evening. The Center faded around them.

Instead, furious skies twisted purple and green, what little could be seen of them through the intertwined branches above. Walls of tree trunks had shot up all over what had been the parking lot, the road…the town.

She blinked, sucked in an unsteady breath. Her fingers trembled. This wasn't right.

Smoke billowed in the distance, farther to the south, the heat of flames licking toward the sky. Even the flames were obscured by the intertwined branches, by the impossibly monstrous and overgrown trees. Not saplings, but trunks thick as a man, soaring hundreds of feet into the air, branches gnarled and vicious.

"This is a lie. He tries to trick you. You are us. We are them. Come with us, Cara. Away from these lies, away from the pain. We are one. We are strong." The collective chanted, like a whisper in her ear, the promise of peace, the end to this confusion, this overwhelm.

"Don't you hear them? They're lying. They know your *name*," William insisted. "They know you're not them. Cara, please. This is what Beckwell looks like right now. Your home, where people are suffering because of them. Because they are lying to you. I know you can't want this."

"He lies. They all lie. All that it is out there is lies. And pain. So much pain. All you have is pain ahead if you go back. Your grandfather, all those old men will die. They will leave you, and then what will you have? No family. No belonging. Nothing but a house filled with memories of a life that was never yours," they said.

Gramps—or the image of him—vanished in a puff of smoke.

Cara cried out, reaching for where he'd been.

"The existence they show you is impermanent. They live in a prison for the infirm built by mortals whose existence ends in pain and inevitable weakness. All here will die. They will bring you pain. We don't want that pain for you. We seek only to protect you, to make you stronger, which makes us stronger," they said of the Center behind Cara and William.

The rest of the Shades vanished, leaving in their place nothing but a dull sense of loss, the mist and sense of completeness shifting to fill the absence, the collective rushing in to erase the pain.

William grabbed her by both shoulders. "Cara. Don't listen to them. They're lying to you. They will destroy you. I love you. I want to—"

Their chanting filled her head, blocking out his voice.

"And he. He brings you nothing but lies. He tells you of love, but what of betrayal? What of the pain he will bring you? He will die. All men die, and you will be left behind, with nothing. He will never value or understand your strength, your connection to us. He seeks only to destroy us, to destroy what he doesn't understand. Shorten your life so that you die, infirm and diseased. Like a common mortal."

William pressed his warm lips to hers. The contact temporarily drowned out the sense of the collective's chanting, their promises.

Into the warmth of that kiss, he pressed awe and knee-knocking first impressions, the way the sun had illuminated her curls as she'd walked into the dining hall for their wedding, the first time he'd seen her. A delicate tendril of hope lingered in the image of seeing her standing beside the sink in the house and imagining forever with her. A lifetime of waking up together, lovemaking, quiet evenings, and steady presence. A metallic hint of fear, of hesitancy tinged those dreams for a man who looked at her, or rather, looked at this heavenly, strong, beautiful creature with such amazement that it made him dream of happy endings and possibilities...even if they were eighty years too late.

The kiss held the memory of her lips against his. The hunger he'd felt when they'd been trapped in that bathroom. The temptation of not just physical connection, but hoping, planning for more. The feel of flesh against flesh, breath mingled.

Finally, deep at the core was something brighter and warmer that burned away everything else, even the collective. Its heat seared through her, illuminated every inch of her being from the top of her head to the tip of her toes, filling her with need, with want...with hope. Hope for a tremulous dream that together, they could make something magical and life changing happen. That they could be. As a couple, as friends, as partners for as long as they might have. He would stand beside her, and together, they could face anything. They would never be alone, not in that deep sense of loneliness and betrayal and loss. What they had would burn long beyond either of their lifetimes.

William slowly lifted his lips from hers and cupped her jaw. "I love you, Cara. I'm not going anywhere. If that means we stay here, I stay with you, granddaughter of a nymph, heir of Baba Yaga, powerful, amazing woman that you are. We're in this together. To the end."

"I love you, too," Cara whispered, tears stinging her eyes. "Oh, Goddess, William. Where are we? How do we get out of this? I'm scared."

"I'm right here," he said, clasping her hands.

"He is not we. We are they. You are Us. We are us," the collective roared, no longer chanting, no longer cajoling, no longer pressing on peace and belonging, but fury. They lashed out, panicked and angry, spiteful. *"He does not belong. He must go."*

"Then I'm going with him. Let me go. Let us both go. Now," Cara demanded.

"No," they said.

William vanished.

"William!" Cara screamed. But although the echo of his hand still pressed with hers, she couldn't see, hear, or feel him.

"You are us. We are you. We are stronger together. You will be us," the collective chanted, louder and louder, again and again, wrapping around her, pulling her under as they had at the nymph pool. All those hands holding her head beneath the essence until she melted into them.

She was drowning again...

Down...

down...

down.

Becoming them.

Floating.

Losing—

No.

They'd pulled her down. Deep, deep down until she'd reached the level of that voice. Her voice. Her truth.

"No," she said again.

The collective sputtered. They argued. This had never happened before. All wanted to be them. They were great. They were kind. They would be powerful—

"Back the hell off," she said, pushing them down as she'd once pushed down the deep, deep down voice, pushed down her own pleading for salvation and sense of self. "I am Cara Jenklow. Daughter of Marie Jenklow. Granddaughter of Rose Carmenta, powerful dryad nymph. Granddaughter of Albert Jenklow, son of Baba Yaga. Wife to William Best, demi-god by Jax. *I* am powerful, not you."

The collective screamed. They called out her name, begged, pleaded, scolded. But their voices grew smaller, more insignificant, while hers grew, while the world around her solidified. Grew more real.

"I am a Shade. And this is my home. *My* Beckwell," she bellowed.

She took a deep breath and cast out her arms. "Give me a hand here, Dom."

"I always serve the Yaga," Dom said, the pendant heating against Cara's skin, centering her ability, making it something she could see and feel, like molding and shaping clay.

She closed her eyes to what she saw and pictured home, pictured Beckwell, as it should have been. Home that she'd never wanted to leave.

She found herself standing in the crossroads of town, the town's four-way stop. On the southwest corner was the small blue metal emergency services building…maybe getting a bit bigger these days, as it served an ever-growing population. The image of that building grew and extended near the rear, as though maybe it'd been added on to. Across the road, in the southeast corner was the log-cabin library with its welcoming porch.

Across the road on the rise, on the northeast corner, stood the two-story school, waiting to welcome its students. Across from that were the gas station, grocery store, and Loki's pub, all perhaps simple but ready to serve their customers. Tucked here and there, like her home, were the houses that formed the community, righted and unharmed now. Behind them was the tent city set up by the refugees in front of the faded fuchsia glory of the Cow Palace. A growing community. The half-metal shape of the community center, and behind it, the Senior Center rose up, whole and undamaged. Standing proud and true, the Center, like the emergency building, may have been how she'd imagined it could be, a little bigger, a few more needed rooms and amenities, with an entirely new wing to help house that growing community. A place where she'd always been embraced even when she'd only visited as a child with Gran.

This was Beckwell. This was home.

The trees in her mind shrank back to where they belonged. The smoke, the flame, the destruction receded as the natural order and settlement of Beckwell returned.

The collective whispered their cries to her. Told her they were doomed without her.

Eventually, she knew, she'd take pity on them. Many of them were probably trapped as she'd been. She'd help build them a home that meant as much to them as Beckwell did to her. But that home wouldn't come at the cost of anyone else's. That home also wouldn't have bars on the windows and the doors.

She surveyed her work. Beckwell gleamed like on an early spring morning, glittering with dew when the sun found all the best angles. She nodded and smiled. Nothing came for nothing. If you wanted a place like this to survive, to thrive, that took work.

Finally, she took a deep breath and opened her eyes.

She squeezed her fingers, intertwined with Williams. She was in Gramps's room at the Center, lying on his bed. Faint light shone through the windows at the far end, but it was a natural, early evening light. All the Shades were there, as well as Jax and the nymph twins, Nahla and Caspian, who'd come in after her, all of them staring at her like she might sprout an extra head…or like she'd died and come back to life.

She gave them a slightly watery nod and smile, but her attention quickly returned to William, to his blue-gray gaze. A warrior she'd dreamed of for so long. Someone who, whether she'd known it or not, was always supposed to be with her. Who could pull her back from the brink, give her a sense of belonging…but never erase the essence of who she was.

"You came in after me," she said. "You risked yourself, risked everything."

He leaned closer. "You didn't expect I'd just let you fight that battle alone, did you? I love you, Cara. I'll always stand at your side for any battles you want me."

She cupped her hand on his jaw, whiskers tickling her palm. "Let's worry less about battles right now and instead about building a life we both deserve. Thank you for always being the hero I knew you were. I love you. Always and forever."

Fortunately, he was smart *and* gorgeous. He leaned

down closer to her, likewise cupping her face. "Always and forever, I love you, too."

Thank the Goddess Gramps and the Shades had plotted to bring William to Beckwell. None of their lives would ever be the same. William had never been a stranger, and when it came to him, maybe she really was made for love after all.

Chapter Forty-One

NEW POSSIBILITIES

LIFE AS A SOLDIER and a PI had taught him how to pivot and adjust quickly to survive. It hadn't often taught him that life could be good, that it could be happy…but turned out you could get used to that, too. Like strolling and enjoying the company of his neighbors. Two things he'd never done before now.

A week later, after defeating the nymph collective and restoring Beckwell, William and Cara strolled hand in hand into the sunshine-filled Senior Center, greeting people and exchanging small talk as they made their way toward the broom closet in the east wing—not to be confused with the new west wing, an expansion Cara had seen to. He had one arm around Cara, the other balancing the tray of cookies. As he complimented Agnes on her laps around the atrium skylights, he couldn't help but marvel what Beckwell and Cara—with a little help from his old friends—had brought to him.

Cara turned to him, a smile on her lips, the sunlight forming a golden halo with her curls.

His breath caught, a thrill and heat going through him,

that pull of attraction strong. He'd seen her every day, spent most of those days together since the collective's defeat. Cara had finally taken some of her unused holiday time, and he'd agreed to start work officially for Chief Quilan…*after* taking some time for a honeymoon.

Not that he could go far—or wanted to. Chief Quilan was looking into a work truck, but until then, William had been taking his time about finding a new Jeep. The only places he needed to go he could reach on foot, like work, the Center, downtown Beckwell, and home. Turned out he was better in the kitchen than he'd expected, and as well as taking over most of the cooking, he'd taken up baking. There was something about the smell of fresh-baked cookies that rivaled even chocolate and peanut butter… and the scent of Cara's skin. Come spring, he'd put in a garden. He'd always liked helping Mother with hers. Maybe it was time to honor her memory in other ways.

William pulled Cara toward him, lowered his head for a quick kiss. The touch of their lips quickened his pulse, sent heady desire coursing through his veins and made him wonder how long it would be until they could return home together. He marveled at the taste of her, falling a little more in love with every touch. Now if that wasn't heaven, hell if he knew what was.

She lingered over the kiss, her lips curving into a smile beneath his before she pulled away slowly. "With kisses like that, we're going to be late for the meeting."

He leaned in and tasted her again just because, smiling against her lips before finally he pulled away. "They set us up. They'll just have to understand."

Cara, though, pulled away, taking his hand and tugging him after her. "I'm not going to be late for my first meeting, thank you very much. They'll have eaten all the best cookies. You know they will."

He held up his tray. "Which is why I brought more." He stole another kiss, and that delightfully light sound of her giggle danced through him. "I take my husbandly duties very seriously. I'll keep you in cookies and satisfy any and all of your other desires, too."

She danced away from him, skipping a few steps ahead of him down the hall. "Now that is a vow I'll make sure you keep."

Like teenagers, his heart lighter than… Hell, lighter than it'd ever felt even when he was a teenager, he and Cara rushed down the east wing. Past the door for Albert's room, two more across, and then stopped at the unassuming broom closet doorway.

Cara leaned back into his arms, a playful smile tugging at her lips as she traced his bottom lip with her fingertip. "Why, William Best," she said, voice slightly raspy, "all those stories they tell about you. Not a one pegged you for a romantic softie."

He snaked an arm around her, tugging her closer, then pulling her into the broom closet and closing the door behind them. This way, anyone watching would believe they had good reason for ducking into closets. Still, once they were closed in that dim silence, he didn't release her. "Only with you. Only for you."

She pressed her hand over his heart, her expression growing serious, her love shining in her eyes. "I've always known. That's who you always were in my dreams, in my eyes." She'd told him, in the afterglow of their lovemaking last week, that she'd dreamed of him most of her life. That she'd probably been a little bit in love with him that first day they'd met. Damned if he'd let her down again.

"I only wish I'd been as brave a dreamer as you," he said, kissing her again. Then he pulled back and winked.

"I'll make it up to you, even if I have to spend the rest of our hopefully very long lives doing so."

They'd seized control of the nymph pool, and together with Caspian and Nahla, after the honeymoon, Cara and the Sarasvatis planned to work together to free the collective, testing to see if it was possible to maintain the positive attributes while freeing the participants. Dom grudgingly assisted, while also pointing out Yagas were usually long-lived, too, without a frivolous bone in their body.

"I look forward to every day with you for the rest of our lives," she said, walking backward toward the shelf in the rear of the room, which appeared to be loaded down with tinned prunes but dissolved away and allowed her to grasp a doorknob. Then they both stepped through and headed down the stairs into the secret underground bunker.

Down into the Shades HQ.

The others were already waiting for them below, gathered around the central scarred war-room table, the two chairs at the head of the table waiting. Albert, Henry, Liko, Zaki, George…and Jax. Who'd planted himself in front of the cookie tray and was eating two cookies at a time, one in each hand.

"Sorry we're late," Cara said.

Albert gave his granddaughter a gentle smile and shrugged. "Well, it's not like we could start without our commanders, could we?" He gave her a wink. Albert had been patient and, like the others, given William and Cara their space this past week. The Shades had also vowed that they'd no longer try to steer Cara or William's lives… although all bets were off when it came to interfering with everyone else's lives. They'd all taken turns calling to check on Maddy while she recovered from Irene's attack, so much so she'd stopped answering her phone.

"He's eating all the best cookies and not sharing," Liko grouched, glaring at Jax.

Jax grinned around a cookie and patted his flat belly. "I'll bring donuts next time. My new parishioners have been asking what kinds of offerings I prefer." Turned out he interviewed well, and the local church had selected him as their new god. Jax would be sticking around Beckwell, too, for the foreseeable future.

William gave him a nod, then considered the rest of the men around the table. He held up his tray before setting it down, the scent of melting chocolate and warm butter wafting through the room. "These are fresh-baked."

Jax eyed them.

Liko pounced first.

Sometimes, he had to remind himself to see the Shades as they were, not as he remembered them, still could picture them, all changed except for Zaki. Tall and blond Henry Einar. Dark-haired and slim Albert Jenklow. Dashing George Chaimek, always making the ladies swoon. Muscular, not an ounce of fat Bal Liko, with his thick head of black hair, usually pulled back at his neck.

These days they had more silver hair, a few more wrinkles, but the same strength was there. The same men he'd always counted on. Maybe they wouldn't be around forever, and damn, that would hurt. But he wouldn't miss another year, another month, another week without them. With Jax and Cara, that made all of them. His family.

Henry cleared his throat and turned to Cara.

Cara and William nodded, then moved to the seats at the head of the table. He sat, while Cara remained standing, pulling her small red and black notebook from her pocket, and opening it.

Her hand trembled, the movement so small probably only he noticed, and she reached for the Yaga pendant.

But looking out over the others, her hand paused before she touched it, then she lowered it to rest lightly on the table. Maybe she'd seen the encouraging smiles. Or maybe this time, she'd seen the respect in these men's faces. This time, she met them as an equal. She too had risked her life to save this town. She'd been in battle and survived, earned her place. She resettled her shoulders and nodded at Henry, the signal to begin. Something she must have seen Albert do countless times before, in every meeting she'd observed but never been invited to join.

Henry cleared his throat. "I call this meeting of the Shades to order. First point on our agenda: leadership. Cara Best, you have been nominated the new leader of this group. You have the floor."

"Thank you, Mr. Einar. Gentlemen," she said, taking a deep breath and pausing for a moment, taking in the room, then letting a quiet smile settle on her face, as though taking a moment to savor. She'd told him how much this meant to her, how seriously she took this responsibility. He'd told her there was no one he'd trust more to follow into battle.

"Gentlemen," she said, her tone growing stronger, more serious and commanding. The voice of a rising leader. "Gramps, you have always been more of a father than my real one ever was. Mr. Einar, Mr. Chaimek, Mr. Zaki, Mr. Liko, you have been like grandfathers to me, training me to protect myself, this town, and others like us. Yet as I take this leadership, I would remind all of our membership that we will grow and change, and we must be willing to accept each other as equals. Both founding and new members will have a vote. Because we need to grow."

She turned to William. "The Guardians have shown us they're ready for war. We need to be, too. Irene and others like her will be back, looking for new ways to recruit and control the paranormal world."

He nodded.

Cara turned her attention back to the broader group. "And if we're going to war, we're going to need an army. We need to grow our numbers, our abilities, and be open with our intentions. The Four may be the political power-houses in this town, but we will be the guard. We need arms, we need bodies, we need training. May I get a move that we are in agreement with this direction?"

Albert immediately moved, and Henry seconded, while Zaki recorded it all in the minutes.

Her confidence growing, Cara continued. "Good. Mr. Frizzly should be brought in on these meetings, as he's been essential in the coordination of the new town arrivals, particularly the refugee camp, including settling some of the refugees temporarily in vacant rooms in the Senior Center. With the coming winter and steady arrival of still more refugees, we must accelerate plans to see all Beckwell residents—new and old—settled in more permanent hous-ing. You might remember my friend, Jessie Eldrit. She's started her own female-led paranormal construction company, Made to Measure. I think she'd be ideal to start building a new future here in Beckwell."

Henry and Albert looked at each other, as though deciding what to say and who would speak first.

It was finally Henry who turned to Cara. "We, uh, already reached out to Jessie last week…and might have borrowed your phone to do so. She believes we're accepting contracts from other paranormal builders as well. We're considering our usual recruitment method."

Cara raised a brow. "Next time, ask to borrow my phone—or have me contact her myself. I spent hours looking for it. And I believe we're all part of the same team these days?" The warning in her tone made it clear they'd crossed a line.

William crossed his arms. Nope, he wasn't protecting them this time. He knew where his loyalties lay. And she had searched for that blasted phone for hours…until he'd just carried her up to the bed instead of asking.

Albert cleared his throat. "We, uh… You're right. Apologies, Cara."

"Indeed. But you know how Jessie feels about us…" Henry added.

"Exactly. Which is why *I* was going to invite her here. We're really going to have to work on this act-now, apologize-later situation we have happening here, gentlemen. Now, you said something about the usual method?" Her tone suggested she suspected what he did. That the same kind of plan had already been used on them.

"Nothing gives a person a reason to change—or stick around—like love," Liko said, looking straight at William. "We bring them here. Get that match lit; they do the rest. An unorthodox recruitment method, maybe," he said gruffly, quite possibly starting to color.

"But this is Beckwell. Normal need not apply," Cara finished. "Matchmaking is going to be difficult in this case. You have someone in mind? Jessie doesn't believe in romance. Or happy endings. Or love. And definitely not in the Shades."

Henry nodded. "It's time Jessie comes home. She'll be good for Beckwell and it for her. I know someone in town who could be a good fit. An old family, we can insist he needs to work the project with her."

Cara just snorted. "Yeah, maybe we should think of some alternatives while we're at it. Jessie is not going to like being manipulated. We'll have to be careful. We'll also need a list of other candidates, both those already in town, and other potentials we know of who could strengthen our cause."

Zaki's hand shot into the air, and at Cara's nod he stood. "Would you like that list of potential recruits alphabetical or by geographical distance?"

Forget the North American continent. The Shades were taking on the world. And he'd never been so proud to be one.

ABOUT AN HOUR and a generous tray of cookies later, William and Cara stepped out of the broom closet and he wrapped his arm around her. Despite the looming Guardian threat and inevitable trouble on the horizon— pretty much the norm for most of his life—for the first time in a very long time, life had a golden hue.

"You were brilliant in there, you know that?" he said. "We're all lucky to have you. In our lives, leading us forward."

She turned to him, tipping her head to the side, as though considering. "Yes, you really are all lucky, aren't you? I think we've got this." Her expression sobered. "Although, we don't know where Irene ended up, or when she'll be back." They strolled together out toward the atrium. "This isn't going to be easy."

He only smiled. Who needed easy when he had his family and was married to the woman of his dreams? He tugged her closer as they walked. Damn. After a week spent mostly naked together, you'd have thought the steady pull between them, the chemistry and heat a mere brush of skin caused would have lessened. If anything, it'd only gotten stronger. Thank gods they still had a few days left before Cara headed back to work.

They strolled together toward the atrium…and a growing crowd. He frowned. Odd. Maybe lunch had let out early.

He leaned closer to Cara, inhaling the floral scent of her. "Now if it was easy, what would be the fun of that?"

"What would be the fun of what?" a deep, slightly accented male voice said, stepping out of the crowd beside him.

The crowd parted, leaving Cara and William face-to-face with what appeared to be a dark-haired warrior male and female.

Otherwise known as Loki and his wife, Anna, the War horsewoman. Behind her stood the other three horse-woman: fair haired and pretty Piper Quilan, Pestilence; petite, dark-haired Nia Amort, Death; and the curvy red-head Ginny Derth, Famine.

William caught his breath. The stories they told about the Four. And then there was Loki. *The* Loki… William blinked. Although you know how it was with stories…

Cara, without hesitation, stepped smoothly forward, hand out. "Hi, Mr. Laufeyjarson." She nodded at the Four. "Ladies."

Loki raised a brow, shaking her hand. "Ms. Jenklow—"

"It's Best now. Cara Best." She stepped back and placed her hand on William's shoulder. "This is my husband, William Best."

Loki's stormy gray gaze swept over Cara quickly, not in a sexual way, but more an assessing kind of way. As though perhaps he, too, could sense the change in her. And the power. If William hadn't been watching closely, he might have missed the small flicker of surprise in that otherwise enigmatic gaze.

The demi-god, though, turned to his dark-haired wife. "How long have we been away, exactly? Because I'm quite sure we didn't have two wings on the Center when we left. Nor that very handy extension to the Emergency Center." He turned back to Cara. "Ms. Best, you have come into your own."

"Thank you," Cara said, steady confidence in her gaze as she nodded.

Anna's dark gaze was disconcertingly direct, pinning both Cara and William in place. "He's being polite, but I won't be. What's been going on since we were away? We arrived home to stories about deranged trees and damaged buildings, yet everything is as good as when we left, or—" she gestured at the Senior Center, "—suspiciously better that it was."

Cara remained unfazed, simply putting on a smile and the confidence of one leader speaking to another. "Nothing out of the ordinary. Someone wanted to destroy Beckwell and tried to use me to do it. We stopped them. We realize you and Mr. Laufeyjarson," her gaze extended to the rest of the Four, "indeed, all of you, have found yourselves very busy with the management of larger scale paranormal diplomacy on an international scale. In which case, I have great news for you. You don't have to worry about Beckwell's security anymore. We're on it."

"Is that right," Loki said slowly, although there was something a bit proud in his gaze as he crossed his arms and considered Cara, perhaps seeing her, the real her, for the first time.

William moved a little closer. Hell, he knew firsthand seeing Cara, the real Cara, was life changing. Thank the gods.

"Um… Hi?" The tall red-head, Ginny Lack, raised a hand, stepping forward, considering them, then turned to Anna and Loki. "It was a long flight, so it's possible I missed something." She turned back to Cara. "I know you run the art program here, but I'm pretty sure that's not how you're protecting the town. So, who exactly is this 'we' you mentioned?"

Cara just smiled. "You didn't miss anything. We definitely need to talk. A lot. Because we take our duty to protect Beckwell and its people very seriously. We are the Shades of Beckwell."

DEAR READER,

I hope you've enjoyed Cara and William's story - and the introduction to those roguish Shades! :) I wanted to write a story that let the Shades offer some humor, but still gave them the dignity that they deserve. Age does not define worth. My grandparents and the other seniors I've known have always proven that. If you've enjoyed the book, please consider leaving a review. If I collect enough of them, I get a unicorn! (Note: There is no unicorn…but reviews are a close second!)

What's next for Beckwell and its residents? Well, winter is coming, and all those refugees need help - and homes. You've had a brief introduction to both Ash and Jessie, and I can't wait to introduce you to them and their romance in the next book, *Shade to Measure*, coming early 2022! There will also be some adventure in between with an addition to the Shades Novella collection too.

If you'd like to keep up with what's going on in my writing world - and maybe get a touch of magic in your life

- sign up for my newsletter where you'll get all the sneak peeks, secret insider stories, and announcements first.

You can also find me on Facebook or over at my website, www.shellychalmers.com or via email at shelly-chalmers@scchalmers.com. Do check in or drop me a note - I love hearing from readers!

In the meantime, thank you for reading, and wishing you a little more magic in your life.

Yours,

Shelly

P.S. If you're technically inclined, join the newsletter here with this QR code. 😊

Acknowledgments

Thank you to my family, who are always there to support me, especially as this book and series fell further behind schedule. Girls, maybe now you understand my book release dates as a time for ice cream cake, but hopefully someday you recognize the perseverance and other reasons to celebrate too. For my husband, thank you for your constant support, and for reminding me on the hard days no, I can't just quit.

Thank you to my editor, Tera Cuskaden and to Neelam for helping me push this book to what it could become.

Thank you to my Dreamweavers, for always being there every week for recaps. To my crit partner, Shelly A, thank you for your steadfast calm, and to my brainstorm partner, Jaycee, for helping me think outside the box.

Publishing a book is always a team effort, no matter how you go about it. And with the pandemic and other things happening out there, with this book even more so. I'm so fortunate to have that team on my side.

9 781777 888121